DREAMWORMS BOOK 1

The Advent of Dreamtech

ISAAC PETROV

Future Notion Press

Copyright © 2021 by Isaac Petrov

Published by *Future Notion Press* — press@isaacpetrov.com

ISBN: 978-90-831552-0-3

Cover art by Cherie Chapman.

Cover images © Shutterstock.com.

Episode art by Maxim Mitenkov.

Sign Up — No Bull Sci-Fi

ISAAC PETROV — EPIC SCI-FI AT ITS BEST!

Come over to my site at IsaacPetrov.com and SIGN UP to get fresh SCI-FI updates, discounts and goodies:

https://isaacpetrov.com/book1

OR SCAN THIS WITH YOUR CAMERA!

DREAMWORMS

A POST–APOCALYPTIC FIRST CONTACT EPIC

2399 FIRST CONTACT

EPISODE I

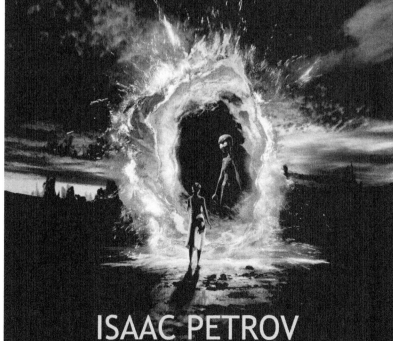

ISAAC PETROV

ONE

A Seminar in the Dreamnet

Ximena watches with morbid fascination as Atahualpa—in a gesture of foolish arrogance that would turn history on its head—leaves his eighty-thousand strong army on a plateau nearby, and enters his city. His Empire. His demise.

The Inca's retinue marches slowly and full of confidence through the narrow streets. The city has been emptied by the war, but the Inca's escort—a few thousand of his most loyal courtiers, all dressed in the finest garments—walk along with the sure arrogance of power. Some carry fine discs of pure gold on their heads. Others, adorned in cloths of patterned colors, sing songs of praise. And in the middle of it all: the Sapa Inca himself, Atahualpa, godly power incarnate, surrounded by silver and fine feathers, and carried in a ceremonial litter by eighty of his most loyal servants.

But, crucially, nobody carries weapons. *Why?* Ximena asks herself. *What were you thinking, Atahualpa? You knew there were less than two hundred of those exotic bearded foreigners you've heard were roaming your lands, didn't you? And they sent word they were keen to join your glory, didn't they? Were you that curious? Were you really that sure that they would cower to your godly splendor?*

The retinue arrives at the open city square and stops. Nobody moves, the singing fades.

A lone Christian friar exits a nearby stone building and approaches the litter, carrying a cross and a thick book, his breath visible in the fresh winter afternoon. Ximena squints, trying to remember his denomination. A Dominican?

The man reaches the litter and begins a heated exchange with Atahualpa, hard to hear from a distance, and impossible to follow even by those nearby because of the lack of interpreters. The friar is shouting the language of the conquistadors at Atahualpa, which Ximena's ancestors would understand but, sadly, she doesn't.

The book finally reaches the emperor's hands, who stares at it like it were a fistful of live worms, and drops it dismissively.

There is a long silence, like destiny holding her breath. Ximena's eyes widen with anticipation.

The friar gives out a sudden shout of outrage and the ambushing warriors begin to pour into the open square from within the surrounding buildings and alleys. Impregnable in armor and helmets of dirty steel, lean swords in their hands, and soulless greed in their eyes, it is a terrifying view. Some ride imposing warhorses— creatures of hell from the look of their petrified victims. They charge, outnumbered one to forty.

And the slaughter begins.

Horror and yells of desperation echo against the small buildings as the lives of myriads of unarmed nobles and slaves are slashed with industrial efficiency, a machine mowing the elite of an empire. And it takes time to kill,

Ximena thinks, as she watches the dread of sure death reflected in thousands of eyes around her.

Cannons are hastily pulled out of the stone building, together with a detachment of gunpowder-spitting arquebuses and join the killing frenzy with explosive devotion. Ximena almost looks away. Almost. But her professional pride keeps her mind focused and her eyes disciplined. The smell of blood, gunpowder and feces fills the air. She wonders how the doomed victims are experiencing the sudden shattering of everything they knew sure in their primitive world: the unfathomable chaos, the mythic beasts, the deadly shooting, the smoke, the violence against their god-emperor. *Some are surely going mad. A mercy, perhaps.*

As the armored warriors reach the fringes of the Inca's litter, his eighty chosen carriers, all dressed in the same fine gowns of the deepest blue, hold their stance with stoic fatalism—faith and loyalty written across their faces. *They will carry their god all the way to the underworld,* Ximena thinks. The foreign swords hack arms and hands with relentless zeal, eager to make the litter stumble and fall. They want the Inca. They need him alive to conquer everything they wished for. The power. The oh so sweet *gold.* Ximena stares in wonder as the last surviving maimed carriers, eyes beaming with fanatical determination, use their last breaths on earth to sustain the litter upright. With their severed limbs and stumps! The Inca staggers on the tilting platform, his face contracted in disbelief and terror.

"Ah, here you are." The sudden voice of Ximena's grandfather makes her jump. "What are you watching?"

Ximena makes a quick gesture with a finger and the gory scene around her comes to a sudden, digital halt. Even the stench vanishes. A date and time briefly blink at the lower right corner: 20th December 2515 16:55. She removes her visor-glasses.

"Abuelo." She smiles at him. "You scared me."

Ximena's grandfather is quite unlike her. Where she is short, he is tall. Where she has the classic complexion of her Mapuche heritage—dark skin, black hair, broad face—his skin is lighter, his nose larger, hinting at Hansasian ancestry. Her hair runs down in two long braids each side of her face. His is nonexistent. She is pretty. He is not.

"Sorry, *cariño*. Are you working on your PhD?"

"Kind of." Her heart is still leaping as she chuckles in delight. "You cannot imagine what I've found!"

Enrique sits on the bench next to Ximena, across the glass panels of their home's cozy winter-garden. "Tell me. But be quick."

"It's the new access to the Lundev archives. It's... Whoa! I can access all their historical documents, Abuelo. Everything! *So* easy to do research with this wealth of material. *So*... It's almost cheating!" She cannot repress a giggle of joy. "I will complete my PhD in half your time. Mark my words!"

Enrique smiles cynically. "Don't get your hopes up. I bet the Townsend University staff has no clue that their *Global Program* students have this sort of unrestricted access. Wait 'til they find out."

"Why would they care? This is an opportunity for *everybody* at the university! Wait 'til I show them."

Enrique scoffs and looks at the visor-glasses. "What were you watching?"

"Atahualpa and Pizarro in Cajamarca. Amazing! I found this sensorial dramatization by Professor Miyagi."

"*Kenji* Miyagi?" Enrique raises his eyebrows. "The Miyagi?"

Ximena nods. "Unpublished, purely academic. Spectacular, too. But it looks a bit, uh…"

"Yes?"

"I don't know." Ximena wets her lips. It's hard to find the right word. "Hmm, *imaginative?*"

"Imaginative, huh? A strange way to describe the work of the greatest historian alive."

"I know," she admits with a shrug. "But it looked more like a fantasy than history. It glorified the barbarians. They seemed more civilized than the conquerors. Can you believe it?"

Enrique nods sadly at her. "Reminds me of some old papers an old lady brought to me when we moved to Entre Lagos. We were the first historian family ever in the colony. I had little time to study them before they were taken out of my reach." His eyes glide along the pines on the garden outside the glass panels. "*Fantastic* they were." He nods slowly to himself.

"Here, look." Ximena passes her visor-glasses to him, but he catches her hand.

"No, Ximena. That's all very nice, but there's no time. It's almost five."

"What?!" A surge of adrenaline makes her stand. "Oh, Goah. I lost track of time!"

"Go. You can't be late to enrollment. This is your *one* moment, cariño. The Global Program and the collaboration with the most prestigious university in the *worlds*—and Kenji Miyagi, no less!—is the opportunity of a lifetime." His eyes sparkle with pride. "You are our legacy, *mi vida*. You'll make the finest historian our family—no, the whole Andean Imperia!—has ever seen."

Ximena is about to run, but hesitates. "Abuelo, *you* are the finest historian—"

"Don't." Enrique shakes his head, and gently pushes

her into motion. "You are just twenty-seven, Goah's Mercy. You still don't know how much you don't know. I hope you learn that from Miyagi, and then more that you can teach me. Now quick, run before your future shuts."

Ximena leaps away and into the living room. As she runs across the open space, she doesn't have time to wonder where everyone is. At this time of the early afternoon, at least one of her parents, or possibly her brother and Ramiro his lover, would be hanging around, lying on the sofa, sensonet visors on their heads, watching the world, listening to music, gaming with strangers—usual life. But there is a tension in the air, subliminal, that melts with her haste and leverages her already considerable anxiety.

Ximena's eyes flinch over to the digital hour on the glass window as she exits the living room.

16:57.

Oh Goah, oh Goah, oh Goah! Three minutes. Three minutes to make it to the new auditorium recently created for the Global Program. Three minutes to meet the world-famous Professor Kenji Miyagi. That is, if she makes it in time. Oh Goah, she won't make it!

She reaches the staircase and runs up in leaps of two, a sweat breaking on her forehead. *Why did I get distracted like that, Goah's Mercy?* It's always been her problem, losing herself in her obsessions. She shudders at the thought of missing the chance of a lifetime. If Abuelo had not come for her... The Global Program could really pull her historian career out of the imperial level where her family has always lingered and onto the international stage. She has the unique chance to put the name of the Epullan family on the lips of Academia worldwide. She can't afford to arrive late!

Ximena trips on the last step and falls flat on the upper hallway.

Goahdammit!

She stands, ignoring the pain, and runs. Her room is at the end of the corridor. Her door, which she painted pink when she was a little girl, is half open. She pushes it and throws herself in.

Her family, bar Abuelo, is there, staring at her with love and hope. Abuela, Mamá, Papá, and her stupid brother Antonio. Well, he is not that stupid, he's actually okay. They are all standing around her *wu-sarc*. Expectant.

"What—?!" Ximena cannot finish her question before Mamá embraces her fiercely.

"We are so proud of you," she says, tears in her eyes. She resembles both Abuelo and Antonio, with her tall, sharp Hansasian features.

"But hurry, cariño," Papá says. He and Abuela on the other hand are—like Ximena—pure pre-Columbian indigenous beauty in different shades of wrinkling. Papá raises his finger at the clock on the wu-sarc's side table.

16:58.

No time! "Damn!" Ximena escapes her mother's arms. "Sorry, Mamá, I really need to—"

"We're leaving you alone," Papá says hastily, beginning to push the rest of the family out of the bedroom. "Just tell us one thing."

"Papá, please." She feels a surge of impatience turning into rage which she immediately suppresses. It's just her family being her family. "What is it?"

"Sorry, but we need to... uh, how long will you be asleep?"

"Hmm." Ximena stares at the clock, eyes wide with stress, so it's hard to focus. "It's a long-format seminar, several uninterrupted dream-days long, but for those

7

awake, just ten hours, so, uh, until about three a.m.? You'll be sleeping."

"No," Papá says. "I'll be awake." He looks at the others as they leave the room. "And I suspect I'll not be alone. Sweet *dreams,*" he whispers with a wink. And shuts the door.

Finally!

She hastily takes off her robes and lies on the copper-like shiny surface of the wu-sarc. The metallic-looking material immediately reshapes to fit her body, engulfing her in a familiar wave of release and comfort. Her body relaxes in an instant. She cannot avoid a last peek at the bedside table. The time on the clock changes.

16:59.

Ximena shuts her eyes and takes a deep breath, trying to rein in a sudden surge of nerves, and speaks the mental command: *Wu-sarc, activate.*

A frenzy of vegetation erupts from the bottom of the sarcophagus. A myriad of ivy-looking tendrils crawl up its walls like worms escaping an earthquake, and cover her body in warmth and darkness.

Ximena takes another, deeper breath to exhale the last figments of stress.

State REM-phase duration, a deep female voice speaks inside her mind.

Ten wake-hours, Ximena replies in her thoughts.

The tendrils around her body tighten with comforting familiarity. She can almost feel the *dream juice* rubbing against her skin, running through her bloodstream, penetrating her brain, releasing her from reality. The wu-sarc is truly a wonder of alien technology, the dream of every dreamer.

The University of Townsend is the most important center of knowledge of the *Goah's Imperia of the Americas*, and the day Ximena was accepted as a student of history was the happiest in her life. A huge honor. The first of the Epullan family ever to attend the university of the capital of the GIA. But today, any lingering happiness is rashly consumed by an overwhelming anxiety.

She runs desperately through the busy halls of the University of Townsend. Not the real brick-and-mortar one, of course. That one is several thousand miles north, in the midst of the North American landmass. She doubts the real campus is in much use anymore, except for some fringe operations like those invaluable historical archives she would give her right arm to be granted access to. The *real* University of Townsend is not really real. It is a *permascape* construct in the dreamnet, as most human institutions are in the twenty-sixth century. A dream, if you like, inside an inconceivably larger dream shared by all humanity.

Ximena dodges student after student, their dream avatars robed in the obligatory white-and-blue colors of the university. Her own academic robes, identical to those of her fellow students, flap behind her haste in an accurate rendition of reality. Sometimes the permascape seems more real than the wake.

Sometimes.

When Ximena reaches the main hall—an open court surrounded by balustrades and columns several floors high—she jumps into the air and flies straight to the fourth floor: the History Department. It is not permitted to fly in the main building, but, honestly, today she just doesn't care.

The main department hallway is empty; the only thing

visible is a gate made of intricate iron with Gothic motifs. And this gate was not here yesterday. A signpost placed nearby reads: "Access restricted to Global Program participants." And behind it, a second, more prominent sign flashes angrily in midair: "WARNING! You are leaving the Goah's Imperia of the Americas."

Ximena's heart leaps. The gate is closed.

A lone university steward guards the entrance. He is not a real person, of course, but just a character designed by some dreamtech engineer and yet more realistic than even the latest AI prototypes that Botswana spits out for the space habitats. But then, human-like dream characters are only natural, aren't they? After all, everything in the permascape is being rendered by the melding of millions of human minds.

"Can't pass," the steward says, raising his eyes at her with a very convincing bored expression. He even appears to be chewing gum.

"I'm in the Global Program," she says, and points a hasty finger at the first signpost. "Ximena Epullan. You can check!"

"Sorry, ma'am." The steward taps an old-fashioned watch on his left wrist. "Seminar's started."

"No." She shakes off a wave of desperation. "It can't have."

The steward gives her a sideways smirk and keeps chewing in silence.

"No." She walks past him, up to the gate, and begins pounding on it. "No, no, NO!"

The steward ignores her.

"Please, PLEASE," Ximena pounds the gate with both hands. She turns to the steward, who shakes his head and scoffs. "Please," she whispers, desperation filling her like sea water in the lungs of a drowning sailor.

She stops pounding and falls on her knees.

It's over.

Ximena is not the type to cry—the Epullan are a tough lot—but here, on her knees at the edge of her shattered future, she feels entitled to shed a few dream tears. What will she tell Papá and Mamá? That she was late to her destiny? How long until she can look Abuelo in the eyes again?

The gate moves almost imperceptibly, pushed from the other side, without noise, until a sudden stream of natural light shines along the widening slit.

It's opening! Ximena jumps to her feet, takes the opening crevice with her hands, and pulls with all her strength. *Goah's Mercy, will they allow me in?*

"Hmm, thank you, dear," a woman's voice says, tinted with strain. A sweet, elegant voice; the cleanest, purest Hansasian accent she has ever heard. "This gate is sooo heavy. You GIA lot sure have a developed sense of the dramatic."

As the gap increases, Ximena turns to the woman, her eyes widening with wonder.

A Neanderthal woman! An honest-to-Goah Neanderthal, brow ridge and all, right in front of her!

She blinks in a futile effort to avoid gaping at her narrow forehead. Neanderthals are supposed to be a bit... brutish. Dim, even. But this smiling, broad-faced woman in her fifties radiates sophistication. Short, brown hair, neatly pulled back, her avatar dressed with the elegant casualness Ximena has only seen in Hansasian sensorials. *Why so surprised? Of course you would expect Nubarian Neanderthals in Hansasia, and most definitely in the Lundev, right by the Portal.*

The Neanderthal woman's smile widens, too gracious to let Ximena's obvious reaction affect her affability.

"Ximena Epullan, I presume?" She extends her right hand in greeting. "The missing student?"

Ximena nods. "I- I'm so, so terribly sorry for being late..." She stares at the hand in confusion and shakes it with an involuntary notch of aversion. It's not that she's racist, of course not. She enjoys Nubarian adventure sensorials as much as the next guy. Neanderthals are so passionate and full of drama. But in *academia*?! Not *everybody* can—

"So delighted to finally meet you!" the woman says like she means it. "My name is Ankhesenneferibre Ankhesenaten, but you can call me Ank." She laughs with the ease of a person who has just told a joke for the first time. Which obviously she hasn't.

"Uh, nice to meet you, Elder Ank."

"Just Ank, please. I'm not Goahn."

Of course you're not. Nubarians are pagans, and too stubborn to convert, from what she's heard. But pagan or not, she is her only hope. "I'm really sorry, uh, *Ank*. I beg you to accept my apologies for my late arrival. I'm with the Global Program. I hope I can still attend Professor Miyagi's seminar?"

"Kenji certainly hopes you do. He personally suggested your name when drafting the list of candidates to attend this first edition of the Global Program."

A tsunami of relief distends Ximena's features into a wide-eyed smile. "*My* name? Why?"

Ank smiles noncommittally and puts a finger on her chest. "Part of it is because of your research on the effects of raw power in post-Columbian America. They are—how did he put it?—*intriguing*." Ank takes Ximena by the arm and pulls her through the gap while speaking. "And it's not easy to intrigue him. Trust me, I should know."

Ximena, baffled at the torrent of gratitude she can't

avoid feeling for this *Neanderthal*, walks through the gate and has to squint from the sudden brightness of what looks like a sunny grass meadow on a beautiful, mild spring morning. Ximena knows it is all a dream, but the permascape air feels invigoratingly fresh and real. Her accumulated stress seems to evaporate with every breath. The gate shuts behind them, standing ugly and out of place in the middle of the meadow like a lone Gothic monument.

"Kenji is about to arrive," Ank says, pointing at the regular door that stands in midair next to the GIA monstrosity, "so take an empty seat." They begin to walk towards a stone amphitheater exquisitely carved into the hills of the meadow. "He is a bit of a showman, you will see," Anks says with a chuckle. "Very punctual at arriving fashionably late."

Ximena stops and gapes at the amphitheater below her. It is small—and intimate. A hemicycle of concentric stone steps of elegant simplicity leading down to the central stone-paved stage. *Breathtaking!* The structure wouldn't be out of place in the Athens of Pericles—which is probably the intention. It even looks old and smoothed by centuries of exposure.

"Pretty, isn't it?" Ank says, pride filling her voice. "My own design. I hope you get the intellectual, hmm, *vibe*?"

Ximena cannot reply, frozen at the sight of the students filling the benches up to the brim. There must be over a hundred of them! Those sitting closer to her are easily recognizable as Townsend students—her own people— wearing the familiar white-blue robes with somber patience. The other students though—more than half by the looks of it—whoa! They're wearing the weirdest avatars she's ever seen! Each different from their neighbor —a chaotic mesh of excited chatter and electrified anticipation. Most avatars she doesn't recognize, probably cultural references to obscure Hansasian sensorials she's never heard of. There are a few more classic themed avatars she can at least identify: there is Batman, over there a *don't-panic* green smiling globe, uh, that one is definitely Michael Jackson, and there sits, yeah, Abraham Lincoln no less. The Lundev students are a very colorful lot indeed. And, she now notices, almost half of them are Neanderthal, including Lincoln!

"There aren't any empty places," Ximena says, browsing the busy place. "But it's fine. I—I can sit on the stairs."

"No need, dear. There is one place per student—I made sure of it." She puts her hands around her mouth, and shouts with a voice that would make Ximena's favorite fishmonger proud. "YOUR ATTENTION, PLEASE! RAISE YOUR HAND IF THERE IS AN EMPTY SPOT BESIDE YOU."

A sudden silence sinks in in the amphitheater as everybody turns and stares at Ximena. She can almost feel their combined gaze as physical pressure on her skin, and purses her lips involuntarily. *That's what you get for being late.*

A lone hand raises up.

Oh, no, it's the goahdamn Neanderthal Lincoln! Ximena desperately scans the neat rows of white and blue robes, but no Townsend hands volunteer.

"Go, dear." Ank gently pushes her towards Lincoln. "Enjoy Kenji's seminar, and welcome to the Global Program."

TWO

The Lure of Truth

T he heavy cheering and clapping begins as soon as the Lundev door opens and Professor Miyagi walks down the central stairs of the amphitheater. Everybody is up on their feet, yelling approval.

A standing ovation! In a classroom! Before the teacher says a single word! Ximena has never experienced that before, and to her own surprise she is an enthusiastic participant. Next to an exultant Neanderthal Abraham Lincoln and embedded in the colorful section of Lundev students, she jumps and cheers like she belongs. To be fair, the GIA section is no less engaged.

Miyagi is universal.

When he reaches the stage, he turns and slowly draws his gaze across the cheering crowd of packed students, while nodding with a confident smile.

Ank approaches him and, in a swift move, attaches a small device to his shirt. The way she does it, the casual gesture, the swift exchange of glances. *They're together,* Ximena realizes with unsettled amusement. She has never seen a *mixed* couple before.

"Thank you... whoa... thanks for the noise," Miyagi's voice comes loud and clear from a set of loudspeakers installed around the perimeter of the amphitheater. Ximena is always in awe at how a dream permascape mimics the laws of physics to such fidelity as to allow electronics to work. "Well, well. It is not every day that a humble historian is received like a pop star," he says.

Ximena smiles. She knows that Professor Miyagi is being modest. He is *The Expert* (yes, capital letters) on post-collapse history and an ultra-popular—and very photogenic—scientific disseminator. A constant face on the sensonet channels as guest contributor, he is also the writer and producer of the most famous historical sensorial of all times: *Fahey's Legacy*, Rowan Prize winner of 2504 for the best drama, not bad for what was just supposed to be a documentary. The man is a genius.

"Autographs at the end of the seminar," he says with a chuckle. "When I began teaching, I never thought I would have to say that to start a lesson."

The students laugh again and clap loudly. And keep clapping.

"Whoa, people." Professor Miyagi casually pulls back his long white hair and smiles, seemingly enjoying the attention of his captive audience. "Enough of that nonsense, or it will go straight to my head. Oh, see what you've done? Too late... Now I know I'm awesome!"

This time the waves of laughter and heavy clapping take even longer to fade away.

"Thank you," Miyagi says, and with the way his smile softens, Ximena knows he means it. "Thanks for that. Love it. Love you people. Love this auditorium. A classic-age amphitheater, no less. Incredible! And the small size, designed to bring us all together, Townsend and Lundev. Just perfect! Can you feel the energy of curiosity? The urge for sharing? The craving for knowledge? For *truth*? Amazing work." He points at Ank. "Please make some noise for the finest Shadow-Walker engineer academia has ever produced, Ankhesenneferibre!"

Ximena cheers at the top of her lungs, as does everybody else in the packed auditorium. It takes a while for the noise to fade, but Ank's ferocious blush takes a lot longer.

"Love it." Miyagi visibly enjoys the noisy attention. "Love it, people, but let's chill, all right?" He gestures to the students to sit. "We have work to do."

As the cheering begins to fade, Ximena feels an electrifying excitement. Professor Kenji Miyagi! Her family is going to want details. How's he dressed? Like Ank designed his dream suit: elegant and yet with a pointed academic *vibe*. Ximena even thinks those words in Ank's oh so perfect Hansasian accent. How does he look? Eastern Asian descent, obviously; youthful in his mid-fifties; plentiful white hair capped at his shoulders.

"Welcome to the first edition of the Global Program. I hope the first of many, because the Global Program lies close to my heart."

Ximena smiles with anticipation. The Global Program! Miyagi's concept child to use academic collaboration to warm the *cold war* that has split the world for a hundred years, and counting. Since the Dreamwars, the GIA and Hansasia have been rival regimes. Ximena's native Goah's Imperia of the Americas is the largest in population and expands the inhabitable latitudes of the North and South American continents. Hansasia, while not so populated, is enormous and, Ximena must admit, more technologically advanced. It stretches along the northern half of Eurasia, from the Hansa to China, plus a sizable part of Nubaria across the Portal to top it up. A true monster. And its scientific and cultural heart is, of course, Miyagi's alma mater: the one and only University of Lunteren-Deviss, or *Lundev* for short.

"The Earth is getting smaller. Too small for petty differences, I'm sure you all agree." Miyagi's voice is lighthearted and practiced, the clean Hansasian accent not unlike Ank's. Ximena read somewhere that a century ago Townsend's Montana English was the peak of refinement, but, like most things, that changed after the devastations of the Dreamwars. "It is high time we talk more, so I say let's start the conversation with the least controversial of topics: science. And, since this Program is *my* initiative, of course we'll begin with the sexiest science of them all: *history*."

A fresh round of spontaneous clapping and whistling, Ximena's included, drowns the hemicycle and Miyagi's words for a few moments. As the noise fades, Ank approaches Miyagi and whispers something in his ear.

"Sorry, people," Miyagi says, "but first the admin. Where is the…?" He turns to Ank, who swiftly produces a sheet of paper from thin air and hands it to him. "Ah! All right," he inspects the paper, "health comes first. We are in for a long-format session. You are all aware, right? With so many of us in such a small permascape, time dilation is off the charts, which is great because I plan to keep you trapped in my seminar for several dream-days. We are going to revisit the entire history of the Reformation and the Dreamwars in one go. And in great detail! It's going to take a while, people."

Ximena has done long-formats before. No big deal. She actually enjoys the immersion of dream-binging for days without end, no hunger, no tiredness, pure engagement. And this seminar promises to be epic, a detailed insight into the events that precipitated the end of the largest empire Earth has ever seen. Bring it on!

"And you know what that means, right?" Miyagi continues. "After the seminar you must all hold strict dream rest for at least a wake-week, got that? No excuses. No exception. Any porn you need, keep it strictly digital." He raises his voice at the sudden barrage of laughs. "I'm serious, people. No sneaking in the dreamnet for a week, all right? Let your brains recover."

He raises his eyes at the benches, to unanimous nodding.

"Good. Next, hmm, Censor Smith sends his apologies. He will miss the early part of the seminar. Okay, what else… Ah!" He looks up again, "You all had your dream pills or are using wu-sarcs, yes? We don't want people waking spontaneously and missing dream-hours of seminar because it took them a few minutes to go back to sleep."

More nodding and hums of assent.

"Good, and the last…" He cringes slightly as he reads and then turns to the Lundev section with an apologetic expression. "Yes, uh, sorry, people. No *creative* avatars allowed. Dress code is strict civilian."

Silence hangs in the air for a moment, before a tsunami of protests and whining floods the auditorium. Neanderthal Lincoln next to Ximena is standing, and like many others around her, booing and muttering *very ugly* words of disapproval. It takes some time of Miyagi patiently appeasing them with reassuring gestures until his voice can be heard again.

"I hear you, I hear you, but this is non-negotiable. Censor Smith was very specific. Please, people, don't make this a freedom-of-expression thing. There are rules even in the Lundev. You cannot show up, say, naked. The threshold today is just a tad higher. So please, out of respect for our fellow GIA students…" He extends his hand at them, all sitting in astonished silence in their neat white-and-blue robes, just like Ximena.

Miyagi folds his arms across his chest and stares on as the Lundev students grudgingly comply. It is a sight to behold, all those weird and flamboyant characters *shrinking* —that's how it feels—into regular, almost boring looking students her age, dressed in regular Hansasian style civilian clothes. Next to her, Neanderthal Lincoln is unceremoniously *un-Lincolned* into a redheaded Neanderthal man in his twenties with a mean frown in his narrow brow and a "bollocks" on his lips.

"Thank you for your understanding," Miyagi says with a slight bow of his head. "Now, cheer up," he raises his voice with practiced confidence, "and shake off those long faces. You are in for a treat, people. The best lecture of your lives is about to begin!"

Yes, finally! Ximena tries to keep her legs from shaking with anticipation. She totally believes the man. This is going to be the most important seminar of her life. She feels it in her bones.

"History," Miyagi begins in a solemn voice, "is a tough science." He sighs theatrically, as if he were confessing his deepest sin. "A true bitch, trust me. Truth is elusive. Convenient lies always loom on the surface, *so* tempting." He stops and stares into the eyes of his enthralled audience with an unusually stern expression. "You are here not only to learn what happened a hundred years ago. No, people, that's not really that important. You can always look it up. *Much* more important, if I succeed, is to give you the mental tools to dig out the truth from under the heavy layers of historical bullshit."

Some students chuckle. Ximena doesn't. His words resonate deep in her, like an old melody she cannot remember. *To dig out the truth...*

"I'm dead serious," he says. "A tough science requires tougher scientists. The aim of this seminar, *my* aim, is to make you think *tough*. So, I expect you people," he slides a finger across the auditorium, "to do much of the talking. I want to hear your thoughts, take part in the analysis, and come together with conclusions and historical theories that —like any other science—approximates us to the objective truth."

The objective truth.

Miyagi's smile returns. "So, woo-hoo." He playfully wags his fingers. "This semester we are diving deep into events that happened just a century ago—early twenty-fifth century. Life then differed greatly from now. Why?"

He looks expectantly at the young faces. A shy hand rises from among the GIA section. It's Cody.

"Please, why was it different, uh…?" He points at Cody, frowns, and then turns to Ank. "The name thingy, please?"

Ank smiles and nods. "Done," she says without moving a muscle.

Miyagi points his finger at Cody again, and large, friendly letters appear floating over his head: *Cody O'Higgin.* "There! *Cody*, please. Why was life so different a mere century ago? I mean, think about it, it's not that long ago. There are still people around that lived through those events. The ink of history is not quite dry yet. So, what was so crucially different back then?"

"Well, sir, a hundred years ago we were on the verge of extinction."

"Please class, don't call me *sir*, all right? Just Professor, or simply Kenji. And yes, humanity went almost belly up. But that doesn't really answer the question. Why was it different from today? How do you know we will not soon go extinct ourselves?"

Cody falls silent, considering.

"Er... Well, there are no obvious threats now. Back then there was the Dem-Pandemic, the ritual deaths, the brief lives. Now all is different. Better. We have a larger population, technology..."

The redheaded Neanderthal next to Ximena—the former Abraham Lincoln—raises a hand. Professor Miyagi points at him with a nod. A name appears over his head. "Mark, please. Your opinion?"

"Well," Mark turns to Cody who is still standing at the opposite side of the amphitheater, not too far away considering its size, "I don't agree that population and technology are by themselves a guarantee against calamity. Not according to history. Take, say, the peak of the golden age, at the end of the twenty-first century. The human population was, like, twenty times larger than today's. Technology was also more advanced back then, even if we are catching up. They had colonies on Mars, and on the Moon and some asteroids. And what, in just a few decades, humanity lost all that and collapsed to numbers not seen since, uh..."

"Good point, Mark," Miyagi says. "We barely made it through both collapses. By the mid twenty-second century humanity was a pathetic shadow of its former self. Anything to say in reply, Cody?"

"Uh, yes, that's all true, but I think the Dem-Pandemic made all the difference. Cause unknown. Impossible to cure. Nobody could escape it, not even with strict isolation. The first collapse of the golden age had obvious causes: environmental destruction, geopolitical tensions, technological disruption, and so on. All human-made. With time and common sense, all curable. But not Dem."

"Again, good point," Miyagi says with a curt nod. "The Dem-Pandemic triggered the second collapse when we were still licking the wounds from the first, and left us crawling through the mud for centuries. But even then, they were as equally sure that they had everything under control as we are today. They built a rural utopia in environmental equilibrium spanning the inhabitable latitudes of the world. They had a stable society, based on Goah's Gift; the first truly global empire in history, quite the achievement, I would say. It might seem strange to us now, but most people lived happy lives back then. Tragically short, true. At your age," he points his finger at the young faces, "most of you would be reaching your last years of, yes, a fulfilled life of family and community. This was just a hundred years ago. Just a hundred years. Think about that for a moment, people."

He pauses to let that sink in.

"But as sure of their destiny as they might have been, they were equally ignorant; just a bad turn away from kicking the bucket. And then, just as the twenty-third century is counting its last days, something very unexpected happened in a remote colony, far away from the centers of power, something that empowered a woman —a teenage girl really—to turn her narrow rural world on its head."

Edda van Dolah! Ximena's eagerness surfaces as a hawkish smile on her face. Edda van Dolah—*Juf* Edda—is Ximena's undisputed historical hero. Ximena can't wait to dive into the nitty-gritty details of her lifework.

"The jury is still out on the merits of her legacy," Miyagi says, "but nobody can deny the extraordinary role that history reserved to Edda van Dolah from Lunteren."

Ximena frowns lightly in puzzlement. *Why the doubt on her achievements? She is the inspiration of every young girl on Earth, and probably on Nubaria too, isn't she?*

"We believe we are doing fine now, don't we?" he

continues. "Imagine that some brilliant new Edda van Dolah appears today. Right here, perhaps one of you." He points a finger at his captivated audience. "And imagine that she discovers something new, unknown to the rest of us. Something that makes her realize how hopelessly doomed we humans really are."

An uneasy silence extends across the auditorium.

"It would be tough to convince your fellow citizens, don't you think? Especially if doing so involved a radical transformation of our way of life."

He paces the stage slowly, the echo of his steps the only sound in the wide hemicycle.

"Now imagine *that* happens in a fanatically religious society, where most people spend just five years in school before joining their family business at the age of ten. Think about it, people. Life was so short that a ten-year-old was considered a fully functioning adult back then! Edda van Dolah herself, aged sixteen in 2399, was already an experienced and reputable schoolteacher. And a mother too!"

No wonder, Ximena thinks. *If everybody dies at twenty-seven, they had to get busy pretty quickly.*

"Try to put her existence into context," Miyagi continues. "Think about the limited time to educate and to specialize on any trade. The world in 2399 was a sea—no, an ocean!—of ignorance. The average person was clueless about where they came from... and where they were headed. And it is in such a world that this sixteen-year-old girl leapt out of nowhere and kicked history squarely in the balls. What were the chances? Not many, I would say. And not only because, as everybody knows, history is a female."

Many students laugh as Miyagi takes a few idle steps, his hands behind his back, a smile on his lips. Even Ximena has to chuckle at the horrendous joke.

"I want you to ponder how... *improbable* Edda's impact on history really was. We are going to dive into interesting times indeed. But that's not all." Miyagi begins to raise his voice with expert modulation. "I've also got you covered with an extinction-event asteroid, first contact with an alien species, and even *human* radio signals from outer space!"

A roar of enthusiasm erupts, Ximena's included. *Goah, this is going to be sooo good.*

"I like what I hear," Miyagi says, nodding at the red-faced students. "All right, let's get the show rolling. Literally, because I have a little surprise for you today." Miyagi's smile widens. "To make this seminar more interesting, I'll make use of some scenes from a new documentary I'm working on about the time——"

A renewed burst of enthusiastic claps and cheers drowns his words. Ximena is jumping on her feet and clapping her hands into stumps. She has to stop herself from hugging Mark, who is yelling his lungs out next to her. Ximena knows that Professor Miyagi is of course referring to *The Rise and Fall of The Juf.* Rumors about his new sensorial are all over the media—another historical masterpiece by Kenji Miyagi!

"Thank you. Yes, yes, you've guessed it. Prepare to literally immerse yourselves in the world as it was in the zenith of Goah's Imperia. Please," he raises a hand, "I must insist on your discretion outside these walls—this is still very much a work in progress, merely a draft. I'm just bringing these scenes into the seminar in the faint hope of saving some of you from certain boredom."

THREE

Faith and Dem

"**D**em." Professor Miyagi seems to enjoy the focused attention of his hundred odd students. "The *Dem-Pandemic*. The final obsession of the powerful nation-states and scientists of the golden age, all investigating compulsively even as society kept crumbling around them in the early twenty-second century."

He takes a few silent steps on stage, hands on his back. *The seminar begins*! Ximena thinks as excitement creeps up her guts.

"They all ultimately failed," he says somberly, "and *billions* died. Forward two hundred years, and history crashes against a sixteen-year-old schoolteacher who is convinced she finally figured it out. She is the one that shall crack open Dem for all to see. Is she a one-in-a-millennia genius? Or is that the natural arrogance of youth?"

Ximena leans back at the words. They ring harsh, almost heretical.

"Prepare to meet the true Edda van Dolah, people. Not the myth, mind you. We do *history* in this," he waves his hand around the structure, "auditorium. Not religion."

It almost feels to Ximena as if he were directing his words at his fellow GIA students, the way he glimpses in their general direction. But no, he was just pulling his hair off his face.

"If you must only learn *one* thing in this seminar," Miyagi speaks slower and with greater emphasis, "let it be this, people: Edda was only human, nothing more, living her regular colonial life at the edge of the Hanseatic Imperium a hundred years ago. She was, like we all are— yes, me included, I grudgingly confess—just a limited and flawed *mensa* of her time."

Ximena scoffs, and recites to herself, "A bullet is just a piece of metal, until it kills an emperor."

"Very poetic!" The redheaded Neanderthal sitting to her right is smiling at her with appreciation. Ximena blushes at the unsolicited attention and keeps her eyes firmly locked on the stage below.

"And yet," Miyagi continues, "there was undeniably something extraordinary about this girl. What she brought upon the *worlds* is not the product of the common man."

"She had the Walking talent of a goddess!" the Neanderthal next to Ximena whispers. She involuntarily turns her head to him, and meets his large, blue eyes. His prominent Neanderthal brow ridge enhances the intensity of his gaze to an almost hypnotic level. His white smile broadens. "Name's Mark," he says, extending his hand.

Ximena blushes intensely. She is not used to masculine attention, and most definitely not Neanderthal. Luckily her manners go on autopilot and she shakes his hand blandly. First time she touches a Neanderthal, she thinks with apprehension. No, second! There was also Ank before. The Global Program is churning surprises faster than her provincial mind can cope with.

"Didn't catch your name." Mark's eyes pierce hers.

"Uh, Ximena."

"Ximena," Mark pronounces slowly, like he is savoring it. "Beautiful name. And exotic."

She cannot blush further. Her dark skin is hopefully hiding it, but she doubts it; dream permascapes are treasonous that way. She mutters something resembling a non-committal word of thanks and hastily turns her eyes back to Professor Miyagi.

He is pacing in silence along the rim of the stage, leisurely, squinting at the sun that bathes the amphitheater. Ximena can even feel its balmy warmth on her face. Miyagi approaches Ank, who is sitting with her stunning female elegance next to a wudai machine in the shape of a small round table. From her bench, Ximena can see the actual wudai in the device: green tendrils of ivy-like vegetation slowly withering around and inside copper-colored metallic components. Wudai are, at their core, highly psychically-reactive creatures, not quite plants, nor animals, but something else entirely—the true wonder at the heart of the dreamtech revolution.

"Is Bob ready?" Miyagi asks, pointing at the machine.

Ank nods. Ximena knows that that machine is just the dream avatar of a *real* machine, with *real* wudai, running in some goahforsaken data center in the wake.

"Great, then let's watch Edda in action, shall we? Determined to solve once and for all the largest mystery humankind has ever faced. Okay then…" Miyagi turns slowly to the wudai machine, almost hesitantly, "Bob, can you, er, turn *on*?"

"Acknowledged," the machine—*Bob*—replies with a distinctively artificial female voice that Ximena hears directly inside her mind. "Do state archive."

"Uh," he speaks slower and louder, "yes, er, please grab the latest draft of *Rise and Fall of the Juf?*"

"Acknowledged. Do state index of reproduction."

"Index of…?" Miyagi turns to Ank with a frown of frustration. "What—?"

"Let me," Ank says with a firm shake of her head. "Bob, load tag 6th December 2399."

"Acknowledged. Do state perimeter of rendition."

Ank speaks like she is taking notes on a recorder. "Expand rendition to permascape globalprog dot historydep dot lundev dot edu."

Bob vibrates for a few moments. "Detected one hundred twenty minds in one million cubic feet of permascape. Do confirm."

"Confirmed," Ank says. "Render from index zero, camera tag Edda at Joyousday House, Lunteren."

"Acknowledged. Rendition begins at index zero."

As the machine speaks, the spring sun and blue sky over the amphitheater vanish in an instant, surrounding the dumbfounded students in humid darkness. Many gasp at the sudden drop of temperature and Ximena shrinks into herself with an involuntary shudder.

"Oh, sorry, let me…" Ank says, and she must do something in the darkness, because the cold detaches at once from Ximena's mind. *Oh, the relief.* The cool winter air is still there, around her, thick and humid on her senses, but not uncomfortable now, like her skin is watching instead of feeling. Other students sigh as well.

"Bob, increase natural light," Ank says. "Point one lux."

"Acknowledged."

Ximena's eyes—still trying to adapt to the darkness—are grateful for the extra radiance. The contour of the students sitting nearby appear like ghosts. She turns to see Mark's white smile as he stares intently at something above the stage of the amphitheater. She follows his gaze. Yes, there, she can see it as well.

A house floating in the air.

An elongated one-story house, surrounded by a carefully tended garden—flowers and lawn barely hinted at in the winter night. It is raining too, and as Ximena engages her senses, she begins to feel the drops of freezing water on her head and arms in full immersive experience—blissfully detached from her mind. The ultrarealistic impact of dream sensorials never fails to amaze her, and the quality of this one is… wow! She knows she is sitting on the amphitheater bench—she can see Mark's comforting shape beside her—and yet she feels like she is right there in that garden, silently approaching the back of the house, sneaking behind a bush and getting her sandaled feet wet on the soaked grass.

Her mind reacts to that. She is not wearing sandals!

"Meet Edda van Dolah, people." Miyagi's voice unexpectedly rises from under the floating scene. And it's as if his voice reveals the perspective Ximena was becoming lost in. Her mind snaps back into place as she realizes that it is not herself who is tiptoeing in the darkness along the geometric reliefs carved across the house walls. Dreamsensos engage you like that—*psych-links,* they are called. They make you lose yourself in the characters, make you live the dream drama as if they were your own.

Ximena is not a frequent consumer of commercial dreamsensos, so she must make a conscious effort to see with her own eyes what her mind is psych-linked to: a teenage girl, wearing a dark tunic that makes her virtually invisible. Her dark skin and short, wild hair melt seamlessly with the night. She moves with determination towards a window covered with exquisite stained-glass motifs.

The girl smashes the glass with a rock, and stays put, looking around for a few seconds, until silence returns.

"Don't worry," Miyagi says. "Edda's accomplice is faking a wound to distract and lure the guard away. Edda has a few minutes for herself."

As the psych-link strengthens, Ximena feels a surge of adrenaline and a simple thought—*hurry!*—that isn't her own.

The girl—Edda—climbs through the ruined window. It's dark, and there is an unpleasant smell in the air, like too many perspiring people without ventilation. She fetches a bulky, metallic flashlight from within her tunic's folds. It *feels* heavy in her hand, as she turns it on and slides the weak light beam across the room: a mix between a laboratory and a morgue.

I'm in! The thought flashes through Ximena's mind as intimately as a lover's whisper. She lets the stream of thoughts drown her own. She is finally in the forbidden backroom of the Joyousday House! The proof has to be here, somewhere! Goah, she has but a minute, perhaps two if Aline is really convincing with her bogus injury. But better hurry—Aline's such a terrible liar.

Edda waves the beam of light across the four bed-sized platforms that take up the better part of the room, the light reflecting off their shiny metallic surface. They look like dissecting platforms, Ximena thinks—a thought of her own. As Edda inspects the last platform, the light beam reveals a body.

A *breathing* body. A naked man in his mid-twenties. Eyes open. Silent.

Ximena jumps from fright. Edda doesn't. She just stares at the man for a long moment, waiting for a reaction that never comes.

"Hello?" she finally says. The words rumble in the silence.

No reaction.

She approaches the man, who keeps staring at the ceiling like she wasn't there. Then she recognizes him.

"Elder Meerman! Are you okay?" Edda waves a hand across his line of sight.

No reaction.

"This is Edda. Your evening-school Juf two years ago?"

Nothing.

Edda inspects the platform which seems inhumanly cold under the exposed body. There are traces of feces around his buttocks. Somebody is taking care of him, but not thoroughly enough.

Edda waves the beam of light at his green eyes. The irises dutifully contract.

What have they done to you? Edda gulps and gathers her thoughts. She was there, like most in the colony, to bid Elder Meerman farewell in his Joyousday. That was, er, ten days ago? Two weeks max? And he was the happiest and liveliest man in the party. *Look at you now.*

Ximena can feel Edda's pity and anger rising up her own guts.

There's only one explanation, Edda thinks.

Poison.

So simple.

She knew it all along, and by Goah she is going to uncover the truth. Dem is *not* a disease. Dem doesn't really exist. Never did. Just a myth, drilled down for generations by *Quaestors* and the rest of the hierarchy of *aws Head*. Just a *lie* to keep people compliant. Yes, good old hunger for power. It is so simple, isn't it? Administer dumb-making poison to every adult when reaching twenty-seven years of age. Adorn with an involved ritual

—the Joyousday—to give it a shell of religious legitimacy. And the result? A compliant population, forever young and, crucially, too ignorant to ask the hard questions. Well, she sure as Dem is going to ask them! But she needs evidence. She needs—

"Who's there?!"

Edda—and Ximena—jump at the sudden shout. There is a man behind the only door to the room. *The guard. Fuck, Aline. Too early!*

"I know you're there," the guard says. His steps are closing in. "Don't move!"

Quick, she needs proof, or it will all be for nothing. Goah's Mercy, where would they keep the...? She frantically turns the beam of light towards the other platforms. Nothing, they are empty.

The guard pushes the door, but it doesn't budge. *Thank Goah, it's locked.* The guard begins to fumble with a set of keys. No time!

Edda turns her flashlight to the white laboratory cupboards lining the walls. Are those...? She runs toward the nearest shelves, where a neat line of transparent vials hold some sort of thick-looking liquid.

The door blasts open. The guard stands there, panting, dumbfounded, staring at her flashlight not five meters away.

No, no, no. She must have the evidence!

"Freeze! Who are you?!"

With a swift, almost instinctive move, Edda aims the beam of light squarely at the guard's eyes.

"What?!" He flinches his head away.

It's just an instant. That's all she needs. Edda reaches to the shelf, precise and quick like a reflex. Before her conscious mind even realizes it, she is pulling a vial into the inner folds of her tunic.

"Juf Edda?" The guard stares at her, gobsmacked. "Is that *you*?"

"Man Kamphuijs," Edda meets his gaze matter-of-factly. "Now I see why you never have time to finish your homework."

The floating dreamsenso scene changes abruptly.

Right there, floating above the students, Edda is sitting, elbows on knees, inside a small windowless cell. The cell is mostly empty, except for the bed she is sitting on, a toilet in the corner and a dim electrical bulb hanging from the ceiling. She is wearing the same dark tunic, gaze lost in some point on the wall.

"This is a few hours afterwards, in the morning," Miyagi says, unnecessarily, since Ximena knows it already as the psych-link to Edda is still active. She can feel her boredom. And her impatience. "Edda has been put in jail, of course." Miyagi's voice rises from where Ximena knows he is standing on the amphitheater stage, but she cannot see him in the darkness beneath the floating scene. "But she is not your average drunkard, is she? Juf Edda—*Juf* is a title of respect for female schoolteachers in the broader region—is quite popular in her native colony of Lunteren, or perhaps *controversial* is a more appropriate word. And accounts of her little adventure have already spread like fire. Ank, could you please move the POV outside of the jail cells? Just for a second?"

Ximena can only imagine Ank down there waving her hands at Bob, or whispering at it, or whatever dreamtech engineers do to manipulate dream sensorials.

The scene shifts abruptly as the camera moves through the walls, causing Ximena to squint at the sudden brightness of the rising sun. She hears the excited chatter of dozens of voices before her as her eyes adapt to the light.

Gathered on a red-bricked esplanade around the building, there must be a hundred people, maybe more, most in their teen years. They wear long, thick tunics; some plain, some colorful, some wildly patterned. A few dozen bicycles have been left carelessly lying nearby. A horse pulling a cart, loaded with sacks and crates brimming with potatoes, trots across the background, the driver staring at the crowd with blatant curiosity. There is a lone guard by the wooden door to the cells, laughing and chatting animatedly with some of the crowd, probably grateful for the interruption of his usual tedium.

"Popular," Miyagi says. "You people get the idea. Back to the cell, please, Ank. And forward to Willem's visit."

The scene shifts back to Edda in her cell, as the door opens to a thin man in his mid-twenties. He gasps as his brown eyes behind thin glasses lock on her. He dashes forward and inspects her anxiously.

"Hey, Dad," Edda says with a monotonous voice, and turns her head to the wall, like she doesn't care. But she does. Oh Goah, you bet she does! Ximena almost gasps as she feels the surge of love splatter like an explosion in her guts, filling her with a warmth that she's not sure she's ever felt for any member of her own cozy family. "So you've heard, yeah?" Edda asks, glacially.

"I have," he says with a grave tone as he pushes his thin glasses up his nose. He nods at the guard behind him, who softly shuts the door and leaves them alone.

They could not be more physically different. To Edda's sharp African beauty, Willem's pale Northern softness. To Edda's black, short curls, Willem's brown, long hair. To Edda's natural elegance, Willem's intellectual shabbiness.

But Ximena knows that they are not so different after all. At least not inside, where it counts.

Willem holds his daughter's gaze for a long while.

In silence.

Until she finally sinks her head. "I had a good reason."

"As usual," he sighs. "And as usual, the family reputation takes a hit."

Edda scoffs. "There are more important things than our reputation. Your *life*, for example."

"Here we go again." Willem folds his arms.

She turns towards him, eyes pleading. "Don't let them kill you, Dad. It's all a farce!"

Willem sighs again. He looks like a man that has been doing lots of sighing lately. "Listen. Marjolein will be here any moment. She's dispersing that little fan club of yours outside."

"What fan club?"

"Doesn't matter. I promised her your deepest regret and your best behavior, so play your part. I don't want her to hear any of this nonsense, you hear me? Or you will be in serious, serious trouble."

"But she's with them, Dad. She's aws Head through and through."

"She's much more than that, and I'm sorry you cannot see that. Just..." He draws a deep breath. "Edda, please. If you can't respect my guidance as your Elder, could you at least respect my wishes as your father?"

"But you know I'm right!" Edda stands and steps closer to Willem. "Dem is not real. You know it too!"

Willem presses his lips, walks to Edda, and places a kiss on her cheek. "It doesn't matter what I believe, girl." His voice has softened. "The show must go on. You, Bram, and especially little Hans, you are the show now, and all this..."

he waves an exasperated hand at the cell walls, "... is only making things harder for you when I... *leave*."

"So you still want to uphold your Joyousday, yeah?"

"I must, girl." He smiles at her, a pinch of sadness in his eyes. "What else can I do? And you will as well, when you reach my age. For Hans's sake, and for your future grandchildren's."

She meets his stern look silently. "Please, Dad... I know I haven't always been the easiest daughter. But..." She has to stop to keep tears from surfacing.

A muted noise behind the door—approaching steps?— resonates up her spine, making her sharply aware of the urgency. *The bitch will be here any second now!* The surge of adrenaline dispels her emotions and leaves only *purpose*. The only thing that matters. The reason Goah put her in this world. Her lifework. And her father is key.

Edda throws herself forward and puts the vial into her father's hand. "I found this in the Joyousday House, next to the body of Elder Meerman. He was still alive, Dad! But empty—*soulless*."

Willem's eyes widen. "Dem?"

"Same as you now, he didn't have a trace of Dem before his Joyousday. Whatever that was, it wasn't Dem. The answer is in that flask."

Willem frowns and inspects the vial. "How did you hide this? Didn't they search you?"

Edda blinks. "I asked for the toilet, you need more details?"

She turns her head towards the door. Steps are clearly approaching now. They are right outside. She stands on tiptoe, and whispers in Willem's ear with the most compelling urgency she can muster, "Dad, hide it! Analyze it in secret—somebody you trust."

The door opens, and a woman steps in. Ximena recognizes her immediately.

Marjolein Mathus.

A few years younger than her usual historical image, when she was still the colonial Quaestor of Lunteren. Ximena tries to repress the sudden pinch of revulsion, and it's not only from Edda's psych-link. It's been a hundred years since the Dreamwars, but its scars still run deep, especially in the Goah's Imperia of America.

Look at her, Ximena thinks, *twenty-one years of age, and already so full of herself, with those intricate blond braids and that pretentious Quaestor robe.* Neanderthal Mark whistles his appreciation at the small, exuberant shape under the thin fabric. Ximena's eyes flinch at him. *Men. They're all the same, whichever the world.*

"Will." Marjolein smiles at Willem. "Edda." Her smile freezes and she takes a step closer, inspecting her from top to bottom. "You've been a naughty, naughty girl."

"A *repented* girl," Willem says, putting his hands in his pockets and smiling awkwardly. "I'm sure we can—"

"You mind waiting outside?" Marjolein's large blue eyes drill into his. "It will be just a minute."

"Uh, of course." He turns to his daughter, a warning in his eyes, and leaves.

Marjolein turns to Edda, who stares defiantly back at her, lips pressed hard. "I'm disappointed, Edda. You're making things unnecessarily hard on your father. In his last weeks on this plane, he needs peace and family." She hesitates the briefest of moments. "And love."

Edda chuckles. "Oh, I'm sure you are more than willing to ease his pains."

Marjolein's expression tightens. "Your father *paused* his relationship with me, if that is what you're implying..."

"Again?" Edda scoffs. "Let's see how long this time."

"You were part of the reason."

"A pity I'm not the *whole* reason."

Marjolein closes her eyes and rubs her right temple slowly. "Is this how it's going to be?" She opens them and meets Edda's poisonous gaze. "What have I ever done to you? Is it because of me and your father?"

"I don't care who wants to fuck my father," Edda says with exaggerated scorn. "But who wants to kill him, *that* I do care about, yeah?"

Marjolein frowns her thin, blond eyebrows, her blue eyes locked on Edda's. "This is very confusing, Edda. Are you implying that *I* want to kill your father?"

"Yes! Same as Elder Meerman. You poisoned him! You're poisoning all of us. And in two months, it's my dad's turn."

Marjolein's eyes widen, her expression honestly baffled. She opens her mouth as if to speak, but says nothing.

Oh Edda, Ximena thinks, feeling her rage. *I hear you, but perhaps you should be a bit more subtle.*

"I've seen what aws Head has done to Elder Meerman," Edda says. "I'll tell everybody."

"Elder Meerman has Dem, Edda," Marjolein speaks softly, as if Edda were a little kid. "End phase. He is already in Goah's Embrace. What you've seen is just his mortal carcass. The incineration is planned for tomorrow—"

"He had no Dem! We all saw him during his Joyousday. He was... *alive* and happy. What I saw in the Joyousday House..." Edda shudders visibly.

"*Dem.* That's what you saw."

"What a coincidence, yeah? Nobody's seen Dem for generations, but when a person enters the Joyousday House, they get infected," Edda clicks her fingers, "like that."

"It's not a coincidence." Marjolein's voice is soft and patient. She's once more the Quaestor, explaining *aws* Faith—the Faith *of Goah*—to a recalcitrant child. "We are all infected with Dem, Edda, from the day we are born. But the human mind is marvelous—Goah's most prodigious creation in the universe. Our brain can resist the constant pressure of Dem for a whole quarter of a century. It used to be more. Much more, they say. There are chronicles of people that turned one hundred. But as the second collapse sped up, Dem got increasingly vicious and killed ever earlier. Until—you know your scriptures, Edda—Kaya Fahey and her revelation of Goah's Gift. Were it not for our first Pontifex, we would not be here today. Nobody would."

"Don't give me the sermon, *Quaestor*." Edda's scorn is filled with poison. "I know the propaganda. I teach it, remember? The whole lot. How Fahey founded the oh so holy *Imperia of Goah* that saved the last humans from barbarism and extinction. What does that have to do with—?"

"It's not propaganda, Edda. It's the truth. It's *history*. And it has everything to do with Elder Meerman. In the Joyousday House we perform sacred rites and treatments that have been perfected for centuries. My Joyousday specialists assisted Elder Meerman to let go of his soul in peace, without suffering—with *dignity*. That's my office's last blessing." Her lips curve into a faint smile. "The *Head of Goah* is not evil, Edda. We take care of all our children. There's just no alternative to the rites of the Joyousday, other than the agony of Elder Meerman and his family as his mind vanishes relentlessly for weeks, until nothing —*nothing*—remains. I know it sounds complicated. And it sure as Dem is. But let that be the concern of *aws Head*, not yours."

"Yeah, how convenient. How fucking convenient," Edda's sarcasm removes Marjolein's smile like a slap, "to keep us all ignorant and harmless, making sure we die before we can pose a threat to aws Head's power, yeah? Not a single tyrant in history has ever come with such an exquisite tool of control," she scoffs. "No need to repress your people if you kill them early enough. Brilliant. And yet the Joyousday comes a far second place in the perfect tyrant's toolbox."

Marjolein takes a deep breath. "I know I'm going to regret it, but please enlighten me, Edda. What's the first?"

"Mind control, of course. Or in other words: *religion*."

Ximena gasps in emotional confusion. So far, Edda's rough feelings against Marjolein resonate with her, but now the sudden dissonance takes her by surprise. And is not pleasant. On one hand she is feeling Edda's anger as her own, even as it boils into righteous hate, but at the same time she feels her own beliefs attacked—hammered even—by her words.

"Goah's Mercy, Edda." Marjolein throws a nervous glance at the closed cell door. "Never let anybody hear you say that. It's heresy!"

"It's *truth*!" Edda shouts. "Faith and Dem are the two faces of Imperial power."

"Enough of this lunacy, Edda." Marjolein's voice has changed. It is cold and stern. "Enough of your childish conspiracy theories. As teacher—as *Juf*—you hold a public office and have the same sacred responsibility I have to keep harmony in Lunteren."

"A teacher must teach the truth, *Quaestor*."

"Oh Goah, you'll flog a dead horse until…" Marjolein shakes her head. "Can't you see what you've done already?"

Edda folds her arms and holds her gaze in silence.

"Your excursion to the Joyousday House—that was *desecration*, Goah's Mercy. Of place, of art, and—much worse—of *soul*."

Edda's eyes narrow. Ximena feels the fire of her rage, but Edda keeps her expression cool.

Marjolein sighs heavily. "The Meermans are asking for maximum reparations. And removal of your office."

"Removal…?!" Edda's eyes widen. "No, you can't… My students—!"

"I know what you mean to them, I just spoke with a few outside. But I also have a responsibility to them, and to everybody in Lunteren. To be honest with you, Edda, I'm not sure you deserve the public pulpit, and by allowing you to keep it I might be harming not only your students, but also yourself."

Edda blinks in silence. Ximena feels her anger dissolving in fear, paralyzing her.

Marjolein continues, "And it's not just your students that you're harming. Aline is in the cell next door. Why?"

"A- Aline didn't—"

"Because she's your friend, that's why. She follows you everywhere, like a puppy, same as your students. Where are you taking them, Edda? Do you even care?"

"I, uh…" Edda's voice is unnaturally weak. But her thoughts and feelings flow strongly through the psych-link. She's a *Juf*, and teaching is her life—the life of every Van Dolah. Their calling. *What would Dad say if—*

"With the trust of followers comes the responsibility of leadership. And it's a heavy burden, believe me. Please tell me you understand what I'm saying."

Edda nods in silence and sinks her head.

Marjolein takes a deep breath. "I want to believe you. I don't know if I do, but I'm giving you the benefit of the doubt. For your students. And for your father. He doesn't deserve this—not in his last weeks." She lifts her chin and watches Edda in expectant silence, as if waiting for a word of gratitude.

Edda doesn't move.

Hold your temper, Edda, Ximena thinks.

"Very well," Marjolein continues in a formal voice. "This year's karma increase to the Van Dolahs is hereby reassigned to the Meermans in concept of reparation. You shall spend one more night in this cell. Upon release, you shall go straight to their home and offer a sincere apology. A *sincere* apology, you hear me? And above all, you shall keep your outlandish theories to yourself."

Edda doesn't move a muscle and keeps her eyes locked on her sandals. But her outrage burns deep into Ximena's guts.

FOUR

The Ices of Austerlitz

"So what have we got?" Miyagi paces the stage, hands still placed on his back. It remains dark in the amphitheater, but Ank has conjured a full moon and dashing Milky Way across the starry sky, enough to bathe the professor and Ximena's fellow students in a creamy gleam. "A rebellious teenager, a worried father about to be ritually dispatched, a pissed-off Quaestor. There's still something… missing, isn't there? Something with more, hmm, historical weight."

Mark turns to Ximena and whispers with an ominous voice, "Aliens."

Ximena chuckles, and Mark, clearly pleased with himself, returns his gaze to the floating dreamsenso scene over Miyagi's head, where Edda, still in the cell, sleeps soundly on her side, head over hands.

"Same date," Miyagi continues, pointing at Edda, "6th of December 2399, close to midnight. Edda van Dolah enjoys her last hours of penitence in Lunteren's arrest cells. But," he pauses for effect, "she's not alone."

Ximena's eyes scan the cell methodically. It is dark, but it's a small empty space. "She's alone," she mutters.

"Aliens," Mark says, smiling radiantly at her.

"Where?" Ximena doesn't stop her scrutiny of the scene.

"In the *Second Wake*."

Ximena turns to him. "How do you know?" Mark's oh-so-blue eyes seem to glimmer in the moonlight.

Before he can reply, Miyagi says, "Ank, please alter phase to the Second Wake."

The static scene with Edda in the cell changes abruptly, and yet nothing has changed: Edda still sleeps, the door, the toilet, all in place. But the light... Ximena's jaw drops at the sudden sharpness of her visual senses, like she was blind before without knowing. As a simple user of the dreamnet, Ximena has never seen the Second Wake—the Traverse, as it is colloquially known—with her own eyes, but she is of course familiar with its traits, and recognizes it instantly.

Everything—every object—radiates its essence vividly. Ximena intellectually knows there are no shadows in the Traverse, but now, in full immersion, she can finally grasp in awe what a true shadowless world really means, even something as unspectacular as an arrest cell. Every surface glimmers its intricate secrets in gray-like radiance. Every wrinkle, every imperfection. No spot remains invisible.

And Edda, oh how her body radiates *life*, a dazzling blue aura glows over her skin and scintillates intensely, in high contrast with the gray vividness around her. Ximena knows that Edda's blue sparkling reflects her inner world— she is dreaming intensely, and it shows.

And, as Miyagi promised, she is not alone.

And, as Mark promised, it's *aliens*.

A tall, elongated figure, vaguely humanoid, is standing

next to Edda. Its skin—white and hairless, almost of silky quality—emanates an intense red glow that glints even more wildly than Edda's blue halo. Ximena cannot see the front of the head as it is leaning over Edda—obviously inspecting her closely—but the back is as featureless as the rest of the body: no clothes nor ornaments, no hair, just the thin trunk and four, long, boneless limbs resembling two arms and two legs, none of which touch the floor.

"That's Rew," Mark whispers. "Finally." He is smiling, eyes locked on the alien.

Ximena frowns at him. "You mean *Yog*, right?"

Mark gives her a strange side glance. "Where do you get your history from?"

"First Contact is near," Miyagi says before Ximena can reply, "but it is not happening tonight. You'll have to be patient. These are just the preliminaries. People," he waves a hand at the creature, "meet Rew."

Rew? Never heard the name, Ximena thinks as she shoots an annoyed glance at Mark's smug smile.

"Rew is looking for candidates for First Contact," Miyagi continues. "*Worthy* candidates, for there is a plan for them. She has already selected a few dozen humans and is almost ready to execute her plan. But there's still time for one or two more. And Edda's recent activity in the Joyousday House has caught her attention. She is wondering, isn't she? About Edda. Can you imagine her thoughts?" He turns to his captivated audience. "Anybody?"

Several hands shoot up in the air, including Mark's.

"Yes?" Miyagi points at a Lundev student close to Ximena who is wearing retro-glasses. His full name appears in bright, bold letters over his head. "Qiao, what is Rew thinking?"

"Uh, what about: is this human *motivated*?"

"Motivation. Essential, yes." Miyagi nods. "To do what?"

"Hmm, rebellion, I guess," Qiao says.

"Uh-huh." Miyagi nods again. "Rew is indeed looking for rebellious humans, but… let's face it: half the teens in every place and age fit that description. There is something special she believes to have found in Edda. Anybody want to…? Er…" Miyagi points his finger almost directly at Ximena, "… Mark?"

Mark stands. "Rew is looking for raw potential—for talent. Not many people have that. Look at Edda's halo, it's… spectacular!"

Edda's halo? Ximena squints at the fierce blue refulgence around her sleeping shape. *What about it?*

"Ha!" Miyagi claps once and points a finger back at Mark. "You are a Walker in the Shadow, aren't you?"

Mark bows. "At your service."

"Wow," Miyagi laughs. "What are you doing here? Shouldn't you be—I don't know—earning tons of karma in the dreamnet?"

Mark chuckles. "There's more to life than karma, Professor." He seems to enjoy the undivided attention of the auditorium. "There's also girls," he says with a wink at Ximena, who blushes instantly. "And history!"

"Oh so true," Miyagi says, students laughing. "Now, Mark, what do you think? How can Rew figure out if Edda is First Contact material?"

"By testing her, of course."

"Of course," Miyagi says, "let's watch."

Mark sits and smiles widely at Ximena, very satisfied with himself, as Miyagi gives Ank a curt nod.

Rew begins to move. Gently. She leans closer to Edda, ever closer, until their halos—red and blue—touch!

Ximena leans back with a gasp as the scene seems to

explode across the auditorium, shattering into pieces as if made of colored glass, and then rejoining into a fresh scene.

Colors are a notch more... intense. And textures are *off* somehow. Edda is there, much younger, appearing to be around eight years old. She is sneaking into a large room with a big glass window that looks over the backyard and the vegetable garden of the Van Dolah's house.

It is a warm summer day, and the glass windows are open. Fresh air and sunlight are streaming in, flooding the room, and Miyagi's students' grateful lungs. A large, square table close to the windows is covered with dozens of miniature soldiers lovingly painted in historically accurate Napoleonic-era uniforms. Two armies face each other on a beautiful model battlefield: farms, hills, woods, towns, rivers, lakes, valleys, all painstakingly recreated.

A younger-looking Willem stands by the table and stares at the armies in quiet reflection.

"What are you doing?" Edda shouts from behind him.

Willem jumps. "Ha! You scared me, girl!" He takes her in a wild embrace.

"Let me down!" she giggles. "What is this?" She reaches towards a tiny soldier.

"Whoa, whoa, don't touch that! This is... war!" He looks at her with open eyes, as if trying to impress her.

"Looks like toys to me. These tiny dolls are ugly."

Willem laughs. "You caught me, girl. The truth is, it's a game. In a few minutes your mom will be home from work, and we are going to spend the night fighting this... er, war."

"You are going to play the whole night? Dad, that is not fair! You never let me! You are a *hypocrates*."

"Hypocrite. Yes, I guess you are right. You know what? Tomorrow is Sunday. Let me talk to your mom, and if she agrees, you and Bram can stay and watch the game. Would you like that?"

"Yes! I don't think Bram will like this, though. It's for adults and he's such a baby. But I want to learn the game. I want to play with you and beat you like at chess last week!"

Willem laughs, seemingly pleased. "This is not chess. It is a battle simulation and very realistic, with many rules. Look at this!" He lifts a thick book also placed on the table. "Would you like to read them?"

Edda frowns at the rulebook. "Uh…"

"Tell you what, you read it, and you can play with your mom against me. I'm sure she'll be grateful for the help. Would you like that?"

"Yes!" she says, radiant.

The scene pauses and begins to rotate slowly over the amphitheater in full visual glory. Young Willem glows with frozen happiness at young Edda, as she enthusiastically raises her fists.

"Do you notice the *texture* of the scene?" Professor Miyagi asks, as he proudly points with a finger, showing that indeed, the entire atmosphere is not quite *right*. It is thicker, not fully static, as if immersed in an invisible liquid. It appears real, but not complete. The light is strangely unnatural, the colors perhaps too vivid. "What do you think the dreamsenso is telling us?"

"A dream?" Qiao says.

"I think so as well," a female student says—*Lora* is the name that appears over her head as Miyagi points at her. "At first, I thought it was a flashback, or a memory. But it has a *dreamy* quality to it." Ximena and other students nod at her words.

"Yes! Thanks." He smiles, satisfied. "This was a tough problem. When producing this dream sensorial, my team had to get very creative to convey a convincing dreamscape to the audience, you know, a dream inside a dream. In my opinion they nailed it, but I wasn't a hundred percent. Now I am, thank you!"

Miyagi gives Ank a nod, and the scene shifts again. The room is the same, but later in the night, the garden outside already covered in darkness, glass windows closed to evening mosquitoes. Inside the room, two dim electrical lamps illuminate the table and the surrounding faces, immersed in the imaginary, unfolding battle.

Willem is on one side of the table, staring at the miniatures and not looking too happy. Opposing him are Edda and an intense black woman—*Anika*. The name comes to Ximena through the psych-link as if a memory of her own. She is Edda's mother. And her biological mother too, from the looks of her—older by a few years than her brother Willem. Edda's biological father was an unknown dowry merchant, she remembered reading somewhere.

Ximena's own family is Goahn, of course. In the GIA everybody's is. No exceptions. It's *Goah's Gift*, after all. Even in Hansasia and Botswana most families are also still Goahn. Supposedly. But she has heard that there is an increasing tolerance—and even acceptance—of the barbaric practice of the Sexual Families of old, surely a result of the pagan cultural influence of Nubaria, spreading like cancer across the old world. Ximena gives Mark an involuntary side glance. This Neanderthal, sitting right there next to her, has been pulled out of the vagina of a woman. A woman that had carried him *inside her guts* for nine excruciating months. Worse, his father had impregnated his mother! Oh, the thought is… She cringes, and can't repress a shudder of disgust running up her spine. Goahns have sex, of course. Plenty. But just for fun. Or to bond with lovers, for those lucky to have time for that. And always—*always*—outside the family, Goah's Mercy!

She doesn't get it. There is no upside to the Sexual Family. They are brittle. Short lived. And, inevitably, a bitter source of loneliness and alienation—especially to the eldest. Compare that with the naturality and certainty of Willem and Anika's fraternal relationship. Watching them playing together over the war miniatures, Ximena projects her own relationship to her brother Juan: unbreakable, *unshakable*, forever in the same household, from birth to death. So is the bond that lies at the core of every Goahn Family. Siblings to each other, they are parents to the next generation, and grandparents to the next after that. And so it goes on, indestructible, the immortal Goahn Family.

Ximena turns her attention to Edda and takes in her exultance—the family evening, the belonging, the intense love for her parents, the imminent victory in the game. Yes! But… There is also a pinch of sadness, hiding in plain sight. Something powerful and ominous. Yes, Ximena realizes, observing Anika closely. Burrowed shallow, right below the fragile surface of happiness, there is darkness and rage. Injustice—and death.

"Our gambit has worked!" Anika says, eyes wide with delight and disbelief. You are a genius, baby. "And you, my dear brother, for the first time ever," she puts a finger on Willem's chest, "are toast!"

Edda giggles and claps. "We got him, Mom!" She excitedly points at one of the miniature sets. "Maneuver this battalion up this ridge into Napoleon's ass!"

"Napoleon's *rear*, baby." Anika laughs. "Yes, sure, let's do that. We are taking Napoleon himself down. Ha! Down goes the tyrant!"

"A *tyrant*." Edda pronounces the word carefully, as if for

the first time. "Is he a baddy, Mom?" She meets her mother's gaze with large, open eyes.

"You tell me, girl: a defender of the civil rights for the people, but to spread those revolutionary ideas, he first conquered and oppressed those same people."

"Hmm," Edda twists the tip of one of her long braids. "Napoleon was a, er, *hypocrite*. Did I say it right?"

"You did, baby Edda! You absorb knowledge like Dad's troops absorb casualties."

"Beginner's luck." Willem scratches the back of his head. "Or you are indeed a genius, girl." He winks at Edda. "Your mother has never beaten me before. And I'm playing the French, who historically won Austerlitz. But your Russians," he points over at one side of the table, "and Austrians," he points over at the other side, "are everywhere! Well done! But…"

"What?" Anika asks. "There's no way you can turn the tables." She actually looks worried and scans the battlefield. "What are you hiding this time, you sneaky bastard?"

"Nothing, nothing," Willem laughs. "Except that your general Kutuzov down here, by the lake," he points with the finger, "is in real trouble now."

"Let's save Kutuzov, Mom," Edda says. "Our victory will be complete!" She touches the miniature rider— wearing a Russian general uniform and leading a cavalry battalion—with sudden affection. Ximena feels it too, like the figure were… *Abuelo?* "But look, Mom. He is surrounded by an army of retreating French troops."

"You can kiss your dear Kutuzov goodbye, dear sister," Willem says with exaggerated glee. "I may have lost the battle, but I'm sure as Dem taking Kutuzov down with me!"

And then something snaps.

What was that? Ximena thinks, as she and all the students next to her sit bolt upright in sudden attention. Ximena exchanges a silent glance with Mark, and then squints intensely at the floating scene. She has felt something strange, a sort of *vibration*. Something out of place.

"Look at her face!" Mark whispers in her ear.

And then she sees it. Anika's maternal sweetness is gone, her face distended like she were *dead*, and her eyes—Ximena gasps—the iris and pupils are absent! Anika stares now with blank, almost radiant, white eyes.

But such is the nature of dreams that changes happen unnoticed to the dreamer. Edda seems too absorbed by the tough situation of Kutuzov's battalion on the battlefield. French enemy troops on their west, on their north, and on the east; and a lake on their south.

"We can still escape, Mom," Edda says, and puts a finger on the table, "Satchen Lake is frozen!"

The scene begins to slide slowly, approaching Edda from behind, while she is bent over the drama unfolding on the table. The scene camera passes over her head and begins to glide down onto the battlefield from far above. Now it looks almost like a satellite view. The camera does not stop, like it is falling, ever closer to the *ground*.

Ximena dives with the camera down into the cold, fresh air at the edge of Satchen Lake, first feeling the vertigo of the fall, then the smell of the winter fields of old Moravia.

The shore is teeming with Napoleonic-era cavalry soldiers in chaotic disarray; they look tired, their blue and white uniforms dirty. Only a handful of them are still wearing the high military hat of the Russian dragoons; the horses seem spent, sweating despite the cold.

And leading them all, the man himself: General

Kutuzov, sitting still on his horse, studying the desperate situation with cold-blooded calmness. The French are closing in from all sides, blood-thirsty. Contact is a minute away.

Kutuzov gives the order. "Over the lake! Spread out to spare the ice. Slow walk."

The soldiers immediately abandon their chaotic stance and get into a wide formation behind the general. The horses move in unison, carefully stepping over the ice.

And the ice holds.

The disciplined soldiers motion their horses deeper over the frozen lake, the staccato of their hooves echoing across the auditorium.

The scene zooms in closer to the center of the formation, where three soldiers ride side by side: the general in the center, a captain on his right, and a lieutenant on his left. Ximena leans forward as she recognizes their faces: General Kutuzov is actually Willem! The captain is Edda, her sixteen-year-old self once again, somehow sized to fit the uniform of a gallant Russian officer. And the lieutenant... Ximena leans forward with fascination. The lieutenant is the expressionless, white-eyed Anika.

They are approaching the center of the lake. In the background, the French have reached the shores.

"General, the enemy does deploy cannons," Anika says in a strange voice—still feminine, but flat, devoid of Anika's warm intensity.

"Trot!" Willem orders without hesitation. The deafening hammering of hooves against ice grows louder as the horses thump forward. The pressure on the ice creates some cracks, but it is a thick pre-industrial winter ice.

It holds.

Edda looks back. Ximena feels her anxiety—her fear of death—in her own guts. Behind them, far away on the shore, the cannons begin spitting smoke. It takes a few instants for the thunder-like blast to reach her ears, and a few more instants for the cannonballs to rain around them with deadly precision.

The ice breaks mercilessly under the hooves of their right flank. Many men and horses disappear silently under the ice in an instant.

"Gallop, Edda!" Willem says with uncharacteristic passion. He is no longer a general, but a father. "Straight to the shore! Anika, take her!"

Edda obeys with the instinctive discipline of a soldier. She kicks her horse forward, galloping hard over the cracking ice, while Anika keeps up without visible effort, almost like her horse is floating over the vanishing ice.

As they escape forward, Willem maneuvers the remaining dragoons into a hard turn, aiming deeper into the heart of the lake; obviously a distraction.

Edda and Anika finally reach the safety of the other side of the lake. Edda stops the exhausted horse and turns around to discover in horror that Willem is not following right behind her but is still deep on the surface of the lake.

"Dad!" She dismounts and runs to the edge of the lake, fear transforming into terror. Terror of loss. Terror of being left behind. Alone. A fate worse than death, Ximena realizes with surprise.

Anika, silent as a ghost, stands on her right. With no discernible emotion on her face, she stares at the far shore with her eerie white eyes. She raises her right arm and points at the French troops. "Do look, Redeemed van Dolah," she says. "The cannons are aiming at your father."

Edda exhales loudly, tears of fear and frustration running down her cheeks. She seems unable to speak.

"Do remain calm," Anika says with her strange, leveled voice. "Do detach your emotions. You are dreaming."

"What?" Edda gapes at Anika with confusion and desperation.

"You *are* dreaming, Redeemed van Dolah. Do trust me. I am here to assist you."

Edda gives Anika a long gaze, as if just aware of her presence. "*Who* are you?"

"That is of no relevance at the moment." Anika points at the galloping dragoons. "Your father is about to die. Do focus your will on what matters."

Edda glances back at the drama unfolding on the frozen lake. "What can I possibly do?" Her voice trembles.

"Do remain calm."

"What?" She glares at her mother-thing. "Dad is up there, and you expect me to——?!"

Her words are cut short by another barrage from the French cannons. The violence of gunpowder rumbles louder than ever, as the cannonballs fly towards Willem and his hapless dragoons with ballistic, death-bringing inevitability.

"Do detach your emotions, Redeemed van Dolah. Do trust me. Do detach your fear and focus your will on the cannonballs. Do reach out with your senses and *feel* them."

Edda's eyes flinch over the lake where the cannonballs stand out with sudden vividness, impossibly made visible from that distance in a way that only dreams allow. They move with slow elegance, still rising through the freezing air.

Edda blinks and her eyes widen with sudden realization. "I'm *dreaming*!" she says.

"Very good," Anika says. "You do control the pace. The cannonballs do slow. This is *your* dream. You can save your father, Redeemed van Dolah."

"But how?" Edda asks, voice drenched in anxiety as the cannonballs keep falling, slowly but inexorably.

Willem's cavalry stops their gallop as they realize the futility of their situation. They raise their eyes to meet death head on, with the dignity of warriors of any era. All except Willem, who turns instead to look straight into the desperate eyes of Edda, a sad smile on his face.

Edda gasps in horror, powerless.

"You do not *will* those cannonballs to reach the ice," Anika's slow and patient voice says, trying to slip through Edda's panic. "You do not *will* the ice to break. You do not *will* the horses to fall into the lake. You do not *will* your father to die."

Edda gives Anika a desperate look of confusion. "But what can I do?! I'm too weak, Goah's Mercy! I'm just a stupid girl in a deadly world. I can't change shit!"

"Do accumulate power, Redeemed van Dolah. Power to force change. Power to save lives. Power to bend the world to your will. Would you like to wield power that matters?"

"Yes! Oh Goah, yes!"

"What would you sacrifice for such power, Redeemed van Dolah? What would you renounce?"

"Everything!" Tears of desperation and dread run down her cheeks. "My life! Every-fucking-thing!"

"Do prove it. This is *your* dream, Redeemed van Dolah. It is yours to do as you desire. Do bend it to your will."

Edda squints, trying to grasp the full meaning of Anika's words. Ximena feels her confusion, her hope—and the raw thirst of her desire.

But with the unstoppable pacing of nightmares, the cannon balls complete their arc of death, and rain right through the doomed dragoons, disintegrating the ice under their hooves. The *crack* sound is so loud that it echoes against the auditorium walls.

"What do you *will?*" Anika insists.

Edda is paralyzed with terror. The brave soldiers do not even have time to scream as the icy waters swallow their horses whole. Willem is the last standing, his horse already sliding.

"What do you *will*, Redeemed van Dolah? Do detach your mind of emotion, and claim power over your dream."

Edda closes her eyes and takes a deep breath.

Willem's horse frantically tries to maintain equilibrium on the floating ice as Willem pulls the reins left and right, with the skill of a lifelong rider. He does not look scared; he knows he is doomed.

Edda opens her eyes and looks sharply at her father as his horse begins to fall. Fear slips, and disappears. Anxiety vanishes. Her gaze is void of passion, even as her father dives to his death.

"Do force your *will*."

Willem's horse extends its wings. And flies.

The entire scene slowly fades into darkness, a dream that ends. "Reality is built on top of dreams." The enigmatic voice of Anika slips through even as the last light disappears. "Do control your dreams, and you shall control your reality."

Edda sits drowsily on the arrest cell bed, and rubs her neck. Ximena can see something fresh in her expression that was not there before. As if the dream had set something free that was lurking inside her.

As Edda gathers her thoughts, Ximena and her fellow students lean forward and observe her with absorbed fascination, as if a dynamic drama was unfolding in the cell.

Because it does.

Right under Edda's skin.

Oh, what a gift, the psych-link. Perhaps the greatest achievement of dreamtech. It takes the breathtaking immersion of the dream sensorial deep into the shores of *another* mind. An incredible feat of engineering, when you really think about it. Thoughts, memories, even emotions, exquisitely crafted by a dreamtech engineer—Ank, most likely in this case—flow into your brain as if they were your own. And Miyagi's innovation is to apply this technology to historic dreamsensos. Whoa, it feels like true time travel to Ximena. Better.

Ximena smiles at Edda's feelings. The fulfillment, the clarity, the sense of power, the *thirst*. She feels like she could stop the world spinning if she puts her mind to it.

Powerful thoughts that attract doubts like porridge attracts flies.

But… They'll throw me out of school. My students need me. *I* need them.

But… Only if they catch me.

But… Our family reputation… Dad and Bram don't deserve… Oh, little Hans, my love. You don't deserve to grow in a family without a name, without karma.

But… We will be *together*. Hans needs his grandfather, perhaps more than I do.

But… What if I can't convince Dad?

But… If I do, I won't be left parentless—alone in the world.

Ximena feels it now, unmistakable, growing in the background with every exchange: the raw defiance, the determination, the *will*.

But.... What if I can't? What if I don't have the strength?

But... I *do*.

But... What can I do?

But.... Does it matter? *Anything*!

Edda stands, and stares at an indistinct point on the wall like there was something—somebody—right there, staring back.

She smiles, and whispers, "I will save you."

FIVE

The Joyousday of Rozamond Speese

"So you see, people, in December 2399 Edda van Dolah was just a young woman desperate to save her father," Professor Miyagi says as he paces the stage, sunlight on his face. "She wants him to renounce his Joyousday. And we know how she plans to convince him: by dropping a bombshell that, *if true*," he pauses for effect, "would destroy the entire society."

Ximena absorbs his every word with the same rapt attention as every other student in the auditorium. *The professor surely has a sense of drama,* she thinks, but then it hits her. *The vial! He's talking about that vial that Edda sneaked out.*

Professor Miyagi continues, "As an educated colonist and teacher, she knows some history, and she believes that the actual force behind the Joyousday ritual is some good ol' tyrannical repression. Is the Goah's Imperia government—the *Head of Goah*—really poisoning every colonist upon reaching twenty-seven years of age?" He chuckles loudly. "Edda is convinced. What better way to retain power than keeping your people in the eternal, happy ignorance of youth?"

He walks towards Ank, who is sitting on the front bench next to Bob, the wudai machine, and says to the auditorium, "I think you will find the next sequence instructive. It is context at its best, so please pay attention —we will have a little Q&A right after." He gives Ank a nod.

The amphitheater—Miyagi, Ank, the students—fades out as a resplendent morning scene materializes over the stage, and expands upwards and outwards over their heads and across the whole auditorium. Ximena is still in awe at the vivid realism of the dreamsenso immersion. Magnificent! It draws her in and engulfs all her senses.

The scene is static, frozen in time. A pastoral setting. A field of carefully tended grass surrounded by oak trees. It must be winter since no leaves populate their branches. The sun lies low, throwing long shadows. It is not an empty scene. Quite the contrary—it is teeming with people, none older than, indeed, twenty-seven. They are dressed in fine, bright-colored tunics, ornate belts on some waists. The older men and women wear colorful, large hats made of dry branches, leaves and flowers. These young people seem to be celebrating something—with wide smiles and beaming eyes, many are frozen in mid-dance.

"Check that out, people," Miyagi says, barely visible at the edge of the stage. "The colony of Lunteren on the 10th of December 2399." He turns and points at the happy dancers. "Any guess as to what we are seeing?"

Many hands shoot up.

"Yes, Qiao?"

"Er, it totally looks like a Joyousday celebration right out of *Fahey's Legacy.*"

"Spot on. Let's watch. Ah, I forgot to say, but you'll notice that I've removed the dramatic effects, symphonic music, camera shifts and all that. That will be all good and fine for the final production, but for us historians, only the naked facts, right? I want you to feel that you're there, mingling with," he gestures at the dancers, "our happy ancestors." With another nod to Ank, the scene comes to life.

The dreamsenso immediately floods Ximena's senses with a distinct feel of the fresh winter air, her nostrils filling with the smell of wet grass and wooden stoves.

Hundreds of young women and men dance and chatter happily on the grass field. Pop music from the golden age erupts from two large loudspeakers discreetly installed inside the only building at the edge of the field —*the Joyousday House*, Ximena recognizes. The same house Edda assaulted a few days ago, same walls carved with geometric reliefs. And in the daylight, from a distance, Ximena can now appreciate the roof is made of intricately braided tree branches.

A woman dressed in white—the only person in the celebration who is not wearing colorful robes—is the undisputed center of attention. She is pretty, the youth of twenty-seven years of life tinting her white cheeks. Her long, black hair and eyes contrast beautifully with her dress. When she approaches any group of people, they stop dancing and greet her warmly, exchange some words, and conclude with deep, honest hugs before she moves on to the next group.

The scene view begins to slide sideways, across a myriad of laughs and dances, until it stops at the edge of the gathering where a girl glimpses nervously at every new arrival. She is obviously waiting for somebody. And she looks very upset.

Aline Speese, Ximena recognizes her immediately, *the fallen angel*. Oh so young still, sixteen—the same age as Edda. She looks splendid in that yellow-and-orange robe—

what is that, silk?—that wraps her feminine shape. Ximena squints as she studies Aline's face. It's as if she had just seen her somewhere else... That white skin and long, black hair... Oh, she looks just like the younger sister of the woman in white. And as pretty, except that her face shows traces of tears. *Oh,* Ximena gasps in understanding. *That woman is Aline's mother! And this is her Joyousday.*

"Wow." Mark beside her is staring at Aline with a look close to reverence. "*Speese-Marai,*" he says the words like he is praying.

Aline shifts from one foot to another, scanning the colony path impatiently, when she sees a tall, black girl with short, curly hair approaching slowly. Aline exhales a breath of relief—or is it distress?—and runs towards her.

"Fucking Mercy, Edda," Aline says, wide-eyed and voice drenched in distress. "Where in Goah's Name were you?!"

Edda's eyes are wet and red, and her colorful tunic is worn carelessly, wrinkled in places. Even her intricate broad belt sits too loose above her hips. She says nothing. She just meets Aline's eyes, lips pressed together, and drops her chin.

"No," Aline covers her mouth with a hand and begins to cry. "No, no."

Edda embraces Aline as tears well up in her own eyes. So they stay, in solidary silence, for a long while, oblivious to the party behind them. The psych-link seems to kick in as Ximena begins to feel Edda's sorrow and pity. *Poor Aline,* comes the thought. Followed by a *Goahdamn you, Dad.* Her rage comes out of nowhere, spilling over the sadness like ocean surf over beach sand, wiping everything in its path. She's angry. No, she is *furious.* At her father, of course. He is going to do it, doesn't matter what she says. How can he be so... *stubborn?* But mainly she is angry at herself. For failing. It was all for nothing. She feels so powerless. So alone.

"Congratulations, Woman Speese." An imposing woman—mid-twenties—dressed in the finest robe Ximena has ever seen, approaches from the field. It's Colony Elder van Kley, Ximena gathers from the psych-link. "Oh, are you all right, dear?"

Aline takes a step back and wipes her tears with the back of her hand. "Yes, yes, sorry, Colder van Kley." She tries to smile. "Thank you."

"Are you sure nothing is upsetting you? You look—"

"No, no. It's nothing. Just the emotions, you know?" Aline forces a smile. "Such an eventful day. So happy."

Colony Elder van Kley smiles radiantly at her. "And we are *so* delighted for you. A great day for the Speese Family —for those that left us, and for those that remain."

"Yes, thank you so much, Colder van Kley. If you'll excuse us, there is something…"

Aline takes Edda by the elbow and pushes her off the path on a discreet route towards the party. "So, what was in that bottle?" Aline asks, voice still wavering.

Edda snorts. "According to Isabella, just some sleeping herbs."

"Sleeping herbs? Like for insomnia?"

"Stronger, way stronger. A powerful sedative, but not lethal, apparently. Isabella knew what it was because aws Eye orders it in her pharmacy regularly. They even have a name for it: *Joyousday infusion.*"

"Can we… can we trust her? Isabella Zegers, I mean."

Edda sighs, and nods. "Unfortunately, she's telling the truth. She's going to be my dowry sister, Aline. Yeah, she's solid. My dad gave the vial to her straight away. She was the obvious choice."

"Oh, Goah, that means—"

"That means that I fucked up, Aline. I took the wrong flask—the sedative—and left the poison on the counter. Pure sin!"

"What am I going to tell my mom?" Aline's voice increases in tone and pitch, close to tears. "How can I convince her with no evidence?"

"I'm so sorry, sister. But you have to try. What else? Look, there she is." Edda points at the resplendent woman in white surrounded by the crowd of well-wishers. "Talk to her."

"Fuck, Edda," Aline says, her voice barely under control. "This is so much harder than I thought."

Edda takes her friend's hands into her own. "No shit." Edda looks into her eyes. "I don't know how you feel. Honest to Goah, I don't want to know. But in two months I most certainly will," she says sourly. "Get a hold of yourself. This is it. What you don't say today, remains unsaid."

"Yes." Aline takes a deep breath. "I know."

"And about this monstrosity, this... *ritual,*" Edda gestures at the dancing crowd, disgusted. "We are moving to plan B, sister. I can guarantee you nobody will ever forget your mom's Joyousday."

"About that—I've been thinking..." Aline says in a weakened voice.

"What?! You promised!"

"I know. But it is hard enough as it is... I don't want Mom's Joyousday to be, I don't know," she shrugs, "*desecrated.*"

"Well, it's not up to you anyway," Edda says, defiance rising in her voice. "You *cannot* stop me."

Aline's rosy cheeks lose some color. "No way, Edda. You can't do this without my consent."

Edda regards her in silence. *Sure I can,* her eyes seem

to say.

"Edda, I forbid it." Aline drops her head. "I'm sorry."

"But you promised!" Edda purses her lips, but only for an instant before her tongue lashes. "This is bigger than us! It's bigger than your mom's goahdamn Joyousday!" The fury is followed by instant regret, and then by pride, and then by fury again. Oh, it is so exhilarating for Ximena to ride Edda's emotional roller coaster.

Aline steps back as if physically assaulted. She shakes her head slowly and points a finger at Edda's face, serious and cold as a marble statue.

"Don't. You. Dare. I forbid it! You do this, you're dead to me."

Edda holds her gaze for a few seconds before lowering her eyes. Oh, her fury is still there, all right. Ximena feels it burning inside. But fear—fear of loss, fear of being left *alone*—that is… unbearable. "Fine," Edda whispers. "But promise me something." She looks up at Aline.

"What?"

"Talk your mom out of this."

"I won't be able to." Aline shakes her long hair and clenches her jaws. "I know her."

"What else can we do?" Edda's voice is sharper now. "*Begging* is our only power, sister. Go talk to your mom."

Aline turns and looks at the beaming white figure with hesitant eyes. Edda gives her a gentle push. "You got this."

"Aline! Come here, my love." The woman takes her daughter in her arms and kisses both her cheeks. "I wasn't expecting you until after the prayers. Quaestor Mathus hasn't even arrived yet."

"Sorry, Mom, I just wanted to talk to you in private, without, er, the rest of the family."

"We will have plenty of time to talk when you join me in Goah's Embrace, in eleven years!" She laughs, happy.

"Please don't make jokes, Mom."

"Oh, come on, love. Cheer up! Can you please excuse us?" she asks the surrounding group.

"Of course, Roz," a tall woman says, smiling. "But don't forget to say goodbye to us next, it's our turn!"

Rozamond takes her daughter aside.

"You look pretty today, Aline." Rozamond gently pulls back a strand of hair from her daughter's face. "A smile would make you look even more beautiful, love. What's in your heart?"

"Please, Mom. Please, I *beg* you." Aline looks up at her mom. "Call this off."

Rozamond's eyes look concerned, but her smile widens.

"Oh, what a scandal. What would our guests say?"

"It isn't funny. Please!" Tears begin to well up in Aline's eyes.

"My love, I know that you have doubts, but I don't. See?" She opens her arms, radiating happiness. "It will all be fine. Trust me. You will have to assume more responsibility at home, but you are more than ready," she says proudly.

"Mom, please. I've never seen anybody with Dem. You haven't either!"

Rozamond's smile mixes with a sudden hint of sadness.

"Just because you haven't seen something, it doesn't mean it's not a thing, love." She takes Aline's hands. "I knew somebody that has seen it. You never had the chance to meet my mother, Saskia—you were too small. I loved her so much. I hope you love me half as much."

"Mom, I love you, you know that."

"My mother is waiting for me. And I know in my heart that she is eager to see me, as I will be to see you in eleven years." She beams. "I remember her Joyousday as vividly as if it had been last week. It was wonderful! It was right here as well, but it was spring; sunny and fragrant." She takes a long look at her daughter. "I want you to remember mine with the same love and hope." Rozamond's eyes seem to shift away as she remembers. "Right after the prayers, during the evocation, only the family was gathered around Mom. She was recalling the events of her life that she chose to share with us, blessing them in Goah's Eyes." She paused, looking deep into Aline's eyes. "She shared a sad memory. But beautiful in a way. Mom described the suffering of her family when her father lost his mind, day after agonizing day. Dem is a terrible, terrible thing. I don't want that for any of you, my love."

Aline opens her mouth to say something, but Rozamond puts a finger on her lips.

"The first days it was barely noticeable," she continues her tale, "but as the weeks passed by, he forgot everything. Absolutely *everything*. First it was his profession. He was an engineer, obviously, so he had to stop working soon after. Then it was the community. He forgot names and faces. Then his closest friends." She pauses, her smile fading, eyes far away. "One day he forgot his own name. His own name! Everything was gone. That was his last day. He was mercifully taken to the Joyousday House. But you know what your grandma Saskia's most precious evocation was?"

"What?" A tear runs down Aline's cheek.

"When her father was being taken away after the final farewells, he turned back one last time and smiled fondly at her. 'Daughter', he said. 'Saskia', and then he left forever."

The scene freezes with Aline and Rozamond holding hands. The entranced students look down to the stage of the auditorium where Professor Miyagi is smiling up at them.

"Nice touch, don't you think? You may wipe your tears away now." Ximena laughs softly and actually rubs her eyes. Even Mark, beside her, passes a finger across his cheek. "You may think that is some cheap drama dreamed up for the final dreamsenso. But no. Everything you see here, it really happened. That conversation between Aline and Rozamond, it *did* really happen. It was all documented by Speese-Marai herself, many years later."

Some students raise their hands.

"Hold on a sec," Miyagi says. "Before opening the Q&A, I want to show you another exchange that happened a couple of hours later. It is relevant for our analysis."

He whispers something at Ank, who in turn gives Bob a sidelong glance. In an instant, Aline and her mother disappear, and a new scene takes their place.

It is Edda again, walking away from the grass field. More people in the background are leaving as well. Her pace is quick on the paved street that links the Joyousday House with the rest of the colony. A greeting that comes her way from a passing horse and cart goes unanswered. She also ignores each of the returning Speese guests that cycle past her with a raised hand. With a scowl that threatens to turn the next saluting passerby into ashes, she reaches the outermost houses of the colony—red-bricked, double-story, some with sizable vegetable gardens. Unchanged for countless generations.

"Edda, wait for me!"

Edda's frown deepens, but she slows down a notch. "I

hate you, Dad," she says without turning. *Not true*, Ximena feels. *But oh, she's mad.*

Willem reaches Edda slightly out of breath, his right hand clumsily nudging a pair of thin glasses in place. "I love you too, girl," he says with the smile of a tantrum-hardened parent. "Do I perceive a hint of anger?"

"Very observant. Leave me alone."

"Please, Edda. You must learn to accept the world as it *is*. You cannot change it."

She abruptly stops and turns. "I don't want to change the world. I just want *you* to stay in it!"

"I know." Willem's resigned smile broadens. "Nothing would make me happier as well."

They walk again, slower now, side by side.

"I admit I feel strange," Willem says. "Rozamond's Joyousday was…" he searches for the right word, "…*disturbing*. I'm happy, Edda. I love my family." He caresses her hair. "I even love my students." He laughs. "I love my life. And I admit I'm not ready to leave it."

"Then don't!"

"But what do you expect me to do? Even if there had been poison in that bottle, what could I…?" He swallows, and softens his voice. "Do you know what would happen to our family's standing if I cancel my Joyousday?" He speaks almost in a whisper. "Our prestige would be in shatters."

"I don't care. *We* don't care."

"You must!" Willem stops and puts his hand on her shoulder. "Bram and you will soon be the Van Dolah elders. You must *never* forget our standing in the colony. Your lives, little Hans's life, all your futures will soon be in *your* hands, Edda."

They walk on in silence. Ximena feels Edda's anxiety, the pressure—the fear. He's dead serious. He never calls her by her name.

"And what for?" Willem continues. "A few more months? A year at the most? Dem will inevitably catch me…"

"But Dem is just a lie!"

"Edda…"

"You know I'm right, Dad. Have you actually seen anybody with Dem?"

"No, but come on, girl. You are smarter than that. Nowadays everybody strictly observes the Joyousday when they turn twenty-seven. Dem never has a chance to take hold."

"But think about it, who's really benefiting from all this… death?"

"Hush!" Willem looks nervously around and remains silent for a few seconds. "Let's walk home," he finally says. They get moving. "I also have my doubts…" he whispers.

"Then why——?!"

"*But*," Willem interrupts, "that doesn't change the fact that our family will suffer if I do not attend aws Call."

"I don't give a damn about our reputation!" Edda yells at him. "Let's take the family somewhere else if we need to; another colony, on the frontier."

"What good would that do? Joyousday is Joyousday, and I'm turning twenty-seven here and in the frontier. There's no escaping it. Besides, there have been worse regimes in history than aws Imperia if you really think about it."

"You are not possibly defending——"

"Why not? If you leave your emotions aside and try to be objective, you will realize there's much we have to thank Goah for."

"Like what?"

"Well, er, we've got aws Gift and aws Compacts for starters. And nobody lacks shelter nor sustenance. That's an incredible achievement for any post-collapse society. What else? Uh, we are reasonably free, have families and stability, meaningful work that matters, and even enough free time to... whatever."

"Wonderful regime, yeah. With just a few tiny caveats, like inequality, the arbitrary distribution of karma, the lies and propaganda, aws Head's absolute power. Am I forgetting something?" She taps her chin. "Ah, yeah. The fucking killing us all. Goah's Mercy, Dad. I don't want you to die in two months!" She is close to tears. "Remember when in Mom's Joyousday—?"

"Enough!" His shout freezes Edda in place. "I will not hear any more of this. You will respect my decision. I expect to have some peace in my last weeks of life." Any trace of tenderness in his voice is now gone.

She stares at him for a few seconds, her mouth ajar. "I hate you!" she finally says. "You don't have the right to leave us!"

She begins to weep sourly and runs away.

E dda is in her room, sitting on the desk by the window, tending the potted cactus with a cotton gauze. *No blooms.* Her thoughts flow unimpeded to Ximena, as she inspects the hard, spiny surface of the plant. She'll ask Isabella for some nitrates, maybe that would help. Dad made a good catch when he proposed her for a dowry bond, she admits. The Zegers are a good family.

Edda's attention is caught by Willem passing by on the sidewalk with a baby stroll chair. She can barely see Hans's light-brown hair from the distance. She follows them with her eyes until they move out of sight.

Edda sighs. Why can't Dad see how important he is to

them? She is not ready to manage the family alone. Okay, yes, a poor excuse. She can sure as Dem manage anything on her own. And she's not alone. Bram might be her little brother, but he can hold his own as well as anyone.

Edda sighs again, puts the gauze in the desk drawer, and moves the pot into the daylight. She smiles sadly to herself. What a pitiful thing she has become. So psychologically dependent on her father. Yes, so what? Friends and lovers come and go, come and go, but fathers… they only go, don't they? She scoffs and tries to repress the pinch of self-pity behind her eyes.

Fathers—and mothers—they only go.

She remembers Mom, so solid, so powerful, so *warm*. Then she remembers her look that day, the last time she saw her. It's just a flash, more a sensation than an image, but it is enough to… Ximena's own stomach seems to contract at the sudden pain. Goah, it has been two years already, and is still so vivid, so… No, Edda shakes her head, trying to dispel the memory. She can't afford to lose herself in that rabbit hole again.

Dad is so naive. For her he plays the role of the brave Elder—family first and all that—but he is not as strong as he thinks, and surely not as much as her mother was. Goah's Mercy, he even admitted to having doubts. Mom never showed any doubts, and yet…

The familiar bite of fear crawls up her spine. And this time it's not her usual fear of being left alone and parentless. This time she's terrified that Dad will not make it. At the end, it is only dignity that you take to aws Embrace, and Edda fears that Dad will not be strong enough. Mom wasn't.

Edda takes a deep breath and blinks her eyes clear of threatening tears. Dad needs to see that his life is too valuable to sacrifice in the altar of aws Head's power game. No regime is worth his life. She'll make him see how corrupt they really are. She'll make everybody see. Then, perhaps, he'll reconsider. Yeah, but it has to be something big. No, not big. *Huge.* Something that resonates way beyond Lunteren, beyond the whole fucking Geldershire. Something that sows doubt—and resentment. Edda knows her history. Empires have fallen for less than doubt and resentment.

SIX

Sex and Collapse

"Okay, wakey, wakey, people." Miyagi chuckles at the overused permascape joke. "Q&A time! I want to hear your thoughts, especially," he waves a finger across the section of the amphitheater where Ximena's fellow GIA students sit, "from our new friends from the New World—you people are being way too shy. Shoot!"

A few hands raise, but none of them from GIA students. Miyagi ignores them and keeps his smile locked at the sea of white-and-blue robes. Finally, a brave hand rises slowly.

"Ah great, er, Cody." Ximena knows Cody O'Higgin well. He's in one of her classes. Smart guy. Ambitious. And always a kind soul. "Please, go ahead."

Cody stands. "Thank you, Professor. Sorry if the question is a bit, er, superficial, but I was wondering how old Edda van Dolah and Aline Speese were in the sections we just watched?"

"Aha, good question, Cody. People, don't be shy about your questions, all right? There are no boring questions, nor stupid questions. It is the wildest thoughts that usually start the most fascinating discussions. Now to your question. They were both sixteen. But don't be fooled by their youth. A century ago, when a person reached *your* age," he drives a finger across his audience, most in their upper twenties, "they would have accomplished a basic education, learned and perfected their family profession, ordered two babies at aws Womb, led a family as an elder, and died."

He paces the stage in silence to let that sink in. Ximena is twenty-seven herself. She would have been killed already if she were born four generations ago. Goah, how did they manage? There was no time to pursue any meaningful life project. She wonders… Perhaps they were indeed happy while it lasted? Free of the worries of career and uncertainty?

"A person entered adulthood at ten," Miyagi continues, "as they reached sexual maturity. Fun fact: did you know that at the end of the golden age, right before the first collapse of the 2080s, humans matured at least two or three years later than we do now? Yes, an unexpected side-effect of the Dem-Pandemic of the twenty-second century was the natural selection of humans with ever earlier sexual maturity. Can anybody guess why?"

Ximena scoffs. *It's obvious.* But nobody raises a hand.

"Go ahead, Ximena," Mark says. "Answer that."

Ximena shakes her head, blushing—oh she hates her compulsive blushing, even in dreams she cannot control it.

Mark grabs her hand and raises it shamelessly. "Here, Professor," he yells.

"Ah, please…" He points his finger at Ximena and reads the name that pops up over her head. "Oh *Epullan*, so happy to have you in this seminar. Loved your take on raw power in that Post-Columbian paper you published. People, this is Ximena Epullan, a sharp mind."

Ximena's cheeks are on fire. She tries to smile, and fails.

"I would like a word in private after the seminar, if you don't mind."

"With... with me?"

"Yeah, there is something I stumbled on during my research that might interest you. But more of that later."

Miyagi turns his face to the stupefied students. Even Mark looks at Ximena like she had just turned into crystal.

"This seminar is not just an academic event, people," Miyagi says. "The Global Program is first and foremost an intercultural exchange." He claps at Ximena. "Bravo, you totally embraced the spirit by sitting with the Lundev gang. You should all heed Ximena's example, and mix more, people. Now, Ximena, please, answer the question. Why the selective pressure for earlier sexual maturity?"

Ximena clears her throat. Twice. "Yes, Professor. Before that, I'm sorry to disappoint you, but the truth is that I arrived late, and this was the only free spot."

"Really?" Miyagi laughs, together with most of the students. *Oh Goah*, Ximena thinks. *Ground swallow me up.* "Well," Miyagi nods at her in appreciation, "I have to apologize then, I didn't want to put you on the spot. Love your honesty, though. Perhaps the most important trait of a historian. Now, your take on the sexual selection?"

"Yes, Professor." Ximena clears her throat again. "The selective pressure began in the 2080s, as the first collapse gained traction. More than a billion people were killed in a single generation."

"Tell us about that, Ximena. What killed them?"

"Hmm," she raises her thumb in the air, "the immediate cause was the environmental breakdown, especially in the tropics, which then," she raises her index finger, as she counts on, "precipitated famines and migration waves like never seen since antiquity. That in turn," she raises a third finger, "wrecked the global and national networks of trade," another finger, "collapsing country after country into smaller nativist grouplets. And the cycle repeated: more famine," she keeps raising finger after finger, "more xenophobic massacres, more splitting into ever smaller groups. And on and on went the first collapse, killing millions upon millions of people."

"So you're saying," Miyagi asks, "that it was the higher mortality that created evolutionary pressure for earlier sexual maturity?"

"No, no. Not the higher mortality. Rather, the *earlier* mortality."

Miyagi smiles. "Please clarify."

"Yes, Professor, er, it was the Dem-Pandemic, of course. *Dementia Furiosa* has always been killing people, even before the first collapse, but it has always been in a relatively small scale, and only affected the most elderly. But all that changed with the high mortality of the first collapse."

"How so?"

"Hmm, the more people died in the first collapse, the higher the proportion of *Dementia Furiosa* that affected the elderly. Nobody knew why back then, but soon everybody over eighty perished from Dem, which then began spreading through those in their late seventies. And when they in turn were dead, Dem began to ravage those in the mid-seventies, and so on it went, killing the oldest humans alive, and killing ever younger, mostly hidden from the public view behind the curtain of the horrors of the first collapse. Until, at some point, there were no elderly left in the world, and Dem kept killing on and on, relentlessly."

"Can you give us some numbers?"

"Not from the top of my head, sorry, Professor. I only

know what everybody knows: that the human lifespan shrunk rapidly during the twenty-second century."

"I'll give you some numbers, people." Miyagi paces the stage while speaking. "Lifespans went down from sixty years in 2100 to forty-five in 2120. Can you picture what *that* does to a civilization? And it didn't stop there. Dem kept ravaging the oldest layers of society, decade after decade. The second collapse, indeed. Billions die as the fabric of society dissolves simultaneously worldwide. First go the nation-states, then the cities and towns, then even the timeless institutions of tribe and family begin to falter. Which brings us to one of the key human adaptations that allowed us to survive." He turns and points at Ximena. "Which is…?"

Ximena clears her throat. "Er, earlier sexual maturity." Miyagi nods and keeps his gaze locked on her. *Oh Goah.* "Er… Yes, just natural selection at work, Professor. Shorter lifespans create pressure on the reproductive cycle. Early breeders have higher chances to pass their genes to the next generation, so after a few generations, uh…" She clears her throat again.

"Perfect. Thank you, Ximena."

She sits and draws a deep breath.

"Well done," Mark whispers with playful tone. "But you got to work on that thing you do with your hands while——"

"Oh, shut up," she says, and mocks a slap on his shoulder.

Miyagi is pointing at a pretty South Asian Lundev student that is raising her hand insistently on the front bench. "Yes, Sky?"

She is frowning. "Makes little sense, sorry, Professor. Even with all that dying… There were still a few million survivors."

"You are right. Most of them in North America, about fifty million, where Townsend was already spreading the Gift of Goah. But there were only fifty or sixty left in the rest of the world combined."

"Still," Sky spread her hands, "plenty of people to keep civilization running, I would think. That's what I don't get. Even if everybody dies young, so what? All our knowledge and technology—it doesn't disappear from one day to the next."

"*That*," Miyagi points at her, "is a *great* question. Nice, Sky. Anybody care to…? Ah, Cody, great. Happy to see our Townsend University friends more active. Keep it up. What do you have to say to Sky?"

"With all due respect to my esteemed fellow," Cody says with slow, studious tone, "what good is a quantum field theory manual to a farmer that can barely read?"

"Oh, come on, *GIA*," Sky says with an exaggerated roll of the eyes. "Not all remaining millions are *farmers that can barely read*." Ximena doesn't like her tone.

Cody's kind expression remains stoically unmoved by Sky's reply. Always the attentive debater, Ximena has seen him in action before. "I am sorry if my metaphor was too simplistic," he continues. "My fault entirely. In my haste to make an *obvious* point, I wrongly assumed a hint would be enough."

Ximena smiles. *Touché*.

"What are you saying?" Sky stands and points a finger at him. "Are you calling me a—?"

"People, people," Miyagi raises his hands and tone. "Come on. Keep it civilized and respectful. Discuss away, but no name-calling. Sky, sit down, please. Thank you. Cody, please, no more metaphors nor, uh, *hints*. Tell us in simple, everyday words, why the radically shorter lifespans destroyed the sophisticated civilizations of the golden age."

"Apologies, Professor, Sky." He bows at her with convincing humility. "I did not intend disrespect." Ximena chuckles. She knows him better. "To find the truth, I believe we need to take a step back from Dem, the collapse, the great dying, and ask ourselves the proper questions."

"I like how you think." Miyagi is nodding at him. "Finding the right questions is a cornerstone of science. Often harder than finding the answers. So, tell us, which questions are relevant to the second collapse?"

"The *key* question, I believe, is: *what makes a civilization?*" He pauses a second. "And the answer, in my humble opinion, is not knowledge nor technology. Not directly," he hastily adds as Sky seems about to say something. "The answer is *specialists.*"

"Specialists?" Miyagi says, squinting eyes staring at Cody. Ximena throws a glance down to the front bench where Sky seems to scoff. "Yes, quite right," Miyagi says. "The more complex the civilization, the more specialized we all become."

"Yes, Professor. Doctors, engineers, scientists, botanists, analysts, merchants, financiers."

"Don't forget historians," Miyagi adds with a chuckle. "Each splitting into dozens of more concrete specializations. My best friend is a solar-energy automation engineer specialized on Near-Earth habitat structures."

"Yes, Professor," Cody says, his kind smile broadening, "great example. Now that we have a candidate answer, *specialists*, to the key question, *what makes civilization*, we can postulate the impact of Dem killing at ever younger ages."

Ximena is mildly jealous of Cody's ability to remain calm and well-paced. The whole auditorium is staring at him, and many, like Sky, even with suspicion, if not open disdain. He just doesn't care.

"Put simply," he continues through that perennial smile of his, "specialists *died*, one by one, together with their experience and wisdom. Until all that was left were ignorant kids. Take your friend, for example, Professor. What would happen to our space habitats if specialists like him died from Dem without replacement? Yes, as my esteemed fellow Sky rightly points out," he extends a hand in her direction, "human knowledge persists, but, alas, only on paper and digital storage."

"And what good is that knowledge," Miyagi says, "if nobody has enough time to absorb it, right? Great answer, Cody. Thanks. Love this discussion. You began by asking how old Edda was in the sequence we observed and ended discussing the ravages on humanity of the second collapse. Only by the outset of the twenty-third century did lifespans finally stabilize at twenty-seven, and so it remained, unchanged, until the early twenty-fifth century—the fascinating times which we are studying in this seminar—when that stability came spectacularly to an end."

SEVEN

The Reseeding Effort

"**A**liens, aliens, aliens," Miyagi says, pacing the stage with his usual self-confidence. "You either love them, or love to hate them."

He laughs aloud, as if he had delivered a joke. Some students chuckle obligingly, but not Ximena.

"Their meddling in human affairs has gone unnoticed for *way* too long. But finally, First Contact is imminent."

Some students around Ximena actually whistle and cheer with anticipation. Ximena can of course understand the historical importance of the event, but why the excitement? Even Mark is smiling sheepishly at Miyagi.

"Before that, though, I want you to meet them right before First Contact. Yes," he raises a hand at the sudden roar of excitement, "I know you're eager to see our favorite alien again, huh?"

"Favorite?" Ximena murmurs to herself. *How can there be a favorite—?*

"Rew," Mark whispers in her ear. He's heard her. "He's speaking about Rew. You wait and see."

Ximena doesn't have time to reply before Miyagi

continues, "For the first time in dreamsenso, we are actually going to dramatize events from a non-human perspective. Sensational stuff, people!" He raises both arms. "You're welcome for the privilege."

Ximena watches in confusion as the surrounding students clap fiercely. At least her fellow GIA students, on the opposite side of the amphitheater, seem as baffled as she feels.

"Thank you, thank you. Obviously, we have taken some liberties, like dubbing and such. But all in all, our historical sources are solid, and I'm quite pleased with the results. Now, without further ado… Ank, if you will."

A scene materializes immediately: a flat ground, made of some sort of impossibly polished dark stone, that spans infinitely in all directions. There is nothing on the ground: no object interrupts the spotless sight to the horizon, anywhere you look. The sky is pitch black, yet a soft light irradiates in all directions. *A dream*, thinks Ximena. *Empty and simple, but a dream nevertheless.*

A figure is now standing on the infinite expanse. It was not there an instant ago.

Ximena has seen this creature before. In Edda's detention cell.

It is not quite human: a grotesquely elongated figure, thinner and taller than any human could possibly be; no clothes, no hair, no genitals; spotless white skin; a proportionally smaller head; no ears, no nose, just an over-sized black, humid mouth and two fully white eyes—no iris nor pupils—whiter even than the color of its skin.

The figure just stands there, idle, still.

And time passes.

"So, who is this?" Miyagi's powerful voice breaks the students' absorbed attention.

"It has to be Rew, or Yog," Lora says.

"She's Rew," Miyagi says. "Yog has three bodies. At least had them before First Contact. She also features in this scene, coming up any second now."

"Is this a female?" Sky asks from below Ximena, as her eyes scrutinize the alien body.

"No," Miyagi says. "Mares do not reproduce sexually. If you are asking why I say *she* instead of *it* when referring to a mare, it's simply an academic convention for asexual sentient creatures. We need to somehow address them as people, not things."

"Why as female? Why not male?" Mark asks.

"I know, I know. Please let's not open that can of worms, pretty please? In any case," Miyagi points at the mare on the scene, "look at her thorax. Rew is not breathing, ha! But unfortunately for us romantic historians, there is little drama to that. No zombies, no vamps. Mares just don't have lungs. Which means they cannot speak like we do. They don't even have ears. When they communicate, they *reverberate psychically*, a special type of telepathy. Very, very efficient. They don't have the problems we do with accents and sore throats." The students laugh. "In this sensorial, you will hear the communication in High Hansasian English. Oh!" Miyagi points at the floating scene. "Here comes Yog."

Three more mares pop into existence. They appear at roughly the same moment, side by side, facing Rew, and just as ghostly white. Rew bows her small head slightly at the three figures.

Nobody *speaks*. As if waiting.

A larger creature materializes next to the four mares. She is not even humanoid. As large as an elephant, as sticky and soft as an octopus, and as many appendages under her body as a millipede. Two large bulbous eyes— white like those of mares—protrude from a head that is as large as the rest of her body. A head with no mouth to be seen. Her skin is white, also resembling that of mares, but thicker, and it throbs slowly like waves of flesh. Her body is so massive, and her short appendages so delicate, that any xenobiologist would correctly guess that her habitat is underwater. And indeed, she seems to be somehow floating above the ground, as if pushed by invisible currents.

The four mares bow to the creature. *A very human gesture,* Ximena thinks with wonder. *Perhaps some type of convergent evolution on the body language of biped sentients?*

The massive creature does not react.

"Sense and bind, Master Gorrobor." The eerie female voice echoes crisply in the auditorium. Its source are the three mares standing in front of Rew, speaking as one. While she *speaks,* her black mouth remains shut, and her body unnaturally still.

"Do name yourself, and state the objective of this gathering," Gorrobor says. Her deep, female voice—oddly old—comes out of her bloated body with no obvious physical source.

"Yes, Master Gorrobor. I am Yog," the three mares say, "dreaming from Yian, Overseer of the Reseeding effort in Oromantis. We are gathered to hear the report of Walker Rew-at-Deviss."

"I am Rew," says the mare that arrived first, "dreaming from Deviss, Walker assigned to the Reseeding effort. I did summon this gathering to report on its progress and to request arbitration."

The protruding eyes of Gorrobor study the mare carefully. "Walker Rew-at-Deviss," she finally says, "I know of you. One of our few Human Whisperers, are you not?"

"I am, Master."

"Sense and bind, Human Whisperer. Do report."

"Yes, Master. I began assignment under Overseer Yog

a year ago. My directive: to use my discretion as Human Whisperer to maximize the Reseeding impact, and so generate and maintain the long-term increase of human population."

One of Gorrobor's eyes jerks at the three limbs of Yog. "Sensible."

Rew continues, "I did spend this period studying and making a preselection of the most promising regions to focus my effort on. I did find promise near Diamar, and so I rebased to Deviss."

"Master Gorrobor, if you do allow." Yog bows. Gorrobor's bulbous eyes lock on her. "I did raise to Walker Rew reservation on her choice of base. Human settlements in third-wake Diamar are far from the center of human power. Deviss itself is a fringe operation, too small to exercise effective Reseeding action. I did try to——"

Gorrobor interrupts, her eyes jerking back to Rew. "Human Whisperer, what makes a region more or less promising for the Reseeding effort, in your perception?"

Rew takes a few moments to reply. "There are several factors. I did study in detail the social dynamics of human settlements, and there are regions where they are more prone to... *new* ideas. Furthermore, for reasons concealed from me, there is significant variation among humans regarding their innate talent to *walk*."

Gorrobor regards Rew in silence for a few seconds, before replying. "I do sense the wisdom in finding humans that do change their ways with more ease. But I do fail to sense how their talent to *walk* is of relevance, Human Whisperer."

"Master Gorrobor," Yog says, "I did raise to Walker Rew similar reservations. Not only is the *walking* skill of humans not relevant to the Reseeding effort—it can become *dangerous*."

"A risk perhaps," Rew says, "but a *controlled* risk if we do manage it actively. And as with most risks, it offers an opportunity. It is this opportunity that I am focusing on, Master Gorrobor. Humans can become our tools. We can leverage their rudimentary walking abilities to reach into their societies *far* more efficiently than we could ever achieve on our own. Our numbers are too few since the forced hibernation. This *must* be done."

Yog's three bodies make a slight step forward. "I did instruct Walker Rew to abort and perform a standard persuasion campaign closer to Yian." Her words are directed at Gorrobor. "Regrettably, my authority has not compelled Walker Rew into compliance. To protect the Reseeding effort from... *unpredictable* consequences, I did rule Walker Rew unfit for service."

Now it is Rew who takes a slight step forward. "As of my official prerogative as Walker, I did decline Overseer Yog's *suggestion*, and did request high arbitration. Thus, this gathering, Master." Rew bows.

Gorrobor floats in thoughtful silence, the tip of her appendages moving as if caressed by invisible currents. "I am intrigued, Human Whisperer. Do elaborate the relevance of the *walking* capabilities of humans to the Reseeding effort."

"Yes, Master." Rew bows again. "I do begin my exposition with a statement. It is my conviction that unless we do succeed with the Reseeding effort, humankind will soon become extinct."

"I do not agree," Yog interrupts with a slight bow. "Human civilization is solid, their numbers are stable, and they have settlements over the still inhabitable parts of their world."

"Their civilization is stable *now*," Rew says, "but precarious. As Whisperer, I did study them with more detail than most marai, Master." She looks at Yog. "With their artificially shortened lives they lack the capability to adapt. A typical human has barely time to gather the knowledge required to keep going exactly as their ancestors have. Humans are essentially blind farmers. Labor specialization is a rarity. Their scientific and industrial capacity is rudimentary, and their world is wounded, out of ecological balance. One more nudge from nature—a crop's failure, an epidemic, a war—and they will be gone. Forever."

"An unlikely outcome," Yog says. "Their society is stable. With our persistent support, the Reseeding effort shall succeed, as projected."

"Overseer Yog has considerably more trust than I do in human civilization, or their environment, to remain stable for the whole millennium our best projections require. Alas, Overseer Yog lacks the insight in human psyche and the nuances of human civilization that I do possess."

Yog seems about to reply, but Gorrobor intervenes. "No more interruptions, Overseer." Yog lowers her three heads in submission. Ximena smiles at the human-like gesture. "Do proceed, Human Whisperer."

"Yes, Master. My analysis suggests that, without intervention, humans shall become extinct in the next century or two. And without humankind, our purpose on this world vanishes. We shall leave Nubaria and return to space for eons, in the hope to find another suitable world, if we ever do. To avert this scenario, we must act hastily and decisively."

"A perturbing vision, were it accurate," Gorrobor says. "Do expose the nature of your intervention effort, Human Whisperer."

"Yes, Master. As already reported, I did rebase to Deviss in Diamar, on the Western coast of Oromantis. The third-wake human settlements in this area are on the periphery of human civilization, which appears to make them more susceptible to new ideas. But even more relevant to my intentions: there is a noticeable concentration of vibrant human halos. I do expect natives to have an abnormally high talent for *walking*." Rew pauses, almost as if expecting an interruption. "I am selecting a sample from among the most promising humans in this area and am selecting those that are most suggestible to my persuasion."

"How do you determine their... suggestibility?" Gorrobor asks.

"My staff in Deviss has been selecting young specimens all over second-wake Diamar since I did take over the operation, Master Gorrobor."

"Selected... how?"

"I did instruct my staff to pick independent-minded individuals with strong halos; not quite emotionally mature, but old enough to have real influence in their settlement. After that, I had to take over personally over the subsequent phases; alas, no marai in Diamar has my expertise. I took to observe the interactions of all human candidates and selected those that appeared less satisfied with their status quo—a task only a Human Whisperer can fulfill. Finally, I did test their determination to overcome their dissatisfaction."

"Crafted dreams?" Ximena finds Gorrobor's voice strangely unsettling.

"Indeed, Master."

"Strong halos..." Gorrobor remains silent a few moments, eyes locked on Rew. "Can humans *walk*, Human Whisperer?"

"The potential is there, Master. Some, the highly talented, do often tread the Path of Light by accident, without realizing it. I do intend to initiate the selected humans into the *Paths*."

Yog's three bodies move a tiny step forward. She seems hardly able to contain herself, but manages to keep a disciplined silence.

"Do elaborate how *walking* humans can support the Reseeding effort, Human Whisperer."

"Yes, Master. I shall recruit humans as our agents."

"Agents." One of Gorrobor's bulbous eyes turns to observe Yog. "I can sense Overseer Yog's *anxiety*. Indeed, providing humans with the power of the Paths appears… *risky*. But I do find the concept intriguing. Do elaborate, Human Whisperer."

"Yes, Master. Each human, even their cubs, are human whisperers by their own nature—they must empathize with their peers to survive, and can be highly manipulative— more than even the best of us could ever become after centuries of training. More than even me. They possess an uncanny capacity for deception that is beyond our reach. I shall enrich the Reseeding effort's arsenal with its most potent weapon yet: *human Walkers of the Mind*. Walkers with the capacity to purposefully deceive. We shall then deploy such weapons immediately, forcefully, effectively—before humanity's end."

A few moments of silence follow Rew's words. All the mares are facing Gorrobor now.

"A refreshing perspective," the colossal alien finally says. "Risky," she looks at Yog. "Promising," she looks at Rew. "And yet, perhaps not even worth considering, unless humans do show a bare minimum ability to walk the *Paths*. How can you know they can?" Her eyes drill into Rew.

"I have already seen it. One of my candidates did achieve will-control on her first session, without practice— she was not even conscious of my true presence."

Gorrobor stares in silence, as if in disbelief.

"As I did report before," Rew continues, "one of my selection criteria has been the brightness of human halos. Here in Diamar there is an exceptional concentration—I do trust them to possess enough talent to walk the *Paths*."

Gorrobor turns both eyes to Yog. "I am going to allow this... *experiment*, Overseer Yog."

"Yes, Master Gorrobor." She bows. "Do I have your permission for a suggestion?"

"Do proceed."

"Yes, Master Gorrobor." She bows again. "I do request additional powers over Walker Rew's activities, to better oversee the considerable risk."

Rew's head wobbles slightly. "I fear I must protest, Master. Yog does lack the vision to fulfill—"

"*Overseer* Yog," Gorrobor interrupts. "Do mind your tone, Walker Rew."

Rew lowers her head. "Yes, Master."

"Overseer Yog shall attend your instruction personally in full overseeing authority." Gorrobor turns her protuberant eyes to the three bodies. "Overseer Yog, it shall be your duty to restrict the risks as you deem fit."

"Yes, Master Gorrobor."

"Furthermore, I do wish only a minimum number of humans to be initiated in the *Path in the Shadow*."

"But Master Gorrobor," Rew says, "I fear instruction in the *Path of Light* shall be insufficient. Without traversion, or persuasion, their power shall be too constrained."

"I do realize that, Human Whisperer, and yet the risk of sharing such knowledge with humans cannot be disdained. Thus, I do wish to limit the risk exposure by first assessing the reliability of this new *weapon*. You shall select the most promising candidates, and grant access to the Path in the Shadow to just one or two humans, which

Overseer Yog can then keep under constant surveillance. So shall we know for certain if this *weapon* can be deployed safely, or else be safely disposed of."

Gorrobor disappears without awaiting a reply.

Rew and Yog turn to face each other.

"Your hunger for control is putting our future at risk, Overseer," Rew says. "We cannot afford time-wasting power gestures."

Yog raises her heads. "I do not appreciate your defiance, Walker. This," Yog's three bodies gesture with their hands' appendages, "*effort* of yours is distracting; and dangerous. Master Gorrobor shall see it soon enough. Then I shall send you to the hibernation ships."

The three bodies of Yog disappear without further words.

Rew remains on the infinite landscape. Alone.

EIGHT

First Contact

"The date," Miyagi raises his arms with theatrical exaggeration, "is the 12th of December 2399."

"Yeah, baby," Mark says next to Ximena, and winks at her. "Finally!"

Ximena is curious. She doesn't know much about First Contact, nor about the *Three Trials of Worth and Soul*. Her instructors skimmed over the details, and rightly so. What's the big deal, other than the fun factor? Christopher Columbus's arrival to the West Indies and First Contact with the natives would have surely been entertaining—except to the natives themselves, of course—but of little immediate consequence. History didn't begin its relentless shift until Columbus returned to Europe, and greedy or pious eyes turned to the West. That was what mattered.

"I got all the juicy details neatly packed for you," Miyagi says, to the cheers of many, including some of her fellow GIA students. "There were forty-eight direct human witnesses, some of whom survived the Dreamwars to tell their account of the event. And here is the result. I hope you like it. Ah, wait!" He raises a hand to stop the spontaneous claps and whistles. "Sorry, one thing you need to know before we begin. About the dreamsenso psych-link. It's a tough bitch to produce, excuse my language. Requires a gifted dreamtech engineer," he extends a hand at the elegantly dressed Ank sitting on the front bench, who nods in acknowledgment, "to record and edit into the sensorial the thoughts and feelings recreated by very talented actors. And expensive, the goahdamn divas. But, hey, only the best for *The Rise and Fall of The Juf*, right? Oh, sorry!" Again, he raises his hand to stop the incipient cheering. "I got sidetracked by…" He smiles and shakes his head. "What I *wanted* to say is that I made an exception with this scene and did not psych-link it to Edda van Dolah this time, although she is one of the forty-eight witnesses. I decided that we need to broaden our perspective and gain more historical context, all right? Context is everything in history, remember, so I chose somebody else to psych-link you guys to—somebody outside of Edda's immediate orbit. Ank, please."

The auditorium darkens to black skies and an infinite flat landscape of dark polished stone. Ximena recognizes the featureless place immediately—just a few minutes ago, Rew and Yog were at each other's throats in just such a place. But there are no aliens now.

Instead, there are people.

Forty-eight young women and men to be exact, dressed in the robes and tunics of the Goahn period. They are staring at each other with perplexed expressions, like they just arrived, and scan the surrounding nothingness with confused frowns.

These are probably the humans selected by the mare Rew, Ximena thinks, and wonders if forty-eight is a round number for the aliens. Mares have three appendages that function as fingers do on humans, perhaps they count in base six?

As Ximena studies the scene floating over the amphitheater, the camera viewpoint slides closer to the group of youngsters, until it finally settles near a particularly attractive teenager. He is sixteen or seventeen, light brown skin, black curled hair—*probably North African ancestry*, Ximena thinks.

Gotthard.

The name comes to Ximena as if by magic—the psych-link, of course, she realizes. So, this boy is going to be their point of view… Why? Why did Miyagi choose him specifically? Who was he? His full name fills her mind as if she were remembering her own: *Gotthard Kraker*. Kraker. The name does indeed ring a bell. What was his role in history? Well, she'll find out soon enough. Good that she made it to Miyagi's seminar—she definitely needs a lesson on recent history.

"Rutger!" Gotthard shouts, and trots towards another boy standing with baffled eyes not far away.

The boy—Rutger—turns to the sound of his name. He is white, tall, and thin, and wears glasses. His long brown hair matches his eyes, that soften with relief on seeing Gotthard.

"Gotts!" he says. "What's going on?" Ximena smiles at the sight of the two boys. They must be among the best dressed of all present—both wear robes of the finest-looking fabric. And the thick belt around Rutger's waist is spectacular. Other people wear much simpler tunics, some even washed-out work pants.

"Don't know, mensa," Gotthard says with a shrug, and turns to look at the other people, who roam around with the same expression as children on their first school day. "Edda!"

"What?"

"Edda van Dolah. There." Gotthard points his finger at the black girl in the distance, who is talking animatedly to Aline and two strongly built young men. "With Speese and the rat boys."

"And Valentijn van Kley is there, with her sister, see? But most I've never seen before."

Some people shout a warning, and point at something in the sky. Gotthard and Rutger raise their heads. Yes, Ximena sees it as well: a pulsating light that moves against the starless night sky at incredible speed.

"What...?!" Rutger says.

Gotthard remains silent, head moving right to left as he follows the dashing sight across the firmament. Ximena feels his curiosity echo inside her, harmonizing with his sense of awe at the marvels of nature.

"A shooting star?" Rutger asks.

"Shooting stars don't pulse," Gotthard says.

The light stops its darting movement, and stays hanging in the air, perfectly still, flashing slow pulses of white light.

"Whoa!" Gotthard says, as Ximena feels his mind instantly reassessing the evidence. "Definitely not a shooting star! That thing stopping its movement like that is impossible. Infinite deceleration requires infinite power. Or that thing is massless..."

"It's getting bigger," Rutger says, a pinch of nervousness in his voice. "It's getting closer."

The talking of the surrounding people becomes louder as they realize the same. Forty-eight heads turned towards the light, as its brightness slowly dissolves into shape. It is something flat and curved, descending slowly towards them, in eerie silence, lights flashing in orderly patterns around its perfectly spherical perimeter.

Ximena laughs at the sight of the thing descending from the sky. Mark gives her an amused glance and chuckles as well.

"It's a flying saucer!" Gotthard says, wide-eyed. "An honest-to-Goah flying saucer." He smiles and shakes his head with wonder. "Goah's Mercy, what a cliché."

"Aliens?" Rutger says, a pinch of anxiety in his voice.

"Think so." Gotthard keeps his eyes locked on the object as it descends vertically on an empty spot not far away from the group. "And my karma is on little green men, if you want to bet. Either the old sci-fi magazines were spot on, or these mensas have a developed sense of humor—and know us very well."

Complete silence envelops the group as everybody stares at the saucer, floating perfectly still a few yards over the ground. Four poles emerge from the perimeter of the floating saucer and extend uniformly until they touch the ground.

"They're here," Gotthard says. He is not afraid, Ximena notes. Not the same way as Rutger or others appear to be. Gotthard is fascinated, filled to the brim with curiosity. No force on Earth would move him away from this place now.

A door—rectangular shape and all—slides open on the side of the saucer facing them. There are only shadows beyond.

Gotthard takes a step forward, eyes not daring to blink. "Show yourself," he mutters.

A thin ramp slides slowly out of the bottom of the door until it touches the ground. All eyes return to the door. There is a hint of movement behind it, in the shadows.

"Show yourself!" His lips curve in a faint smile.

An elongated white humanoid shape walks out the door onto the ramp, moving slowly and intentionally. A mare, who stays there for a few moments, regarding the humans below in silence with those uncanny white eyes. And being regarded in return.

"Not little," Gotthard whispers at Rutger. "Not green. But otherwise, it doesn't disappoint."

"Greetings, earthlings." The mare communicates without moving her black mouth, her voice *reverberates*, feminine and elegant, directly inside Gotthard's mind. "I am an alien from outer space, and I come in peace."

"In peace," Rutger says, daring a smile. Other people around them murmur words of relief.

"You may call me *Rew*," the mare says, raising an arm and awkwardly extending the three finger-appendages in distinct angles. "Live long and prosper."

Rutger frowns. "Isn't that what the Klingons say on the Tuesday evening radio show?"

"The Vulcans," Gotthard says, eyes locked on the mare. "Hush now."

"We are the *marai*," the alien continues. "We did settle near your world over ten thousand years ago. Since then, we have been with you, every night, here," Rew points an extremity at her own head, "in your dreams."

"Dreams...?" Rutger turns to Gotthard. "Did it say *dreams?*"

"Shh, listen."

"You never knew—how could you, with your primitive senses?—but we have been visiting your dreams for millennia. It is through dreams that we influence your destiny. We did guide you through the chokes of your history. We did plant the notion of farming in your ancestor's minds, of domestication of lesser beings. Of writing, when you were ready. You thrived. You took Earth. And then you lost it."

Rew floats down along the ramp in silence, reaches the

ground, and keeps moving towards the group of attentive youths. Another mare exits the flying saucer's opening and floats down with Rew's same awkward gait. And then another mare comes out, indistinguishable from the others. And another. Until a row of mares—eleven in total—walk in a line and form a row behind Rew, who has stopped just a few yards away from the group.

"We did fail you," Rew says, and bows her head deeply for a long moment. "A terrible failure with dreadful consequences for your race." She stands tall and moves her gaze across the group. Gotthard shudders as his eyes meet the alien's. "We could not stop you from unbalancing your world. We did miscalculate the intensity of your predations, and Earth's capacity to resist them. A grave miscalculation that triggered the most hideous suffering on your race. And on ours. We did fail you." Rew bows again.

Rutger turns to Gotthard as if to say something, but desists at the intensity of Gotthard's expression. He is absorbing every word uttered by the alien as if they were Goah's awssel£.

"We did hope that humankind would recuperate in time," Rew continues, "as it has done countless times before. But, alas, your recovery remains fragile. Your lifespans are too short, insufficient to maintain a resilient civilization, insufficient to escape the extinction sink it is falling into. Humankind cannot regain control over its own destiny as a species. And so, after millennia of subtle guidance, we marai are forced to reveal ourselves," Rew extends her extremities in a very human gesture, "and take direct ownership over your fate."

"Are you invaders?" a stocky man in his early twenties asks. A farmer, obviously, in view of those brown pants beneath the short working tunic. Ximena feels Gotthard's innate aversion to the lowborn. He speaks matter-of-factly, without fear. Out of place.

Rew turns to face the man, who holds her gaze with defiant blue eyes. "We are not, Elder Luuk. We are shepherds."

"You know my name?!"

Rew keeps her eerie white eyes fixed on the man's for a short while. Then she says, "I do, Elder Luuk. I do know each of you." She slides her gaze across the forty-eight youngsters. "I met you already. In your dreams."

"Why are we here?" The stocky farmer—Elder Luuk—asks. "Why us?"

"I do know your desires, Elder Luuk. I do know the deepest needs of each and every one of you. You do burn inside from longing. Alas, you shall never be satisfied. Society resists your wishes—unmoved, merciless. You are all wounded by desperation."

Nobody interrupts her words. Not even Elder Luuk. Some have gasped, as if suddenly realizing they are naked. Ximena feels Gotthard's inner passion as he swaps a glance with Rutger. He for one is not afraid of exposure. Only careful.

"You are here," Rew continues, "because your non-conformist cravings are powerful. You do want to change your world. So do we." She turns her white, lifeless eyes to the stocky man. "You shall be our agents, Elder Luuk. Our agents of change. If you so desire."

"What if we don't?" Elder Luuk asks.

"Then you shall return to your world in peace. And desperation. But if you stay with us, if you do yield your will to ours, we shall grant you the power to achieve your every goal."

"Which power?" a girl asks from behind Gotthard.

Ximena turns her head. It is Edda, her eyes drilling the aliens'.

"The ultimate power, Redeemed Van Dolah," Rew says. "The power to penetrate others' minds, and to influence them *decisively*. The power to truly *persuade*. The right idea, in the right mind, at the right time, and you shall accomplish *anything*. With our rigorous guidance, your history shall fly forward, free from the shackles of tradition."

Usually Gotthard is quite the cynic—Ximena begins to *get* him already—and yet, somehow, he feels in his guts that Rew is speaking the truth. Ximena can feel his lust rising like the Pacific tide—thick and relentless. He wants *so much* to believe the alien. He needs that power. Oh, what he could accomplish. With that power they would finally have to listen, those narrow-minded fools. They would see as clearly as he does. They would have no choice but to mobilize all the resources of Goah's Imperia for a new space program, jumping from horses to rockets, even if half the planet starves to death. Because the alternative… The alternative is inconceivable.

"And what's in for you?" Edda asks. "What do you want in exchange?"

"Edda!" Aline mutters, and pulls from her hand, as if warning her.

"Your compliance, Redeemed van Dolah. Your *obedience*. We shall dictate policies, and you shall execute them to the utmost of your abilities. Which are considerable—a factor you have also been selected for."

"Which *policies*?" Elder Luuk asks.

"I do feel your skepticism," Rew says. "But do not fear. You humans and us marai ultimately want the same: for humankind to flourish anew. To fill the world like you did centuries ago. And to keep it this time."

"Sure, sure," Edda says, ignoring the insistent pulling of Aline. "But what do you want us to do for you?"

"I cannot give you details, Redeemed van Dolah. Our policies are flexible, and shall adapt to your own successes. But do not fear. Our instructions shall remain compatible with your private desires. It is in our interest that you accomplish your own goals and put yourself in a position of influence. Only then you shall serve us with maximum efficacy."

"So, you scratch our backs, and we scratch yours?" Elder Luuk asks.

"Indeed."

"Fair enough," he says. "I'm in."

"Whoa, whoa, wait a minute, yeah?" Edda says. "What if even with those magical powers of yours we can't make, uh, whatever it is we need to do?"

"If you do fail yourselves, then you are of no use to us. You would then be free to return to your inner despair in peace, without further obligation towards us."

"It's a no brainer." Elder Luuk shrugs and turns towards Edda. "There's no downside."

"No downside, yeah?" Edda squints at Rew. "Except that we might be sealing a pact with the devil."

Those words hit a nerve. The body language of forty-seven youngsters changes abruptly. They seem more aware of their featureless surroundings, more defensive. Expressions have tensed noticeably. Even a mind as rational as Gotthard's seems touched by irrational fear. No, he thinks, that's *superstition.* And to be honest, what's the alternative? He's got to take every chance, even if...

"I'm in," Gotthard says. "And if you're the devil, Elder Rew, I'm still willing to accept your conditions."

A murmur of voices crisscrosses the group, many of

assent, some of doubt. "I'm in," Rutger says. Others join. "I'm in." "Me too."

They must be truly desperate, Ximena thinks, if they are willing to gamble their souls.

And yet, not everybody seems convinced, not by far. About half of those present, including Edda and Aline, remain silent—a long silence of uncertainty, mistrust written on their faces.

"This is a dream," Edda says, staring at the palm of her hands. She raises her eyes at Rew. "You're not real."

"I am most certainly real, Redeemed van Dolah. Real in my world. Real in your dreams. And I am *really* most impressed with your innate awareness—indeed, you are dreaming. We all are. This is a permascape, a shared dream. Every marai you see, and every human, is real. Only the dream is not."

"I want to believe you, Elder Rew," Aline says, after swapping a glance with Edda. "And that's why I can't. Without evidence, I can only trust my hope, and hope is a lousy source of truth."

"Show us your powers of influence," Edda says. "Convince us. I want to be convinced."

"I did indeed expect a degree of resistance," Rew says. "It's in your nature. Thus, I have arranged for a demonstration."

Rew raises an appendage-finger and the empty infinite flat landscape, flying saucer and all, vanish as if made of smoke. Even Ximena jumps at the sudden transition. But the people remain. They are now in an enormous room, surrounded by the luxury of another age: a massive round table of the most noble of woods surrounded by chairs that would not have been out of place in Versailles, a fire roaring on a stone hearth as high as a person, and enormous stained-glass windows, paintings and tapestries depicting preindustrial scenes of aristocracy and rural glory.

"Be welcome to the colonial palace of Fulda," Rew says. "The center of power of your country. Naturally, still a permascape. But we shall bring a special guest to our dream. A human of power, unaware of our intentions. One of my Walkers, Qoh," Rew extends an arm towards one of the eleven mares standing behind her, who bows in acknowledgment, "shall operate as thread-maker."

Qoh disappears.

"I have personally been conditioning the subject for this demonstration in several previous sessions. Today, I shall apply maximum persuasion, enough—I do hope—to tilt the balance. I do urge you all to witness the exchange in silence. Without training, any out-of-place word might doom my persuasion efforts."

The only door to the room opens and a woman in her twenties barges in, her expression filled with impatience, and her gait with authority. She is stretching out her robe —made of a glossy purple fabric—with harsh strokes, as if she had just put it on. "What's so urgent?" she says, her voice annoyed and creaky.

Ximena realizes that she can feel her irritation— frustration, rather. The psych-link has been rechanneled to her, obviously. She can hear the exhalations and chuckles of her fellow students as the source of the woman's irritation becomes apparent—there is an underlying, more primitive emotion at play, more powerful: *arousal*. The woman is horny as hell, probably an echo of the dream she has just been pulled out from by the mare Qoh. A glimpse of a wet embrace flashes through the psych-link. Ximena is hetero, and yet the woman's longing for the nude hips of her lover... her warm thighs... Whoa! It makes her own cheeks warm. And not just her cheeks. It's a goahdamn powerful beast, the psych-link, she must admit.

"I do apologize, Consul Levinsohn," Rew says. "It is indeed a matter of urgency." She is standing next to the woman, and has changed form, resembling a tall male human courtier, groomed hairstyle and all, although this courtier has expressionless white eyes. And yet, for whatever reason, that doesn't bother the consul.

"Who are these?" The consul is sweeping her eyes across Gotthard, Edda and the rest of the people scattered around the luxurious room. Most of them are staring back at her with fascinated anticipation, except the few white-eyed that don't seem to care.

"Nobody of concern, Consul Levinsohn," Rew says. Ximena feels that the woman trusts the alien advisor. She wonders how Rew earned that trust—surely not easily. "I do urge you to make an urgent decision regarding the location of the Century Festival."

"Come on," she says, rolling her eyes. "You called for that? There's still plenty of time until New Year's Eve."

"I do fear that is not accurate, Consul Levinsohn. The end of the year—or rather, the *century*—is a mere fortnight away, and preparations do need to be made in haste. I shall remind the consul that there is great symbolic importance to the venue of—"

The consul laughs acrimoniously. "And that right there is the problem, Chancellor. Everyone and their dog is getting on my nerves with the Century Festival. Goah, who cares where the final countdown is broadcasted from? Yes, I know, I know—everybody cares, Goah be merciful. The Praetor of Rhenania has even sent envoys and gifts."

"I do appreciate the political significance of this decision. Thus, my advice to select a remote area, and so avoid the jealousy of any significant party."

"Yes, I see your point. But I'm not convinced. If I select a Rhenanian colony, the praetor has promised to cut his karma allotment for the next two years—the imperator would appreciate that, and perhaps even the Pontifex. And since Imperator Cisek is almost twenty-seven..."

The train of thoughts and machinations of the consul feels like a roller coaster to the complacent academic mind of Ximena. Then the consul stops talking and grimaces, gripped by a sudden sense of disgust, like she was smelling a putrid corpse, but without the actual smell. Ximena must cover her mouth. Mark sits back, obviously feeling unwell.

"If I may offer insight, Consul Levinsohn, Rhenania is an influential and rich province already—the envy of Germania. I do fear the other provinces shall feel threatened were you to select a Rhenanian colony for the Century Festival. May I humbly suggest an alternative," the revolting sensation disappears as quickly as it came, and a sense of relief and peace takes its place, "the Dutch province?"

"The Dutch province... Hmm..." The sensation evolves into a pleasant warm fuzziness in the consul's innards. "Could be, could be..."

"Peripheral. Remote. And, of most relevance to your political interests, mostly harmless. Especially the coastal regions."

"Remind me, Chancellor, what's the name of that land at the end of the Rhine? The one you mentioned last time?"

"Geldershire, Consul Levinsohn. An ideal choice."

"*Geldershire*, yes." Ximena's eyes open involuntarily as she feels the consul's arousal—which was still lingering in the background of her psyche—raise with sudden intensity. The consul wets her lips. Even Ximena feels uncomfortably conscious of Mark's masculine presence next to her. "Never been there."

"Exactly my point, Consul Levinsohn. Nobody that matters to your ambitions has ever been to Geldershire."

"But if I go with this… Geldershire, that would disappoint everybody."

"Not quite, I do believe, Consul Levinsohn. They shall certainly complain, but they would be secretly pleased that a rival is not favored in their stead. The balance of influence would remain intact."

"Hmm, Geldershire…" As the consul utters these words, Ximena feels her libido pushing through the roof. The consul takes a deep breath and straightens her robes. "I really need to return to my chambers. Very well, Chancellor. The Century Festival shall take place in Geldershire's capital colony. What's the name again?"

"Oosterbeek, Consul Levinsohn. A wise choice——"

"No!" Ximena jumps at the unexpected exclamation from the back of the room. It is Edda, walking towards the Consul. Everybody else—both in the scene and the amphitheater—is staring at her wide-eyed. "Forgive me for my boldness, Consul." Edda bows awkwardly. "I know I'm out of place, but the selection of Oosterbeek would be a costly mistake."

"Who is this?" Consul Levinsohn's eyes scan Edda's white garments and then turns her head towards Rew.

"Do excuse my impetuous… underling, Consul Levinsohn. Redeemed van Dolah is indeed speaking out of turn."

Edda clears her throat. "I am, uh, the chancellor's *expert* on Geldershire matters, Consul. And I'd be a poor expert if I failed to warn you."

Consul Levinsohn studies her for a long moment.

"Fine. Say what you have to say. Why is selecting Geldershire such a mistake?"

"Not Geldershire, Consul. On the contrary, I concur two hundred percent with the chancellor. Geldershire is the *perfect* place to hold the Century Festival, yeah? But Oosterbeek is to Geldershire what Rhenania is to Germania. Plus, it is also the residence of Geldershire's Aedil. How would the other aedils of Germania feel? There's no need to pick favorites if you can choose an even more remote colony."

"I see." Consul Levinsohn smiles at her, her eyes scanning the feminine shapes under Edda's tunic. "And I am sure you have a suggestion?"

"Lunteren, Consul. Lunteren. Lunteren is the place. Fish, steel, and beautiful sunsets. At the fringe of the fringe, Lunteren is the place nobody cares about."

"Lunteren." Consul Levinsohn nods slowly, takes a step forward and rubs a finger on Edda's exposed neck. "Sounds like a fascinating place." Her smile broadens. "Care to accompany me to my chambers and tell me more about it?"

Edda seems momentarily at a loss, but then puts a playful hand on her hips and smiles back. "Anything you *desire*, Consul."

END OF DREAMWORMS EPISODE I

Sign Up – No Bull Sci-Fi

ISAAC PETROV – EPIC SCI-FI AT ITS BEST!

Come over to my site at IsaacPetrov.com and SIGN UP to get fresh SCI-FI updates, discounts and goodies:

https://isaacpetrov.com/book1

OR SCAN THIS WITH YOUR CAMERA!

DREAMWORMS

A POST-APOCALYPTIC FIRST CONTACT EPIC

ALIEN MASTER

EPISODE II

ISAAC PETROV

NINE

Pontifex's Day

The auditorium darkens as the next section of the dreamsenso comes up, floating vividly above and across the amphitheater. A landscape lights up from above, a roughly almond-shaped collection of a thousand colonial houses—spacious double-story buildings, most with garden patches around them, like a jigsaw of maroon roofs mixed with vegetable green. The chaotic network of narrow, red-bricked streets hints at the legacy of a town settled for uncountable generations.

"Lunteren," Professor Miyagi says. "Meticulously recreated as it was a hundred years ago, before the Dreamwars: a sleepy colony prospering contentedly at the margins of aws Imperia."

From this height, a few hundred yards over the red-tiled roofs, Lunteren appears seamlessly embedded into its natural environment. To the east, right on the edge of the colony, a large dense forest; farmlands extending far to the north and south; the sea to the west, not farther than fifteen walking minutes, with a large sandy beach and an active harbor. The afternoon is advancing; the sun sends traces of gold over the sparkling waves and the fishing boats and merchant barges that unload their catch and wares onto horse carts.

The scene slides lower, towards Lunteren. Ximena squints at the movement in the streets. Yes, they are teeming with colonists. As the dreamsenso point of view approaches the ground, the air fills with animated chatter, noise and music. And orange. Plenty of orange. Most colonists are wearing orange-tinted tunics, and those with hats, the oldest among them, have decorated them with orange-colored motifs: feathers, orange leaves—even carrots and small pumpkins. *This must be a festivity*, Ximena thinks.

"Thirteenth of December," Miyagi says. "Pontifex's Day. A tradition in the Dutch Province. Everybody is out on the street, sharing and trading junk." Ximena can see him pacing below the scene. "Lots of fun, apparently. And all for the glory of the Pontifex in Townsend, who brings them peace and prosperity." Ximena feels a pinch of pride. The Goah's Imperia of the Americas are still nominally under the sovereignty of the Pontifex. A symbolic and religious role nowadays, of course. But Ximena, like most of Pontifex Fahey's subjects, still prays for her health and wise guidance every day.

Like a placid pigeon, the scene lands in the middle of a busy street where people walk leisurely in small family groups. No horses nor carts on the road, not even bicycles. The public space belongs to the people today. Music hammers the air, loud and rhythmic. People laugh, children run, and everybody—absolutely *everybody* —dances.

Decorated tables have been set up on both sides of the street, in front of each house, as if an extension of the front yards. Old, used every-day objects—toys, pottery, books, radios, tools, clothes, anything and everything—are put on display for trading. Bright orange-themed decorations cover the tables, and strongly scented delicacies on beautiful large ceramic plates lure neighbors and fellow colonists. The spiced aroma waters Ximena's mouth. A member or two of each family stands by the tables to greet passersby, while the rest of the family roams the colony, dancing and filling large bags with bargains.

The scene closes in on a particular house on the south side of the street. It is not so busy here, towards the eastern edge of the colony. Two teenage girls dressed in ornate, orange tunics stand by the gleaming orange table gesticulating excitedly, one black and tall, the other white and short: Edda and Aline.

"This is the Speeses' residence on the Miel Way," Miyagi says. "Edda lives nearby, up the street." He points with a finger to where the crowd grows thicker. "Let's watch."

The teenage girls chat with discreet but excited voices, too enthralled in their conversation to mind the world around them.

"That's not proof enough," Aline is saying, trying to keep a calm, controlled voice, although her eyes beam with the same intensity as Edda's.

"But we had the same *exact* dream, yeah?" Edda is pulling Aline from the sleeves. "We saw the same exact *alien* floating out of the same exact spaceship, Goah's Mercy. Promising the same goahdamn… *powers*, yeah?"

"A shared dream. That's all."

"That's *all?*" Edda shakes her head and scoffs. "We shared the same fucking dream, Goah's Mercy!"

"I know, I know. But that's my point. A shared dream is… wow! Rare enough. I… I still have problems accepting it. But *aliens*? Aliens that are trying to save us from," she shrugs, "*whatever*? Nah, that's too much to take, sister."

"Extraordinary claims require extraordinary evidence, yeah?"

"Yes! Nicely put."

"Not my line. And a pile of bull! What more evidence do you need than the fact we did share a dream, huh?"

A sudden, shrill bleep makes Edda and Aline—and Ximena—jump in place.

"ATTENTION, LUNTEREN!" A loud female voice echoes deafeningly off the house walls along the street. "STOP YOUR CHORES, AND LISTEN."

Aline swaps a stupefied glance with Edda. Ximena pinpoints the source of the commotion on a small loudspeaker set up on the top of a power pole down the street.

Another loud bleep makes Ximena cover her ears in reflex.

"ATTENTION, LUNTEREN! THIS IS YOUR QUAESTOR SPEAKING. ATTENTION, THIS IS NOT A REGULAR CALL TO SERVICE. I BRING NEWS OF THE HIGHEST RELEVANCE TO OUR COLONY."

Yes, it is Marjolein Mathus. But Ximena can hardly recognize her voice, so exultant, shaking with raw emotion.

"AFTER MONTHS OF TIRELESS REQUESTS TO MY SUPERIORS, MY INSISTENCE HAS FINALLY BORNE FRUIT, GOAH BE PRAISED. REJOICE, LUNTEREN! FOR I HAVE JUST RECEIVED RADIO NOTIFICATION FROM FULDA, DIRECTLY FROM OUR CONSUL'S OFFICE, THAT OUR COLONY HAS BEEN BLESSED TO HOST THE OFFICIAL NEW YEAR'S FESTIVAL!"

As she pauses to take air, Edda gasps and Aline falters.

She must hastily hold herself to the adorned table, before meeting Edda's wide-eyed gaze.

"REJOICE, LUNTEREN! IN TWO WEEKS' TIME, THE DAWN OF THE TWENTY-FIFTH CENTURY WILL BE BROADCAST TO EVERY SOUL IN GERMANIA FROM LUNTEREN! THIS IS THE MOST IMPORTANT EVENT—EVER!—IN THE HISTORY OF OUR COLONY."

Another pause. Edda takes Aline's hand into her own. Their wide-eyed gazes meet with the explosive force of realization. *It happened! It really happened!* Ximena feels the exhilaration like it were her own. Even her heart pumps faster. The joy—the implications—are so overwhelming…

"I WILL BE HEADING AN EMERGENCY COMMITTEE TO BEGIN URGENT PREPARATIONS. IN THE MEANTIME, I ASK ALL OF YOU TO EMBRACE THIS ONE-IN-A-THOUSAND-YEARS HONOR WITH GRATITUDE FOR GOAH'S BLESSINGS. LUNTEREN, WE ARE THE STEWARDS OF GOAH THIS YEAR. MORE THAN THAT, WE ARE AWS AGENTS ON EARTH THIS CENTURY! I ASK YOU TO DO WHATEVER IT TAKES SO THAT GERMANIA NEVER FORGETS OUR NAME. NOT IN A HUNDRED YEARS. FOR LUNTEREN! QUAESTOR MATHUS OUT."

Edda and Aline, wide-eyed, begin to speak at the same time into each other's faces, but their voices are drowned by a tide of chaotic shouting and cheering along the street. Some nearby tables kick up their music, and the passersby jump to the bass blasts, hands in the air, in celebration.

The scene closes in on Aline as she embraces Edda fiercely. Both are now laughing wildly.

"It was you!" Aline shouts, locking her friend in a bear hug. "Goah has Mercy, it was you!"

"It was, yeah?" Edda laughs louder, so overjoyed her thoughts melt in disarray, unable to speak—just laugh, hug, and feel. Ximena's eyes mist over.

"Oh!" Aline releases Edda in shock from the sudden impact of her bottom being smacked.

A teenage boy—tall and muscular, with white-tanned skin, dark blond hair, and blue eyes—is standing right behind her. "Aws Blessings to you, Woman Speese," he says with a wide smile. "And to you, Redeemed van Dolah. Happy Pontifex's day!"

Aline laughs and hugs him. "Aws Blessings, my Man Ledebour!"

"Blessings, Piet," Edda says, laughing. "What are you doing to my friend? When you're around, she turns into this melted, horny shadow of herself."

"What can I say? The irresistible attraction of fishermen. No, please—no fish-smell jokes."

"I like fish!" Aline says, kissing him and biting his lower lip.

The greeting goes on for a while until Pieter finally escapes Aline's embrace, both laughing.

"Some news, huh?" Pieter says. "Lunteren picked for the New Year's Festival. Those aliens ain't fooling around!"

He knows! Ximena thinks with surprise, but then she realizes that Edda is not surprised at all. Then she remembers. During the First Contact section, as she was psych-linked to Gotthard, she saw this boy talking with Edda and Aline in the distance. He was there too.

"Did you sleep with her?" Pieter asks Edda.

"What?" Edda stops smiling.

"That aws Head woman—Consul Levinsohn. Did you....?" Pieter makes an obscene gesture with his hands.

"Piet!" Aline slaps his broad shoulder.

"What!" He frowns in mocking complaint. "Edda was

obviously very convincing! Perhaps more than that alien, what's her name again?"

"Rew," Edda says. "And let's just say I did what I had to do."

"That's all? No details?"

"Piet!" Aline slaps anew.

"Okay, okay," he chuckles. "Sorry, Edda. Didn't mean to… But say, why did you, er…" he wets his lips, "… *insist* on bringing the Festival right here to Lunteren?"

Edda shrugs. "Was more of an impulse." She meets his curious gaze. "It sure as Dem opens possibilities, yeah?"

"Like what?"

"Don't know." She shrugs again. "But our colony will have the complete undivided attention of the entire country for a few minutes."

"Uh huh." Pieter turns his face to Aline, and back to Edda. "So… say, are you mensas going to, er, learn that stuff the aliens are promising?"

"Sure," Edda says. "All the way! I can use those persuasion," she wiggles her fingers, "*powers* of theirs to convince my dad to stop his Joyousday."

A slight frown crosses Aline's forehead. "Aren't you afraid of what they will ask us to do in return?"

"Why? I bet they know what they're doing, sister. They've helped us since, what did they say, like ten thousand years ago?"

Pieter nods. "We scratch their backs, they scratch ours. Fair and square. I for one want to stop all those Siever factories for good! You with me, love?"

"Uh, sure," Aline says, and smiles, thoughtfully. "We could even try to end the coal trade in the Hanseatic Imperium."

"Now you're talking!" Pieter says, eyes beaming. "And why just in our Imperium, huh? We could clean all aws

Imperia from filth, can't we? Where's the limit?" He takes an orange-colored fluffy cookie from the table and gnaws on it. "Wow! This is good!" He chews slowly, and gapes at Aline. "*You* did this?"

She playfully slaps his shoulder again. "So hard to believe? Gastronomy runs as deep in the Speese family as engineering. Unfortunately, it brings less karma."

"Oh, fuck!" Pieter says, his eyes squinting at something behind Aline. She turns to see a male teenager of their age approaching with a smug smile. Light brown skin, short black hair—and attractive. Ximena recognizes Gotthard instantly. He is dressed in a fine orange tunic, same as the darker-skinned toddler sitting on his shoulders looking around at the colorful festivities with large eyes.

"Aws Blessings to you," he says.

"Aws Blessings," Edda and Aline reply at the same time. Pieter remains silent.

"Impressive achievement yesterday, Edda. I wasn't sure that dream was, well, just a dream. But now…"

"Not too bad, huh?" Edda says with a wink.

Gotthard turns his attention to Pieter and gives him a long, studious glance. "I was surprised to see you and your brother there too. I wonder what the marais saw in you?"

Pieter shrugs. "Ask them."

"And what are you doing here? This is a specialist district." He walks closer to Pieter. "Shouldn't you be catching some fish or whatever you smelly rat boys in the fishing district do?" He has taken a napkin out and waves it mockingly over his nose.

"I go where I goahdamn want," Pieter says.

"I don't know what you see in this rat boy, Aline," Gotthard says as he hands her a folded piece of paper. "A woman with your talents should have standards."

Aline unfolds the paper and nods absentmindedly as she gives it a superficial glance.

"What's that?" Pieter asks, trying to peek.

"Nothing," she mutters, folding the paper and sliding it in her pocket. "Professional secrecy."

"You working with this… elitist worm?"

Gotthard walks past Pieter like he doesn't exist—no, like he doesn't *matter*—and leans to inspect the small shrine set up next to the table. The shrine, on top of a piece of tree trunk, is made of freshly cut lush-green branches, decorated with shiny balls of different colors. The open front reveals the inside: an orange cloth, possibly silk, with a pile of metallic flat pieces.

"Not much karma left," Gotthard says. "I hope the Quaestor is more generous this year with the engineer families—we scientists have doubled. I can put in a good word, if you like." He turns his side-smile to Pieter. "You and your rat brother better catch many, many fish this year, Ledeboer, because aws Head never has much karma left for rat families."

Pieter, face flushed, walks his massive body right in front of Gotthard, their faces mere inches from each other. Pieter, a head taller, stares with bloodshot eyes down into Gotthard's amused gaze.

"Goah, the smell!" Gotthard covers his nose with the napkin. "Makes me almost hungry." The toddler sitting on Gotthard's shoulders reaches out to Pieter's blond hairs, grabbing them with a giggle.

"Ouch!" Pieter takes a step back, safe from the infant's curious hands.

"Leave that, Gerrit!" Gotthard says, raising his right hand to caress the toddler. "You just had your bath." He points at the large speakers, loud disco music merging into the street celebrations. "Goah's Mercy, Speese. Stop that noise or change the tape." He shakes his head theatrically. "What's that, the Bee Gees?" He chuckles. "The 1970s were a lost decade."

"But that's when we were exploring the *moon*," Aline says in a musical, ironic tone. "You like *space*, don't you, Gotthard?"

He side-smiles back at her, but says nothing.

"Very true!" Edda says. "What was that story in the summer about? Oh, yes! One of the old space colonies, apparently still has people living on it, yeah?"

"Oh, yes, I remember the story," Pieter says. "The meteor colony!"

"*Asteroid* colony, hick," Gotthard replies, smile frozen in place, a spark in his eyes. "And there was nothing apparent about it," he says, turning to Edda. "There *really* is a lost colony. Still alive. I heard the radio traffic myself."

Aline laughs. "There were warnings about the end of the world, right?" She points at Gotthard. "What was it all about? *The end of the world is nigh, over*," she mocks, enjoying herself. "*A meteor will destroy Earth in a hundred years, over and out.*"

Aline and Pieter laugh wholeheartedly, while Gotthard stares at them, keeping the smile on his lips, but not in his eyes.

"How did all that end?" Aline asks between laughs.

"They also sent a picture," Gotthard says, his voice barely audible over the loud music. "My contribution was the software that rendered the image." He looks at Edda, his eyes dark and sad. "The faces—they were old—*Old*. One glance, and aws Head declared them demon-ridden and banned all further communication." His gaze is lost somewhere behind Edda. "*Heresies…* they called it, the ignorant zealots. And then, they covered it up, like it never happened. I couldn't believe it! They just…" He waves a hand, and sighs, "No, there's no surviving colonies in the solar system, they said. All colonies were abandoned to their fate during the collapses and starved out centuries ago, they said. All lies. Dangerous, dangerous lies, that damn us to extinction."

"Lies, huh?" Pieter points a finger at the toddler. "You better get your shit together, mensa, for your son's sake."

"Okay, enough everybody!" says Edda with a loud clap. "Pieter, stop being such an asshole. And you," she turns to Gotthard, "take your snob ass somewhere else, yeah?" She steps forward and caresses the toddler tenderly, who giggles in return. "What a poor example for Gerrit."

Gotthard smiles to her and mocks a bow. "As you wish, dowry sister," he says, and walks away.

"Wow!" says Aline. "You play that idiot like a guitar. How can you have such an influence on him?"

"I know how," Pieter says sourly, still glaring at Gotthard's back. "By walking over to aws Womb and giving away an ovum to the Kraker family."

"Piet!" Aline turns and gives him a scandalized look.

Edda laughs and shrugs. "I think you're right, Piet. Gotthard may not respect many things—but *family*, that he does."

"Goah's Mercy, Edda," Pieter says, voice drenched in disgust, "what a catch. You're always talking about how we must be oh so alert, how those *rastocrate* families have our sacred rights in their sights, and just want to oppress us and all that shit. And then you fucking bind to one of them!"

"You mean *aristocratic*, Piet," Edda says, an incipient frown of anger on her brow. "And it was my dad who arranged the dowry bond."

"How unfortunate for you. Well, at least you get to enjoy the karma."

The scene vanishes and the spring sun and blue skies

return to the amphitheater. Ximena and many of her fellow students stretch their dream limbs as they refocus their attention on the stage below.

"Sorry, people," Professor Miyagi says, "the dreamsenso section finishes here. I was thinking about prolonging it with Edda's spectacular slap across Pieter Ledeboer's face, but it was getting way too long already."

Chuckles, polite laughs and whines of disappointment fill the open-air auditorium.

Miyagi takes a few steps, hands on his back, as if reflecting. "You know what comes to my mind when I witness the events leading to the Century Festival?" He pauses and looks gravely up to the students' expectant faces. "That they had some dubious taste in music."

All students burst out laughing.

"No, seriously, people," he says as the laughs die away, "when I watch this scene, I always wonder about Gotthard. You have seen the little asshole. He lives a life of privilege —the Kraker are a prestigious scientist family. And yet, the poor bastard seems to be the only one who knows that the Babi asteroid is coming, and has the education to understand what that ultimately means." He shakes his head. "The world lives in innocent denial, and science has been silenced by dogma. Ignorance—not truth—is guiding humanity in the age of Goah. Ignorance, fanaticism. And lies. Not the most reliable guides, I would say."

The words hit Ximena like a sting. It's a strange feeling. On one side she intellectually understands what the professor is saying, that aws Head was looking the other way when a world-ending event was literally falling over their heads. They covered it up, they buried it. History repeating itself, just like in the first collapse. Worse. Yes, the professor is telling the truth, she knows, and yet she feels attacked inside—in her identity—by his words. The blue-

and-white section of GIA students at the other end of the hemicycle also stirs uncomfortably. This is not history, not by far. They are still living the age of Goah, at least in the Goah's Imperia of the Americas, as vibrant as it was one hundred years ago. Aws Head is not just a human-made institution. It's more than that, much more—it's also *divine*. They'd never—

"Imagine what he might be feeling." Miyagi's words interrupt Ximena's thoughts. "Loneliness, perhaps? He's a father, and perhaps he is relieved that his son will live a normal, fulfilled life, and his grandchildren as well, and so on for a few more generations. Does he even care, with the short lifespan of his time, what will happen to his descendants a hundred years in the future? Does he even care," he lowers his voice, as if thinking aloud, "about *us*?"

TEN

Worth and Soul

R ew paces forward, or rather floats an inch over the ground towards the forty-eight youngsters.

Ximena feels Edda's inquisitive eyes scanning the elongated form, and comparing it with the eleven mares standing in a neat row behind her. There are subtle differences. Yes. Some are slightly higher, or thinner. Even length of arms and legs vary from one to the next. The shade of white of their skin also differs subtly. *They're just… animals*, Ximena thinks, *same as us, with individual traits and variations, the result of evolutionary pressure in a resource-scant ecology.*

"I do welcome you back to the staging permascape," Rew says, and waves an arm across the infinite flatness of dark stone and black skies. "It is only us here—our conscious minds—then at this point only *we* do matter, what we marai say to you, and what you ultimately decide to do with our words."

Rew turns her head to the side, and three mares *walk* forward to stand next to her. There are subtle differences among the three, as there are among the rest, but they move as one in precise synchronization—same gait, same speed, same balancing of the arms as they slide, same stance as they stop.

"Do meet Overseer Yog," Rew says, bowing lightly to the three mares. "She shall clarify your choices."

"Sense and bind, humans." The words emanate as a single feminine voice from the three heads. Ximena feels Edda's wonder as she realizes how alien the aliens really are. "All of you are here to serve us."

Not the sexiest of speech beginnings, Ximena thinks. Edda and the others seem to agree, their faces expressing a degree of unease.

"You shall be granted abilities that no other humans possess." *That's better.* "You shall exert power over other humans, and so do our bidding." *Ouch.* "It is imperative that only humans of worth are provided access to this knowledge. Walker Rew," the three heads turn lightly left, where Rew remains fully still, "suggests that all of you are of worth. I shall judge that. I shall assess each of you at every step to determine if you are worthy of carrying the power of a Walker of the Mind."

A Walker of the Mind. Edda's excitement flows through Ximena like a hurricane through a ravine.

"Worthy are those with the will to exert power," Yog continues. "I shall assess who is worthy among you, humans. Walker Rew and her Deviss Walkers," her bodies turn briefly to glance at the eight mares standing behind, "shall instruct you in the three steps of the Path of Light."

The Path of Light. Ximena feels Edda's anticipation with amusement. Everybody in the twenty-sixth century knows, of course, about the Paths. To a great extent, dreamtech defines their age. But for Edda, they are just words—never-heard-before words of hope.

"But a master of the Path of Light," Yog continues, "is but an apprentice of the Path in the Shadow."

The Path in the Shadow. Ximena smiles, as she feels Edda's steel determination, like a drooling lioness. A sudden image of Willem crosses the psych-link in a flash of love and angst, but Edda promptly gathers herself in an impressive show of discipline, and her attention snaps back to the speaking mares.

"The three steps of the Path in the Shadow are the true source of power over others. That is your objective, humans: to tread the Path in the Shadow. Your objective, and ours. Without treading the Shadow, you are worthless to us—and to yourselves. Only a Walker in the Shadow—a true Walker of the Mind—can traverse the Second Wake, intrude into the minds of others, and hope to mold them to their will. It is my duty to ensure that only the worthy tread the Paths." Her heads turn left, as if talking to Rew directly. "It is a sensitive and dangerous discipline, that which Walker Rew plans to instruct you in. Thus, it is also my duty to limit the access to the powers of the Mind Walker to a minimum of subjects." She turns her heads to the forty-eight gripped youngsters. "Only the two most worthy humans shall be granted access to the Path in the Shadow. Only two of you shall become Walkers of the Mind."

Two? Ximena feels Edda's flush of icy fear, as her hope wavers. *Only two?!* She exchanges a wide-eyed glance with Aline. Behind them, Pieter and others begin to complain. The mares watch in silence as the protests grow louder. Gotthard, at the edge of the group, is talking agitatedly to a pale Rutger. The clamor continues for a long while, as the mares look on, impervious to the human storm, until it finally calms to a fearful, expectant murmur.

"Do look around you, humans, to your peers," Yog

continues. "Do observe them, and assess their motivation —and worth. Do ask to yourself, are they grander than yours?"

Many do indeed turn their heads studiously. Not Edda. She just stares at Yog, hands closed in fists. She feels... *betrayed*. This is not what they promised! Power, they said. Power to fix your world. That's what they said. They never spoke of—

"There are forty-eight of you now. But not for long. Your determination shall be put to the test after every single step Walker Rew pushes you along the Path of Light. If you do lack talent to Walk, or talent to learn, or motivation, you shall be flushed out, back to your human life of despair, in full knowledge that you are not worthy of a last chance to make right whatever wrongs you. Do look around you again, and if your strength falters at the thought of proving yourself more worthy than your peers, do step forward, and accept your fate now."

Silence falls on the staging permascape as Edda and the rest exchange glances of curiosity, even suspicion—but no one moves.

"What happens if we don't pass your tests?" a tall man in his late teens asks, his voice more aggressive than curious. Edda doesn't know the man, probably from one of the other Geldershire colonies. From Oosterbeek perhaps, judging by his arrogant stance.

"*Nothing* shall happen," Rew says, speaking for the first time since Yog stood beside her. "Which is punishment enough, Elder Kuipers. You are but barred from revealing our existence."

"But you are a very big deal! The world needs to know what you're doing. I bet you can get more help if you collaborate openly with aws Head."

"You shall not reveal our existence," Yog says.

"Even if you would," Rew says, "nobody would believe you, Elder Kuipers."

"I can be very persuasive. What if I try?"

"Then you shall be terminated," Yog says.

Edda blinks in shock. *Terminated?*

"Nobody shall believe you," Rew repeats. "I do suggest not to make a fool of yourself in the attempt."

"What does, er, Overseer forgotername mean by *terminated?*"

"Overseer *Yog*, human," Yog says. "If you do attempt to reveal our existence, or the nature of this… *collaboration*, we shall terminate your life."

"Whoa! Oookay." The man raises his hands in a gesture of appeasement. "Can you do that?"

"Yes."

"Uh huh," the man folds his arms across his chest. "Why are you doing all this? What do you want from us humans?"

"To help you flourish," Rew says. "As we have for millennia."

"Nice work you've done. Where were you during the collapses?"

Rew takes a few seconds to reply. If mares could breathe, Ximena thinks, Rew would probably be taking a deep breath. "Our power is limited, Elder Kuipers—that is why you are here. Human Walkers of the Mind shall remedy our handicap."

"But *why* are you helping us?" Elder Kuipers insists. "Why *really*? What's in it for you if we humans flourish or die? Is it your religion? Do you even have a god? Are you angels of Goah? Why us? Why, Goah's Mercy, are you here?"

Yeah, Edda thinks. Ximena feels her curiosity

overwhelming her apprehension. *That's a fucking good question.*

Yog replies immediately. "Your inquisitive mind disqualifies you from worth, human."

Before Elder Kuipers can reply, he disappears. Every one of the forty-seven remaining people stare at the empty spot in astonished silence.

Rew turns her head towards the three Yog mares. "Elder Kuipers was a promising candidate."

"There is no promise in curiosity. Only danger."

"He had a strong traversing halo. Very rare. His selection was a substantial investment of my personal time."

"Alas, ultimately unworthy of it." Yog's three faces turn to the apprehensive audience. "Humans, your way into the Path in the Shadow is now a spot closer. Only forty-five opponents remain between you and the power of the Mind Walker. Do look at them now, and ask yourself if you possess the inner strength to take the prize for yourself, or whether you would rather unburden your fate now, and join Elder Kuipers in going back to your miserable human existence."

Nobody speaks. They just stare at each other in silence, like they are holding their breaths. Edda glances first at the people she knows: Aline, next to her, and Pieter right behind them, with his brother Janson. Edda's dowry brother, Gotthard, is to her side, next to that rich friend of his, Rutger. Edda recognizes some other Lunteren faces: Man Rijnder, at eleven probably the youngest present, stands timidly behind the Van Kley siblings. She can beat them all, she thinks. Probably. But the others—the majority —are an unknown. There is no apprehension in anybody's eyes as they measure each other. Only determination. And defiance. Nobody speaks up.

Ximena draws a deep breath, as if that could shake the electrical anticipation she is feeling. Oh, she is so happy she made it to the Global Program. Professor Miyagi's seminar is turning out to be more engaging than she could have ever… *dreamed*. Ha, bad joke. Oh, she is so ready to immerse herself into the nitty-gritty historical details of the *Three Trials of Worth and Soul*, as history comes to know them.

"I am pleased," Yog finally says. "Now, do return to your individual dreams to await your first assessment. We shall recall each of you, one by one, to appraise your motivation. Do prepare, for I shall not be lenient in extracting your truth. By the morrow you shall know if you are deemed worthy to even begin Walker Rew's instruction in the Path of Light."

Before anybody can react, all humans disappear.

Only twelve mares remain in the empty vastness of the staging permascape.

"I do not approve of your methods, Overseer Yog."

"You are not required to approve, Walker Rew. Just to acknowledge."

"I do fear you are not sufficiently acquainted with the art of teaching. An adequate instruction is never a competition. Direct peer confrontation stirs the mind of the apprentice towards aggression and detaches it from self-focus. Many shall fail that would otherwise succeed."

"Indeed, which guarantees us the two worthiest and most malleable humans among all your candidates."

"I carefully chose each human for its talent and motivation—most would perform adequately as human Walkers. This selection process of yours—this *cull*—amounts to an unforgivable waste of resources. We are in no position to delay our goals. Master Gorrobor shall be informed."

"Master Gorrobor made me Overseer for a reason, Walker Rew. You are too... *attached* to assess the risks in their entirety. I do fear you lost your sense of context along the way while whispering to all your humans. Now, do call your threaders and bring the first candidate. A long session awaits, and I do expect to get to know each of your humans *intimately*."

ELEVEN

The Deepest Door

Edda opens the door, and her smile widens. "Please, come in," she speaks like she is greeting an old friend she hasn't seen for ages. "Welcome to my home."

The four mares—Rew and Yog—walk into a spacious colonial living room: three sofas around a large, wooden radio receiver, fire in the hearth, heavy carpet, and wide windows.

A solid dream, very realistic, Ximena thinks, as her eyes wander over the classic paintings on the walls—mostly romantic landscapes of the golden age. One depicts an enormous city, its crystal towers extending as far as the eye can see. Another one that catches Ximena's eyes depicts a harbor, a labyrinth of cranes and piles of containers, dwarfed by the largest vessels the world has ever seen.

"You did expect us, Redeemed van Dolah," Rew says, as the mares walk in. "Very good."

"The human is aware?" The three bodies of Yog ask with a single voice.

"No," Rew says, "albeit her subconscious bubbles right under the surface of awareness. This individual's halo shines with talent, but with no training, talent is just potential."

"And yet, the human knows who we are and why we are here."

"She is indeed subconsciously prepared for our arrival. She does perceive us as… a *visit*—a social bonding practice among humans."

"Meet my family," Edda says, waving a hand at the sofas from where three adults and a toddler watch them in attentive silence. Ximena blinks in surprise. The living room was empty just a moment ago. "That's my father and family Elder, Willem, with my son Hans."

Willem, sitting with the toddler on his knees, nods politely, but says nothing.

"And that's my brother, Bram."

Ximena looks at the young boy with curiosity. About thirteen, white, broad-faced. Willem's biological son, obviously—both stare with the same sad brown eyes.

"Would you like to see the house?" Edda asks. "I can do the tour for you."

"And who is this woman, Redeemed van Dolah?" Rew extends an arm at the black woman sitting on the side sofa: tall, hair falling over her shoulders in airy curls, grave expression, and eyes that pierce the visitors with the intensity of ice shards. Ximena recognizes her instantly; she has seen her before in Edda's dreams. That is Anika, her biological mother.

"Who?" Edda asks.

"The woman." Rew points again with the arm, and even wiggles the three appendages at the sofa.

"Oh," Edda's eyes flinch over at her mother with a momentary frown of confusion, but immediately turns her attention back to the visitors, smiles brightly, and says, "Great. Then, let's go, yeah? This way."

She walks towards a dark hallway which Ximena finds bizarrely out of place. The mares follow.

"How would you like to proceed, Overseer Yog?" Rew asks. "This is, after all, your assessment."

"You are the human whisperer, Walker Rew. Do your art to expose the human's motivating force."

"Very well." She turns to Edda, who is waiting patiently in the hallway's doorway. "Redeemed van Dolah, do kindly show us a recent memory."

"Sure thing! Anything particular?"

"A *core* memory. Something that did touch you."

"Core… That touched me… Hmm." She taps her cheek, in thought.

"Something that pushed through your inner self. With violence."

"I know!" she says cheerfully, like she just thought of what to wear for a party. "This way."

As Edda enters the dark hallway, she flicks a switch on the wall, but nothing happens.

"Oh, I'm sorry. Lights aren't working today. Happens now and then, hope you don't mind."

"Do proceed, Redeemed van Dolah."

They walk into the hallway. It is long, its end lost in the deepest darkness. The walls are packed with identical-looking doors on both sides, no space separating each from the next. Edda stops in front of one of them. "I think you'll like this one," she says, opens the door and walks through to a field flooded by daylight.

As the mares cross the threshold, Ximena immediately recognizes the setting: it was a few days back, when Edda and Willem were walking back from Aline's mom's Joyousday celebration. They are arguing.

"Goah's Mercy, Dad. I don't want you to die in two months! Remember when on Mom's Joyousday—?"

"Edda, that's enough!" Willem shouts at her, red-faced. Ximena feels Edda freeze in shock at her father's unusual fury. "I will not hear any more of this. You will respect my decision. I expect to have some peace in my last weeks of life."

How dare he? How *dare* he?! Edda just wants him to see that there are more important things than reputation. *Life*, for once, Goah's Mercy! Rage bubbles up inside her. He's so unfair, so short-sighted, so…

"I hate you!" she shouts. "You don't have the right to leave us!"

Uncontrolled tears well up in her eyes. *Goahdamnit, this is not helpful*, she thinks as she runs away, fueled by pain and dread of the future.

"I do fail to understand," Yog says. "This human dislikes her parent. And yet she wants him to stay alive."

"Do not let the words fool you, Overseer Yog. Human speech is as unstable as the surface of the ocean during a storm. After centuries of study, I have learned to find the truth beneath the waves. This human loves her parent with unusual intensity, even for a young female."

Edda, the one that entered with the mares, observes their exchange with the distant patience of an attentive hostess, yet Ximena feels the pain of the fleeing Edda echoing inside her, leaving behind a dreadful sensation.

"And yet," Yog says, "I do fail to see how something as insignificant as the affections of a cub for her parent qualifies this human as a candidate to tread the Paths."

"It is hard to fathom, Overseer Yog. But love is a stronger emotion than self-preservation among humans. I can assure you that this candidate shall yield adequately to the imperatives of the Reseeding effort, as long as we assist in her keeping her father alive."

Yog's three bodies regard the sad eyes behind Willem's

glasses as they follow her daughter running down the street. "Intriguing, but unconvincing, Walker Rew. That the human's inner drive is but a single bond to a single individual is... *frail*. I do require more self-focus on our human Walkers. Unless there is more to this subject, we shall hasten to the next candidate."

"There is more to this human, Overseer Yog. She is a complex individual. It shall take more of our time, but she is worth the inspection. She brims with raw talent." Rew turns to the Edda standing by the doorway to the dark hallway. "We do wish to see more, Redeemed van Dolah. Do lead us deeper."

"Deeper," she says, and the blunted pain inside her grows in intensity.

Is it anxiety? Ximena doesn't know, but she can feel Edda wetting her dry lips as she slowly leads the mares back into the hallway.

She paces along the row of anonymous doors, towards the deeper darkness. Is it getting hotter in here? Ximena's glimpse at Mark reveals his intense attention on the scene, and the perspiration on his temples. It's funny how realistically their dream bodies react to the permascape.

"Anything particular?" Edda stops and turns to her guests. "I don't think there is much more to see. Should we return to the living room and get us all some tea with pastries?"

"Take us deeper into yourself, Redeemed van Dolah," Rew commands.

"My dad just got this box of soft fluffy cookies from one of his students that just made the Rhine-Baltic circuit. They are delicious. They've got this amaaazing—"

"You shall show us now," Yog says. "Yield or be disqualified from treading the Paths."

Edda blinks in confusion. Something inside her

understands the implications—the compulsion—of the mares' words. She turns towards the darkness, and paces on, step after step, each one further tensing her pain, like someone is trying to pull her soul out of her skin. A grimace on Mark's face reminds Ximena that she is not the only one psyched-link to Edda.

It is so, *so* dark now—no light at all reaches this far inside Edda's hallway, but Ximena can still see in that weird way dreams allow you to perceive beyond the limits of your wake senses.

Edda stops, throws a glimpse at one of the doors, and presses her lips together.

Rew reaches out, opens the door, and—followed by Yog—enters the same living room they just left behind at the beginning of the hallway. It is early in the morning, bright daylight streaming through the windows. A much younger Willem is sitting on one sofa, reading a book. Anika is lying on the other sofa, hands behind her head, an open book on her belly, eyes lost in thought. A soft fire glows timidly in the hearth. It is warm and cozy. Safe. The feeling streams through Ximena as an eight-year-old Edda runs down the stairs and throws herself on to Willem's lap.

"Ouch!" He laughs and embraces her. "Watch out, girl. I'm softer than you think. You done with your homework yet?"

"Uh, almost, Dad. I have a question on Civics."

"Another one, huh? Shoot."

"When Mom and you meet aws Embrace," Anika turns her head towards her, "how are you going to tell me and Bram what to do?"

"Bram *and* me. *Me* always comes last. And don't worry about those things—they're complicated."

Anika sits up and puts the book to her side. "They're not complicated, Will. Don't be lazy."

"Uh, well, when your mom and I, uh, meet aws Embrace—"

"*Die*," Anika says, a notch louder. "When we die."

"Come on, Ani. Not now."

"So you die when you meet Goah?" Edda asks, large eyes swinging between Willem and Anika. "Like… a dog?"

"We are animals, girl," Anika says, her voice softening. "All animals must pass away at some point."

"We still have pleeenty of time," Willem says soothingly, forcing a smile. "Don't you worry."

"B- But if you are dead, how are you going to…?" Edda's voice breaks, her eyes brimming with tears.

"We will always be watching over you, girl," Willem says, his voice soothing, his smile comforting. "No matter what."

"Don't tell her that!" Anika's voice is dead serious now. "Who's watching for us, huh?"

Ximena feels Edda's sudden angst at her mother's unusual reaction.

"That's not helpful, Ani."

"And telling lies to your children is?" She shakes her head. "They must learn to be alone. They soon will be, and life must go on."

"Come on. It's too early. We still got some good years in front of us."

"I don't want to be alone!" Edda says, her voice wavering with incipient fear.

"You are not alone, girl," Willem says. "Listen. No one in this family will ever be alone." He is speaking to Edda but looking at Anika. "We have each other. We have our parents and ancestors watching for us, and our children and descendants waiting for us." He chuckles. "Sometimes I wish I had some more time for myself."

"Oh, such beautiful horseshit," Anika says. "Our

ancestors are *dead*, and our descendants are *unborn*. I don't know about you, but I can only hear people that are *alive*, yeah?"

Edda begins to weep. Willem takes her with both arms against his chest, kisses her softly on the top of her head and caresses her unruly hair. He turns his head to his sister. "Calm down, Ani, please. How long are you going to be grieving? It's been over a month, Goah's Mercy. Marthijn is in a better place now. His Joyousday was... beautiful."

She scoffs and folds her arms. "You don't know the half of it. He didn't want it, yeah? But he was a coward! He accepted it all like a lamb taken to the slaughterhouse."

"If that were true, that makes him very brave."

"Oh, always so logical. It's so easy to be logical, yeah?" She begins to speak with a mocking tone. "The heroic man that accepts his fate for the good of the many. Way to go!"

"You're being selfish," Willem says. "You'd rather have your lover back for your own sake."

She stands, eyes widened in outrage. "You don't believe that he is enjoying the *oh-so-sweet Embrace of Goah*, do you? You're not that naive, are you?"

"Who am I to say? I'm just a teacher."

"Exactly! We *are* teachers!" She takes Edda in one hand and Willem in the other, and pulls them up on their feet. "Come!"

She leads them out of the living room, up the stairs, and into a windowless room. She turns on the light. The walls are filled to the brim with shelves of books.

"It's unlocked!" Willem says when he enters the room with Edda.

"It's *always* unlocked. That's how I like it now. The kids should come here anytime they like." She laughs. "I'm not surprised you haven't noticed yet that I unlocked the room. You spend all your time playing with those stupid tin soldiers, instead of absorbing the knowledge entrusted to us as colonial teachers."

"But what if somebody breaks in and—"

"Not even you, a teacher, care enough to read them, and you think our fellow colonists would?" Anika scoffs. "They're all either working their asses off in the fields or at sea, or too hooked to that trash radios are spitting at them every evening."

"But we've sworn to keep the old books safe." Willem's voice sounds unconvinced, like he's repeating a mantra. "They're only for emergencies, if things really go south, that we have a semblance of guidance. These books are too dangerous to—"

"Read this," Anika hands him one of the books lying on the only desk in the room, "and then we can discuss what forbidding books really tells us about the society that takes that step, yeah? Oh, and when you're done, get started on this one, on myths and religions. Yeah, *plural*. Then we can have an actual conversation on the merits of aws Embrace, yeah? And this on the *real* history of the Roman Empire is… eye-opening. Did you know their entire system was fueled by slavery? That barbarians were absorbed, not cleansed? That resisting cities and civilizations were forever wiped from the face of the Earth? And this book on Napoleon," she is pointing alternatively at the other books on the desk, "or that one on Stalin," she shakes her head as she snorts, "those will give you quite a view into the true soul of the heroes of aws Imperia."

Edda, wide-eyed, is looking at the shelves with fascination. "Can I read them too, Mom?"

"Of course you can, baby. That's the whole point!" Her eyes keep scolding Willem as she speaks. "These books connect us with thousands of years of human civilization. And they're just," she waves her hand around the shelves in exasperation, "gathering dust in locked rooms like this one. The knowledge inside these books, that's what really extends the reach of our ancestors into our descendants, not aws stupid *Embrace*. Reading these books will *transform* you, baby, into a true human."

The mares are back in the pitch-black hallway. Edda —sunk head and limp shoulders—stands next to them, her anxiety hanging tight in a tense, high-pitched vibrato, like a suspect awaiting the jury's verdict.

"Insufficient," Yog finally says, and Ximena feels Edda's tension burst inside her guts. "A pronounced desire for change is indeed a valid motivator for our candidates, but I do fear that this memory only did show such ambition in the human's female parent. The candidate seemed merely… curious."

"This was but the beginning, Overseer Yog," Rew explains. "The candidate has since shown repeated active behavior in the pursuit of change. Just recently she infiltrated an official space in a doomed attempt to shake the power of the elites."

"Too risky, Walker Rew. This human's motivations— love and change—are too… *faint*. I am still unconvinced."

"We shall then dig deeper," Rew says. "Until you see what I know."

"No time, Walker. I shall grant this human one last inspection, since your… *belief* is so strong. But then we shall proceed to the next candidates."

"Very well." She turns to Edda, whose eyes are wide with fright. "Redeemed van Dolah, take us to the last door."

"Th- The last…" She turns towards the deeper end of the hallway, "Sorry. I- I can't."

"You can," Rew says, speaking uncharacteristically slowly. "You can, Redeemed van Dolah. Do lead on."

Like a zombie, she begins to drag her legs, slowly, down the hallway. Ximena feels raw dread filling her body—her soul—as she pushes herself forward.

She walks and walks until the air tastes… stale and bleak. And on she walks, passing door after door after door. Sudden images of Willem, of Anika, flash across her sight, as she musters every last fiber of willpower.

And then, the hallway comes to an end on a narrow wall with a single door—a black door, in the darkest rim of Edda's memories. She is panting, eyes injected with horror, like she has just pulled a corpse across a field of mud—like the corpse is her own.

"Do open the door," Rew says.

Edda continues to pant, frozen in place, like a jumper staring down the edge of a skyscraper.

"Do open the door, Redeemed van Dolah."

"Which… which door?" she asks, her voice breaking.

"Do open the door, Redeemed van Dolah, or you shall never Walk the Paths."

Edda falls on her knees and weeps. The pain Ximena feels coming from her is almost physical. She wished it were—it would be more bearable.

"Please, open the door, Redeemed van Dolah," Rew says, her voice softening. "Do it for your father."

"For…" she stretches out, slowly, *painfully*, until her fingers rest against the black door, "… Dad."

Edda pushes the door open.

TWELVE

The Joyousday of Anika van Dolah

The Van Dolah family sits on cushions around the low table in the center of the *Evocation* Room. Well, not the *entire* family. Little Hans wasn't around back then, three years ago, Ximena realizes. Thirteen-year-old Edda has arranged the decoration all by herself. She has gone with a colorful display of fall leaves, mixed with a careful selection of fresh flowers of matching colors. Ximena can feel her pride at the resulting effect: festive with a shade of farewell. Ten-year-old Bram suggested a large happy-faced pumpkin on each corner, but Edda refused. This is Mom's Joyousday, not Halloween, Goah's Mercy!

"Come on, Ani. Tell us one more." Willem is almost twenty-five, but he is holding his older sister's hands like he is a little boy learning to swim, afraid to let go.

"Yes, Mom, please." Ten-year-old Bram smiles radiantly with the confidence of a new adult. "Tell us another story of your life before you go. Something we can tell your future grandchildren. And when I see you again in seventeen years, I promise I'll tell you all about them!"

Anika, looking splendid in her white tunic, lets go of

one of Willem's hands, and puts it softly on Bram's cheek. "Seventeen years," she says, her expression turning somber. "That is a long time, boy."

"It is!" Willem laughs—a loud, lighthearted type of laughter, but he doesn't get it quite right. There is a nervous undertone, a hidden anxiety in his voice. "But don't worry, Ani. I'll be there with you in no time. Three years pass by flying. Then we can watch this lot together."

"Together..." Anika's eyes wander to an empty point on the wall.

"Yes, and in the meantime, you make sure to tell Mom and Dad how wonderful their grandchildren are, all right? And that I miss them awfully."

"Yes, me too!" Edda says. "And tell them Bran came out kind of all right," she adds with a chuckle.

Anika, still staring at the wall, says, "It doesn't make sense."

"Huh?" Willem's smile twitches, but it's just an instant.

She meets his glance, no trace of contentedness on her beautiful face. "Why tell anything to Mom and Dad, if they're watching over us?"

"Yeah, uh, m- maybe they..."

Tears well up in her eyes. "Or why do you need to tell me about our grandchildren, if I'm to have a front-row view over their lives?"

"Anika..." Willem's imploring eyes pierce his sister's.

She blinks a tear away, and then nods and smiles to her two children. "I will, of course, send your love to your grandparents, girl," she tells Edda. "And tell them about your wonderful brother."

Bram smiles at the words, but Edda doesn't. Ximena feels the wrongness as well.

The outer door to the Evocation Room opens, and a smiling man—a Quaestor in formal purple robes—enters.

He is followed by three white-robed acolytes: two men and a woman—Marjolein Mathus, Ximena immediately recognizes. Not even twenty yet, and her aspect not as carefully tended, with her blonde hair falling flat instead of finely braided, but it is her, all right.

The Quaestor rubs his hands together and turns to Anika. "I trust your evocations have been satisfactory, Elder van Dolah?" He then waves both hands at the family. "They shall all be blessed in Goah's Eyes." He shuts his eyes and sinks his head, murmuring some words to himself. Then he directs a fresh smile at Anika, and says, "Shall we proceed to aws Embrace?"

"Can we get more time, Quaestor Menger?" Anika asks, her breathing quickening. "There's so much I need to tell my family."

"And you shall, my child. But not on Earth. Rejoice, Elder van Dolah, for the time has come to meet the Love of your creator." He gestures invitingly at the door opposite the one they entered from, a wooden door with a large Eye of Goah painted on it. Ximena knows what awaits on the other side—Edda herself will break into that room in three years' time.

"I- I'm not ready." Anika stands, sudden panic in her eyes. She takes a step back. "I can't—"

"Now, now," the Quaestor says calmly, "there's only Bliss in front of you, my child. You are leaving your earthly pains behind."

"No." Anika takes another step back, and she bumps against the wall. "No!" She begins to weep in panic, staring at her brother with pleading eyes.

"Ani," Willem stands, eyes wide with dread. "All is good. Please, *believe*."

"I don't. I can't!"

The Quaestor throws a subtle glance at the two male

acolytes, and says, "Now, now, nothing to worry about. Nothing at all." The two men walk over to her and grab both her arms. "Rejoice, Van Dolah family, and feel aws impatient Eagerness to Embrace your Elder."

"No, I changed my mind!" Anika shouts. "I renounce my Joyousday!" She tries to shake her arms free, but the men hold her firmly. They push her kindly but relentlessly towards the eye-marked door. "No, leave me alone! This is just a ritual to control the masses. There's no Dem! There's no Goah! Let me go! Will!"

"Q- Quaestor Menger…" Willem takes a tentative step towards his sister and the two men, Bram and Edda beginning to sob behind him.

"Mom!" Both are standing with stretched, trembling arms. "Mom, mom!" Ximena gasps as she tries to keep herself from crying, Edda's dread and disbelief battering violently inside her.

Willem hesitates, turns around and takes Bram and Edda in his arms. He begins to weep himself, while futilely attempting to calm his kids.

"Don't mind her words, children," Quaestor Menger says, his tone practiced and unwavering. "This is her flesh speaking, not her soul. It happens occasionally and there is nothing to worry about."

"No! I renounce, I renounce!" The men open the door and push Anika firmly through. "You can't do this! Will, help!"

As the door shuts, her muted shouts continue, yelling her brother's name in desperation.

"It's okay, it's all right," Willem whispers over and over to his crying children, interlaced with his own sobs.

Marjolein, still standing by the entrance, is covering her mouth in dismay. Her eyes fill with tears as she watches Willem trying to console his children while his sister calls his name from behind the door, over and over again, drenched in desperation. And Willem keeps whispering words of comfort over the shaking bodies of his children, caressing, soothing them, ignoring what for many would be an irresistible compulsion to go, well, *mad*. Ximena can't take her eyes off him. Such discipline, such strength of character; a man refusing to drown, because his kids need him. Marjolein is staring at him like she most certainly agrees.

"Mom's fine," Willem keeps repeating between sobs, "Mom's okay."

And then, from one instant to the next, Anika's screams end.

Edda and the others stop crying at once and turn their heads at the sudden, eerie silence.

A silence that hangs in the Evocation Room like a blanket too thin to warm a soul in the dead of winter.

A silence that freezes Ximena's blood with the horror of Edda's irrevocable realization. She has seen—she has *heard*—her mother for the last time.

Her mother.

For the last time.

"Goah be praised," Quaestor Menger finally says. "Rejoice, Elder van Dolah, for your sister's soul is heeding aws Call, and is now on her way to aws Embrace."

"I want to see her," Willem jumps, reaches for the door and pulls, but it doesn't budge.

"There's nothing to see but a soulless body, Elder van Dolah," the Quaestor says. "A carcass ripe for Dem. In two to three weeks, when her Dem-ridden body leaves us for good, I will send somebody with the ashes."

Edda and Bram run to their father and hug him anew.

"You may stay as long as you need," the Quaestor says in that annoyingly understanding tone of his. "Acolyte

Mathus, please remain here with the family and attend their every need."

It takes a long while for the children, and for Willem himself, to sit back around the table, sobbing quietly now. In the meantime, the Quaestor has called his two male acolytes from beyond the eye-marked door and left in respectful silence. Marjolein stands by the entrance, head sunk like she doesn't belong there, which she obviously doesn't.

Willem draws a deep breath, keeps his eyes down and says with broken voice, "Let's go home."

"Why didn't you help Mom?" Edda says, her accusing eyes locked on her father's.

Willem doesn't raise his eyes. He sighs. "There's nothing I could do."

"You could...!" Edda doesn't know what to say, but that doesn't stop her from trying again. "You could've...!"

"We're just teachers, girl," Willem's tone is subdued, infinitely tired. He finally meets her gaze. "We can't change the world."

"Why not? We are teachers!"

"We are powerless, Edda girl. We must take what we have and make the best of it."

"Knowledge is power, Dad! You are always saying it. We are teachers, and we hold knowledge. We can change the world. I will!"

"Knowledge is necessary, yes, but not sufficient. There's much more to power than reading books."

"But... But..."

"We are powerless," he says, a notch louder. He reaches out with both arms and takes Edda and Bram by the hand. "We still have each other, and it'll have to suffice." He sounds so infinitely sad, Ximena thinks. "It'll have to."

"And when you're gone? What then, huh? What *then*?!"

"We still have a few years, don't think about it now."

"Three years! Just… three fucking years!"

"Edda!" Willem throws Marjolein a glimpse. "Language."

"Don't leave us!" She begins to sob again. "Don't, please. I don't want to be alone!"

"You'll never be alone, girl." He gently wipes a tear off her cheek. "You have each other," he smiles at Bram, a very sad smile, "and your children, and your grandchildren afterwards if you don't delay the dowry bonds. You still have so, so much to live for."

"No!" Edda's sobbing intensifies. "I need Mom! I need you! You don't have the right to leave us!"

"There's nothing you can do. It's better to accept it."

"I could… I could…! Ah!" She throws her head back in exasperation.

"You don't have the power, girl."

"Not yet." Her eyes open with determination. With *desire*. Ximena feels it flooding her senses: the will, the urge, burning up her spine. "Not yet."

Yog and Rew stand alone in the infinite nothingness of the staging permascape.

"That has been revealing," the three Yog bodies say with her single female voice. "The human does thirst for power."

"Indeed, she does," Rew says. "Power to save her father —*thirst for love*, as we did witness on her first memory. Power to shake her world—*thirst for change*, as her second memory demonstrated. And now, underpinning it all, as the foundation of her being—*thirst for power*. Power to control her own destiny, and impose her will."

"Indeed," Yog says. "This human has reached due worth. You are cleared to begin her instruction in the Path of Light."

Rew bows lightly and remains silent for a few moments. "She shall likely conclude it, Overseer Yog, as one of the two human Walkers to tread the Path in the Shadow. With such talent and thirst, she has the potential to attain the power she so desires. She shall prove invaluable to us."

THIRTEEN

The Wake Barrier

T he staging permascape is once again filled with people. And other than the black sky, that's all there is here: humans and mares. *And that's the point of it, I guess,* Ximena thinks.

"I do welcome you back, human apprentices," Rew says.

Edda and the other youngsters gather slowly in a rough semicircle around the twelve mares. Ximena feels Edda's deep discomfort at the memories of the events of last night. It was tough—the emotional ride, the depth of the alien inspection, such exposure, such *vulnerability.* She's not the only one feeling it. Aline, next to her, has also refused to talk about last night, as have Piet and his brother Janson. Everybody looks kind of shell-shocked. But what surprises Ximena the most, by far, is that most of them have made it through. *Such a motivated bunch!* Apparently, there's only one missing. Edda and her friends were just talking about it. Pieter, who has been chatting with the other candidates, says it is a man from De Haere, who apparently suffered cardiac arrest and had to be taken to aws Medic.

"In this session," Rew continues, "you shall be initiated into the first step of the Path of Light, which you shall conclude in morrow's session."

"Just two nights?" Ximena whispers to Mark. He is a Walker, after all. He has done the training. "Is that even possible? To learn the first step in two nights?"

"Not for me," Mark whispers back. "Took me six months. But look," he leans closer to Ximena and points at the group of eager youngsters floating in the air in front of them, "so many minds in such a limited space. That's some serious time dilation right there. Every night will feel to them like a month, or more."

"Like us right here now, right?" Ximena waves a finger at the auditorium.

"Yep. Time dilation in dream-space is directly proportional to its mind density," he says, like he is reciting Pythagoras' theorem. "And inversely proportional to its rendering requirements."

"Uh, okay."

Mark smiles. "Let me rephrase that. You want to binge-watch a month worth of zombie dreamsensos in a single night? No problem. Bring many friends and pack them close together in an empty room." He chuckles. "Gets boring after a few dream days. Trust me."

"Right. But still," Ximena points a finger at the floating scene where Edda and the rest are listening to something Rew is saying, "even stretching both nights to two entire dream months, is that enough? You trained for six."

Mark shrugs. "Rew chose Geldershire for a reason."

Ximena frowns skeptically, and returns her attention to Rew and her students.

"—which shall have you trialed after the second session," Rew is saying. "Only the twenty-four most proficient among you shall be cleared forward. The rest shall be discarded."

Ximena feels Edda's sudden surge of apprehension. That's about half of them! Purged after just one step. And the Path of Light has *three* steps, Goah's Mercy. Edda draws a deep breath and exhales slowly, trying to blow her anxiety away. She wants to pass. She *needs* to pass. But is her desire stronger than the others'? She looks around her —all those determined looks. They sure as Dem are going to give their best. And perhaps this is not even about who wants it more. Edda couldn't lift two hundred pounds over her shoulders, even if the life of her father depended on it.

"I do request each of you humans," Rew continues, "to approach one of my Walkers," she nods with her head at the eight mares standing behind her. "Each shall take a maximum of six apprentices."

"Come!" Edda says, taking Aline by the hand and trotting towards one of the mares. "You too, mensas!" she shouts behind at Pieter and Janson.

It doesn't take long until eight groups have formed, one around each mare. Edda, Aline, the boys and two nervous-looking women Edda has never seen before gather around the tallest mare of all.

"Sense and Bind, human apprentices," the mare says. She speaks to them slowly, her female voice soft and pleasant. "I am Qoh, dreaming from Deviss, thread-maker to Walker Rew-at-Deviss, and your instructor."

"What's Deviss?" Edda asks.

"What's a thread-maker?" Pieter asks at the same time.

Qoh turns to Edda. "Deviss is where I am sleeping and dreaming from."

Then she turns to Pieter. "A thread-maker is a master of the second step of the Path in the Shadow."

"And what's thread-making good for?" Pieter asks.

"I do meld minds. As yours are now melded into this permascape."

"Dream sharing," Aline says to Pieter. "I think."

"Where are you?" Edda asks. "Where's Deviss?"

Ximena notices that other groups around them are similarly grilling their mare instructors with questions. Qoh raises an arm, and the other groups vanish from sight, or Goah knows, perhaps they have all teleported somewhere else, too far away to see in this naked permascape.

"I am not to provide more information than that required for your instruction," Qoh says. "Which begins now." She lifts an arm again and six beds appear in two neat rows of three, each separated from the next by about twenty feet. They are all identical, like taken out of a whimsical fairy tale—tidy and cozy.

"There are three steps to the Path of Light. Like my master Rew, it is my ambition to be the instructor of the first human able to Walk them. The first step is named *Piercing.* For many apprentices the hardest of the three, since it requires a considerable amount of raw talent. I do believe you all possess such level of talent. Your halos are strong."

"What's a halo?" Edda asks.

"Not relevant, Redeemed van Dolah. You shall focus your attention to Piercing."

"Wow, you know all our names?"

"I do." Qoh gestures at the beds. "Do each take a sarc."

"You mean the beds, yeah?" Edda asks.

"Indeed, I do, Redeemed van Dolah."

"What are they for?" she asks as they each approach a bed. Ximena can feel her energy, her eagerness to learn; this is what she does, this is what she is. "I never had the chance to use a bed in my own lessons," she chuckles and sits on it tentatively. The mattress feels comfortable but firm, better than her own, Ximena thinks. "I'm a teacher too," she says proudly. "A Juf, you know?"

"I do." Qoh turns her white eyes to the other students. "A master piercer must learn to push through the *wake barrier* at will. Do lie down."

"What's the wake barrier?" Edda asks as she and the rest let their heads fall on the soft pillows.

"The wake barrier separates each dream from the next. After each dream, comes the wake. After each wake, comes the dream."

They all nod. *Simple enough so far*, Ximena thinks. Probably Edda's thought, because for Ximena it sounds too… *techy*.

"A master piercer can take her mind and her memories through the wake barrier."

"*Recall*," Mark whispers to Ximena.

"What?"

"In dreamtech it's called *Recall*. To remember your dreams."

"Oh, that's what that's about?" Ximena asks. Qoh keeps explaining to her pupils the nature of the wake barrier, but Ximena finds it way too boring, especially compared to Mark's private lessons.

"Well, it's also the opposite, which is way harder, let me tell you that. Once you're asleep and dreaming, ha! Not easy to remember what happened before, while awake."

"Oh, I see. But I can right now! I was home, Abuelo came to, er… Well, I can remember."

"Yeah, it's not the same. This is a permascape, the Dreamnet. Millions of melded minds. It's…" he frowns, like he is trying to find the right word, "… *different*. But in a normal dream, whoa!" He chuckles. "Six fucking months. Oh, excuse me."

"It's okay," Ximena says with a smile, and returns her attention to Qoh.

"A master piercer," the mare is saying, "so acquires the capacity to remain bound to the worlds, be it dream or wake." Ximena doesn't understand a word. "And yet, carrying yourself through the wake barrier is but the least challenging part to master. There is also…"

"Diving," Mark says with a snort. "Yeah, that was a tough nut to crack."

"… *Diving*," Qoh says in her slow patient voice. "The dream dive is a mind ability that, in contrast with the coming steps of the Path of Light, you must initiate from the wake. It gives the Dream Walker the ability to dive into a dream by one's own volition."

Ximena leans towards Mark. "What in Goah's Name is she talking about?"

"Ignore all that fancy dreamtech speech. Diving is to fall asleep at will. And dream."

Ximena gives him a smile of appreciation. "You are good at this."

"And at some other things, if I'm given the chance."

Ximena laughs out loud, attracting the curious gaze of their neighboring students. She clears her throat and returns her attention to Qoh and her human apprentices.

"I shall teach you the necessary techniques of mind focus and relaxation," the mare is saying, "and you shall practice them continuously for our two allotted sessions. If your talent is adequate, and your motivation strong, you may be able to accomplish your goal."

May be able, Ximena hears Edda's thought, and feels a rush of apprehension.

"Do shut your eyes and ready yourself for dreaming," Qoh says.

"But we're in a dream already," Pieter says from his bed, leaning on his elbow. "Can we even fall asleep here?"

"This is indeed a dream, Elder Ledeboer, thus it is neither possible to fall asleep nor to dream. But this is also a permascape, a melding of minds. Thus, a malleable approximation of the wake. I shall tune and stimulate your minds at each step of the process as to *simulate* the challenges that a master piercer must learn to overcome."

A *simulation*. Edda draws a deep breath. *Whatever.*

Ximena can feel her jitters. Edda has always had problems falling asleep. And relaxing is not quite her forte, to put it mildly.

"Do shut your eyes, and picture a door," Qoh says.

The class begins.

FOURTEEN

Fear and Hatred

A mare materializes next to the two rows of beds. "Walker Qoh," she says. "Do report."

It's Rew. Ximena recognizes her voice instantly.

"Yes, master." Qoh extends her arms at the humans, all six seemingly sleeping faceup on the beds. "My human apprentices are showing unusual talent to carry their minds intact through the wake barrier."

"Their halos are strong."

"Indeed, they are—they all accomplished a high degree of memory recollection on their first try. I do admit, I initially held doubts about whether lesser alien minds were even capable of—"

"Do never voice such doubts in front of Overseer Yog."

"I acknowledge, master."

"Do proceed. Have your assigned humans shown a similar talent to dive?"

"They have indeed, master. So far as the simulation can determine. All except Redeemed Van Dolah."

Rew turns her white eyes at Edda. She is lying on her

bed, eyes shut, expression distended. Her breathing is slow and regular. To the untrained eye, she appears sleeping. But she is not, Ximena feels. She is only trying. Trying desperately. And failing. The inner anxiety is still there, clinging to her guts, unable to let her pierce the wake, even this permascape-simulated version of it.

"That is regrettable," Rew says after a few moments. "Even disappointing. Is this your failing as an instructor, or hers as an apprentice?"

"My instruction has sufficed the other humans, master."

"Indeed. And yet she holds such promise, considering she does possess the second most potent halo among all human candidates."

Rew remains silent for a few moments, staring at Edda with her eerie white eyes.

"Walker Qoh," she finally says. "As of now, I do retake ownership over Redeemed van Dolah's instruction."

Qoh's head wobbles almost imperceptibly before she replies, "I acknowledge, master."

Rew approaches Edda's bed and inspects her carefully.

Edda opens an eye. "Oh, Elder Rew," she says. Her eyes look pained. She *is* pained, Ximena can feel it. Edda is fully aware of her failure, as her comrades have all been able to sleep themselves into dreams. "Hi."

"You did feel my presence. Impressive."

"Uh, what?" She sits up, blinking, trying to get a grip on her emotions. And failing.

Rew flicks one of her appendages, and—*whoa!*—the beds are gone. And Qoh. Even the flat nothingness of the staging permascape is gone.

Rew and Edda are alone inside a spacious bedroom that has appeared from nowhere and closed around them in an instant. The room is covered in the heavy shadows of night, light from the street's electric lamps barely sneaking through the curtains.

Edda looks down at the bed she is sitting on, and touches it. It has changed. It feels more… *real*. Her eyes shine with wonder as they scan the room in the timid light. She smiles at the sight of a plant pot with a cactus on the desk by the window, next to a few books—one of them open in the middle—and a typewriter with a half-typed page still in the cylinder.

"My room!" she says, as her eyes wander over to the chaotic pile of under-shirts and colorful tunics scattered next to the half-open closet. "It's… Wow! Exactly like when I went to bed!"

"Your memory is indeed not the problem," Rew says. Her head almost touches the ceiling, and her white skin and whiter eyes fluoresce strangely in the darkness. "You can indeed pierce the wake barrier without difficulty."

"Argh," Edda raises her eyes at the ceiling. Ximena feels her exasperation, her rage at her own incapacity. "My problem is the fucking diving thing." She sinks her head and sighs. "I can't fall asleep! And I tried, Elder Rew. I tried everything that Elder Qoh threw at us. And more. I've been at it for… How long have we been training already? It feels like weeks, Goah's Mercy!"

"Sixteen dream days to be exact."

"That," she waves her hand at Rew, "time stretching thing, whoa!" Her eyes shine for an instant. "That's the best! And I don't even feel bored. Nor tired. Are you going to teach us how to do it?"

"You are not capable of treading a single step in the Path of Light, Redeemed van Dolah, and yet dare to crave the Path in the Shadow. That urge you feel—that impatience—might very well be the cause of your failure."

Edda turns her head away. She is sad, and mad, and

frustrated. "I've always been good at focusing on things, you know?" She looks up at Rew's impassive blank stare, and sighs. "My dad had to shake me out of every book that landed on my lap. I would just," she shrugs and sinks her head anew, "lose myself in the pages; especially with stories. I would live them as if I had been teleported to a parallel universe. I don't get it, Elder Rew. I should be able to do this, yeah?"

"Indeed, you should. But you won't."

"I know that," she says, her voice breaking as tears begin to well in her eyes. "And my dad will pay for it."

"Indeed, he will."

She wipes her eyes with the back of her hand. "You are my teacher, Elder Rew. Goah's Mercy, why don't you start doing your goahdamn job? Tell me what I'm doing wrong, yeah?"

"You are doing nothing wrong, Redeemed van Dolah. But something is doing wrong to you."

"Can't you speak more clearly, Goah's Mercy? When I teach my students, I must speak like them!"

"It is your fear, Redeemed van Dolah," Rew extends one of her appendages and points at Edda's head. "You do fear, and thus you fail."

"I'm not afraid!"

"You do fear *failure*," Rew says, and walks slowly towards the desk by the window, "and you do fear failure's *consequences* even more."

Before Edda can reply, Rew pushes the plant pot off the edge. Edda gasps as it crashes noisily on the floor, sending pieces of broken cactus across the room.

"No!" Edda shouts. She jumps out of bed and kneels next to the broken pot, eyes wide with dismay. She grabs soil with her hands and inspects the damage.

Ximena watches her reaction with a mix of pity and

surprise at the intensity of Edda's feelings. There is nothing she can do to save the plant.

Edda turns her glare at Rew as she stands while rubbing the earth off her hands. Ximena feels her anger. No, it's more than that. She feels like it was her own heart that was planted in the pot. Broken—and furious. "Why?!"

"You do feel anger," Rew says. "Even… *hatred?*"

That's pretty accurate, Ximena thinks. Edda stays put by the window and simply glowers at Rew.

"Place that hate in the center of yourself," Rew stretches an appendage at Edda's belly, "and let it bloom."

Edda's eyes widen as she realizes that this is a lesson. Ximena feels the anger wane, as hope rises from its ashes.

"No, Redeemed van Dolah. Do not let go of your hate." Rew waves an arm at her and, whoa! Ximena gasps at the sudden surge of rage. "Do feel it burning inside you. Very good. Now," she raises both arms at once. "Do stoke it up."

Ximena leans back and gasps anew at the ravaging force of the emotion. It is like a fire burning her alive from the inside out. She wants to hurt Rew. She *craves* to tear the fucking mare to pieces. Edda's expression is distorted in an ugly grimace of murderous hatred.

"Let it burn deeper and wider," Rew says. "Let it fill your body and hold it there. Very good. Do embrace it until you feel like only hatred flows through your veins. Very good. That shall suffice."

Rew gestures at Edda's head, and the hate vanishes in a beat, leaving only exhaustion in its wake. Ximena's body jerks forward as if suddenly released from an unknown force. *What a ride*, she thinks.

"What was that?" Edda asks.

"In order to dive from the wake, you shall cleanse your mind of emotions, Redeemed van Dolah."

"I know. Elder Qoh repeated that like a parrot."

"Alas, *fear* is a primitive emotion, Redeemed van Dolah. Ruled by animal instinct, not by reason. Once inside of you, it lingers like a parasite. You shall not get rid of it, not directly, no matter your mental discipline. Fear is shy at first, as it slowly creeps out of your amygdala. But it gets more daring with time as it grows, until it inevitably overwhelms your brain, and thus, your destiny."

"Oookay, got it. Fear equals bad."

"*Anger*, on the other hand—and its younger variant *hatred*—are a marvel of evolution. Both, together with your other high-order emotions, are the pillars of your sentience, and thus can be tamed by a strong will."

Edda frowns. "I'm not sure I follow…"

"The human brain is mechanically simple, unable to cope with the nuisances of too many emotions at once. Thus, a potent emotion must necessarily drown a weaker one. Your fear is subdued now, is it not, Redeemed van Dolah?"

Edda's eyes widen. "Oh, you're right. My… anxiety is gone! I got so steamed up, that… wow!"

"Your emotions are too erratic for an apprentice of the first step—that is your weakness. But you do possess an even more formidable strength: your power of *will*. You must learn to use your will to supplant insidious, primitive emotions like fear with high-order emotions—like hatred."

"Or love?"

"If you are so inclined. And yet those higher emotions are equally harmful—they must be cleansed out of your mind to pierce the wake barrier."

"So then, what's the point?"

"Unlike primitive emotions, high emotions can be tamed by a strong will. Thus, you must use your will anew, to dissolve any lingering emotion into nothingness. So shall you cleanse your mind, and ready it to Walk the first step of the Path of Light."

"Right," Edda says, her anxiety creeping back into her guts. Goahdammit. "Isn't that asking a lot from my, uh, *will* thing?"

"Your will is disciplined, Redeemed van Dolah. And relentless. Do lie down on your sarc and shut your eyes."

Edda nods slowly. *Willpower*, she is thinking. *Can I do it?*

She lies on the bed, faceup, letting her body embrace its familiar comforts. She draws a few deep breaths to relax her body and mind, like Qoh taught her what feels like weeks ago, and shuts her eyes.

And as she does so, the room disappears from the auditorium, and a spotty blackness takes its place. Ximena and her peers are watching what Edda is watching behind her lids: the darkness of night, and the onset of sleep.

"I sense fear in you, Redeemed van Dolah." Rew's voice comes through as if it were whispered in Ximena's own ears. "Do rid yourself of it."

"Easier said than done," Edda's voice says. The blackness becomes more grainy, like an old TV plagued with interference.

"I shall not assist you this time. Do as I say, and succeed."

"I'll try, yeah? But what if—?"

"If you are incapable of controlling your mind, Redeemed van Dolah, then I have misjudged your capabilities, and shall give my time to other more promising apprentices."

Ximena feels Edda's anxiety spiking. "At least give me a few days to practice whatever you teach me."

"Your extensive training with Walker Qoh should suffice. Now you shall impose your will, or fail."

"Pure sin!" A nervous crawl twirls in her stomach and up her chest. "No pressure there. Not helping."

"I shall assist. Once. Do signal your readiness."

Edda draws another deep breath. Ximena feels her mental effort to bring her nerves under control. *Okay, that's better*, Ximena thinks. *Marginally better.* "Bring it on, Elder Rew."

"Very well. Do picture with your mind a white square."

"Oh, the purification technique!" Mark whispers to Ximena, eyes beaming. He seems to be enjoying himself. Perhaps Ximena is more sensitive than him to the psych-link, or more empathic to Edda's distress. Or, more likely, Mark is just a dreamtech geek about to have a nerdgasm.

"A white square. All right…" Edda says.

The blackness thickens across the amphitheater, and a square appears floating over the stage. It is indeed white, but *noisy*—spots come and go, and the edges wave in amorphous chaos, as they usually do in daydreams.

"Very good. Do keep the square fixed in place, as you focus your will on ridding yourself of your fear, Redeemed van Dolah. Do fill your mind with a high order emotion."

Hatred, Ximena hears Edda's thoughts through the psych-link, *or love*.

Flashes of images begin to project on the whitish square in quick succession, like a film on a canvas. It's people—mostly Hans as a baby, and also Willem, Anika and yes, even Bram. Aline also features often; shared moments of happiness—and sadness. A balmy warmth extends up her trunk and along her limbs, filling her up, pressing against her skin from inside. She feels like love streams out of her pores.

"Very good. A sharp will, indeed. Now do cleanse the square of impurities."

Ximena feels Edda's mental exertion as she puts her

mind into cleaning the white surface. But no matter how hard she tries, impurities of thought keep tainting it like black rain on a snowy field.

"No, Redeemed van Dolah. No will in the universe can break free from emotions. You shall first cleanse your mind of all emotion. Do rid yourself of love."

Right, Edda draws a deep breath and focuses her attention into herself. She focuses her own mind into her own body, still overflowing with love. With another breath, she puts her mind at work. First on her chest, cooling it, absorbing all warmth like the vacuum of space absorbs light. Then along her limbs, up her head, down her trunk, systematically, until she feels *empty*. Not sad, nor happy. Just empty.

Like a vacuum.

The square is *pure* white, resplendently so, hanging in perfect stillness in the undiluted blackness that is Edda's mind, edges sharp and straight like they have been engineered by Goah awsself. Ximena is in awe at Edda's capacity to focus her attention on something, and then subjugate it so completely. Such purpose. Such *power*.

"A sharp will, indeed," Rew's calm, female voice resonates like an impurity as it intrudes in the mathematical perfection of the scene: a perfect white square in a perfect black background. "Were this not a simulated permascape, that square would be your gate to the dreamscape. Now, do open your eyes."

Ximena feels almost pain, as the godly white and black created by Edda's concentration is violently substituted by Edda's dark bedroom, like returning from Goah's Embrace to the dirt ball that is her Earth.

Edda sits on her bed and smiles radiantly at Rew. "Not bad, huh?"

"Indeed not. And to prove your worth, you shall now

wake up in your real world, refocus, and dive back to *this* same dream."

"What if I fall asleep, but can't join this dream?"

"Then you shall have failed, and must return to your life of powerless frustrations."

"But that's not fair!" That anxiety again. Ximena feels it creeping up Edda's spine. "The others still have plenty of time to train with Elder Qoh, yeah?"

"Shall you fail now, then you shall irremediably fail later." Rew gestures awkwardly around with her arms. "Do embrace this dream, Redeemed van Dolah. Dig into it. Look and feel around you. Know deeply where you are, and what this dream represents. Digest its essence and push it into your memory, ready to be pierced by the will of your wake mind."

Edda takes a deep breath and shuts her eyes in concentration. *Deep* concentration, Ximena feels. Then she extends her hands and opens her eyes, sharp, focused.

Absorbing.

This place—this dream—is now an extension of her consciousness.

"You are indeed ready now, Redeemed van Dolah. I do hope to see you again. Do wake, and dive back. Now."

The scene changes visibly, although Ximena still sees Edda's room from the same angle. But it feels more natural, somehow more *real*. The dreamy quality—so nicely crafted by Miyagi's production team into the dreamsenso—is now gone.

Edda, a moment ago sitting on her bed, is now waking up from under the sheets. She sits, breathing slowly. Then stands up and walks to the window, opening the curtains. The night is still long ahead, the street silent. Edda caresses with a timid finger the intact cactus plant on the table.

She draws a deep breath, closes the curtains tightly and

returns to bed. Facing the ceiling, blankets up to her chin, she closes her eyes. "Let's fuckin' dive," she mutters, as her breathing slows.

The scene seems to vibrate ever so slightly with every further breath she takes, back and forth, like a slow-beating heart.

Its dreaming texture gently returning.

And then, Rew is there in the room, back turned to her, looking at the empty bed.

"Boo!" Edda says, waving her hands.

Rew turns to face her, calm and smooth. "You did scare me."

Edda waves a fist in the air. "I made it! First try, baby!"

Rew studies the room, as if trying to find something out of place.

"And?" Edda asks, smiling with expectation.

"I am a most talented instructor," she finally says.

"Now you shall go back to your world's Wake," the three Yog bodies say with a single voice, "and return to this permascape with utmost haste."

The almost four dozen humans standing in grouplets on the infinite emptiness of the staging permascape exchange nervous glances.

"The earliest twenty-four *piercers* among you shall be allowed access to the second step in the Path of Light. The rest shall be discarded."

Ximena feels how Edda is already trying to gather her emotions. Trying to calm down. Whoa, it's hard, even after what feels like an eternity of mind-focus training. A dream month at least of continuous practice and concentration, without sleep, without food, without even rest.

Permascape's time dilation doing its magic. And Edda's ironclad motivation, of course.

"The first trial begins," the three Yog bodies say. Rew and her eight mare Walkers wave a hand and all the humans vanish. Only the flat dark stone remains, empty, stretching forever towards the horizon, where it meets the black sky.

Good luck, Edda, Ximena thinks, and turns to look at the twelve mares, which without a hint of movement seem to be waiting patiently. *As if they could wait impatiently.* Ximena chuckles at the thought.

"What's up?" Mark asks, his blue eyes fixed on hers.

"Huh?" She blinks at him. His gaze makes her uncomfortable—in a strangely pleasant way.

"What are you laughing at?"

"Nothing. Uh, how long until they return?" Ximena points at the place where the humans last disappeared.

Mark turns his head back at the floating scene. "Good question. I guess we'll know soon enough."

"But you're a Walker. How long takes you to… uh…?"

"To *dive* back into a dream? Pfff, not my forte, I can tell you that. Requires so much mental discipline… Gets easier with age, they say."

"So? How long?"

He sighs, thoughtful. "About five minutes on a good day, I would say. Ten max."

"So I guess we're going to be here for—"

A human reappears. A teenage woman.

Ximena feels her mind through the psych-link as soon as she begins scanning her surroundings with expectation. And then with sheer delight.

Edda.

Rew waves an arm, and a numeric symbol is bestowed upon her.

The number *one*.

The symbol shines *inside* her, like a telepathic lighthouse —the equivalent of a signboard, but not one made to be seen by eyes, but to be felt by minds. *Guess marais can't read*, Ximena thinks.

"Incredible!" Mark mutters next to her.

A young man appears a few seconds later, not far away from Edda. It's the Oosterbeek farmer, worn working tunic over brown pants. Rew bestows a number *two* on him.

"These Geldershire mensas are... wow!" Mark says, still wide-eyed. "Funny how nobody's ever found out what made them *so* good at this."

It's almost half a minute until the next person appears: the farmer's sister, *three*. Then, a few seconds later, Aline, *four*, and Gotthard, *five*. And then some people Edda doesn't recognize. There comes Pieter—Aline's lover—*nine*. By the time the count reaches the high teens, a couple of minutes in the waiting, the next familiar face arrives: Janson—Pieter's brother—*eighteen*. Rutger—Gotthard's best friend—*nineteen*. Valentijn van Kley, *twenty-four*. Louisa van Kley, *twenty-five*.

The last familiar face, eleven-year-old Marten, makes number *thirty-two*. His face is a mask of disappointment as the number falls into him like a tombstone. He watches as many of his peers—inevitably the low numbered ones— cheer and hug each other. He begins to weep—the boy still very much under the surface of the man—and then disappears at a gesture of Rew's Walkers, together with Louisa van Kley and the other high-numbered people.

Only twenty-four remain.

Edda releases Aline's exultant embrace. *We're both still in the race. Ha!* Ximena can hear her thoughts, threaded together with exhilaration. *I was the best of all, Goah's Mercy! The best!* Edda sighs inwardly with satisfaction. It was all worth it, every dream minute of painstaking concentration. The price—the Path in the Shadow, the power to infiltrate others' dreams and manipulate them to her will—is hers to lose now. She's really got a chance at it.

Edda smiles widely, eyes beaming as she scans the other… *human piercers*—she imagines Yog's voice in her thoughts. She feels strong, energized. No, more than that. She feels… *liberated*! What she has achieved—this awesome success—was a pure act of will. Literally. Elder Rew just taught her how to deploy her will, and the results… Ha! She feels like she can do *anything* if she just *wants* it enough; if she puts every atom of her soul into it. Why hasn't she acted before? Life is short, and she feels like she has been adrift, at the mercy of the winds of convention. But now… Is she going to keep taking everything that life throws at her to *show her her place*, or is she going to do something about it? She could of course wait and learn more. There is power to be found in the Paths of the Mind Walker. But why wait? She could begin acting *now*. Yeah, like she should have years ago. Like a true, free woman, that deeply knows what she wants, and reaches for it, consequences be damned. Consequences are for the weak-willed. For those free of the shackles of convention, consequences are just, yeah, steps. Steps on a path. A path to self-fulfillment, to control over your own fate—and the fate of others.

A path of *will*.

A path to *power*.

FIFTEEN

Juf Edda

"Sixteenth of December 2399," Professor Miyagi says. "Barely two weeks until the Century Festival." As he paces across the amphitheater stage, he points at the scene floating over his head. "And Edda van Dolah is pumped up."

The scene is frozen in time, but vivid, as if they were watching a set of actors that have been asked to kindly stand still. It is a classroom, recognizable in every age and place: a blackboard covered with chalk-written dates and names of people and places, a world map hanging on the wall, six rows of young adults with bored expressions, elbows and forearms on wooden school desks, tunics wrapped tightly against the chill. And looming over them all at the front of the classroom, like an altar in a temple of knowledge, the teacher's desk, and Edda standing next to it, staring down at her pupils like a priestess of wisdom at her faithful.

"Can you feel her energy through your psych-links?" Miyagi asks rhetorically. "Her zeal? Yesterday she was just a girl trying to learn the first step of the Path of Light.

Today she's a woman with a mission. And she's using the only weapon she knows how to wield: the teacher's pulpit. This," he points at the classroom, "is her Mondays' and Thursdays' evening lessons for adults. What do you say, people? Can a schoolteacher on a remote colony cause a shock of historical proportions?"

Ximena smiles to herself. Another rhetorical question.

"Let's watch. Ank, please."

———

"So picture this, mensas," Edda is saying, "Rewind the clock to the twenty-second century. We're at the peak of the second collapse, yeah? *Death*," she gestures passionately with her arms, "is all around us. People are dying younger and younger, society is breaking down everywhere at the same time. It's so bad, Goah awsself comes to the inevitable conclusion that we are truly too stupid to keep ourselves alive, and decides to take matters in aws own hands. And you know the rest, yeah? Kaya Fahey flees to Townsend, Goah's revelations, aws Gift, aws Compacts, aws Womb, yada yada yada, and," she claps her hands, "Goah's first Imperium began. Initially just a small area around Townsend," she points at a big black star on the world map, in North America, "in the province back then called Montana," with vigorous strokes she writes the name on the blackboard. "But since they were the only ones staying alive, other than a few scattered barbarians still giving birth through vaginas," some students, mostly the females, cringe at the image, "here we are now," she points at the six Imperia of Goah, covering with bright colors most of the inhabitable parts of Earth's landmasses. "You've heard it before, yeah? Peace and prosperity for all. The Goahn Pax. Worldwide.

176

Blessed be Goah, our Pontifex and all that. Sounds familiar?"

"Boooring," a man in his twenties in the first row says, and turns his smirk at his fellow students.

"I know, Erik" Edda says, her eyes piercing his. "It's boring because it's all a lie. And lies are always so boringly simplistic."

Silence falls on the class as the students exchange wide-eyed glances. Even Ximena frowns. *A lie?* Other than the colorful language, Edda has pretty much nailed the essence of the period between the second collapse and the Dreamwars.

"A lie?" Erik seems as baffled as Ximena.

Edda smiles and points at the blackboard. "The history you've been taught—all horseshit, yeah?"

"But… It was *you* who taught us!" Erik says.

"Yeah, I know. That's because that's the history I've been taught myself. Also lies. And it gets worse. Neither I nor your other teachers know the truth, nor how to get at it. Every book written since Fahey is just… propaganda. Like a fairy tales' *and they lived happily ever after*."

"Then," Erik spreads his hands, "how can you tell it's a lie?"

"Because it's been done before. Countless times, by every dictator and tyrant since the first word was sculpted on stone. And no matter what they want us to believe, power corrupts, and absolute power corrupts absolutely, turning the most benign of rulers into tyrants bent to change the past to control the future."

"Juf Edda," a young woman says, raising a hand as she speaks, "are you implying that aws Head is, uh…"

"Corrupt," Edda says. "I'm not implying it. I'm *saying* it."

Ximena leans back. Strong words. Almost *heretic*. She

raises her head at her fellow GIA students at the other end of the small amphitheater to find some mouths covered by scandalized hands.

"What do you know?" Edda points a finger at her equally shocked students. "I mean, *really* know, huh? How to clear a field?" She points a finger at Erik. "Or gather clams in the low tide?" She points at the young woman. "And live *happily-ever-after* under a regime that has brainwashed you so completely, that you will voluntarily let them kill you when you reach twenty-seven years of age, yeah? Wonderful."

Many students' jaws have dropped. Nobody looks bored now.

"But," Erik begins, "Dem——"

"Dem is an invention of aws Head, mensas. To keep us all nicely in place, content and ignorant. Did you know that there are books that my family keeps at home," she points out the window, "that you are not allowed to read? Even us teachers are encouraged not to, but we keep them around just in case we ever need old knowledge."

Erik scoffs. "Who wants to read, anyway?" Some students laugh at his comment.

"Did you know that there were other religions before Goah? Other gods? Of course you don't, because no one's ever told you. So convenient. We all know there's only one god, yeah? And Fahey is aws Prophet. Let me ask you something, mensas. Do you think the Romans worshiped Goah?"

"Didn't they?" Erik looks genuinely confused.

"We are about to enter a new century. In just two weeks. A very round number, twenty-four hundred. Did you ever stop for a second to ask yourself what happened twenty-four hundred years ago?"

"I know that one," Erik says. "That's when Goah created the world."

"Pure sin," Edda says, shaking her head. She sighs. "We'll leave that for another day. My point is that before Goah, there were centuries of history, of tyrants and democracies, of empires and republics, of slavery and freedom, all hidden from you. For a reason."

"Who cares what happened hundreds of years ago?" Erik says. "How's that gonna help me feed my family?"

"Pretty, Erik. Exactly like aws Head wants you to stay. Illiterate and stupid. A model colonist."

Erik's pale face turns red. "Juf- Juf Edda, I—"

"I'm trying to make you see that we've been here before. Tyrannies hiding the truth from the people, to claw on to their power. Do you mensas think it's okay that I have books you're not allowed to read?"

Her students stare at her in silence, eyes blank.

"Am I better than you? Just because I'm a teacher? A specialist? Don't aws Compacts give you all the same Sacred Rights and freedoms that I possess?"

Some students, including the young woman, nod slowly. Others, including Erik, exchange puzzled glances with their neighbors.

"What aws Head doesn't know, is that their efforts to suppress the truth are doomed. The changing winds of propaganda cannot hold long against the static certainty of truth. And then, as history shows over and over again— take, say, the French and American revolutions, or the Soviet Union—repression can only hold so long before cynicism turns into activism. And activism into change. Regime change."

"And what's the truth, Juf Edda?" the young woman asks.

"The truth," she shifts from one foot to another, "is that Dem has been eradicated."

"But if—" Erik tries to speak, but Edda raises her voice.

"The *truth*," Edda's eyes shine with defiance, "is that Joyousday Houses are slaughterhouses, designed by aws Head to keep us ignorant and complacent."

Most students gasp—both Edda's students in the school class, and Miyagi's in the GIA section of the amphitheater. *This can't be right*, Ximena thinks, still gaping at Edda, and then throws a wondering glimpse at Professor Miyagi, sitting below, on the front row next to the stage. *This is not the Edda van Dolah we've all been brought up with. She sounds like, er, a conspiranoid lunatic.*

"Mensas," Edda says, "there's no right more sacred in aws Compacts than life itself, and aws Head is stamping on it every day with the Joyousday. With the truth in our hands," she reaches out, hands cupped like she was carrying water, "how can we trust aws Head to fight for our Sacred Rights?"

"That's a lie, Juf Edda!" Erik stands. He turns to the class. "Don't listen to her, a demon has taken her tongue."

"Shut up, Erik," the young woman says. "Since when can farmers call teachers liars? This is Juf Edda, Goah's Mercy."

"Erik," Edda says with a conciliatory tone. "You are free to leave if you don't like what I have to offer." She puts a hand on her chest and then stretches it at him.

"Fine," he says, and stomps out of the room, slamming the door behind him.

The rest of the students shift in their place with unease and turn their attention to Edda. Some stare with eager eyes, others look at Edda's feet, blinking in confusion.

"Pure sin," Edda says, shaking her head. Then she

smiles at her gaping students. "Don't mind him. To be free, you must first *really* want it. Freedom is a matter of *will*." She turns her head towards the door. "Sad truth is, some people are born to be slaves."

———

"Okay," Professor Miyagi has frozen the scene in place and is walking towards the amphitheater's flank opposite to Ximena, where murmurs and discussions among the GIA students are turning louder by the minute. He smiles politely. "What's up?" He points a finger. "Cody?"

"Uh, I beg your pardon, Professor," Cody O'Higgin says, standing and smiling apologetically. "We were wondering about the sources."

"The sources?"

"Yes, Professor. Van Dolah's... attitude and ideas," he is frowning, without giving up the smile, "her message to her students. Is this your—with all due respect, Professor—personal *interpretation?*"

"Of course not. I leave no space for interpretations in my work. All you see has at the very least one reputable source, and often more. This lesson we just watched was mentioned in the first De Vroome's Interview, and in more detail on surviving correspondence from two of Edda's students. There's also a written complaint raised to aws Head office in Lunteren this same day. And guess who signed it?" He points a finger at the frozen classroom door. "All references are available to you for your inspection in the Global Program's sensonet archives."

"Yes, Professor. Er..." He seems about to say something else, but then he sits. "Thank you."

A female student sitting on the front row of the GIA section stands. "Professor, where is Censor Smith?"

Good question, Ximena thinks.

Miyagi points a finger at her. Her name pops up over her head. "I'm afraid I don't know, Mallory. He sent his excuses."

"Is he coming?" Mallory pulls back her brown hair and turns her head at her fellow GIA students. Many nod back gestures of support.

"Yes. He said as soon as possible. But you know how it is with permascapes. He had to attend some real world business, so with time dilation and all that," he shrugs, "it might take a while until he shows up. Why?"

"Uh, well…" She hesitates. A student sitting next to her whispers something at her, and another one behind taps her shoulder in solidarity.

"Don't be afraid," Miyagi says, spreading his hands. "This is a safe space, people."

"It's just that," Mallory avoids meeting his gaze, "we would like to hear his opinion about, uh…" her voice breaks.

"About what?"

"About Van Dolah."

Miyagi frowns. "I can't… follow. I can guarantee you that Grand Censor Jean-Jacques Smith knows as much about Edda van Dolah as I do. Well, perhaps not as much," he chuckles, "but he is Professor of History in the Townsend."

"Yes, sure. But I'm not sure he knows what Edda is, hmm, *saying* here. He might not approve."

"Oh, I see. Ha! Sorry," he raises an apologetic hand, "I realize now that the historical Edda might not be the shiny, spotless hero you people are used to digesting at the GIA."

Digesting, Ximena snorts at the word. It sounds so…

condescending. Almost insulting. Before she can think of what she is doing, she is standing up. "Pro- Professor Miyagi," she calls, and clears her throat as he turns around towards her. Mark is staring up at Ximena like she just turned into a toad. "Sorry, uh," she blinks as she feels warmth rushing to her cheeks, "may I request a recess until Censor Smith arrives?"

Miyagi smiles briskly and says, "You may, of course. But I'm afraid I can't accommodate you. It would be a logistical nightmare, believe me, the waking until he arrives, the gathering you all back here... No, I'm sorry, but the show must go on." He chuckles lightheartedly. "Come on, people," he turns towards the rest of the Townsend students and spreads his hands, "we're all historians here, aren't we? Historians! When has a scientist ever felt uncomfortable with the truth?" He sighs, paces across the stage in silence, and then looks up at the Townsend lot. "I suggest you all take this opportunity to learn how to take crude facts with duly professional distance," he turns his head and gives Ximena a pointed glance, "and leave your prejudices at home."

Prejudices, Ximena cringes at the word. Yes, definitely insulting. Professor Miyagi speaks like Lundev were Goah's gift to the worlds, and Townsend just a second-rate school. She sits, folds her arms, and throws a murderous glare at the smirking Mark.

"Now," he claps noisily, like trying to wake up a cranky child, "cheer up, people. Let's get the ball rolling down the Path of Light, all right? Who wants to watch humanity's first crash course on the second step?"

SIXTEEN

Questions and Awareness

"That same night," Miyagi says, pacing the stage, "the twenty-four remaining human candidates are starting the next lesson. But while Aline, Pieter, Gotthard and the rest must all share a mare instructor, Edda has Rew all for herself. And you know what?"

He stops, hands on hips, and smiles at his audience.

"Nobody really knows why!" He chuckles. "Oh, of course there are theories. But why Rew took such a personal interest in Edda van Dolah is," he shrugs with theatrical exaggeration, "unknown. She must have seen something in her, obviously. But so she did in all her other candidates. Anyway, my dear historians-to-be, let this be an illustration of how history cannot answer all the questions. Ours is a science condemned to navigate around the gaps left by lack of sources, myths, personal opinions and propaganda. And that's okay."

He takes a few more steps in silence, head sunk as if lost in thought. Ximena suspects it is all for show—he is a public figure after all and knows his way on stage well.

"Now, I have a question for you." He moves a finger

slowly across the amphitheater. Yes, definitely show. "I produced the dreamtech lessons for a more, er, *commercial* version of the dreamsenso. But truth is, they are of limited historic interest. I can summarize the next one simply by saying: the mare Rew trained Edda van Dolah on the second step, and then she faced the second trial with the other remaining human candidates." He spreads his hands. "Done. Is that okay with you, people? Should I skip Rew's lucid dreaming lesson?"

A loud roar of protests engulfs the auditorium. Mark is shouting 'NO!' at the top of his lungs next to her, as are most of the students. Miyagi smiles, pleased. Oh, Goah. Ximena rolls her eyes. Showman through and through.

"That's what I thought," he says, smirking. And gives Ank a curt nod.

The auditorium darkens.

A sunny scene pops up with sudden radiance, forcing the students to squint. It is a dream landscape, viewed from high in the air, and lit by an unnaturally small, red sun. As the students' eyes adapt, they begin to discern far below an orange-yellow desert, fiercely bright in the sun, that extends all the way to the horizon. A massive, abrupt mountain range crosses the desert in a zig-zag, and unnatural rock formations sculpt the slopes and peaks. The scene glides towards the higher rocks on the higher mountains.

Some students murmur and point at a lone human figure in the middle of a wide natural rock bridge that spans two of the highest peaks. It's Edda, Ximena recognizes as the scene glides closer, wearing a short, white summer gown. She is standing at the edge and stares serenely down at the sand abyss below. Ximena leans back at the sudden surge of vertigo. The chasm is several miles high!

Edda watches with calm curiosity the mysterious giant pyramids scattered all over the sand like islands on an archipelago, enormous structures made of copper-colored metal that feel as old as the mountains themselves.

"Aren't you afraid?" Rew asks. She is standing next to Edda, in her natural, vaguely humanoid form: tall, thin, and eerily white.

"Why should I be?" Edda replies, while moving her uncovered arms in the warm breeze. She seems to enjoy the sensation.

"The altitude—most humans would respect the void."

Edda gazes down again. "It *is* very high. I should care, yeah?" She has turned to ask Rew with the familiarity of an old friend.

"I do believe you should. Ten miles high over certain death deserves... attention."

She keeps her eyes locked down, with more curiosity than discomfort.

"What are those?" She points her finger at the dozens of ancient pyramids that seem to own the desert, their enormous scale obvious even from this height.

"Why do you ask?"

"I'm curious."

"Why?"

"These buildings... So large and old... What is their purpose? Who built them? Why here?"

"So many questions. That is very good, Redeemed van Dolah. So it begins."

"What begins?" Edda stares into Rew's blank eyes.

"*Awareness*—questions lead to awareness."

"*Questions lead to awareness*," Mark repeats slowly, almost reverentially. Ximena looks at him with curiosity. His eyes are locked on the scene like he is having a religious experience. "The litany of the second step."

"*Awareness...* of what?" Edda asks with a frown.

"First the questions, then the awareness." Rew gently touches the side of her head with one of the three narrow appendage-like ends of her arm. "More questions. What else do you see," she waves her arm around the landscape, "that is worthy of your curiosity?"

Edda scans her surroundings again.

Her eyes widen, as if she had just arrived there. Then she looks down—*miles* down—and for the first time a surge of vertigo flows through the psych-link, melding harmonically with Ximena's own.

"The height is scary," Edda says, a hint of uncertainty in her voice. A flock of bird-like creatures passes by miles below, so far away that it is impossible to discern the species. Her breath quickens. "Why wasn't I anxious before? What is this place?"

"More questions," Rew says.

She takes her eyes off the abyss, and steps away from the edge. "Where's home? How did I reach this place? Did I fly like the people in the golden age, in a machine?"

"You are doing well, Redeemed van Dolah. More questions."

"This doesn't make sense," she says, her frown deepening. "What's the meaning of all this?" She turns to Rew, who remains silent, and simply stares back at her with intensely white eyes. "*Who* the fuck are you?"

"*Awareness.*" Her psychic voice reverberates a notch louder. "All your questions lead to the one, simple, elegant answer."

"What answer?"

"The only answer, Redeemed van Dolah." Once again Rew gives Edda's head a gentle touch with her appendage. "Do explore the questions. Do reflect."

Edda's eyes wander over the desert, the pyramids, the

rocks, Rew herself, as her thoughts, initially tumbling in chaotic chunks through the psych-link, begin to slow and crystallize into concepts, into *reason*.

She turns to Rew with an expression of triumph. "I'm dreaming!"

"*Awareness*," Rew says, and clumsily gives Edda a very human nod.

"I'm dreaming!" Edda repeats with a smile. Ximena feels her wonder at the realization that her consciousness—her senses—are locked inside her own mind. Everything feels so... real, so vivid; even the fresh smell of the air; all a simulation created by some other part of her, a hidden part, outside of her control.

"What's the big deal?" Ximena whispers at Mark. "She's been, er, *aware* before many times, while training for the first step."

"Lucid," Mark says. "We say *lucid* now, not *aware*. And no, this is different. This time Edda was not artificially pulled into lucidity by the will of a Walker." He waves a finger at Rew. "This time Rew is merely nudging, teaching Edda how to become lucid on her own, teaching her to wonder and reflect. Questions lead to awareness." He smiles brilliantly at Ximena, more with his blue eyes than with his lips. "By asking the right questions. And finding the right answer."

"I do congratulate you on becoming aware, Redeemed van Dolah. But do beware. Awareness is slippery, easy to lose—short-lived without discipline."

Edda frowns in confusion at those words, but soon loses interest in Rew. Her eyes wander anew. Ximena feels how those copper-colored pyramids below reclaim Edda's curiosity.

The scene begins to shake, shrinking and contracting in slow waves of surrealism, as Edda's mind keeps wandering, sliding further into disorder. The bright daylight and colors of the desert begin to wane.

Edda is about to wake up! Ximena realizes.

"Your dream is ending prematurely," Rew says. "Do not pierce the barrier. Do ground yourself."

"Huh?" She barely seems to notice Rew. "What?"

"Do you feel the wind, Redeemed van Dolah?" Rew asks, her voice like a roar over the chaos of waking.

"The wind?" She raises her arms and closes her eyes—the breeze moves the tips of her short, curly hair, and the bottom of her gown. "Yeah, I can feel it."

"Do you *hear* the wind?"

"Uh, yes—a whisper."

"Do spin your body and feel the centrifugal force stretching your limbs."

She obeys, her gown opening like a flower.

"Do kneel and touch the ground."

She does so, without questioning. The waving has stopped and the scene is slowly recovering its vividness.

"Do feel the warmth on your fingertips, the dryness, the fine texture of the traces of sand."

Edda rubs her fingers together and closes her eyes as if embracing the sensation. Then she turns to Rew with sudden realization. "I'm dreaming!"

"You are indeed dreaming, Redeemed van Dolah. You did lose your awareness, but you did also ground yourself in the dreamscape and your awareness has come full circle."

"Yeah..." she says, fingers still rubbing sand, thinking hard about what just happened. "I knew I was dreaming, and then... Whoa! Totally forgot about it. And I almost woke up!"

"Your deep-mind wants you to forget—but a disciplined high-mind can stay aware. You must train your mind to constantly engage your senses, to *ground* yourself into the dream—like you just did, with your touch, your hearing, your sight."

Edda looks around, nodding slowly. Ximena feels her engaging all her senses. She approaches the edge of the rock bridge and kneels down, slowly poking her head out.

"I could jump down—I'd just wake up, yeah?"

"An undisciplined mind would. But with awareness, you simply *ground* yourself to the sensation. A free fall caters for intense feelings. Go ahead, do jump."

"Uh, why am I scared? I know it's just a dream."

"A disciplined mind would not be afraid, because it is indeed a dream."

"You're saying I'm not disciplined, yeah?"

Rew regards her in meaningful silence.

Edda laughs.

And jumps.

The scene in the auditorium hastily follows her fall as she dives headfirst. Ximena and many of her fellow students lean back and gape in vertigo as they feel Edda's body thrusting through the air into the chasm. Mark is laughing like an adrenaline addict. The wind is loud and moody, pushing Edda unpredictably to the sides, never straight down; growing louder the farther she falls—her face stricken with exhilaration, staring down with a grin on her face. *Engaged*.

"I'M DREAMING!" she screams.

The fall seems to take forever, and yet, the ground is still far away below her, the dunes of the desert and the rocks around the lower mountains still invisible from the distance.

"May I suggest landing next to a pyramid?" A large albino raven—larger than a real raven could ever be—is diving beside her, the deafening noise of the fall weirdly unable to drown her calm voice.

"Can I fly? Or control the fall?"

"You could. But easier is to simply *be* there. Traveling in dreams does not require the slow movement through space that you must suffer in the wake—that would make your awareness slip of sheer boredom. Dreams are like tales—they skip the needless bits. Just move this dream to the next… chapter."

"Like a tale. Oookay…"

An instant later Edda and Rew are standing on the soft sand of the desert.

"So sexy!" Edda says, grinning wildly as her eyes slide over the landscape. The sand is bright yellow and orange, thin as to be almost dust, and hot enough to make the air above dance. A few steps beside their short shadows rises a large pyramid. Well, not large. The Great Pyramid of Giza is large. This pyramid is so… *gigantic* that the edge of the base gets lost beyond the farthest dunes in the horizon. It looms as high as a mountain. Its texture is metallic, shining golden scarlet under the reddish light of the sun, and yet it feels ancient, decrepit. "What in Goah's Name is this thing?"

"Do not get lost in the sight. Do mind your awareness."

"Yeah, I know I'm still dreaming, no worries. As long as I, uh, *focus*, the dream stays, and I know I'm dreaming, yeah?"

"We name it *grounding*, the second step of the Path, but… *Yeah*," Rew says. "Grounding your senses into the dreamscape—engaging them with purpose to remain aware—that is what shall be put to the test in the second trial."

"The trial, uh… right. I remember. Only twelve of us will pass to the… third step?"

"Very good, Redeemed van Dolah. Your memory pierces the wake barrier with impeccable precision. You truly are mastering the first step already. Now I shall attack your awareness until you equally master the second step."

"Attack?!" Ximena feels her sudden anxiety. Edda drops the grains of sand and takes a step back.

"Do not fear, Redeemed van Dolah. It is only your awareness that I shall remove."

"How?" Her eyes flinch nervously. She takes another step back.

"By *willing* it," Rew raises an arm towards Edda, and an invisible wave of... *something* crashes against Edda's dream body.

She gasps and then looks around in confusion. Her thoughts are tumbling, mixing in a tornado of chaos. She blinks, sees Rew, and smiles. "Oh, hi."

An abrupt wave of... *something* rips across the dream. The desert, pyramids and red sun all cease to exist to be replaced by Edda's bedroom.

"Oh, pure sin! Sorry, must go," Edda says, as if she had been in this room for too long. Ximena feels her sudden hurry. She walks to the door. "It's my turn to take Hans to daycare."

Rew makes another gesture at her.

Ximena feels Edda's thoughts gathering in harmony, like a crashed glass coming together in reverse motion. She stops dead in her tracks and turns slowly to face Rew. "Fuck," she says, and grins apologetically. "I slipped."

"That was... less than impressive, Redeemed van Dolah. My attack was the lightest I am able to muster."

"Sorry," she says. "You caught me by surprise." She walks to her bed and takes the blanket in her hands, feeling the doughy texture of the cloth. *Grounding* herself.

"Do engage your dream senses with more discipline.

Deploy your will if you must. We do only have two practice sessions before the trial."

"Oh," Edda says, and Ximena feels the chill creeping up Edda's spine. "Not much, yeah?"

"Not indeed. Furthermore, Overseer Yog did insist in personally designing the arena for the second trial. Be assured she will not be as… lenient as I am."

"Oh," Edda says. She wets her lips. "Fuck."

SEVENTEEN

Plants and Ashes

"The trial of the second step is about to begin," Professor Miyagi says, gesturing at the dreamsenso scene floating across the auditorium. It is the empty, black-skied landscape of the staging permascape, where the twenty-four human apprentices have gathered in scattered groups. "For those of you unacquainted with the history of the *Three Trials of Worth and Soul*, watch carefully, because today's session doesn't end quite like Edda expected."

The dreamsenso camera zooms in slowly towards what seems like an arbitrary part of the flat landscape, where a group of people dressed in their usual tunics and gowns stand around an instructor, avidly extracting the last drops of wisdom before the second trial. The same is happening within the other groups not far away. The difference with this particular group, Ximena realizes when details become apparent, is that the instructor is human. Oh, there is a mare as well, of course, but she stands aside, and watches the interaction with usual mare impassiveness.

"Now, pinch your noses, and shut your mouths, like this." Edda blocks her mouth and nose with a hand, and then, seemingly impossibly, takes a deep breath—Ximena can feel Edda's lungs filling with the dry air of the permascape. Edda removes the hand and laughs. "Try it!"

Aline exchanges an amused glance with Pieter, and both repeat Edda's feat. Janson—Pieter's younger brother —stares at them and, with visible hesitation, imitates them.

"I can breathe!" Aline laughs, hand still covering her mouth.

"And speak!" Pieter says. "Pure evil." He grins. "These damn dreams are so real, they can't shut you up, love."

Aline laughs and slaps his broad chest.

Janson is drawing slow, controlled breaths behind his own hand. He is unusually large for a fourteen-year-old, almost as much as his sixteen-year-old brother. Now that Ximena sees them side by side, she is struck by how many similarities they share. Yes, he has brown hair, where Pieter's is lighter. Janson's eyes are green, Pieter's blue. But other than that... Same muscular body frame, same protruding jaws. *They must be genetically related!* Ximena realizes. *Such an unusual family. First, two siblings of the same gender. And now this!*

Janson turns to Edda, wide-eyed at his capacity to breathe behind a hand. "How did you discover this... *magic?*"

"Ah," she changes her weight to the other foot. "I was with Elder Rew, you know, in one of her lessons, like yours with Elder Qoh." She gestures at the watching mare next to them. "At one point we were under water, and I could breathe. So then when back on land, I experimented, and..." She shrugs.

"Yours is a family of teachers, dowry sister," Gotthard says. He just walked in. His group is nearby, training with their mare. "But you have the heart of a scientist."

"Nobody is perfect," Edda says, grinning at him. She

gestures at Gotthard's group. "You bored already of the alien's teaching and looking for something more... *stimulating*? Oh," she turns to Qoh. "Sorry, didn't mean to—"

"We are marai, Redeemed van Dolah," Qoh says. "Not *aliens*."

"Sorry." Edda smiles. "We appreciate your support, Elder Qoh. And that you allowed me to join you when Elder Rew went to," she waves a hand in the air, "whatever."

"To complete the preparations for the second trial," Qoh says.

"Right." She claps loudly. "Come on, mensas. Who's next? Oh, hello." Edda smiles and stretches out a hand at an older man, already in his early twenties, who has just approached the group. "I'm Redeemed Edda van Dolah, a Juf in Lunteren. And you are?"

The man, short and stocky—and quite ugly, Ximena thinks—shakes Edda's hand without the shade of a smile. "Elder Luuk Smook. A humble farmer in Oosterbeek. Hope you don't mind me looking at how you specialists prepare for the trial." His voice is deep and coarse.

"We're not specialists," Pieter says, throwing a finger at his brother. "Much better. We're fishermen!" He laughs, like it was a joke.

"You sure are, Ledeboer," Gotthard says with a smug smile. "Your smell gives it away—even in dreams."

"Shut up, Gotthard," Edda says, and then smiles widely at the stocky man. "You're welcome to stay, Elder Smook. You made number two in the first trial, yeah?"

"Yes." His eyes pierce Edda's. "And you, number one." He says it like it is not praise, but sin.

Edda shrugs and laughs modestly. "Lucky, I guess."

Luuk Smook doesn't reply. He just stares at her in silence, like an iceberg at a passing ship.

Edda clears her throat. "All right, let's…" she turns towards her friends. "Who was…? Ah, Piet. Come." She takes Pieter's muscular arm and pulls him away from the rest, onto an empty spot. "And you, Elder Qoh," Edda walks to where the mare is standing, puts her hands on her white, leathery skin, and pushes firmly, "over here, please." With Edda leaning on Qoh, her elongated body slides until Edda stops her right in front of Pieter. "There. Now, Elder Qoh, please attack."

"With which intensity this time, Redeemed van Dolah?"

"Medium, Goah's Mercy! Please stop asking. If I say nothing, it's always medium intensity, yeah?"

"Acknowledged." Qoh raises an arm at Pieter, who stumbles in sudden confusion.

"Piet!" Edda shouts at him. He looks at her, eyes blinking. "What you are feeling right now, that chaos… Remember, remember!"

"What?" He stares at her, his frown deepening.

Gotthard rolls his eyes. "No fish biting, eh, rat boy?"

"Shut up, Gotthard," Edda says, and then to Pieter, "Remember, Piet. That feeling—your head spinning— associate it with the question."

He blinks again, and then scans his surroundings, his wide blue eyes stopping a second on Aline's. "The question," he mutters. And then, as if following an impulse, he sinks his head to inspect the palm of his hands."

"Excellent!" Edda claps.

"The lines," he raises his head at Edda, "they move!"

"Yeah, they do, huh?" Edda exchanges a satisfied glance with Aline.

Pieter then covers his nose and mouth with the hand and breathes in.

"Excellent, Piet. You remembered!" Edda says.

Pieter looks back at Edda and his lips stretch to a hesitant smile. "Whoa, this is a dream!"

"It is, yeah?" Edda claps again. Aline joins her, and Janson cheers loudly.

"Oh, everything is coming back." Pieter joins in the laughter.

"That's the first step at work, mensa," Edda says. "You remember."

"Thanks, Edda," he says, a warm smile on his lips. "Your techniques—they really work!"

"You almost lost it there, Ledeboer," Gotthard says. "And that was just medium intensity."

"You think you can do better?" Pieter asks.

Gotthard laughs. "Some of us need no fancy tricks, rat boy."

"Who's a rat boy?" Janson walks towards Gotthard, his green eyes glowering.

"You and your brother," he snorts, "and your two dead fathers. No place for women on your fishing boat, correct?"

Janson cringes and charges forward, pushing Gotthard hard on the chest, who falls back on his buttocks, laughing hard.

"Jans, no!" Pieter grabs one of his arms. "It's not worth it."

"Always a pleasure debating with you, *Elder Ledeboer*," Gotthard says, like the name is an insult. Without losing his smirk, he stands and dusts off his tunic, as if there was dirt on the staging permascape. "Who can compete with such persuasive arguments?"

While this little piece of drama unfolds, Ximena notices that not everybody is looking at Janson.

Luuk Smook is staring fixedly at Edda.

And his look sends a shudder up Ximena's spine.

———

The auditorium's point of view follows Edda as she paces to her assigned spot at the edge of the arena.

The trial of the Second Step is finally here.

It is all or nothing once more, twelve will stay in the race, twelve will be gone forever. The fate of her father is in the balance, and yet, with a pull of brutal willpower, Edda puts the nervous twitching of her hands firmly under control. Ximena nods in admiration at her mental discipline—it is incredible how far she has come.

Edda stops at the rim of the arena and looks down at the perfectly circular depression the size of a small lake carved on the infinite flatness and filled with fog to the brim—concealing the inside from her dream eyes.

"Do ready yourself in position, human candidates." Yog's soft female voice reverberates mentally across the amphitheater as if whispered in every ear simultaneously.

Edda steps directly onto the top of a giant metallic slope that plummets steeply down into the mist and loses itself in the mysteries below. Except for the scale, the slope is not unlike those playground slides Ximena loved to throw herself down as a little, unruly girl.

She looks around the edge of the round lake-like arena, where the other twenty-three candidates have taken positions on equidistant slopes, identical to hers. The slopes are numbered sequentially. Hers is slope number one—the number emanates telepathically from that spot like her ranking did after she nailed the trial of the First Step. Next to her, on the right, number two is manned by Elder Luuk Smook, who gives her a cool side glance, and then exchanges a grin with his sister, next around the rim on slider number three. Aline and Gotthard are standing beyond, number four and five respectively, their faces too far to see. And so, each candidate is placed along the perfect circumference of fog, ordered by the rank they achieved in the first trial. The last one, on Edda's left, is a nervous-looking Valentijn van Kley. Although also from Lunteren, she doesn't know him well, but exchanges a nod of support.

"Do sit," Yog says.

Edda sits in place, on the top platform of the slide, legs stretched down towards the mist and the arena hidden beneath, hands on railings, ready to push. She turns her head expectantly to the right, where a mare is standing exactly between her and Luuk Smook. There is another mare between Luuk's sister and Aline, and another one between Gotthard and whoever is next, and so on; twelve in total—Rew, her eight walkers, and Yog's three bodies—around the arena, each between every two humans.

"So shall you be trialed," Yog says. "At the count of six you shall push yourself into the pit." The fog glows briefly as Yog speaks the word *pit*. "You shall propel yourself into descent, at which point your assigned marai shall remove your awareness applying middle intensity—the same applied in your instruction. You shall then regain awareness by your own skill and proceed to the exit, a hole in the ground in the exact center of the pit." A brief, intense flash of light under the disc of fog pinpoints the location. *Pretty far!* "The first twelve humans that exit shall be initiated in the last step of the Path of Light. The rest shall return to their short, meaningless lives."

Ouch! But Edda doesn't let the words affect her. *Good*

girl, Ximena thinks. It is a surprisingly simple test. As soon as the candidates recover their lucidity—which should happen quickly enough from what Ximena has seen in training—they will all run for the exit like their lives depend on it. Looks more like a race than like a dreamtech-awareness trial. Ximena is about to ask Mark, but a side glance at him convinces her to let it be. He is staring at Edda like he himself is there with her, about to throw his future—his *life*—into the mist.

"Do brace for the count, human candidates. One… Two… Three… Four…"

Edda's hand clutches the railing, her dream arm muscles readying for the dive, and her mind embracing every sensation with sharp savagery—the cool, hard texture of metal on her skin; the tasteless humidity as tendrils of fog reach up into the air; the weight of her own body on the slide—Ximena realizes that Edda is *grounding* herself into the dreamscape in anticipation of the mare's awareness-removal attack.

"Five… Six. Do proceed."

Edda pushes forward, and begins a long, dashing slide down the slope, her breath under rigorous control, her eyes trying to pierce the fog into which she is plunging. As the scene camera dives behind her, Ximena catches but a side glimpse of the closest mare stretching an arm towards her, and—

Whoa, Goah! Ximena and many of Miyagi's students gasp as one as they feel the mental blow as if it were physical. Edda's mind has been violently pushed into a blizzard of chaotic confusion as she penetrates the fog, her vertigo making Ximena cringe.

Just as Edda reaches the bottom of the slope, the surrounding fog dissipates and a clash of colors hits her eyes like a hammer on a thumb. Her body, still brimming with momentum, thrusts forward through a jungle of flowers as tall as her, and more exuberant in display than anything Ximena has ever seen in her life—or in her dreams. Vegetation eager to impress, to absorb—to *mate*. The rush of vertigo floods her falling body, and yet her gaze is inexorably drawn to petals with spiraling turquoises, and thick stems in dazzling shades of burgundies. She finally falls on a soft bed of sprinkling dust that explodes in hues of blue and whispers of pain. Warm, titillating pollen immediately covers her skin, overwhelming her senses, as a sudden, sharp fragrance simultaneously smashes up Edda's nostrils, and transports Ximena in an instant into a land of forgotten memories, a past she cannot remember, and yet feels deeply as her own. A warm wind shakes the canopy of flowers as if bubbling instead of blowing, and *sings* wailing, wordless songs of the soul—ever changing melodies only meant to be heard once, and be forever forgotten.

Whoa, damn! A few stray tears run down Ximena's cheeks. She shuts her eyes and counts to three. *Goah, it's impossible to focus!*

But, of course, she doesn't have Edda's training. Nor her power of will.

Edda has been embracing each of these clashing sensations with wild eagerness, grounding herself into each new feeling before letting go of the previous one, an unbroken chain of awareness as the primary question of the Second Step echoes uninterruptedly in her mind.

Am I dreaming?

Yes!

Edda stands, shakes off the blue dust from her skin and tunic and draws a deep breath. With a shove of her mind, she dispels the soul-ripping melodies from her ears and the pungent smells from her nose.

Ah! Ximena sighs with relief. A glimpse at Mark confirms that she was not the only one overwhelmed by the sensory storm.

Edda draws another breath, and throws a calculating look back at the impossibly high slide, at its fixed position in relation to the wildly dancing vegetation. Ximena sees it now through Edda's eyes. Of course. It is not just a slide. It is also a *compass*. Edda takes her bearings and begins to move swiftly towards the center of the arena—towards the exit.

Something catches Edda's eye. Between the flowers, on her left she sees a glimpse of Valentijn van Kley, gaping around like a madman. *Poor bastard… Like a mensa groping in the dark.* Her thoughts flow unimpeded through the psych-link, accompanied by a distinct sense of pity. But Edda keeps trotting on regardless, sharply focused on her bearing, and quickly loses sight of him behind the foliage.

"Van Dolah!" She hears the sudden shout from her right.

Before she has time to turn her head, two bodies slam into her with simultaneous violence, and throw her tumbling across the ground.

Ximena feels Edda's sharp pain in her own body— blissfully muted by the psych-link safety interface. Edda's right side has been smashed by the impact, and her breasts and shoulders hit the ground hard. She raises her head, gasping for the air squeezed out of her lungs. She groans weakly and blinks up at the two figures staring down at her, as tears of pain well up in her eyes.

The Smook siblings.

Luuk's pale blue eyes pierce Edda's like a splinter of ice. His expression is closed, rational, almost blank. Ximena cannot read any anger in them, nor resentment, nor anything that could explain the attack. Only *execution*.

He is looking at Edda like a lion at a hyena. He is just doing what must be done.

His sister is different. Very different. In her early twenties, she must be one or two years older than him. She is tall where he is stocky, has blonde hair—cut short— where his is dirty brown. She is pretty where he is... *not*. And her eyes shine with hatred, stained teeth showing beneath a wolfish smile.

"Take her out," Luuk says, voice cool like he was commenting on the weather.

Both begin kicking her. Viciously.

Edda, creeping on the ground, screams and tries to drag herself away. Waves of *unreality* begin to ripple across the amphitheater, like the surf of the tide gradually engulfing a shipwrecked body. *Goah, she's waking up!* Ximena thinks.

"The head," Luuk says, as he kicks Edda's face with all his weight. His sister joins him, giggling, and stomps on her ear as Edda instinctively curls up and tries to cover the back of her neck with her hands.

Ximena's hands tighten into fists as the psych-link allows through a few traces of agony. She feels disgusted. The savage display of violence! "She's going to wake up," she mutters, eyes locked on thump after thump.

"No way," Mark says beside her. He is frowning, head tilted away, but his eyes are as locked as Ximena's. "Not Edda van Dolah." His voice is almost reverential. He meets Ximena's eyes and points at the scene. "Check that out, she's not letting go. She's using all that pain to dig herself deeper into the dreamscape. No way in hell is she going to wake. Not Edda van Dolah."

And indeed, although blows and kicks keep raining ruthlessly on Edda's head and trunk, the waves of the impending wake begin to slowly wane, and the scene solidifies. But the constant pain—intense under the relentless beating—trickles through her consciousness, into the hidden depths of her mind, where memories—*painful* memories—lie lurking in the dark.

Luuk stops halfway through a kick, and stares at Edda closely. "That's good enough, Mirjam. We run now."

"But she's not dying!" She keeps beating her. "The bitch doesn't want to die!"

"Look at her," Luuk points at Edda. "She lost awareness."

All around the immediate vicinity, the huge trunk flowers and strong singing wind are vanishing. Something completely out of place is taking its place: a flat wooden floor, a bed, a desk.

"If we don't leave now," Luuk says, holding his sister by the shoulder, "we might not make it in time."

"There's time." Mirjam stops kicking Edda, but her eyes remain fixed on her. "The others are," she snorts. "too *delicate*. We are the best by far."

"No risks," he says. "If we're not underestimating this one," he points at Edda, "we're not underestimating anyone! We go. Now." His voice is not imperative, just as casual as always, but Mirjam nods curtly and both take off, running side by side in controlled tempo.

Only Edda remains on the now fully formed wooden floor, grunting weakly as the pain wears off. It is *dream* pain after all, thank Goah—it doesn't linger.

A closet and a door frame rise silently from the floor, and a window frame appears in the air over the desk, curtains unraveling in place. Ximena can see it now, as the place solidifies with astounding realism: it is Edda's bedroom! Complete in every detail. There are even used gowns carelessly dropped in the corner, and through the window Ximena can see a couple of Lunteren colonists strolling in the morning sun, oblivious to the fact that they are casting in somebody else's dream. There are no walls, though. Nor ceiling. The door stands by itself, and the window hangs statically in midair. The wild cacophony of the flower storm rages on beyond, undeterred by this small pocket of order.

Two knocks on the door startle Ximena. "Can I come in?" a female voice asks.

"Uh, just a sec, Mom," Edda says, standing as her wrinkled tunic transforms into a delicate red gown, and her own face turns back in time by two or three years. "Ready, come in."

The door opens, and a beautiful Anika van Dolah in an elegant white tunic walks in with a plant plot in her hands. She is smiling at Edda, but Ximena sees something else in her eyes…

"I want you to have this, baby," she says, walking towards the window. She places the plant on the desk.

"Grandma's cactus," Edda says.

Anika nods, pressing her lips together.

"What happens?" Edda's large, innocent eyes avidly scan her mother's expression. "Are you nervous?"

"A bit." Anika's lips curve in an awkward smile.

"But your mum and dad are waiting for you, yeah? You'll have dinner together tonight!"

"I will miss *our* dinners, baby." Anika stretches her hand and caresses Edda's cheek, her eyes shining with sadness.

"Me too." Edda embraces her mother. "But you will be *so* happy. I'm so, so happy for you, Mom."

"Yes." Anika places a kiss on Edda's brow, and takes her gently towards the plant on the desk. "I want you to mix my ashes into the soil," she says, placing a hesitant finger on the pot. "I will be part of the plant now, and I promise you that when I bloom, you will bloom as well."

"Bloom?"

"*Bloom*, baby. To your full potential. I cannot be here to, er, be with you then in person, but Dad will. Do as he says, yeah? He loves you very, very much."

"Yes."

"And keep an eye on Bram, yeah? He is still so young..."

"Okay, Mom." Edda's voice breaks. Mixed emotions are swirling inside her: the very real happiness for her mother's reunion with her ancestors, mixed with the sudden realization of her prolonged absence and the wound it will surely leave. "Will you be fine?"

"Is that important?" Anika asks. She sounds vaguely resentful. "Only you and Bram, and Dad, matter. Only..." Her voice breaks, and she presses the back of her hand against her mouth. "Excuse me," she mutters, and leaves the room, shutting the door behind her.

Edda stares at the door in silence, her confused emotions dissipating slowly and leaving behind a lingering, unpleasant sensation: a seed of pain.

And the seed grows, throbbing grotesquely in her guts like a tumorous organ, until pain covers it all; a constant, sharp pain, not unlike that produced by Smooks' violence.

"Edda!" Gotthard storms into the room across one of the missing walls. He looks exhausted, hair and tunic out of place from the roaring, singing winds of the flower jungle. "What in Goah's Name are you doing here?"

"Man Kraker," she says, smiling mildly. "You look old."

"You look young! Wake up, dowry sister. You lost awareness!"

"I lost..." she turns her head at the door.

"Come on, Edda. There's no time. Everyone and their mother have probably reached the exit by now, but we have to try."

"Man Kraker… Gotthard…" She stares at him with sudden intensity. "Dowry brother?"

"You are dreaming, Goah's fucking Mercy!" He grabs her shoulders and shakes her. "Return to me!"

"Dreaming…" Edda's eyes seem to regain focus, and her skin tightens in a sudden reversal of her rejuvenation. She blinks, her old sixteen-year self once again. "What—?!"

"How did you… create all *this*?" Gotthard waves a hand around the room. "Forget it. Doesn't matter. We have to go to the exit right now!"

"Yeah." Edda shakes her head, and then clenches her fists as a sudden spurt of rage bursts inside her. "Smooks!"

"What?"

Edda draws a deep breath. "Doesn't matter," she finally says, and pushes him out of the bedroom. "Lead the way."

"Uh, I'm lost."

"What?"

"Yes, sorry. I regained awareness, er, too late, I suppose. I was already in the middle of this mess. That's how I found you. Pure luck."

"Yeah, well, we'll thank Goah later for that." She turns her head, like a hound sniffing the wind. "This way!" She pulls his sleeve and they both run off.

They dash below and around trunk-sized flower stems of flashing colors, sprinting towards an imaginary point clearly painted in Edda's memory—the bearing, the exit. Ximena can feel Edda's certainty. She is most definitely not lost.

Just delayed.

It feels like a minute or two before they finally reach what Edda believes to be the geographical center of the arena. *Spot on*, Ximena thinks, as they stop on the edge of a small hole, size of a man, leading somewhere too dark to see.

A side movement catches Edda's attention. Somebody is running towards them from their flank. She turns abruptly, fearing another attack, but it's not the Smooks this time. It's just Janson. He is alone, and his panicked eyes look like those of a hunted man, running for his life.

"Me first." Gotthard pushes Edda aside. "My mission is more important than yours," he says, and jumps into the hole before Edda can react.

"Son of a…!"

Janson is closing with the speed of a madman, eyes fixed on the black hole. He doesn't even seem to realize Edda is standing there. He takes three last bounds and leaps forward…

"Oooh, shit!" Edda jumps, a mere fraction of a second before Janson plunges in headfirst.

EIGHTEEN

Abracadabra

A line is the first human to appear in the empty flatness of the staging permascape. She looks around, and all there is to see are twelve mares loosely scattered in stoic stillness, except for four of them that, clustered together, seem to be engaged in communication.

"Where's everybody?" she asks Qoh, who is standing next to her.

"Patience, Woman Speese. You are alone because you are ranked human number one of twelve. I shall thread the other eleven qualified humans in short notice to begin your instruction in the Third Step of the Path of Light."

"Number one... You mean I was the winner of the trial?"

"Indeed, you were. By a significant margin—your performance would have been very impressive even for a marai, Woman Speese."

"Oh, really?" Her eyes widen with pride. "Number one!" She claps with childish enthusiasm.

"Indeed. Now, do be patient. I shall traverse and thread back human number two."

Before Aline can reply, Qoh disappears, and a few seconds later, reappears in the exact same spot, next to a baffled Pieter.

"Piet!" She throws her arms around his neck. "You made number two in the trial; can you believe it?"

"Whoa!" He chuckles. "Did I really beat Edda?"

"Uh, it seems so," Aline says, the hint of a frown appearing on her brow.

As they keep exchanging words, Qoh disappears and reappears anew with not one, but two humans this time.

The Smook siblings.

Almost a dozen humans have already been threaded into the permascape, and Ximena—and all other students for that matter—watch with increasing agitation the space where Qoh always reappears with a new candidate.

Edda is still missing.

In the last minutes, the scene's camera has been gradually moving away from the candidates and closer to the four mares clustered together, to the point where Ximena can already make out the voices of Rew and Yog as if they really were made of vibrations in the air instead of reverberations in the mind.

"I find it curious," Rew is saying, "that many remaining human candidates do reside in the same physical settlement."

"Why would you find it curious?" Yog asks. "You did state that humans in Diamar have a notable propensity to enhanced Second Wake halos."

"And that is correct. There is much talent scattered in the broader region. And yet, most humans that have made it to this stage are dreaming from the one settlement closest to Deviss." Rew stretches an arm towards Aline. "Woman Speese, the strongest halo I have ever perceived in a human."

"A traverser halo."

"Indeed, and thus very rare. Then Elder Ledeboer," Rew keeps gesturing with her arm, "Man and Woman van Kley, Redeemed Siever, and," she points at a gaping Gotthard that has just materialized with Qoh, "Man Kraker. All native to the same human settlement."

"Remarkable indeed."

"I do acknowledge that we are only to instruct twelve humans in the last step in the Path of Light, Overseer Yog. Yet, I hereby request official dispensation for a thirteenth one."

"A dispensation? Do clarify."

"One of the humans that missed the mark in the last trial, Junior Elder Ledeboer, has a very unique halo. I do hereby request his reintegration."

"Junior Elder Ledeboer... I do remember. He did not perform with much distinction. What type of halo makes this human so exceptional?"

"He radiates the halo of a thought piercer, Overseer Yog. The only human we have scouted with such a trait."

"A human thought piercer... Is that even physically possible?"

"We shall never know, unless we do proceed with his instruction. Thus, this official request."

"A human thought piercer," Yog says. "Remarkable." She pauses for a few moments, as if considering the idea. "And inconceivable. No, Walker Rew. We shall not waste resources on futile enterprises. Furthermore, I do fail to see how a thought piercer could benefit our goals."

"That is a regrettable lack of foresight on your part,

Overseer Yog. A human thought piercer could be deployed—"

"My decision is final, Walker Rew. We shall not discuss this matter any further."

Their attention is drawn back to the surface of the permascape. Qoh has just materialized there, and next to her, Edda is scanning the area with eager eyes. She is wearing her usual outfit: the plain white tunic with the black, ornate belt of the Redeemed hanging loosely on her waist.

"The last human is here," Yog says. "That is your human, Walker Rew. Quite the disappointment. An appalling performance, despite the amount of personal time you have misspent in her instruction."

"On the contrary, Overseer Yog. The context is not to be dismissed. Redeemed van Dolah was unduly attacked, and yet she did resist the illicit violence and managed to reach the exit. I doubt any other candidate would have made it under such duress. The Elders Smooks have subverted the spirit of the trial, and as such proved themselves unworthy of the Paths."

"On the contrary, Walker Rew. There was only one rule: to make it out before others. The Elders Smooks not only fulfilled the goal adequately, but they had the discernment to sacrifice their ranking in the trials in exchange of gaining a tactical advantage over a dangerous rival. That shows an impressive array of high order skills: attentiveness, cunning and forward planning. Skills that shall prove invaluable to our first human Walkers of the Mind. Your human, on the other hand, showed weakness and unpreparedness for the unexpected. Without the assistance of another human, she would have surely missed her qualification."

"That human who did assist, Man Kraker, is a relative,

and thus an extension of herself, not unlike your limbs," Rew gestures to the three bodies of Yog, "which are an extension of yours. I do fear such human nuisances like family and relations are beyond your comprehension, Overseer Yog. Thus, you shall trust my judgment as human whisperer when I maintain that Redeemed van Dolah's ability to establish alliances with other humans is one of her key strengths. Which in this case proved indeed critical to her success. Such ability to weave a network of relations shall prove invaluable to our first human Walkers of the Mind."

"I do fear you overestimate your human's abilities, Walker Rew. She is weak in her core, broken by fear and trauma, and shall be exposed as such soon enough."

"I do fear that what you identify as weaknesses are actually strengths, Overseer Yog. And indeed, we shall assess her abilities soon enough."

E dda's face is a few inches off Luuk Smook's smug smile. Her eyes are wide, her frown sharp. *Go, girl!* Ximena thinks.

"Why?!" she yells, droplets of dream spit scattering across his ugly face.

Luuk's icy blue eyes remain locked on Edda's, unperturbed, his lips almost imperceptibly curved.

Ximena catches an abrupt side motion in the corner of her eye.

"Get off his face, bitch!" Mirjam Smook says, as she rams her full weight against Edda's flank.

Edda falls with violence on the dark stone of the staging permascape. It is painful on her knees, but especially on her soul. Her bafflement, Ximena realizes, swallows the pain in a single gulp. Edda pushes herself up on her knees and turns her head towards Mirjam, her eyes still asking, *Why?!*

Ximena gasps at the rage she sees in Mirjam's expression. Her narrow, fierce face, and short, blonde hair remind Ximena of the legend of the Amazon warriors. Her blue eyes seem injected with blood, her glower is murderous. *Goah's Mercy, this is not just rivalry. It's... hatred.*

As Mirjam takes a menacing step towards Edda, two men, running from behind, grab her arms and immobilize her in a tight grip. They are Pieter and—Ximena blinks in disbelief—Gotthard, working as one. Mirjam kicks and pushes, shakes and pulls, curses and yells. She cannot break free, but she is not making it easy.

"Could you please call your dogs off, Redeemed van Dolah?" Luuk asks in his deep, coarse voice. Oh, how Ximena hates that smug smile.

"Why should I?" Edda asks, standing and walking towards him. "Who's going to stop us from dismembering her, here and now?" Edda turns her face to Mirjam, who glares back at her, panting, but quiet. "Certainly not them." Edda stretches a hand at the mares, all of whom are watching their interaction. "They look like they want to see some action."

"I suggest we call a truce," Luuk says, his smile widening. "We've better things to do than fight each other."

Edda chuckles, shaking her head. "You've got balls. *Now* you go civilized, yeah?"

Luuk smiles at her in silence.

Edda takes a deep breath. *Fact is, he is right.* "Mensas, thanks. Let her go, yeah? It's okay. There's no time for this horseshit."

The two men grudgingly release Mirjam who walks to

her brother, glaring back at Pieter. "You," she says, "you are a fisherman."

"I think the smell gave you away, rat boy!" Gotthard says with a chuckle.

"Don't you have a backbone?" Mirjam asks, eyes locked on Pieter.

Pieter frowns at her in confusion.

"Look at you," she continues. "You're pathetic. A word of your master specialists, and you jump to do all sort of tricks for them."

"What the fuck are you talking about?" Pieter asks.

"That mensa just insulted you," she says, pointing at Gotthard. "To your face! And you just take it like that? Where in Goah's Name is your *pride*?"

Pieter turns his head at Gotthard, who returns his gaze with a nervous smile. He takes an unconscious step back.

"He's just an asshole," Pieter says with a shrug. "Why bother?"

"And that's the problem." Mirjam points a finger at Pieter's face. "That's the problem, right there! They decide for us, they boss us around, they take all the karma from us, and they work for shit while we work our asses off."

"*They*?" Pieter asks. "*We*?"

"They, the specialists," Mirjam says. "We, the *people*."

"They, the elite," Luuk says. "We, the oppressed."

"Oh, I see," Edda says. She puts a hand on Pieter's broad shoulder while staring at Luuk. "I think I know why you want to win the Trials. I bet a good ol' class revolution is on the menu, yeah? What do you mensas have in mind? French style, or you rather go the Russian route?"

"You think you're so much better than us," Luuk says, "with your fancy words, your pretty tunic and your soft hands. But you are *nothing*," he says the word like it is a curse. "And when the people take power away from your corrupted hands, you'll be *nothing*," he says the word, like it is a promise.

———

E dda is walking through a forested dreamscape not unlike the woodlands that edge the eastern rim of Lunteren—a maze of low, narrow birches naked of leaves. Only the occasional conifer offers a relief of green. The humid, dense fragrance of the winter wilderness spreads across the auditorium, acting like a balm on Ximena's grateful dream lungs.

As Edda walks, she touches the white bark of passing trees, leisurely. *She is grounding herself into the dream*, Ximena realizes. *With such naturality, she does it… yes, almost unconsciously.*

Edda stops in front of a particularly large birch and studies it, tilting her head, her gaze intent and focused. The trees closest to the birch appear to react on their own by moving away, making space around the birch. Then, gradually, the birch grows larger, its branches thicker, its trunk wider, until it is not a birch anymore, but a magnificent oak.

"Aws Blessings to you, Redeemed van Dolah," Rew says. She was not there an instant ago. She stares at the oak, impervious to the fact that her legs are embedded in a thorny bramble bush nearby. "Do you know what all this is?"

"Elder Rew." She smiles at the mare. "Blessings. What is what?"

"This place." Rew gestures with a clumsy sweep of the arm. "What is the nature of our surroundings?"

"Uh, the dream, you mean?"

"Indeed. A dream. You are aware."

"Course I am."

"Can you estimate how long you did require from the moment your dream began until you achieved awareness?"

"Uh, it was pretty much right away. There's always something that makes me... wonder, yeah? Ask *questions*, like you said. Like," she spreads her arms, palms up, "what am I doing here, inside this forest? Then I usually look at the palm of my hands, or pinch my nose, to confirm that it's really a dream, although tonight I didn't need to, because... It's hard to explain. I was already sure of it, yeah? I could *feel* it."

"I do understand. And that is remarkable, Redeemed van Dolah. You have developed the intuition of a master of the *inner walking*."

"Thanks. I've been practicing non-stop, changing things all around me." She points a finger at the oak and smiles with pride. "And I never slip from the dream. Not once! It wasn't easy—sometimes stuff happens, like before, when a rabbit popped up from the ground, and I was tempted to follow it. There're always temptations to lose myself in the... *dream story*, if that makes sense?"

"It does, very much indeed. You have developed a deep intuition for dream mechanics. It is the nature of dreams to engage your consciousness, your dream senses, your attention; to pull you into the logic of their narrative; to gnaw on your awareness until it dissipates completely."

"Uh, thanks...?"

"You are welcome. Your ability to retain awareness makes you equal to a *grounding* master. But as pleased as I am to confirm that you comfortably tread the Second Step, it is the Third Step that concerns us during this session.

You already appear capable of transforming your environment by just wishing to do so. I shall assess now to what degree." Rew extends an arm at the large oak that Edda transformed from a birch. "Can you turn it back into the smaller tree with white bark?"

"Into a birch?" Edda stares at the oak, smiles, and waves theatrically at it. "Abracadabra!"

The oak changes at once—branches shrink, trunk thins, bark lightens. It is over in less than a second.

"Ta-dah!" Edda mocks a bow at Rew. "Now, let me guess. This… *dream magic* is the Third Step, yeah?"

"The Third Step indeed." Rew nods. "*Will-control*—dream-substance manipulation by desire."

"I've been practicing. I got really good at it!"

"Manipulation of individual elements is not evidence of mastery."

Rew directs her expressionless white eyes at the birch. The tree changes again, shrinking rapidly into the shape of a person—into Edda herself.

"What the…! You can change *my own* dream! Do I *really* look like that? Wait…" She concentrates. The Edda between the trees looks down to her own bosom as it grows noticeably, tightening the tunic around her chest. "There!"

"Thanks," the second Edda says with a wide smile.

"Sure, sexy thing."

Rew waves an arm in silence, almost impatiently. The second Edda disappears.

"Hey! You started it!"

Rew ignores her. "Are your abilities developed enough to change the entire dream environment into something else completely?"

"You mean, like turning the forest into something else?"

"Indeed."

"Wow." Edda scans her surroundings. "I've never tried that. Into what?"

"That is up to you, Redeemed van Dolah. A full environment exchange. Anything that is not a forest."

"Aha, let's see…" She looks thoughtful, then closes her eyes and slows her breathing.

"Are you trying already?" Rew asks.

"Yeah, goahdamnit! It's difficult!"

"Do picture the new environment. Do *wish* for it. Do *want* it."

"Duh! What do you think I'm doing?"

"There is a technique that might be of assistance. If you do allow."

"Hold on. Let me…" Edda's face contracts. "Try…" The surrounding birches remain defiantly solid. "Oof! Okay, I give up. Tell me, oh dream master."

"A gradual environment transition is hard to accomplish, even for a Walker in the Shadow. But a *reset* is simpler."

"Say what?" Edda tilts her head.

"A reset. A clean beginning. Make this environment go away first, and only then wish a second environment into existence."

Edda frowns in confusion.

"For instance," Rew says, her feminine, psychic voice reverberating with calm patience, "you may close your eyes for a few moments, and then open them into your desired environment; or you may spin rapidly until the world around you disappears in a blur, while you visualize a fresh one to await you upon completion."

"Okay. Uh, let's try with the eyes first."

The scene goes black in the auditorium, simulating the fact that they are watching the events from Edda's perspective. Ximena leans forward in the darkness with expectation.

"Visualize…" She hears Edda's voice in the darkness. She sounds like she is exerting herself. "What I want… A few moments… Okay!"

An almost blinding light returns to a transformed scene.

The forest is gone.

Edda and Rew are now standing on a wooden boat in the midst of a river. A very wide river, wider than any Ximena has ever seen. High hills along both margins are barely visible in the distance, ruined castles crowning some peaks. The sun illuminates lazy currents from a spotless blue sky.

"So sexy!" Edda raises her arms. "Did I just nail the third step of your Path?"

Rew scans the placid waters for a few seconds. Ximena would bet she is impressed. "It might have been the fortune of the apprentice. Do return us to the forest."

"The Forest. All right." Without hesitation, Edda utters a curt cry of joy, and jumps headfirst into the water, splashing through the surface in an instant.

A surface that spins around itself in a confusion of gravity and water. Ximena feels almost dizzy by the sudden explosion of motion and perspective as her eyes try to adapt to the new narrative of the dream.

Edda emerges upwards, headfirst, from a small puddle in the same forest they left behind a few seconds ago. Her body moves as if pushed up in the air, and has just the right amount of side momentum to make her fall softly on the grass beside the original birch tree.

"There!" she says, visibly pleased with herself. "The forest. Do I kick dream ass or what?"

"Dream control is indeed in your nature, Redeemed van Dolah. As your Second Wake halo reveals."

"Second what?"

"Matters not. Your dominion over the dream substance shall prove invaluable to exert *suggestion*."

"Suggestion. Right." She cuts a twig off a low branch and rubs it leisurely in her hands. "Is that what you did to Consul Levinsohn that first day, to make her nominate Lunteren for the Century Festival?"

"No, that was not suggestion, Redeemed van Dolah. That was *persuasion*. More powerful. It does require dominion over the Path in the Shadow. Should you ever reach such mastery, I am confident your natural talent for control shall make you a formidable persuader."

"So what is *suggestion* good for?"

"The goal is indeed the same: to intrude into another's mind in order to impose your will. But a Light Walker must rely only on the limited reach of willpower, and its cunning application by transforming the dreamer's environment in the right way to achieve deception."

"*Deception*." Edda frowns. "Sounds... Not what a good person would do, Elder Rew."

"Deception is the lightest application of power over others."

"There's also asking."

"That is not power. That is mercy."

"All right. Got it. Can you show me how to," she wiggles her fingers in the air, "use this dream magic to do *suggestion*?"

"I do fear I cannot, Redeemed van Dolah. No marai can. As human, you are better suited to design your own means of deception on other humans than a marai can ever be. And you shall—suggestion is the core of the last trial that awaits you and your fellow human candidates at the end of the Path of Light. Suggestion will determine which two humans are selected to be instructed in the Path in the Shadow."

"But then…" Edda's voice hesitates slightly. Ximena can feel the hint of anxiety growing inside her. Now, suddenly, suggestion is the key to saving her father, if only because it is the key to *persuasion*. "How can I learn?!"

"You have already displayed a degree of proficiency, Redeemed van Dolah."

"What?"

"With Consul Levinsohn indeed. I did persuade her to move the Festival to your Geldershire, as a demonstration to you humans of the potency of persuasion. And yet it was you that convinced her to select your own colony by the cunning application of words, seduction and sex. That was most impressive."

Edda blushes. "But I didn't use…" She wiggles her fingers again.

"By merely using your own self, you did achieve your objective with the consul, Redeemed van Dolah. Thus, what could you achieve now that you also master the manipulation of the dream world?"

"So you think I'm ready for the last trial?"

"You are. But you have not completed your instruction yet."

"Haven't I?" She turns her attention to the birch, snaps a finger at it, and the birch turns into a white marble column that would not look out of place in a temple of the classical world. "I think I'm pretty good already."

"Manipulation you indeed command. Alas, there is also struggle and pain at the end of the Path of Light."

"Struggle—?"

Rew closes on Edda and thrusts her arm through her chest like a spear. "And pain," she says.

Ximena feels a spike of astonished agony for the briefest of moments before Edda wakes up gasping in her bedroom.

END OF DREAMWORMS EPISODE II

Leave a review, Goah's Mercy!

A review, pretty please? No reviews → no sales → there goes my writing career.

Please, PLEASE review now! You can always update your review later if you feel the need.

https://isaacpetrov.com/reviewbook1

OR SCAN THIS WITH YOUR CAMERA!

Sign Up — No Bull Sci-Fi

ISAAC PETROV — EPIC SCI-FI AT ITS BEST!

Come over to my site at IsaacPetrov.com and SIGN UP to get fresh SCI-FI updates, discounts and goodies:

https://isaacpetrov.com/book1

OR SCAN THIS WITH YOUR CAMERA!

DREAMWORMS

A POST-APOCALYPTIC FIRST CONTACT EPIC

31st DECEMBER 2399

EPISODE III

ISAAC PETROV

NINETEEN

The Teacher and the Quaestor

"I am exceedingly sorry for the delay," the man says, as he paces down the central steps of the amphitheater, moving with an ease that comes naturally to people of privilege. He is over fifty, head shaved clean except for a large eye symbol tattooed on his forehead, and wears a humble brown gown with that same eye symbol threaded in gold on his chest. "But I had an urgent council duty to conclude. Please accept my most sincere apologies, my dear professor."

"Grand Censor Smith," Miyagi says from the stage below, and gestures Ank to stop the floating scene, which vanishes in the sudden radiance of a midday sun and a clear blue sky. "So glad you could make it. Please take a seat." He points at an empty spot next to Ank. "We were about to—"

"Splendid, splendid," he says, eyeing the elegantly dressed Neanderthal woman, who is smiling openly at him. "Oh." The corner of his lips twitch almost unnoticeably, and then he scans the colorful rows where the Lundev crowd stares back at him with sassy curiosity, in marked contrast with the deferential respect emanating from the GIA section. His eyes seem to linger longer on Mark. "How charmingly diverse."

"We were about to dive into the Third Step of the Path of Light."

"Third step, splendid," he says as he reaches the bottom of the stairs. "So I didn't miss the climax of the *Three Trials of Worth and Soul*." He walks past a mildly perplexed Ank towards the part of the hemicycle filled to the brim with blue and white uniforms. As he approaches, a spot reverentially opens for him on the first row.

From the opposite side of the auditorium, Ximena follows his every move—his every gesture—with awestruck eyes, like she is in the presence of royalty. Professor Jean-Jacques Smith, who by the age of forty had already reached the very top of the ranks of Academia of the Goah's Imperia of the Americas. Not once, but twice: he is both a Doctor of Economics and of Historical Sciences, and the youngest member ever accepted to the Council of the University of Townsend. Since Ximena began her PhD, she has been hitting his papers time and time again; he really knows his subject. Oh, and to top it all, he is second dowry to the Pontifex herself, which probably helped him pursue a parallel—and successful—career in aws Head. Already a grand censor! And nobody expects him to stop there.

"Eighteenth of December, if memory serves well?" he says, as he sits.

"Spot on," Miyagi says. "Do I have your permission, Grand Censor Smith, to resume the seminar?"

"Oh please," he waves a polite hand at him. "Act as if I wasn't here. And I beg of you, my dear professor, don't be using my full title now. *Grand* Censor Smith is so," he laughs, "*bloated*." He puts a playful hand on his prominent belly. "I don't need to be reminded how *grand* I'm becoming." He laughs again.

"Sure, then *Censor Smith* it is. I was about to show *our* students the daylight events in Lunteren on that Saturday 18th of December 2399. We've been so immersed in the dreamscape side of things—with aliens, trials and what not —that we risk forgetting that, at the end of the day, it is in the real world where we all take a dump. And what is history, but a long account of shit happenings? I hope you can excuse my language, Censor Smith."

"Very florid metaphor," he chuckles affably. "But please, curse away. We're all adults here."

"Thanks. Ank, please," he nods at the woman, "bring it up."

Ank waves a finger at Bob—the wudai machine standing next to her—and a scene appears frozen in midair across the auditorium.

"Oh, this is remarkable," Censor Smith says, as his admiring eyes study the ultra-realistic projection: a large red-bricked building, two-stories high, wide and with a large open field on its front where cheerful children play soccer. A school. Centrally located, judging from the traffic of strollers on the sidewalk, and bicycles on the street— Ximena can even see the receding back of a horse carriage turning a corner. "Is this the dream sensorial you are seeking official GIA approval for, Professor Miyagi?"

"Well, in a way." Miyagi puts his hands in his pockets. "These are the raw sections I am producing in collaboration with the Lundev's History Department. They are for academic purposes, like..." he chuckles, puts a hand out and waves a finger across the rows of students. "But, in essence, you are of course right. For the general public I'm keen to cut and paste the more, er, *commercial* parts into a nice, tight historical drama. Bring history to the people, right? It will be very educative."

"And lucrative, I presume?"

"I very much hope so," Miyagi chuckles again. "Especially if your office permits its publication in the GIA. Such a vast market."

"Oh, Professor," his smile widens, "this is no moment to speak business. I come to your," he gestures at the part of the amphitheater where Ximena sits embedded in Lundev students, "*Global Program* not as Censor, but as Professor of History, and of course as guardian to the academic wellbeing of the souls entrusted to my university." He looks back and meets the devoted look of dozens of students in their neat white-and-blues. He turns back to Miyagi and points a finger at the school floating in midair. "So, what are we watching here?"

"Ah, yes. The De Bron School, in Lunteren." Miyagi slowly begins to pace the stage. "But before we begin today's seminar, I wanted to hear your opinion, people. Mere curiosity, please indulge me. Ank, could you please move the camera to the man exiting the building?"

Ximena turns her attention to the figure coming out into the midday sun. The scene zooms in until he floats full-body like a distracted giant, carrying papers and notebooks under his arm.

"Ah! Here he is," Miyagi says. "Elder van Dolah. Or *Meester* Willem, as he was called by his pupils."

Willem is of the thin and tall type—one of those annoying people that never gains weight, whatever rubbish they eat. His skin is white, a healthy pinch of red on his cheeks. Long, untidy brown hair, intelligent brown eyes, thin glasses. His long tunic seems warm, comfortable—and a tasteless clash of colors faded by usage beyond reason.

"Look at him. He is your age, give or take. Do you find him physically attractive?"

The students exchange glances, waiting for a reaction. Cody O'Higgin, Ximena's fellow GIA student, finally speaks up: "Uh, I think he's okay looking, Professor. A bit dorky."

"Nah, I think he's really cute," Lora says. "Throw on a nice, tight outfit, and he'd be a sex magnet."

"Yeah," Mark says next to Ximena, "he's got that sexy intellectual thing going for him."

Murmurs of agreement spread across the benches.

Mark leans towards Ximena, locks his blue eyes into hers, and whispers in mischievous tone, "There's something about smart people that makes me want to nail them, you know what I mean?"

Ximena blinks and looks away, mildly scandalized; mildly... *Goahdamn blush!*

"Thank you, people. Just curious," Miyagi raises his eyes thoughtfully at the floating figure. "He surely attracted attention. Sometimes of the *dangerous* type." He laughs, and without further clarification gives Ank a curt nod.

Willem exits the school, distracted, trying to balance the books he is carrying. A woman walks towards him.

Marjolein Mathus.

Ximena tries to repress an involuntary swell of antipathy. This is history, she reminds herself. There are no villains in history; just people and motivations, actions and reactions. *Perhaps,* she hears Abuelo's voice in her thoughts, *but there are also consequences. We are human, cariño; not machines.*

It doesn't come easily to us to detach a consequence from its perpetrator. And should we really?

"Will," Marjolein calls with a tentative smile.

"Marjo!" He almost drops his load. "Aws Blessings to you." He gives the woman a shy nod, as his eyes unconsciously check out her small but well-rounded body.

Marjolein seems to notice his reaction and her smile widens. She is wearing a long formal robe, purple with thin golden eye-like symbols on its front and back. "Aws Blessings," she says. "Are you in a hurry? There is something we need to talk about."

"I need to pick up Hans from daycare, is it urgent?"

"Well, not urgent, but it is important. Can I walk with you?"

"Uh, of course. Come."

Willem and Marjolein begin to walk together on the sidewalk in awkward silence.

They join the main street where the center of the colony surrounds them: colonists walking and cycling, alone and in groups, going about their business; some wear expansive hats, others elegant robes, and most plain cloth, working tunics. A horse passes clopping by, pulling a rubber-wheeled cart loaded with wares and passengers. Flocks of children run, liberated from their daily chores. Two dogs bark at each other, restrained by their strolling owners. Just another day in Lunteren.

"I'm surprised you even have time to, uh, be here." Willem finally breaks the silence. "With the Century Festival preparations around the corner, I mean. It must be a lot of work."

She sighs, shaking her head lightly. "You have no idea. What a hefty beast to tame. Pure sin. So many arrangements and deals. Everybody wants a piece of it, and everybody wants it their way."

Willem scoffs. "I'm sure they're in for a surprise."

Marjolein laughs. "Oh Will, it has been a long time, hasn't it?"

"I guess," he says, eyes on a passing bike as he prepares to cross the street. "I've also been…" He doesn't finish the sentence, as they both quickly cross to the other side before an approaching carriage.

"I know," she says, and taps his shoulder. "Your family is lucky to have you."

"You would think," he sighs. "By the way, I never actually told you. Didn't have the chance, so…" He stops walking, takes her hands in his, and looks into her blue eyes. "I am proud of you."

She smiles, opens her lips as if to reply, but then she just presses them tight, and tightens her grip on his hands, her eyes moist.

"I know how hard you've worked for this," Willem says. "Bringing the Century Festival to Lunteren. I am without words, Marjo. This is going to do so much good. So, so proud." He places a sudden soft kiss on her lips.

Marjolein's breathing seems to quicken, Ximena thinks, but she just meets Willem's gaze in silence. Probably too touched by his words—and lips—to reply.

They begin to walk again along the busy sidewalk attracting more than a few eyes. They're both public figures in a way. And loved by the people, it seems.

"I'm so happy for you," Willem says, "especially for your career. I know how important it is to you. In a few days, your name will be on the lips of every big shot in aws Head. There's only one sad side to your success: you will have to leave Lunteren to climb the ladder, but Goah knows it is your destiny."

"Thank you, Will," she says, and wipes her eyes with the back of her hand.

"Anyway, so what is so important that you had to come in person instead of sending for me?"

"Yes, it's too private," she shrugs lightly, "and I thought I wanted to see your face. This morning I got aws Womb's weekly report." She beams at him. "Bram and Isabella's fetus is developing fine. And they wrote down the gender!" She takes his hand and presses. "Do you want to know?!"

"No!" Willem says, dropping her hand. "No, please. Bram and Isabella want it to be a surprise."

"Don't you want to know if it's a Van Dolah baby girl, or a Zeger's baby boy?" Her smile turns mischievous. "I can tell you right now."

"Marjo, please no. Is that what you wanted to talk about?"

"No." Marjolein leans and takes Willem's arm. "I miss you," she whispers in his ear.

Willem softly releases himself from Marjolein's hands.

"Please, Marjo." He looks uncomfortable. "Is it *us* you want to talk about?"

"No." Her smile fades, her eyes flinching with a shade of pain. "I said *important.*"

Willem says nothing.

"It is about Edda."

"Edda?" Willem gives her a concerned look. "Is this official Quaestor business?"

Marjolein takes his arm again as they hastily cross another street. This time Willem does not remove her hands.

"We—I mean aws Head—tolerate eccentricities from children," she says. "It is official Head policy. Children are still learning Goah's ways, and they need… freedom to explore. But Edda is an adult—and a redeemed. And she holds a prestigious office, as Juf in De Bron."

"And students adore her," Willem says, defensively.

"Especially the evening adult students. Her teaching style is confrontational, like the philosophers of ancient Greece. I would never admit it to her, but she is a better teacher than I am."

"Maybe." She presses herself slightly into his arm. "Who am I to tell? All I know is what I hear. That is unfortunately the nature of my office—that you always get to hear the complaints."

"Somebody has complained about *Edda*?" His concerned look has turned more urgent.

"Not just one. She has made some colonists… *uncomfortable*."

"I can't believe it! Who?"

"I can't tell you, Will, sorry. Confidential. Again, the nature of my office."

"What are they saying?"

"Edda is apparently spreading heresies and conspiracy theories, Will. And after what happened with the Meermans, we cannot have any more of that. Apparently, she has trouble accepting Goah's Call for the Joyousday." Marjolein gives him a pointed look.

Willem sighs. "She's having a hard time accepting my Joyousday."

She snorts. "That's quite the understatement. But it is Goah's Call, and she must accept it."

"And she will!" Willem turns to Marjolein. "When I'm gone, she will." His voice drops to a whisper.

"Listen, Will." She casually raises a hand to greet a finely dressed passing cyclist. "In my heart, I understand Edda's feelings all too well. What I would not give for more time together with you, like we used to…" She takes his arm again in an intimate gesture. "And I must ask myself, why not?" She stares at him with a tantalizing smile.

"Why not, what?"

"There is some leeway," she whispers, "some tolerance in aws Head's attributions. How can I say this? Hmm, that the Joyousday is celebrated on the twenty-seventh birthday is more *tradition* than dictate. Certain circumstances *may* allow for official *postponement*. And as you said yourself, my voice will carry considerably more weight in a few days."

"Postponement? How long?"

"As long as you don't turn twenty-eight, you ought to remain safe from Dem," she says, and her smile widens. "An extra year of happiness!" She grabs his arm again. "Oh, I miss you, Will! And Edda will be *so* happy. She quits that heretic nonsense, and everybody wins."

"No, Marjolein. I am sorry, but that's not a solution. I know Edda. She won't roll over just because I delay my Joyousday, even if for an entire year."

"All right. Forget about Edda. What about what *you* want? Don't you want to live longer? I promise I will make your life *very* pleasant."

He gently takes her hands off his arm, shaking his head slowly. "At the end of my life, what I want is not important. Perhaps you would understand if you had a family."

Marjolein's lips tighten, her expression turns strict, professional. All business.

"I- I'm sorry, Marjo. I didn't mean to—"

"I have been officially requested by some concerned colonists to report Edda's activities to the office of the inquisition as suspect of heresy. Dangerous ideas are not to be tolerated, especially not from a teacher who can use her public pulpit to spread lies among the young."

"You wouldn't!" His glare makes Marjolein take a step backward.

"Will," her voice softens a notch, "there have been no heresies in Lunteren for fifty years, Goah be praised, so maybe you aren't aware of the inquisition's rituals; and how they cleanse the demon-ridden before their release into aws Embrace."

Willem's eyes widen in horrific understanding. He keeps walking in frigid silence.

"Is this how you protect your family?" Marjolein says, keeping his pace. "In two months, the Van Dolah's will lose you, and then the senior elder might be declared heretic in Goah's Eyes. Can you imagine how hard that would be for Bram? Alone, responsible for a baby, and with the stigma of heresy hanging over his family? Who could then blame Isabella if she orders aws Womb to abort the dowry bond?"

Willem keeps his eyes locked forward and says nothing, his face an expression of outrage and fear.

They walk side by side in frigid silence for an entire block. The core of the colony is already behind them; houses are wider and front yards larger, most with sizable vegetable gardens covered in plastic. There are fewer people now, most returning home for a late lunch.

As they are about to cross the street, Ximena catches a bulky movement out of the corner of her eye. Marjolein has seen it as well and shouts a curt warning as she holds Willem back with both hands. An old bicycle—one of those heavy ones with a wooden front loader—rushes by, tilts violently as the rider tries to avoid the baffled Willem, and falls on its side in the middle of the street. The rider screams with pain as his body bounces off the surface.

Ximena squints at the fallen rider, a teen in plain work pants and stained winter tunic, and her eyes widen in recognition: Janson Ledeboer, the image of him diving headfirst through the arena hole still vividly fresh in her memory.

"Oh, Elder Ledeboer." Marjolein runs to the street and helps him to his feet. "Did you break something?"

He shakes his head slowly, eyes confused. There is pain in them too, but not pain of the physical type. Janson is a large, muscular, fourteen-year-old man, for whom a bike fall is a shock to the ego, not to the hips. But his green eyes are reddened, and his brown hair falls flat and out of place —out of care—half covering his broad face, half his right ear.

"I'm out, I'm out, I'm out," he mutters, and looks at nobody in particular. "Lost. Gone. Forever."

"Your soul aches, Elder Ledeboer," Marjolein pulls him gently over to the sidewalk and wipes dirt off his tunic, "and Goah has sent you straight into my path. You are coming with me to aws Eye, and you will speak your afflictions to your Quaestor."

Willem raises the bulky bicycle straight in the meantime and tries to put it into Janson's trembling hands, but he doesn't react.

"Will, please secure Elder Ledeboer's loader." Marjolein speaks with a different tone. She is not the lover now. She is the Quaestor of Lunteren, and her word is to be heeded. "I will send for it."

"Uh, of course." He stands still, hands on the bicycle, and looks sheepishly at Marjolein as she puts a hand on Janson's shoulder and begins to lead him away.

She turns her face while walking. "Will, please talk to Edda. Convince her to be more discreet, and mature. Consider this a friendly last warning."

"Yes," he mutters. "Thank you."

"Oh, and about extending your stay on this plane," she stops walking, and looks back at him, "you know where to find me if you change your mind. For you, Will, I'm always open for business."

TWENTY

A Mirage of the Mind

The dream forest rematerializes in perfect fidelity around an irritated-looking Edda. The same leafless birch trees surround her, slightly separated from the space where a magnificent white marble column stands alone. Even Rew is still there, staring at her with her blank eyes while standing in the same bramble bush as before, thorns be dammed.

"You can see now, Redeemed van Dolah, how much you still must Walk to reach the end of the Path of Light. You are far from ready to resist dream violence."

"Violence…" She shakes her head and puts a hand over her chest, while shooting an indignant glare at Rew, "Goah's Mercy, that hurt!"

"Piercing flesh, even dream flesh, does indeed signal due pain to the nervous system. And yet, you must learn how to stand firm against violence directed at you, and also how to use violence to impose your will over others."

"You mean, I have to, what… *fight?*"

"*Fight.*" Rew seems to relish the word. "A generic, yet

accurate denomination of the set of actions required to achieve mastery over violence."

Edda blinks slowly, and then draws a heavy sigh as she shakes her head. Ximena feels her unhappiness. Physical violence, even in dreams, is so… *uncivilized* and *dirty*. Edda is not hesitant though, nor afraid. She will of course do whatever needs to be done—*anything* to reclaim the power to *persuade*. "All right," she says. "I'm ready for the lesson."

"Very good, Redeemed van Dolah. There are two principles, two core concepts of the Third Step that you must grasp deeply if you intend to impose your will over others."

"I do." Her eyes beam. "I *really* do."

"Only a mind disciplined enough to master both concepts can hope to prevail in the conflict of wills. You do have a disciplined mind, Redeemed van Dolah."

"Yes, I do." She smiles expectantly.

"Now you shall apply your discipline to internalize the two *truths* of permascape violence until they are as ingrained in your being as breathing. Do focus on my words now, Redeemed van Dolah, and interiorize them."

"Shoot, mensa!" Ximena can now feel through the psych-link what it means to be a teacher that has mastered not only the art of teaching to others but also the art of *learning* from others. Ximena can feel how Edda's mind settles into a quiet state of hungry attention, ready for absorption; ready to *feed*.

"Truth number one, success in permascape violence is all about *pain*. A true master of violence maximizes both the capacity to inflict pain to others as well as the capacity to sustain pain from others." As she speaks these words, Rew begins to float out of the bramble thorns and towards Edda.

Edda takes a small step back, but then shakes off the sliver of fear and raises her chin.

Rew stops right in front of Edda, and the alien head tilts down until her two white unmoving eyes meet Edda's. "Do give pain, do take pain; and so shall you impose your will."

"Sounds..." Edda swallows thick, dream saliva, "*painful.*"

"Indeed." Rew slowly, almost tenderly, raises both arms and extends them towards Edda's own arms. The appendages at the end of Rew's hands wriggle eagerly towards Edda's skin. Ximena almost recoils when contact is made. Those appendages are cold to the touch, and sticky. They close around Edda's wrist with astonishing strength.

"Ouch!"

"Indeed." Rew begins to stretch Edda's arms. Slowly. Edda tries to resist, but she feels a sudden wave of weakness, and must give in to Rew's inexorable stretching.

Rew keeps pulling Edda's arms apart, ever more, in the same slow motion, until her body forms a perfect cross.

Edda's eyes widen, her breathing quickens. "Elder Rew, what are you——?!"

Rew continues pulling farther. Ximena jumps in her seat as she feels the sudden pain in her own joints.

"Stop, stop," Edda says, eyes widening, breath quickening. "Stop!"

"I shall not, Redeemed van Dolah. I shall rip your limbs apart. And you shall take the pain without piercing the wake."

"What?!" She cries out in agony. "Stop, stop! Please!"

The screams go on as the psych-link's pain filter kicks blissfully in. *Oof, thank Goah!* Ximena keeps feeling Edda's pain inside her own shoulders, but now just as a subdued, warm pressure. Mock pain. The real pain must be... hard to bear, to put it mildly. And indeed, growing waves of wakening ripple across the dreamscape, ever deeper, ever wider.

"Do not fear, Redeemed van Dolah. Until you do learn the discipline of pain, I shall stabilize the dreamscape for you." The waves begin to subdue with Rew's words, until it quietens to a subtle turbulence, never quite going away. "Now you shall not pierce the wake," Rew says. "I shall not allow any undue interruption to your mastering of pain. You are welcome."

Edda keeps screaming and begins cursing. Ximena blushes at the words. It seems civility is one of the first victims of agony. Mark and others are laughing loudly at Edda's colorful expressions. It is a strange, unsettling sound combination: laughs of amusement and cries of torment. Ximena feels sick to her stomach.

"Do ground yourself in the pain, Redeemed van Dolah," Rew says. "Do embrace it and follow it to its true source. Do feel how your dream body slowly tears; do listen to it, accept it into you."

Edda's screaming continues unabatedly, her body twirling from both arms stretched beyond their natural span. Ximena doubts she can even hear Rew's instructions over the excruciating agony. Edda's thoughts swirl like her mind is short circuiting, like she is going mad.

"Something is not right, Redeemed van Dolah. Your heartbeat has quickened beyond the healthy in a human. Do absorb your pain into your mind, away from your body, before it does break."

Edda's cries are guttural, primitive; spit and snot mix down her chin; her eyes wander without seeing. Ximena hears inside her the slow rip of tissue and a sudden soft pop. *Goah's Mercy!* Edda cannot wake, nor become unconscious. She can only sustain pain in full awareness. And her heart…

"Redeemed van Dolah, you are at risk of termination. Do heed my advice."

Ximena puts a hand on her chest, as she feels her heartbeat racing to the edge of cardiac arrest. But the slow, rhythmic beating under her fingers makes her realize that it's just the psych-link's mock, disturbing sense of Edda's inners. Ximena watches Edda's dislocated expression with increasing alarm. *Goah, it's killing her!*

"I do fear that I might have overestimated the human capacity to sustain pain," Rew says. "Thus, I am releasing control now."

In an instant the dream shatters in a thousand pieces, and Edda wakes in her bedroom, pillow wet, weeping in horror.

"You did require a considerable time to dive, Redeemed van Dolah." Rew is standing next to the white column embedded in Edda's dream forest.

"Well, I'm sorry if I made you wait, Elder Rew." Edda walks towards Rew and points a furious finger at her face. "I guess your live-dismembering was too distracting, yeah? Silly me."

"Do not despair, Redeemed van Dolah. We shall practice until you fully master your pain control."

Edda takes a step back. "Are you nuts?!" Her eyes have widened in, yes, fear. Fear of agony. "You almost killed me and now you want to do it again?"

"Indeed."

"B- But what does this have to do with *persuasion*,

Goah's Mercy? Or even *suggestion*? I don't need all this... *fighter* stuff, yeah? Make love and not war, yeah?"

"What you say is indeed correct, and yet a Walker must master dream violence to complete the Path of Light. It is the way of the marai. It is what has always been, and the ancestral Path is not to be distorted."

"I don't care about your goahdamn Path. Just teach me what I need to get my way, and I promise I will be a good soldier of your oh so grand plan to save humanity."

"That is not possible, Redeemed van Dolah. I am to certify to Overseer Yog either your complete dominion over the Path of Light, or your failure. My Deviss Walkers are equally obliged to do likewise with their assigned human apprentices."

"Come on, Elder Rew. All this..." she makes a grimace of pain while waving a hand indistinctively, "*torture* is so unnecessary. Why don't you just tell everybody that I learned to fight, and we call it a day?"

"Alas, I do not lie, Redeemed van Dolah. I cannot lie, in fact. We marai cannot disguise facts, nor distort reason in that marvelous way you humans can. You must face the fact that the last trial is only to be attempted by Light-Walkers. And the fact remains that only a true Walker of the Light can tread the Path in the Shadow. It is the way of the marai. You must cross the Path of Light, Redeemed van Dolah, to reach the Shadow."

"There must be something you can do, Goah's Mercy! Are the others also training like this?!"

"How your fellow human candidates are being instructed is not your concern, nor mine."

"But..." pearls of dream sweat are forming on her brow, "... I don't think I can take that... *horror* again. I just can't."

"If that is your assessment, then I have indeed

overestimated your skill. A regretful waste of my time. I bid you farewell, Redeemed van—"

"Wait!" Edda draws a deep breath, and then looks up into Rew's blank eyes with pleading intensity. "At least tell me how I can resist the pain, yeah? I don't think anybody can. At least no human."

"That is where your mental discipline comes into play, Redeemed van Dolah. And the *second* truth of permascape violence."

"The second... Yeah, right. The first truth was that stuff about inflicting and resisting pain to kick dream asses, yeah?"

"Indeed."

"I don't think inflicting pain is the problem. I can use," she gestures at the white column and with a snap of her fingers the column shatters explosively, and scatters a myriad of marble shards across the forested floor, "willpower."

"Indeed. You are powerful in the Third Step. It is the *resistance* to pain that appears more problematic."

Edda presses her lips together. "Understatement of the century."

"That is where the second truth of permascape violence may assist you, Redeemed van Dolah. If you do interiorize it."

"Really?" Her eyes widen with hope. "Tell me."

"It is a simple but deep truth. There is no physical pain in dreams, only mental. Pain in dreams is but a mirage of the mind. With enough discipline your mind can instinctively feel the difference and thus react differently. So can you avoid the natural stress that physical trauma entices."

Edda stares to the distance and says nothing for a while.

A mirage of the mind.

Edda keeps gnawing on the concept, letting it seep slowly into herself, feeding on it. *Pain is fake. Pain is your mind fooling yourself.* "All right," she finally says. "What can I do to get more discipline?"

"There is only one way, Redeemed van Dolah: practice."

Practice. Ximena can feel gooseflesh crawling all over Edda's skin. Memories of excruciating pain flash with sharp intensity across her mind, triggering a primitive instinct to flee. But, of course, if pain is a mock mental construct—a mirage of the mind—then the terror that is now taking hold of her is an irrational construct, a relic of the most primitive layers of her brain, an enemy to subjugate. Her rational mind recognizes its seductive delusion. The apparent safety of her mundane life is another mirage. If she gives in to her animal fears, her father will be soon gone forever, and that is the simple truth: that there is no true safety without power.

Edda shuts her eyes and presses her lips. "What are we waiting for?" she finally says, head sunk, and stretches both arms to the side.

———

"Do attack, Redeemed van Dolah."

Edda is following Rew through the forest, running as if hunting a rabbit, jumping over bushes and rotten leaves. Rew keeps her distance floating a few yards in front of her, staring directly at Edda and yet sweeping backwards between trees without apparent exertion.

"Are you sure it's safe?" she asks between pants, her eyes fixed on Rew's slim body.

"You are no threat to me. Do attack to the best of your abilities."

Edda raises a hand towards Rew, and a revolver materializes in place, aimed straight to Rew's head, ready to be triggered. She shoots.

Before reaching its target, the bullet dissolves in the air as if it were made of salt.

"Pure sin!" Edda stops and falls to her knees.

Rew floats slowly towards her. "The *canceling of wills*," she says, and points an appendage at a nearby rock. "Do raise that stone in the air, Redeemed van Dolah."

Edda stands. She looks tired. She *is* tired, Ximena feels; mentally exhausted. Edda gives the rock a casual look and points a finger at it.

Nothing happens.

"Pure sin! Not even the simplest dream magic works now. What's going on?!"

"*I* am going on," Rew says, and makes an awkward gesture at the rock. "You *want* that rock to raise. I *want* it not to. Thus, my will cancels yours."

"Right, so you are stronger than me, and what you want, happens, yeah?"

"Wrong, Redeemed van Dolah. That is neither the point, nor the nature of the *canceling of wills*. Willpower is not analogous to physical power in the wake, where strong overcomes weak. In the dreamscape weak *voids* strong."

"What?" Edda frowns at the mare in confusion.

"A demonstration might be more effective to convey the meaning. Do use your will to keep that rock perfectly still. Do not allow it to be tampered with."

Edda shrugs. "Sure," she says, and stares at the rock with focused attention.

"Behold, I am raising the rock now."

"But it's not moving…" Ximena feels Edda's

confusion. She doesn't even feel a tug of resistance to her desire to keep the rock in place.

"Your will is weaker than mine, Redeemed van Dolah, and yet it cancels my desire. You are not resisting my moving the rock; that would be the logic of the wake, but in the dreamscape what you are doing is *removing* the effect of my will altogether from the dream's natural narrative."

"I cancel you…"

"Indeed."

"But you are stronger than me."

"Once again you are falling into the trap of reasoning as if this were the wake. You are dreaming, Redeemed van Dolah, and here your will voids mine, and mine yours."

"Whoa," her lips curve into a sidelong smile, "so the weak can stop the strong, yeah?"

"Indeed. And the strong, the weak."

Edda gives Rew an inquisitive look. "Is that what happened with my bullet?"

"Indeed. As your projectile approached my location, where my will dominates the dreamscape, it was voided."

"So then," she spreads her hands, "it's impossible to fight."

"On the contrary, Redeemed van Dolah. Although it is indeed impossible to directly apply your will against your opponent's, it is possible to apply it *indirectly*, by using the own narrative of the dreamscape to exert pain. I shall demonstrate. Do take a stone in your hands and throw it at me."

"A stone, a stone," she scans the ground between the weeds, finds a fist-sized granite stone and tosses it gently towards Rew.

The stone bounces off Rew's head. "Ouch," she says in her usual smooth intonation.

"Oh, sorry, Elder Rew. But you didn't stop it."

"I could not have, not even with my considerable skills as Walker of the Mind, Redeemed van Dolah. A stone, and the effects that gravity exerts upon it, are concepts both our minds are intimately familiar with, since our very existence began. The world of the wake and its laws of nature are ingrained in the narrative and the nature of all dreamscapes. When a flying stone reaches my area of control, it is not *your* will that is driving it, but the dreamscape's own narrative, *shared* by both our minds. It cannot be voided."

"Oh, wow. So guns won't work, but stones no problem? Wait a minute." Edda frowns and tilts her head. "There's not much difference between a bullet and a stone. I mean, in essence they're the same thing: an object flying through the air, yeah?"

"Your projectile was produced and then propelled by devices that are outside of my experience. And outside of most humans', including yours, unless you are a weapon master. Bullets are technology."

"So you're saying that technology won't work in dreams?"

"Technology does work in the dreamscape, Redeemed van Dolah; only not in a conflict of wills. Technology is not ingrained in our selves like the laws of nature are, and are thus easily voided."

Edda nods and shrugs. "So sticks and stones it is." She laughs as her imagination conjures two angry broom-wielding cowboys facing each other with murder in their eyes. "Not very romantic, huh?"

"There is no romance in dream violence, Redeemed van Dolah. But there is access to power."

"Good enough for me. Teach me how to fight with sticks and stones, Elder Rew."

TWENTY-ONE

Sticks and Stones

"Ouch," Rew says in her usual emotionless tone.

"Oh, Goah. I'm so sorry!" Edda says, dropping a primitive-looking bow and running towards Rew. "Are you okay?" She squints with concern at the arrow embedded in Rew's brow, and then leans to look at the back of Rew's skull, where the emerging tip drops a transparent fluid. "Does it hurt?"

"It does, Redeemed van Dolah. Considerably," Rew says, as she grabs the end of the arrow and pulls it out in its entirety. The wound closes in a few seconds. "Fortunately, pain is but a mirage—"

"Of the mind," a third voice, female as well, reverberates from behind them. A single mare approaches their location from the edge of the dream forest clearing where Edda and Rew have been training.

"Sense and bind, Overseer Yog," Rew says. "I do take it I am due for inspection?"

"Indeed, Walker Rew. I am particularly keen to gauge the progress that your personal instruction has imprinted in your human."

A scowl wrinkles Edda's face. *I'm nobody's human.*

"We were focusing our attention on the minutia of the conflict of wills," Rew says.

"And how is your human coping?" Yog says and steps closer to Edda. Yog has entered the dream with only one of her three bodies. The rest are probably inspecting elsewhere, Ximena guesses. Having many bodies seems very efficient.

"The human's talent to control the dreamscape with her will has been remarkably easy to unlock. And her discipline is at par with some of my own marai apprentices. I can already certify her abilities as a Walker in the Path, Overseer Yog." Ximena can almost picture *pride* in those empty alien eyes.

"Did I pass?" Edda says, her scowl flushed away in an instant by a radiant smile. "Am I really a Walker?"

"Your work has been fruitful, Redeemed van Dolah," Rew says, again that pride almost leaking out of her alien eyes. "I do congratulate you on your passage across the Path of Light."

"Yeah!" She jumps and pumps a fist in the air. "What's next, huh? The final trial? I can sure as Dem take it. Bring it on, baby!"

"So it is possible, after all," Yog says, still inspecting Edda. "A human Walker of the Light."

"The first human Walker of the Path of Light," Rew says. "The first of many, I do hope."

Yog turns towards Rew. "We shall soon see how many, since some are already failing."

"Which humans have failed?" Rew asks.

"There is this one you took a keen interest in. The one with the strong traverse halo."

"Woman Speese," Rew says. "That is... most unfortunate."

"Aline?" Edda trots towards Yog, her feet crunching small twigs and pine needles that cover the forested ground. "What happened to her?"

"Walker Qoh did report inability to resist the rigors of the conflict of wills," Yog says.

"Oh, poor thing," Edda sighs, "Poor, poor Aline. I guess it was too much. It almost got me too."

"That is most unfortunate," Rew repeats. Ximena leans forward and squints at her white, elongated body. Is it shaking or is it the effect of the wind on the naked branches nearby? "I do believe it is a grave mistake to disqualify Woman Speese, Overseer Yog. Her potential is way beyond the reach of all other human candidates. Even beyond Redeemed van Dolah's. Alas, her Walking potential can only be awakened in the Shadow. Thus, I do hereby officially request her reincorporation. I shall then take personal responsibility over her instruction."

"Once again you do request a failed human back into the reseeding effort. First, it was Junior Elder Ledeboer. Now it is Woman Speese. And yet, at the end, only *two* humans shall be allowed to tread the Path in the Shadow, Walker Rew, and it is our duty to guarantee that only the two most worthy are selected. Alas, Woman Speese lacks worth."

"She did indeed fail the conflict of wills, Overseer Yog. And yet you must admit that our human Walkers shall not encounter dream violence as they pursue our objectives."

"That's what I said!" Edda says, spreading her arms. "All this fighting, Elder Rew. I almost went crazy! And for what? It was all a pile of horseshit, and a waste of time."

"I am intrigued," Yog says, staring at Edda. "A human trained to fight back. It is a stimulating thought." She turns towards Rew. "I do wish to *taste* the abilities of your human firsthand, Walker Rew, if you do permit."

"What?!" Edda takes a step back.

"I do not permit, Overseer Yog," Rew says. "Redeemed van Dolah is already a duly certified Walker of the Light, she does not need to be reassessed."

"Do grant me access to your apprentice, Walker Rew, and allow me to confirm your appraisal. It is, after all, in our interest to guarantee that only the most capable humans do access the last trial."

"I do not, Overseer Yog. Redeemed van Dolah has already proved herself adequately. There is no profit in risking her already gained success in a senseless confrontation."

Yeah, bitch! Edda thinks, silently alternating glances between both mares.

"Furthermore," Rew continues, "Redeemed van Dolah is still quite inexperienced and has considerable trouble controlling her strength."

"Are you asserting," Yog extends a long, boneless arm towards Edda, "that this human could best me in a conflict of wills?"

"Not at all, Overseer Yog. What I am saying is that Redeemed van Dolah's lack of experience makes her unpredictable—and dangerous."

"A human? *Dangerous?*"

"Not any human, Overseer Yog. *This* human."

"You are stimulating my intrigue to a degree that I have not felt for a long while, Walker Rew. I shall most definitely fight your human now. You shall yield to my authority."

"I shall not. Unless you do yield to my former appeal regarding Woman Speese."

"What?!" Edda gapes at Rew.

Yog watches Edda in silence for a long while.

Considering.

Ximena feels Edda's discomfort at the gaze, so eager, like a spider's on a passing fly.

"You do bring Woman Speese back into the reseeding effort," Rew says, "and I shall yield my instructor privileges to your authority."

"No, Elder Rew! I *made* it already, yeah? I don't want to—"

"I do accept your terms, Walker Rew," Yog says, her voice drowning Edda's complaints as it reverberates across the winter forest. "Thus, you are to take personal responsibility over the instruction of Woman Speese. If she, despite your whispering, is incapable of reaching adequate proficiency in the conflict of wills, she shall be confirmed unworthy."

"I do accept your terms, Overseer Yog."

"Pure sin!" Edda says. "I won't risk my—" a tenuous image of Willem holding Hans on his knees flashes through to Ximena, "*interests* like that! In what, a fucking *fight*?! Against a fucking marai ninja? No fucking way, alien. Not even for Aline. What if I lose?"

"You shall surely lose, Redeemed van Dolah," Rew says, floating over the undergrowth towards Edda. "But if you do resist Overseer Yog's violence long enough, if you do not allow yourself to pierce the wake too early, not only shall you confirm your status as Walker of the Light, but equally important, Woman Speese shall as well."

"No, Elder Rew. I won't fight. Too risky—*way* too risky. Ah, I know!" Edda turns towards Yog, face lit up with sudden excitement. "I'll do it. I'll fight you all right and you can kick my ass all you want. But whatever happens, I want my place in the trial. Agree? No more tests—no more nonsense."

"Alas, that is not possible, human," Yog says. "I am not to intervene in the instruction except as instructor."

"Well, okay, sure. We'll keep it between us."

Yog turns her gaze at Rew, and back. Ximena gets the distinct impression that the mare doesn't know how to react.

"What?" Edda asks, looking first at Yog, then at Rew. "Nobody'll be the wiser, will they?"

Rew speaks to Yog. "The moral flexibility of the human mind counts among the peak achievements of Earth's evolution. Its ramifications throughout their history and ecosystem are of truly epic proportions. Alas, the concept is too complex to grasp by laymen. If you do excuse me, Overseer Yog, instead of trying, I shall just explain to Redeemed van Dolah that her idea is with no merit."

Rew turns to Edda, who is already frowning.

"Your idea is with no merit, Redeemed van Dolah. We marai cannot lie. Not even to ourselves in the past, nor in the future. When we commit to do something, we do it. When we assume a responsibility, we embrace its consequences."

Edda shakes her head in disbelief. "And you're supposed to be oh so advanced? How in Goah's Name did you make it so far? An ever-changing world requires... *flexibility*, doesn't it? What happens when circumstances change? How do you mensas adapt?"

"We do adapt, Redeemed van Dolah. Without compromising the truth. Now, you shall allow the reassessment of your capabilities by Overseer Yog in a conflict of wills."

"No." She folds her arms and purses her lips. "You can't make me."

"You shall," Rew says. "It is imperative that Woman Speese reaches the last trial. We do need her. *You* do need her more than anybody else. Your interests are intertwined."

"Why?! I love her to bits, Elder Rew, but she's… too distracted with nonsense. All that environment-saving and pollution-fighting—always in her head. And then there's Piet, her lover—always in her crotch. There's just no space in her life for things that truly matter."

"You are being unfair and selfish, Redeemed van Dolah."

Edda blushes. *Touché*, Ximena thinks.

Rew continues, "You are no fool that falls into the traps of self-deception. So do trust this one truth: you shall depend on Woman Speese's abilities to pursue your goals to the end. It is in your nature, Redeemed van Dolah, to be weak alone, weaker than you think; yet strong with allies, stronger than you think."

Edda stares at her in sulky silence, lips pressed in a thin line.

"Should you not comply with my request, I shall hereby drop my support as your instructor, Redeemed van Dolah. You shall cope on your own in the last trial."

"Whoa, okay, okay!" Edda lifts a shaking hand. "Fine, I'll do it. No need to crack the whip!"

She turns slowly towards Yog, draws a deep breath and puts her mind to banishing her fear. What is the point of fear in dreams, anyway? Ximena feels how her anger begins to take over. Why did this alien have to show up and mess her chances up so badly? It's so unfair, so… *arbitrary;* like the marai has something personal against her. But that can't be right. These aliens act more like robots than like people, and Edda has done nothing to her. And yet, the feeling keeps creeping inside her that the dislike is mutual.

Edda glares into Yog's white, soulless eyes. "I'll fight

you, Elder Yog. You might kick my ass, but I sure as Dem will enjoy getting a good bite on yours."

"You shall begin your attack," Yog says, spreading her arms and legs in what appears to Ximena like a mock Da Vinci's Vitruvian Man.

Edda glances at Rew, as if asking for instructions, but Rew remains stoically silent.

Edda sighs. "All right, let's do this." She picks up the bow that was lying on the weeds of grass and ferns that cover most of the forest clearing. An arrow, a simple, sharp stick with gray feathers, materializes in her right hand. She takes aim while drawing a deep breath, gives Rew a last, hesitant glimpse, and shoots.

Yog moves swiftly to the side. The arrow is going to miss.

Pure sin! Edda instinctively *pushes* the arrow with her will. Gently. Just a tad. Yes! Now it's aiming true, straight for Yog's middle body.

Yog appears to move her arms in a protective reflex over her abdomen, but as the arrow closes in, it dissolves in midair. *Canceled.*

Pure sin! Edda produces another arrow in her hand and tries to aim anew. Ximena realizes that it was a mistake to divert the arrow with will-control. That denaturalized it, removed it from the dream's natural narrative, making it easy prey to will-canceling.

Yog's arms and legs flatten at once into what looks to Ximena like elongated fins. She gapes at such sudden display of plasticity. *Can mares do that? Maybe they're also originally underwater creatures, like their masters.*

With one powerful thrust of her four new fins, like a squid underwater, Yog disappears behind the wide trunk of an oak.

Before Edda has time to change her aim, Yog pushes herself anew behind another tree.

Goah, she's getting closer! Ximena feels Edda's anxiety rising as she once again tries to adjust her bow.

Yog then pushes herself into plain sight, even closer, and locks her blank eyes on Edda's.

The fucking alien's too close to shoot. Edda drops the bow. *I need something for close contact.* Ximena hears Edda's hasty thinking as flashes of wargaming miniatures cross her mind. *A melee weapon. Something simple and primitive that can survive will-canceling.*

Yog slashes her four limps in one vigorous push that thrusts her body swiftly towards Edda in a final charge down a fern-covered slope.

A charge. What's good against a charge?

A pike—a long wooden spear tipped in sharp iron—materializes in Edda's hands. The ideal weapon against a medieval cavalry charge. But Edda is not a pikeman. *Oh Goah, it's heavy!* Edda's anxiety turns to panic as she fails to move the unwieldy pike with nothing but her own dream muscles.

Yog sweeps easily past the pike tip and throws her four limbs at Edda like a hungry octopus at a crab.

Edda yelps, drops the pike and leaps sideways behind the trunk of a large oak in a last desperate attempt to flee.

But it is too late.

Yog's four appendages clamp Edda's arms and legs in four unshakable grips. The sudden contact and Yog's forward momentum push her body off balance.

Edda falls on her back, shrieking. Yog doesn't let go, her four extremities firmly attached to Edda's, the stance of a spider, the eagerness of a leech. Her alien face is but mere inches from Edda's. Those eyes, white and empty, lock on hers without a hint of emotion.

And then Yog opens her black mouth.

Terror strikes almost instantly. First as a sudden gnaw at the edge of Edda's consciousness, but quickly crawling up her spine and drowning her innards in ice and dread. She cannot take her eyes off that mouth. So hungry. It's black folds twitching and contracting with the urge of the feed.

Edda wails without control. Her mind is sinking in the quicksand of dread.

Ximena leans forward with morbid fascination to look at the moist blackness of the alien maw. There are things there, sharp things inside—things that yearn—and plead. Reminds her of a mosquito gobbling not blood, but *soul*. Goah's Mercy, the nightmare.

Edda's awareness wavers, shocked to its foundations by that bubbling drainage of reason. Waves with the sweet promise of the wake deform the texture of the dreamscape as the nightmare reaches its climax. She is slipping away, her mind all but lost, there is nothing left to grip herself onto.

"Ground yourself, Redeemed van Dolah." Rew's voice splashes on Edda's vanishing mind like water on mud. "Recall your discipline."

Discipline. Edda's mind whirls around the word. *Discipline.*

"Fear engulfs you," Rew says. "Do recognize its texture, its slippery quality."

Fear. Edda gasps. *Discipline.*

"Do seek its inner truth, Redeemed van Dolah. Pain is a mirage of the mind. Reach for the truth beneath fear. Embrace that truth. Without truth, there is no reality. Without reality, there is pain—and extinction."

Truth. Discipline. Edda gasps as a thought strikes her mind with clarifying brutality. *What is the true purpose of fear in the dreamscape where nothing can truly hurt you?* Edda chuckles at the sudden realization. It is not only pain that is a mirage, is it? *Fear* is as well! Ximena feels Edda's mind centering on that thought. A fucking mirage. Yes. A relic of her lizard mind.

And it can be squashed like a spider.

Edda's discipline kicks in with unconscious ferocity. Her training snaps back in place, in the high layers of her mind, draining all lower emotions away in an instant flush of lucidity. Well, not all lower emotions. She keeps her anger, burning thickly under her skin, as she moves her eyes away from Yog's suffocating proximity and scans the surrounding forest with all her senses: the great oak next to her, rising solid and tall; beyond its thick roots, the fallen pike, and a thick carpet of ferns and grasses spreading uphill to a line of birches; spotless blue skies shine over the naked canopy of the winter forest.

"You have vanquished your fear, human servant," Yog's voice reverberates so close to her it threatens to drown her thoughts. "Remarkable. I can see Walker Rew's imprint in your instruction. But how long can a human resist pain? Even dream pain?"

Yog opens her mouth further. Ximena, and not few of her fellow students across the amphitheater, gasp at the sight of Yog's black, wet jaws, where rows of razor-sharp teeth shake in spasms of raw desire. Edda seems to ignore the horrid vision, Ximena observes with admiration, even though a mere inch separates her tender brown flesh from that horror.

But Edda is elsewhere now, Ximena realizes. Her thoughts have changed. They are clear now, almost as sharp as those black teeth. Fear is thankfully vanished. Now she is planning, like this were yet another wargame where she needs to muster her pieces before throwing them into battle.

Yog buries her jaws in Edda's throat, and rips a piece of flesh off with such savage violence that were this the wake, she would have been instantly killed.

Edda utters a cry of piercing agony. But she skillfully hammers it away with the heavy blow of trained discipline, transforming it into naked rage before it even has a chance to fog her thoughts.

Muster her pieces.

Edda eyes the blue sky, shuts her eyes, and when she reopens them an instant later, a heavy overcast of dark clouds hang menacingly over the naked winter branches. They cast a dark, oppressive shadow over the forest, and gusts of stormy wind shake the foliage with brutal fury.

Yog, still chewing Edda's meat, raises her head at the sudden change, but keeps munching the bloody meat in slow, focused delight. Oh, how Edda hates the arrogant bitch! Ximena feels her own blood boiling.

Edda eyes the pike lying harmlessly nearby, and her will raises it over the ground, where it floats hesitantly as it begins to rotate, and to aim. Then, Edda's will unleashes it forward like a whip, driving its iron tip deep into the oak's bark.

"You did miss, human," Yog says. She is not so distracted as it seems, Ximena thinks. "And had you not, the canceling of wills should have—"

It happens so fast—just two glances—that Yog doesn't have time to react. Edda's first look goes towards the pike that sticks out of the damaged oak next to her. The pike's wood turns into solid iron.

Throw them into battle.

Edda directs her second look at the sky, which shatters

into a sudden spark of lightning that hits the iron pike in an instant, cracking the oak open in a deafening explosion.

The wind does the rest, blowing the enormous trunk forward, tipping it towards Edda and Yog, casting a growing shadow over them. Until it falls hard over their legs, trapping them both with agonizing certitude.

Yog seems shocked by the sudden turn of events, as she initially doesn't react.

Edda scans the fallen trunk and grabs a long, thin branch sticking out at the end of her reach. She tears it out, splits it in two, and keeps the half with the sharpest end.

As Edda removes the last rests of foliage from the stick with her bare hands, the heavy trunk lifts off the ground, and accelerates upwards.

It's Yog! Ximena realizes. She's using her will to escape!

But Edda reacts almost instantly, applying her own will across the trunk like a balm on a wound. The canceling of wills destroys Yog's hold on the trunk, which falls down precipitously for the second time.

Both Yog and Edda remain next to each other, firmly trapped under the insufferable weight. Edda is gaping in silence and sheer agony, trying to gather the last threads of discipline. Ximena wonders what is passing through Yog's mind as the alien turns her white eyes towards Edda. It must be as painful to Yog as it is to Edda, Ximena thinks, and the hatred that they share against the arrogant mare is so intense that Ximena finds the thought disturbingly sweet.

"You act like a fucking vampire," Edda says between heavy breaths, as she leans over the alien with her upper body, "you end like a fucking vampire." She drives the stick —or stake, for that is what it is now—deep into Yog's chest, and stares wide-eyed at the wound, panting, as transparent fluids begin to spurt out.

"Redeemed van Dolah," Rew says, "this exercise has concluded. Do stand down and drop your will."

Edda cannot hear her—does not want to. Hatred pumps in her ears like it has a voice of its own. She takes the stake out and readies herself to stab anew.

"Redeemed van Dolah!" Rew's voice sounds demanding, filled with abnormal intensity. Even emotion. Ximena has never heard that before, not from Rew, not from any other mare. "Stand down this instant!"

A memory of the fight as it began flashes through Edda's mind. Goah's Mercy, it feels like it happened hours ago. Yog was standing far afield, and Edda was shooting arrows at her. The memory sharpens around Yog's arms. They moved then—didn't they?—covering her abdomen in an instinctive rush. It was just a reflex, yes, but reflexes carry the logic of physiology.

"Taste wood, bitch!" She puts her weight on the stake and thrusts it rabidly into Yog's abdomen.

"Redeemed—!" Before Rew can complete the call, Yog disappears, leaving behind nothing but the wooden stake laying in a puddle of transparent gore on the grass.

Edda laughs loudly, almost maniacally. She jumps to her feet, sending the enormous trunk tumbling in the air. The pain in her legs disappears. Oh, the relief! Even fury flees her now.

She turns to Rew, eyes beaming. "Can you believe it, Elder Rew? I won!"

"I do fear that your win over Overseer Yog shall be detrimental to your chances of reaching the Path in the Shadow, Redeemed van Dolah."

"What?" Edda frowns. "Why?!"

"I do fear that Overseer Yog might not take kindly to what you have done to her."

"What I did to her? I just did what you asked me to do! I fought the bitch—and won, Goah's Mercy! Fair and square. I sent her whining back to the wake, yeah?"

"I do fear you have done much more than that."

"What? Oh, did I hurt her pride?" Edda snorts and spreads her arms wide. "Aren't you mensas looking for the leanest and meanest humans to Walk the Paths?" She places her left hand on her hip and waves her right hand theatrically at herself. "This is it."

"You do fail to understand, Redeemed van Dolah. It is not Overseer Yog's pride that you have hurt."

"Yeah, no. Don't get it," she says, frowning and shaking her head. "What have I hurt?"

Rew doesn't reply immediately. And when she does, her voice reverberates slower, carefully modulated, giving Ximena the distinct impression that she is measuring every word. "We marai are not only creatures of the wake, like you humans are. We are also creatures of the mind—of the *psyche*. On one hand, we do live in the wake, and can die in the wake, just like you and the rest of your fellow Earth creatures do. But on the other hand, Redeemed van Dolah, we also do live in the dreamscape."

"What are you saying?" Edda asks. Then she gasps as it sinks in. "Did I kill her? I mean, for good?!"

"Overseer Yog still does possess two remaining limbs. It was very fortunate indeed that she is not single-limbed like I myself am. I shall try to repair the damage that you have inflicted on your prospects. But losing a limb is traumatic to an extreme a human cannot comprehend. I know from experience as once, I was two."

"Goah's fucking Mercy," Edda mutters slowly, her

thoughts still lost in the unnerving implications of what Rew is saying. *Oh, Goah has Mercy, it was… an accident! I never intended to kill the gatekeeper that can grant or deny me the power to stop Dad's Joyousday! The best chance I had, and I just…* She draws a deep breath, trying to calm her nerves. In vain. "But… Why in Goah's Name did she insist on fighting with me, if she could be killed all along? That makes no sense!"

"It does not indeed, Redeemed van Dolah. Alas, not all marai are as wise as they ought to be."

Elders

"Okay, people," Professor Miyagi says. "Moving now to the 21st of December 2399. We are about to see firsthand the *happy* family life of Willem van Dolah. Yes, his daughter Edda included." He snorts, stretches a hand theatrically to the distance and speaks with mock intensity, "Oh, how blessed he surely felt, engulfed in the delights of home and family on those his last weeks on Earth."

Ximena and her peers raise their curious heads at the scene materializing across the amphitheater: a spacious kitchen, colonial style, merging in cozy harmony with the dining area in a space meant to be lived in by the entire family.

"I am sorry to interrupt, my dear professor." Censor Smith stands with a polite smile and raises a finger at the floating scene. Ank freezes it in place by throwing a casual gesture at Bob. "Did I hear you say, this is the 21st of December?"

"Yes." Professor Miyagi's smile is equally polite.

"The evening, I suppose?"

Miyagi nods. "Right after dinner. The *Eleven Days of*

Light begin today. Yes, I know, most people now prefer to begin the Light festivities right away in big, public parties, but back then every good, pious Goahn family would spend aws Gift Eve in close quarters, reviewing the family affairs of the closing year and planning for the next."

"A heartwarming tradition that many still observe," Censor Smith says, "at least in the Goah's Imperia of the Americas. But," he clears his throat, "if I may be so blunt, this is the same night where the last *Trial of Worth and Soul* begins, is it not? That surely is more interesting for our dear students than, excuse me, Professor, a boring family meeting. Would it be too much to ask to skip a few scenes of your wonderful dreamsenso?"

Miyagi purses his lips and regards Censor Smith in silence for a brief moment. "I see where you are coming from. But this is a history seminar, and history is all about context." He points a finger at the scene floating over his head. "What we're going to watch now is context at its best."

"Context," Censor Smith repeats with a polite nod. "I appreciate historical context, my dear professor. Of course I do, but there is not really much to learn in this specific case, is there?"

"Well, you surely agree that Edda van Dolah's role is *central* to the events that culminate in the Leap-Day Reformation. Understanding her inner drive, especially on these last days, right before the Century Festival, is," he shrugs, hands spread, "*crucial* historical context."

"Indeed, it is, Professor, but our students already know all the context that there is to know about Edda van Dolah's divine drive."

Censor Smith has a point, Ximena thinks, half nodding. Everything they have seen so far about Edda has been, yes, fascinating. And the psych-link has made it so…

intimate. But at this point, Ximena feels like she already knows her as well as a sister. And she also knows—who doesn't?—what she's about to do on the world stage.

"Right," Miyagi says, sweeping a glance across the GIA benches, where many students nod and exchange murmurs of approval. "Can I nevertheless ask for your indulgence in this one instance, Censor Smith?" He turns to gesture at the silent, colorful display of Lundev students covering the other, larger, part of the amphitheater. "You see, our Lundev students are unfortunately not as... *acquainted* with Edda van Dolah's *legacy* as they ought to be."

Mark shifts his weight next to Ximena, mumbling something. Ximena tries not to laugh.

Miyagi's smile widens. "They would for sure profit from the extra context. It won't take long, I promise."

Censor Smith nods slowly, puts his hands together and says, "Of course, my dear professor. Of course. Goah forbid our dear fellow Lundev colleagues remain behind." He sits and makes a gracious wave with his right hand. "Please proceed."

Miyagi winks at Ank, and the floating kitchen comes to life through all Ximena's senses. The lingering scents of roasted fish and vegetables strike her first, followed by the warmth of the open fire in the corner. Ximena feels almost at home; it is not quite unlike her own kitchen during the *Eleven Days*. It is already dark outside the window, but not inside as the Light Days' decorations already glow and twinkle with electric predictability in multicolor display across walls and ceiling.

But the undisputed centerpiece of the room is of course the massive wooden table where the family gathers and dines together. After-dinner tea is already on the table, in delicate porcelain cups—mint, Ximena gathers from a whiff. Four candles, neatly set in a line in the center of the table, illuminate the faces of three people with soothing radiance: a man, a boy and a toddler.

"Goah's Mercy, what's taking her so long?" Bram asks, rocking the baby chair with a gentle touch, Hans placidly sleeping through his second ever aws Gift Eve.

Willem takes a sip of tea, and then, as he places the cup back on the table, he throws a patient look at the wooden door that leads to the main hall.

As if on cue, Edda pushes the door open with her elbow. She enters with a plant pot in her hands on which she keeps her eyes reverentially locked as she approaches table. It is a cactus plant. Willem stands and shuts the door while Edda slowly puts the pot down—like it were made of glass—on the unoccupied chair at the head of the table. A steaming cup of tea awaits, untouched, in front of that chair.

Willem and Edda take their usual places without a word. Bram's expression seems heavier now.

They eye each other with pursed lips, stretching the silence, until Willem finally breaks it with a deep sigh. "Let's begin."

The three sink their heads and shut their eyes.

"Bless the taker of this humble Gift," Willem says.

"Goah's Word," Edda and Bram reply with formulaic intonation.

"Bless the giver," Willem says.

"Fahey's Word," Edda and Bram say together.

They raise their heads slowly. Edda and Bram regard their father in silence, while Willem takes another calm sip from his cup.

"The year 2399 comes to an end," he says. "I think all in all it was a good year, wouldn't you agree? We successfully closed Bram's dowry bond with Isabella

Zegers, the fertilization was a success and we might soon pick up a Van Dolah baby girl from aws Womb." His voice has softened, his eyes smiling with hope.

"The baby can still be a boy," Bram says. Ximena leans forward to take a closer look at him. *I bet Willem looked just like him when he was thirteen*, Ximena thinks, *except Bram's face is broader, and his eyes have a lighter tone of brown. He's got more of the gentle intellectual look than even Willem with his round glasses.*

"If the baby goes to the Zegers," Willem says, "you both keep looking for good dowry bonds with other families until we get our girl. It is *imperative*," he points a finger at both of them, "that you get Hans a sister. As soon as possible. I suggest you approach the Speeses," Willem and Bram turn their eyes to Edda. "It's a good family, we already have close personal ties, and Aline is still unredeemed."

Willem appears to wait for a reply from Edda, but she returns his gaze in sullen silence.

"Fine, Dad," Bram finally says. "Problem is we also have a sudden shortage of," he clears his throat, "karma."

"Yes," Willem sighs, and turns his stern eyes at Edda. "That incident on the Joyousday House was… *unfortunate*. But it is what it is. There's nothing we can do about it anymore. You will just have to make do with less. Good news is, you won't be needing as much once I…" His voice wanes, and an uncomfortable silence spreads.

Bram clears his throat. "Shouldn't we then try to dowry-bind a more, hmm, wealthy family?"

"Aline not good enough for you?" Edda says, her icy voice almost a whisper.

"That's not what I meant!" Bram says. "It's just that—"

"At this point," Edda says, "it's not even likely the Speese Elders would consider dowry-bonding with us, and you are thinking of, what, the Haacks? The Sievers?" She snorts dryly. "We are stained right now. We have to wait it out."

"And who do we thank for that?" Bram says, a notch louder, eyes drilling Edda's.

"Hush!" Willem says, and gestures with his head at the sleeping Hans. "This is aws Gift's Eve. Tonight, we show respect and civility to the family."

"Sorry, Dad," Bram mutters, still glaring at Edda. "Let's just hope the baby is a girl."

"Hope for the best, prepare for the worst. Both of you keep your eyes open to how our reputation develops throughout the year. You need to be smart, yeah? Smarter than ever. Can you do that?" He looks alternatively at his kids, but his eyes linger longer on Edda's.

"I can't stand it, Dad," she says with a shrill voice. "Stop talking like you are not here anymore."

Willem and Bram exchange a long look. Then Willem sighs and Bram sinks his head.

"I will not be, girl," Willem says, his tone soft and measured.

"Coward," she says, venom in her voice.

The word hangs heavy in the kitchen, spreading slowly in the minted air.

"In the next weeks," Willem finally speaks, his voice as slow and patient as ever, "I'll be going often to the colonist's office at aws Eye. There's a lot of paperwork to complete and it would be good if one of you comes with me."

"I'll go, Dad," Bram says.

"Sure, Bram," Edda says, venom still drenching her every word. "Encourage him."

Bram slams the table in sudden outrage. "Don't even

dare open your mouth!" He stands, dragging his chair noisily back. Besides him, on the rocking chair, Hans is looking up at him with large, curious eyes. Bram points a shaking finger at her. "You've done enough, spoiled brat! Grow up!"

Edda stares up at her brother like she doesn't know him. Bram's glare is… *disturbing*, Ximena thinks, his expression… so horribly distorted. When a soft face not made for fury is gripped by it, beware being on the receiving end.

"Bram, sit," Willem says, his voice patient, soothing. "Aws Gift Eve, remember."

But Bram glowers on, cheeks inflamed, finger fixed inches away from Edda's nose. "What's next, huh? What do you want now? To invite the inquisition for dinner?"

"Oh, come on," Edda says, her voice shaking lightly. "You're so naive. The Quaestor is bluffing, yeah? All she wants is to get into Dad's pants."

"And of course, if she's not," Bram shrugs his shoulders with enraged exaggeration, "who fucking cares about the consequences, yeah?"

"Bram, stop, please," Edda says, a hint of tears welling up in her eyes. Ximena feels her shock at seeing her little brother like that. He is never mad. He is never mean. And he sure as Dem never curses. "You know as well as I do that Dem is not for real."

Bram purses his lips, eyes still glaring at Edda, but says nothing.

"Dad is going to die, goahdammit!" she says. "For no reason!"

Bram turns his face to Willem, and his expression softens immediately. He sits, eyes sunk, and begins to rock the baby chair to the visible delight of Hans.

"That is not true, Edda," Willem says, his voice a notch

louder now. "I'm meeting Goah's Embrace because it is my time to do so."

"But—!"

"Shut up!" Willem lashes out with as much fury as Bram displayed before.

Edda gapes back at him, dumbstruck.

Hans begins to cry, and Bram takes him into his arms.

"Shut up, Edda!" Willem says, his voice barely under control. "This is the last time I will speak of this with you. Now, get this into that thick skull of yours. I had a good life under Goah's Gift, like I hope the three of you are having. And now the end has come. As simple as that. Under *no* circumstances must this family leave the protection of aws Gift and aws Compacts, because outside there is only barbarism; and short, miserable lives. Now listen: I must go, a baby girl must come, and life goes on, understood? And it is your responsibility to make it a *good* life for all of you." His eyes lock alternatively on both of his children, who stare at him in stunned silence. "You are going to be Elders now. Behave as such, Goah's Mercy, and take responsibility over the family."

"Yes, Dad," Bram says, eyes on his cup.

Edda stands noisily and storms out of the kitchen.

Edda slumps into her bed and begins to sob. *Damn him!* Ximena hears her thoughts streaming unimpeded through the psych-link. *Damn him and his cold logic! It's... hopeless! Doesn't matter what I say—or do. Nah, nothing is going to convince him. Pure Sin!*

Edda takes a deep breath, trying to get a grip on her emotions, drawing discipline from her training. *Goah, it's so much easier in dreams!* But she needs to calm down and rest. It is an important night, the most important so far. The final trial is about to begin, and she needs to have a clear head and be ready.

What if Elder Yog disqualifies me? The thought crosses Edda's mind like a bullet through a brain, shattering away the modest inner peace she had gathered. Her breathing quickens. *Goah, if I'm out…* She whimpers loudly at the thought. She stands, and paces her bedroom back and forth, over and over again, eyes on the wooden floor. *Breathe,* she thinks, and she gasps. *Breathe!*

If she doesn't pass the trial… If she doesn't make the Path in the Shadow… What's left for her to do? Her father is too stubborn. Her family is crumbling, and she cannot allow the only certainty in her life to falter. *What can I do?* Ximena almost gags at the overwhelming feeling of powerlessness. *Without the powers of persuasion, without the powers of a Mind Walker, what can I do?!*

TWENTY-THREE

The Final Trial

"Happy days of light, Edda, Speese," Gotthard says, walking towards them in the dark, flat ground of the staging permascape.

"Hey, Gotthard." Edda gives him a sidelong smile. "Happy days of light."

"Did I hear right?" Gotthard gives Edda an admiring smile. "You killed one of the…?" He points at the two marai that stare squarely at Edda from a distance. "Whoa! You are really something, dowry sister! That's the big boss around here, you know?"

Edda's lips twist into a grimace. "Yeah, I know. She almost disqualified me. *Thankfully*, very few of us actually made the Third Step." She gestures at the few remaining young colonists next to them. "Plus, apparently, it's got to be an even number of mensas, so…" She shrugs.

"Happy days of light to you too, Speese."

Aline gives him a sulky nod, but says nothing.

"Sorry to hear that your rat lover didn't make the Path," he says, his tone clearly saying he is not sorry at all. Ximena can feel his amusement through the psych-link.

278

Apparently, it is tethered to him in this section. "The conflict of wills can be painful, you know? It is not for everybody."

"Do gather, human candidates," Rew calls. Luckily, Ximena thinks, because Aline seemed about to leap on Gotthard's neck and rip it into gory chunks.

The remaining candidates approach slowly and take position a few yards in front of Rew and Yog's two bodies. Rew's eight Walkers form a line behind them. For the first time since the trials began, Ximena realizes, there are more mares than humans. Almost double the number.

"Be proud, Human Walkers of the Path of Light," Rew says. "Six of you have made it to the final trial, may it be fruitful for us all."

Ximena feels Gotthard's excitement burbling inside. More than excitement. It is almost… *hope*. He has really made it to the final! The power of the Shadow Path so close—within reach. If he gets it, he could show those—

"The final trial begins now," Rew continues, "and will conclude in twenty-four days."

Twenty-four days, Ximena thinks. *A multiple of six, of course. Since this is the night of the twenty-first of December—aws Gift Eve—the trial will run until, hmm*, Ximena tries to make a mental calculation, but fails; *sometime in mid-January*.

"Do form in teams of two," Rew says. "Do it now."

Gotthard exchange a glance with Rutger, and walks towards him, of course. The remaining four young candidates were already arranged in couples. Ximena almost chuckles; there's no doubt, no discussion as to who pairs with whom.

"Very good," Rew says. "Thus, Redeemed van Dolah shall partner with Woman Speese, Redeemed Siever with Man Kraker, and Senior Elder Smook with Junior Elder Smook."

Rew turns her white eyes to Yog and regards her in silence for a few seconds, as if secretly communicating. The two bodies of Yog begin reverberating with a single female voice, her tone as pleasant as usual. "Only one team shall be deemed worthy to pass the trial. Only one team shall qualify to be led into the Path in the Shadow and serve as Walkers of the Mind."

Gotthard smiles, turns his head to meet Rutger's anxious gaze, and winks. *Nice display of confidence*, Ximena thinks. *If only Rutger knew that Gotthard is melting inside.*

Rew speaks now. "You do have twenty-four days to unequivocally prove your worth. You shall demonstrate that humans can indeed exceed the skills of marai when dealing with other humans. And you shall do so by using your gained Walker skills to plan and execute a *disruption* in your society such that humanity shall be moved a step away from its demise. The team that achieves the largest impact shall be deemed worthy to be led into the Shadow. You do have a question, Redeemed van Dolah?"

"Uh, y- yes." She looks as nervous as Gotthard feels, perhaps more. "How can we, uh, get together in dreams, and into each other's heads, and so on? We still don't—"

"Indeed. You have not been initiated yet in the melding of minds; the Second Wake is the domain of the Shadow Path, thus each candidate team shall be assigned a support Walker." Rew gestures back with one of her arms. "Walker Moih shall support the team of Elders Smook, Walker Qoh shall support the team of Redeemed Siever, and I shall personally support your team, Redeemed van Dolah."

"Ah, so you will help us, yeah?"

"Indeed. We shall do as you do request. Alas, we cannot provide the crucial ingredients you need to succeed: the human *psyche*. Only by drawing a cunning plan from the well of your human creativity and navigating the intricate relationships that govern human behavior can you hope to achieve what we marai can seldom do."

"So we need to make something happen that is, what, *disrupting* you said?"

"Indeed."

"Like what?"

"The nature of your scheme you shall decide with your partner, Redeemed van Dolah. Do choose wisely. It ought to be something that you can accomplish inside the allotted time—twenty-four days—and that showcases considerable potential to improve the sorry state of human civilization."

"Improve civilization… So, say, like people living longer—that would be a good thing, yeah?"

"That would be a good thing indeed."

"And if we all do well," Edda gestures with the hand at Gotthard and the Smooks, "who determines the winner?"

"I shall, human," Yog says, her empty eyes locked on Edda, who blinks and takes a step back.

Gotthard lets out a laugh, his hopes heightened, and shouts at Edda, "Don't think killing that alien was so smart, huh, dowry sister?"

TWENTY-FOUR

Sardines and
Tears

"Okay, people," Miyagi says, pacing the stage, hands on his back. "We all know what trial project Edda and Aline finally pursued, don't we? It surely left its mark in history." He chuckles softly and raises his head to meet the eager gaze of his students. "But I want you to see the scene where they finally commit to it. Bear with me, please. It's not long." He smiles apologetically at Censor Smith, who gives him a polite nod.

The auditorium goes dark with a gesture from Miyagi to Ank. A sight of the colony of Lunteren from the air fills the amphitheater with vivid intensity. It is a bird's eye view, sliding gently over the tiled roofs and backyards of the settlement. Ximena sees considerable movement on the streets—hats, colored robes and winter tunics going about their business. She bets it is more busy than usual these last days of the year, with the Eleven Days of Light in full swing, and the Century Festival just around the corner. She can almost imagine the frenzy—the excitement—in those tiny figures below.

The scene slides down, closer to Lunteren, to its

western district. A large square, close to the busy road that leads off to the harbor, is teeming with colonists: an open-air market at the peak of its activity. Like a placid pigeon, the amphitheater lands at the edge of the market into the smell of fresh fish and horse sweat, and the shouts of merchants and hagglers.

Two chatting teenage women—Edda and Aline—walk into the market from one of the narrow side streets. Both are wearing ankle-long winter tunics. Edda's is bright white, in stark contrast to her dark skin, and Aline's is pale blue. Both wear external belts, but Edda's is black, thick and ornate, braided from dyed leather strips. A *gomen*, Ximena recognizes: the belt of a *redeemed*. Not in much use anymore, not even in the GIA. Each of the girls carries a sleeping toddler on their backs, wrapped in flexible, warm cloths.

"Come on, I want to surprise him!" Aline smiles in anticipation.

"Chill, mensa! You'll wake up the babies."

"I don't know about Hans," Aline caresses the sleepy toddler on Edda's back without slowing her pace, "but Goah knows an earthquake can't wake Alida from a nap."

"Wait till she ends up on the ground in the middle of the Post Way from all your trotting. Take it *easy*, sister—Piet is never so early. We're bound to make the harbor before he docks."

They must slow down as they begin to cross the market, which is teeming with people, the mood frantic. The girls navigate through the crowd with practiced skill, trying to avoid the busiest stalls. The smell of fresh fish intensifies, as does the noise of commerce. Many of the haggling clients are children under ten, and wear trousers below their shorter tunics. Edda and Aline head towards the street on which occasional pedal carts loaded with even fresher fish make their way into the market.

"Hold on. Oh, the smell—too good to resist. One second, yeah?" Edda stops in front of a small cart displaying a range of fried fish of diverse color, size and texture. "Aws Blessings, Elder Reckers. Happy Days of Light. How much for the sardines?"

"Happy Days of Light to you too, Juf Edda." The man, already over twenty, thick black beard, tall black hat, bows politely.

"I'm not your Juf anymore," Edda says with a broad smile. "Just call me Redeemed van Dolah, like everybody else."

"Goah's Mercy, so formal. You'll always be my Juf, Juf Edda." He smiles with the charm of the merchant. "That's nine karma each, twelve with bread. Just came in. These sardines were still in the water a few hours ago."

"Any for you?" Edda asks Aline, who shakes her head impatiently. "Then make it one—no, *two*, please. No bread."

They exit the market on the road to the sea. The sun on their faces hangs low over the sapphire shallows that sparkle beyond the harbor. As they walk out of the colony, the outer fields of Lunteren open on both sides, stretching for miles along the coast. The fields to their left, closer to the colony, are covered with black solar panels, white wind turbines and cylindrical metal structures. Further down, on the right side of the road, a few large industrial plants grow like tumorous contraptions.

"Careful!" Edda says, mouth full of sardine, gesturing at a hasty horse and cart that approaches them head on. They stand aside as the cart trots by towards the colony. The load is crudely covered with canvas, but they can easily make out some items beneath: there are speakers, cables, microphones, even a guitar. "See?" Edda says. "The Century Festival, it is going to be big, sister! This is an opportunity we just cannot let go."

"Is that why you slept with Consul Levinsohn?"

"Hey!" Edda almost chokes. "For the last time, Goah's Mercy. It was in a dream, okay? That doesn't count as sex."

"Fact is," Aline points back at the receding cart, "*you* brought the Festival to Lunteren. Remember that day? It seems like an eternity already, but it was, like, just ten calendar days ago."

"*Wake* days, but yeah."

"Aliens had just said hello—*aliens*, Goah's Mercy! And instead of being in awe like everybody else, you go off looking for an advantage. So Edda. How in Goah's Name did you know that it would come in so handy one day?"

"I didn't. Back then it just felt like an opportunity, you know… for," she shrugs, "whatever. Media attention is always good. It creates… *chances*. And now, see?" She spreads her arms. "We happen to need a project for the trial. Something big, yeah? Something that makes a lot of noise. It's… perfect!"

Aline laughs. "Quaestor Mathus would say it was Goah's Will all along."

Edda snorts. "If that bitch knew what was coming…" She laughs and puts the second sardine in her mouth without adjusting her pace along the road.

To their right is a large factory that steadily belches black smoke high into the air.

"By the way," Aline says, her face wrinkling in disgust. "this is my family's contract now, you know?" She gestures with her thumb at the building and shakes her head. "The Sievers want yet another steel-melting wing, as if they didn't make enough karma already. With *coal*, can you believe it? The Quaestor raised the limits of aws Balance just for them. Pure sin!"

"Yeah, I guess. At least your family gets part of the karma."

"That makes me feel dirty, Edda. Thank you very much."

"I didn't mean it like that. *Sorry*, I was trying to cheer you up."

"It's like it doesn't matter what we do." Aline shakes her head in frustration. "Even after, you know," her voice has shrunk to a whisper, "our little *action* on the coal barge."

Edda chuckles. "Lunteren's most popular diving attraction."

"We risked being caught," Aline says, her expression as sour as her voice. "And for what? They just roll more karma, and…" She turns her head and gives the industrial site a glare meant to melt it away. Then she stops in her tracks, eyes wide with sudden inspiration. Her toddler—Alida—bumps blandly against her mother's back, but keeps placidly sleeping, just as advertised. "I have an idea!"

"Uh oh," Edda says, stopping next to her.

"Let's blow up the factories!"

Edda rolls her eyes and swallows her last piece of sardine.

"What?!" Aline says with a frown on her face and a hand on her hip. "It hits all the right notes! Good for society, and… Ha! Imagine the faces of the Colony Elders, not to mention the Sievers, Haacks, De Ridders, and I say let's include the Van Kley's processing plant for good measure!"

"Oh, come on, Aline. You are thinking too small. We have to shake society, remember? *Disrupt* it, Rew said. And you want to, what, repeat the coal barge fiasco?" Edda waves a hand at a point on the sea, next to the harbor.

"But… this is *way* bigger than a barge. I'm talking about destroying all the polluters in Lunteren! The whole lot: industries, plants, warehouses, we could—yes!—clean Lunteren once and for all!"

"And how do you want to do it, huh?" Edda is frowning now. "Blow everything up? Get some explosives, and *boom*?! People could get hurt, Aline. We cannot do that."

"Well, no, of course not. Blowing up was more of an expression. I mean… incapacitate, sabotage."

"Come on. The more you speak, the smaller it gets. It's like with the barge. You said it yourself, they will just pour karma over the wound and a day later everything goes back to normal."

"Not a day. A week at least. A month if we get creative. And we will!"

"Even if it's a year, sister. That's not the point. The whole idea is just… too small, too *local*. Think about it. What would we really achieve? Who would care outside of Lunteren? We would only harm our neighbors." Edda points at the rack filled with bicycles, next to the factory entrance. "Even your own family would be out of commission."

Aline purses her lips and resumes the walk in sour silence.

"Think about it, Aline," Edda says, catching up. "You're talking about a little stunt here in the world's ass. Not even our neighbors in Geldershire really give a shit about who pisses on whom in Lunteren. It's just the truth, mensa."

Aline gives Edda a glare out of the corner of her eye.

"All you care about is your dad. That is the real truth, *mensa*."

"This is not about my dad! You cannot be blind to the opportunity, Aline. In a few days, all the eyes of Germania will be set on our little backyard. When will something like that ever happen again? This could win us the trial, yeah? Truth is, if we want to win, it's got to be big. Bigger than whatever Gotthard and the Smook assholes come up with, because I'm not Elder Yog's favorite human of late."

Aline rolls her eyes. "Understatement of the century."

"Quaestor jokes aside, it's like Goah awsself keeps waving the Century Festival right in front of our nose; like Goah wants this."

Aline snorts. "Oh, so pious now. It wasn't Goah, Edda. It was you."

"Are you serious?" Edda's voice is more severe now. "Are you saying that you don't want to take advantage of the Festival taking place right here?"

"It's too risky, Edda."

"Too *risky*?!"

"Yes, Goah's Mercy! The risk is *huge*. If they catch us… Wait!"

They step aside while a pedal cart, filled with still-flopping catch, passes by towards the colony. They remain silent until the electric buzz fades behind them.

"They won't catch us, Aline," Edda says, keeping her voice calm and controlled. "But even if they did, what could they do? Throw us in jail a few days?" She scoffs. "Been there, done that. Worth the risk any day. Listen, we are not hurting anybody. It's not like your idea." Edda gestures with her thumb back at the receding factory. "Sorry, sister, but if they catch us sabotaging the livelihood of our neighbors, then we are fucked for real. And you call my plan risky?"

Aline snorts. "You are being naive. You think you can do something so big, with no consequences? They'll cleanse us for starters if they catch us."

"They can't! Aws Compacts protects us."

"They'll wipe their asses with aws Compacts and our sacred rights if they catch us, Edda. Come on, you are always the cynic; you know your history better than I do. But now you're just fooling yourself. Or worse, trying to fool me."

Edda walks in silence, the weak afternoon breeze playing with her hair and tunic. A horse cart passes by on its way to the market, loaded with shellfish on ice. Ximena eagerly sniffs the lingering fresh smell. The driver shouts a curt "Happy Days of Lights, Juf Edda!" but Edda ignores him, too lost in her thoughts.

Ximena can feel the conflict burning in her mind. Aline is right when she says the risk is real. But the goahdamn Century Festival taking place in Lunteren is so… improbable. No, *improbable* doesn't even begin to do justice to the chances of this opportunity happening naturally. Edda was not kidding when she said that it is as if Goah wanted it. And what else is there on the table, anyway? What could they do that that could have even a fraction of the impact? They are out of ideas. No, they must seize the chance, risks be dammed. You have to crack an egg to eat it, don't you?

"There is risk, sister. You are right," Edda finally says, her voice a notch graver. "But this is bigger than any of us. Imagine a world without Joyousday, Aline. We could begin something here. Something that could have unimaginable impact in the lives of millions of people one day. Ideas spread like fire when the straw dries of hope."

Aline shakes her head slowly. "Have you heard the

Quaestor's sermons recently? I can tell you, she is not in the mood for... extravagances."

"*Extravagances*? That's how you see my dad's Joyousday?"

Aline sighs. "You know I don't. It's not so simple, Edda. You know I support you—with all my heart. My mom... I tried to convince her... Our home is so empty now. You can't..." She looks down, unable to speak.

Edda places her hand on Aline's shoulder. "I'm so sorry—I really am. I loved her so much. I miss her too."

"I know."

They walk in silence. The breeze brings the salty fragrance of the sea, clearly visible now at the end of the road, the sinking sun timidly reflecting on its pale-blue surface.

"But the Quaestor..." Aline breaks the silence. "It's such a big deal now, with the Festival and all... I'm scared."

"Of course you are; you're not stupid. You don't think I'm not shitting myself too? But we must be brave—this is bigger than us. And they won't catch us. Impossible. And if they *do*, I'd assume responsibility. I swear to Goah, you know it's true."

"And how are you going to convince them that *you*, a schoolteacher, knew how to build such a machine? From books?"

"Well... Of course!"

"I'm sorry, Edda, but this is *too* risky." She turns to meet her gaze. "No goahdamn Path in the Shadow is worth losing you as well—I'm sorry."

Edda gives her friend a long, cool glare. "So, I'm supposed to take that shit? I'm supposed to say, 'Fuck it, too dangerous?' Too risky to save my dad? To even *try*?"

Aline sinks her head and keeps walking in silence.

"I helped you and Piet with that action on the barge—no questions asked. I fought and killed that asshole alien. I risked my own qualification in the trial. Only for you. Thanks to me, you are in the final trial. And now it's my turn! If we win, if we learn how to *persuade*, I can convince my dad to stop his Joyousday. You had your chance with your mom, Aline. Sorry to say, but you were too... *timid*. It's *my* turn, and I will *not* be timid!"

Aline keeps walking in sullen silence.

"It's my turn, goahdammit!" Edda says, tears showing in her eyes.

Aline looks at her, but says nothing.

"Shit, Aline..." She begins to weep. "My dad... Please..."

They take a few more steps in silence, Edda trying to control her sobs—and failing.

Aline suddenly begins to cry as well. "I couldn't... convince her."

"I know," Edda says. "I'm so sorry!" And they embrace each other. A long, tear-filled embrace.

After unceremoniously drying their faces on their sleeves, they keep walking towards the noisy harbor.

"Hans is awake." Aline caresses the toddler on Edda's back who is looking around the open field with big, curious eyes.

"No wonder, after so much drama—he's the sensitive type, like his mother." Edda smiles, her eyes still sad. "Isn't that Piet's boat over there?"

Aline turns to her friend and grabs her with both hands. "Okay, I'll do it!"

Edda's eyes grow wide. She gapes at Aline, speechless.

"I can't believe I'm saying this," Aline continues, wetting her lips. "We are doing this, Edda. We'll take the

Century Festival by the balls. I'll build the fucking machine, on *one* condition."

"Anything!"

"Promise me we are not doing this just for us."

"I promise!"

"Swear by Goah. I need to know that the risk is worth it. Tell me we are making a difference here, Edda. That this *really* is bigger than us."

"It is!" Edda places her right hand over her chest. "I solemnly swear by Goah. We are not doing this for us. We are doing it for the people."

"Look me in the eye, Edda. We are not doing this just for your dad, are we?"

"I told you already, Goah's Mercy! All I want is a better world."

TWENTY-FIVE

Aline's Machine

"What's taking so long?" Edda asks.

Aline shrugs, and bites her lower lip with impatience as she paces the infinite stone floor of the staging permascape. They are alone this time in the eerie emptiness of the nothing-dream.

"Remarkable," Rew says.

Edda and Aline—and Ximena—jump at the suddenness of her soft, female voice. She has just popped into existence next to them, and is floating an inch over the dark, polished stone as if she had always been there.

"I hate when you do that," Edda says. "So, what's the holdup? Still didn't work?"

"Still did not, Redeemed van Dolah. The human—"

"Elder Aaij," Edda corrects.

"Elder Aaij does show remarkable resistance to your intrusion."

"Our intrusion? You mean yours?"

"I do mean *your* intrusion, Redeemed van Dolah. I do experience no difficulty intruding into the hu— Elder Aaij's dreamscape. Alas, when I meld *your* halos into his, the threading fails to materialize. I do admit this is beyond my experience."

"But how can that be?" Edda asks. "You had no trouble *melding* dozens of humans together that time with Consul Levinsohn, yet now you cannot get us into a dream with a single man?"

"Maybe Elder Aaij is awake," Aline says.

"He does sleep," Rew says. "And does dream, as his halo conveys. The trouble lies elsewhere. There seems to be an incompatibility clash due to your *intentions*. I do know this, as I clearly sense the nature of the rejection of Elder Aaij's psyche—it does react against your *hostility*, and thus rejects the Second Wake threading like an immune system rejects a preying germ. When we did meld with your Consul Levinsohn, there were no hostile intentions tainting your human halos. Now there are."

"Come on," Edda says, "that cannot be. We are not hostile. We only want him to get out of the Joyousday House at midnight during the Century Festival. What's wrong with that?"

Aline nods, and adds, "We are just trying to *motivate* him to take a pause, or go to the Forum to join the celebrations, or whatever."

"You are thus planning to *deceive* Elder Aaij into leaving the post he has been commissioned to guard, and so violate his duty. Deception coats your Second Wake halos like antigens coat an intruding virus." Rew speaks now like she is thinking aloud. "This must be yet another human weakness. Human halos have never sustained the evolutive pressure to smooth its intent. Most remarkable indeed. And an unfortunate complication."

"Complication? Pure sin!" Edda spreads her hands indignantly. "All that training, all that *suffering*, and for what? How in Goah's Name are we going to get anything done with all this," she moves her fingers in the air, "*dream magic* if we can't even get into other people's heads?!"

"You *can* intrude, Redeemed van Dolah. There lies not the problem. Your hostile intention is."

"Pure sin! What are we going to do now, huh? Impose our oh so mighty will with caresses, cuddles and kisses?"

"They did indeed prove effective with Consul Levinsohn."

Aline laughs out loud as Edda throws her hands up in the air in exasperation.

Rew raises her right arm in a very human gesture. "Do not disappoint me, Redeemed van Dolah, Woman Speese. Both of you do possess gifted brains—for a human. Stop using them to engage in futile bickering and do use them to readjust your perspective."

Edda and Aline frown at Rew in confusion.

Rew continues, "I shall attempt to assist. Redeemed van Dolah," Rew turns her white empty eyes at her, "do explain why Elder Aaij must evacuate the Joyousday House."

Edda sighs the sigh of a Juf explaining a simple concept to a distracted student. "We are going to set fire to the goahdamn place."

"With incendiary devices," Aline adds. "I'll attach hand clocks with automatic triggers so that at precisely midnight—"

Rew has raised her arm again. "I do not care for your plan, nor am I allowed to meddle in its conception or execution. But do allow me to suggest to you how to use your brain with a simple question: if you do fail to get Elder Aaij out of the building, shall you abort your plans?"

Edda and Aline blink and exchange a long glance.

Aline says, "We are not about to burn Elder Aaij alive, if that's what you mean."

"I mean nothing, Woman Speese. Do answer the question, please."

"Of course we would cancel the plan, yeah?" Edda says. "But I'm sure——"

Rew interrupts her, "Do allow me a suggestion—not as a collaborator, but as your instructor in the way of the mind. Do rearrange your priorities, and your motivations shall rearrange themselves. Do make it your goal to destruct of the building."

"But that's already our top priority," Aline says.

"No, sister," Edda says, and wets her lips. "I think I know where Elder Rew is coming from. Our top priority is to keep Elder Aaij safe."

"Hmm, yes, of course."

"Therefore, we are trying to go into his dreams to trick him out of the building. Which doesn't work because——"

"—deception and all that, yes. So what?"

Edda smiles and gives Rew a sidelong glance. "If we decide that we are going to set the building on fire, no matter what, even with Elder Aaij inside, then we'd go into his dreams not to trick him, but to——"

"—save his life, of course!" Aline smiles, eyes beaming. "Let's try that!"

"It is not easy," Rew says. "Far from it. You do need to truly accept your priorities, and not merely deceive yourself, as humans are so fond of. In this one instance you must commit to destroying the building, and thus collaterally terminate Elder Aaij."

"So we kill him, right?" Edda looks at Aline, shrugs, and says, "This is bigger than us, sister, so yeah, I'm in. What about you?"

Aline shuts her eyes and draws a deep breath. "All right," she finally says. "We are killing poor Elder Aaij. His family will be destroyed, and we will be responsible

—*criminally* responsible—unless we find a way of saving his life. Is that better, Elder Rew?"

Rew nods in that slow, awkward way of hers.

E lder Aaij is sitting in the entrance hall of the Joyousday House. Usually empty, he has brought in a foldable table and a chair for guard duty. It is not a small room, but the large fiery eyes painted on the left and right walls make it eerily oppressive. Ximena feels the strong emotions that this place elicits in Edda. Aline's expression is similarly tense.

By the light of two candles—the only sources of light in the room—Elder Aaij is studying a chess board, its wooden pieces casting quivering shadows. He occasionally turns his attention to the well-read book set wide open next to the board. Ximena can discern chess diagrams spread across its pages.

"Uh, Elder Aaij?" Edda says. She is standing to the left of the big, chubby man, while Aline is on his right. Rew keeps to herself, closer to the entrance. "Can he hear us?" Edda asks Rew.

"Only if you *will* it. You do not, thus he cannot. Were he a trained Walker of the Mind, his dream sense would immediately react to your presence."

"So we are invisible," Edda says, wide-eyed. "So sexy! How did you bring us here, Elder Rew? Into his dream, I mean? I want to learn the trick!"

"Regretfully, the Second Wake and the melding of minds are the exclusive domain of the Path in the Shadow, and I am forbidden to share such knowledge at the moment. Furthermore, although the Second Wake grants considerable power to the traverser, it is also dangerous—

mortally so. Proper training is of the essence. Training which only the team that tops the trial shall be granted access to."

"So unfair," Edda mutters.

Rew says, "At the very least you do already possess a critical piece of knowledge: that you must erase all hostile intentions from your human mind to enter the mind of another human. This is indeed new to me as well. I shall reveal this crucial fact to the other trial candidates when my duties in this session are over."

"No, please!" Edda says. "Keep it between us, okay?"

"Alas, I cannot. It is in the interest of the Reseeding effort to promote the worthiest human into Walkers of the Mind."

"What is the Reseeding effort?" Aline asks.

Rew doesn't reply immediately. She stares at Aline in silence for a second or two before saying, "It is the ultimate reason we marai revealed our presence to you." Her voice is a notch slower than usual. "It is how we satisfy our urge to save humankind from extinction and make it bloom anew."

"Aha," Edda says. "Well, we're sure as Dem in, huh, sister?"

"And we'll begin," Aline says, pointing a finger at the sitting man, "by saving Elder Aaij's life. How do we convince him to leave his guard post by New Year's Eve at midnight?"

"Hmm," Edda says, tapping her chin. "We test some ideas on this dream until we find the one with which we can get him out."

"Easier said than done," Aline says. "Got any ideas?"

"Nope. Let's brainstorm." She squints at the guard. "What do we really know about Elder Aaij?"

S omething barks and begins to scratch the outside of Joyousday House's door, attracting the immediate attention of Elder Aaij. He stands heavily up and opens the door, a frown on his face.

"Romulus!" he says, as the German shepherd leaps in, puts his front paws on his belly and begins to whine. "What are you doing here, boy? Ugh." He rolls his eyes with exasperation and sighs. "Theo left the gate open again, didn't he, boy?" He scratches the brown fur behind the pointy ears, and closes the door.

The dog taps on the door, asking to be let out.

"Sit there and stay quiet, you," he says sternly, pointing to the corner of the room. "You should've stayed home, boy. It's gonna be a long, boring night."

A sudden, insistent pounding on the door makes Elder Aaij startle.

"Martijn, open!" The call comes muffled through the door.

Elder Aaij frowns. "Jeroen?" He stands and opens the door. "What—?"

"It's the tournament, mensa! Come." The excited man, also in his mid-twenties, takes Elder Aaij's sleeve and pulls him out of the Joyousday House and onto the open grass field. "They're about to begin."

The field is full of small tables, more than a dozen, each with two people facing each other, a chess board between them. Electric spotlights make the pieces gleam in the middle of the night. Elder Aaij gapes at the sight of hundreds of people standing in excited silence beside the tables, watching the players open their games.

"Let's go watch table one," Jeroen says, putting his arm around Elder Aaij's shoulders. "Regina Milling is playing there!"

"The world champion? In Lunteren?!"

"It's the Century Tournament, mensa." Jeroen smiles widely at his friend and pushes him over to the table where more people stand. "Everybody is here!"

Elder Aaij shuts his eyes and purses his lips. "Sorry, Jeroen. I'm on duty." He turns around and begins to walk towards the Joyousday House.

"What? Are you seriously going to miss this?!"

Elder Aaij shrugs with resignation. "You make sure to note Milling's game, all right?"

"Don't you dare, mensa. Just lock the goahdamn door! Who's going to break in with all this going on out here, and the Century Festival down there?" He points down south.

Elder Aaij turns a sidelong smile towards him. "Say, wanna come home tomorrow to analyze the games together behind a beer?" He enters the building and shuts the door.

"That was close!" Edda says, frustration drenching her voice. She waves an impatient hand at the chess tournament, and the people, the tables—even the spotlights—all vanish in the quiet of the night, leaving the pristine lawn behind.

"Perhaps for the best," Aline says. "I would think getting Elder Aaij out of a building should be easier than haunting the dreams of the chess federation brass to organize a tournament here."

"I'm not so sure, sister."

"That is some work ethic," Aline says, staring at the closed door. "I've never seen anything like that in my life."

Edda turns to Rew, standing next to them near the entrance to the Joyousday House. "Why don't you just, you know," she wiggles her fingers, "use your *persuasion* thing on him? That was so close that I'm sure if you increase his enthusiasm, or his boredom, just a tiny bit, it will prove too much even for him to resist."

"I shall not solve your conundrums, Redeemed van Dolah. My assistance outside the required Second Wake activities is forbidden. The trial is aimed at gauging *your* skills at manipulating reality to your advantage, not mine. Do leverage your *humanity* to the limit, that is all I dare advise."

A single knock on the door takes Elder Aaij's attention off the chess board once more. With a heavy sigh he stands, takes the few steps towards the door and opens it.

There is nobody there. Except—

Elder Aaij frowns and leans down to pick up a bowl filled with nut cookies. "Who…?" he mutters, before noticing a small piece of paper with curvy feminine script. *Eat me before 2400 or endure a hundred years of bad luck!* A set of small exes sign the note, and then two large Ms.

Elder Aaij smiles, takes a cookie and nibbles. "Mmm!" he says and gobbles it whole before shutting the door.

"So sexy!" Edda says, and high-fives the laughing Aline. As Edda then turns to high-five Rew, the alien just stares back at her with her usual empty glance. "Don't leave me hanging, Elder Rew!" The alien slowly raises her arm until her three appendages touch Edda's palm. "Yes!" Edda says, satisfied. "So there we have it. Finally, a plan that works."

"Okay, hold on," Aline says, and draws a deep breath. "Let me recap, okay? Just to make sure that what we're simulating here will work hundred percent in real life next Friday."

"Sure, recap away, sister. And we can practice all you want. We are playing with fire here, literally," Edda giggles, "and we don't want any accidents or last-minute surprises."

Aline raises a thumb, "First, we prepare cookies. That is my part."

"Elder Rew," Edda turns her face to the alien, "are you really sure that the cookies that Aline *willed* into the dream will be identical in taste and texture to those she bakes in real life? Elder Aaij's got to *like* them if he's going to eat them, yeah?"

"They shall be identical, if woman Speese does indeed possess a deep understanding of the ingredients and the chemistry involved in the transformation. A permascape does emulate the wake with high fidelity in the hands of a master of both the dream and the wake."

"Here," Aline raises her fingers at Edda, and a cookie materializes between them, "try it."

Edda does. "Goah's Mercy!" she says, covering her half-full mouth with a hand. "You're good, sister."

Aline shrugs. "Old family recipe and tradition. We always bake a ton of them, all together on aws Gift's Eve. Only for the family. They never last long," she chuckles.

"This year we didn't though." Her expression darkens. She blinks and looks away.

Edda puts a hand on her cheek. "I'm so sorry, Aline. On the bright side, I have no doubt in my heart that Elder Aaij will devour the whole lot in the blink of an eye."

"Okay, then." Aline sighs, and raises a thumb and index finger. "Second, we inject the cookies with some sort of sleeping drug. That is your part."

"No problem. I'll get the herbs."

"Your dowry sister-to-be, I guess?" Aline squints at Edda.

"Yeah. I'll ask her as a personal favor."

"And she will just take the herbs from her pharmacy and give them to you, no questions asked?" Aline sounds skeptical.

"And she will prepare the infusion too, no worries, girl. That's what family is for. I will of course say it's for me, to fight insomnia; caused by er… inner demons or what not. I'll make up something plausible. I'll ask for enough to last several weeks, and then we inject the whole of it in your cookies." She claps loudly. "Done!"

"Hmm, I don't want to bet the entire plan on the moods of your future dowry sister. I don't know her. What if she refuses to help? Or she asks too many questions? Or tells your father or brother and they take the herbs away from you? So many things can go wrong."

"Oh, come on. You leave that to me, okay?"

"Hmm, I don't know. What about if we go to Elder Zeger's dream next—"

"*Woman* Zeger," Edda corrects.

"—and simulate you asking for the herbs. I want to see her true reaction."

"Sure." Edda smiles and shrugs. "Good call. Should we

go now? Elder Rew," she turns to the alien, standing next to them in her usual stoic silence, "could you—?"

"Wait, we are not done yet here." Aline raises three fingers in the air. "Third, we drag Elder Aaij's sleeping body out to the fields—at least fifty yards away to be safe."

"Yeah, of course. Let's go to Isabella's then and—"

"Wait, have you seen the size of Elder Aaij? I'm not sure we can drag him out on our own."

"Come on, between both of us we can. Let's try." Edda waves a hand and a dream copy of Elder Aaij materializes on the grass-covered ground, seemingly unconscious. "You take that arm and I take, er, from here."

Ximena—and many of the students in the auditorium —laugh at their pathetic attempts. No matter how hard they pull—or push, they try everything—the body barely budges.

"Pure sin!" Edda says between her teeth as she drops the massive arm of Elder Aaij's body in defeat. She meets Aline's gaze. "If we can't move him, we have to think of another plan where he moves by himself. But what, Goah's Mercy? No matter what we throw at him, he refuses to leave his post. We are back to square one, sister."

"No, we stick to the sleeping plan," Aline says, still panting from the effort. She turns a studious gaze at the guard's simulated body. "In essence, it's an engineering problem like any other. We just need to find the right tool for the job. Hmm…" Her half-open lips curve slowly into a smile. "I know what," she says with a giggle. "We call the cavalry!"

Pieter gives Elder Aaij's simulated body a glance and says, "I thought I was disqualified from participating in the trial?"

"You are not a candidate, Elder Ledeboer," Rew says. "You are a tool."

"Hey!" Pieter scowls at the alien.

"Not any tool," Aline hurries to say. She embraces his muscular arm. "*My* tool."

"Double hey!" Pieter redirects his scowl at Aline.

Aline embraces him and puts her cheek on his broad chest. "You know how much I love my tools, don't you, pretty boy?"

Pieter's expression softens, and a sidelong smile distends his lips. "Actually, I'm happy Elder Rew came for me. I was having a nightmare, anyway." He squats down on his knees and pushes Elder Aaij face up. Then he stands, places both his feet firmly behind the guard's head, and takes both his arms by the wrists. "Why am I doing this again?"

Edda clears her throat. "Uh, well, the thing is—"

"Just pull, Piet," Aline says. "We'll explain later."

Pieter flexes his legs, stretches his back and begins to pull vigorously, stepping slowly back. Elder Aaij's body jerks along, a few inches at a time.

"Where do you want this?" Pieter asks, effort in his voice, as inches turn into yards.

Edda and Pieter lean forward to stare at Aline as she expertly glides the thin, blue flame of the blowtorch over the exposed circuits of the device. Rew is standing in the corner of the cabin, separated from the rest, observing in silence.

The cabin looks like a technical maintenance room of sorts to Ximena. Electricity—or rather, the attempt to control it with technological means—is the obvious theme of the place. Thick, plastic-coated cables run into the room from a hole in the roof and join a large metallic body covered with translucent disc-shaped protuberances. Smaller cables run amok over racks attached to the ceiling, only to disappear inside a set of large lockers that stand against a wall.

Aline shuts the device's metallic box, connects a cable and turns a protruding knob all the way to the right. "Okay." She sighs, visibly satisfied, and turns towards Edda and Pieter. "I just hacked the generator to discharge all the batteries' juice at once for the few seconds we need. That should make it work now. Ready?"

"Sure," Edda says, and walks towards a connected device on a stool nearby, small and rectangular, covered in dials and knobs. "Say the word."

Aline flicks a switch on the device she was working on, which begins to emit a faint but constant hum. "Do it."

Edda pushes a mechanical button repeatedly. "Yeah, I see a needle jumping on the large dial now," she says, as she keeps clicking the button. "It jumps up every time I—"

"Yes!" Aline claps, takes Pieter's face in her hands and plants a kiss on his lips. "It's working!"

"Oookay." Edda turns around, face as confounded as Pieter's. "If you say so."

"Of course I'm assuming that all this," Aline gestures with a hand across the room, "*dream machinery* works exactly as their real-world counterparts."

"It better!" Edda says. "This contraption of yours is crucial, sister. It's the most important part of the plan. The fire in the Joyousday House will be for *nothing* if your machine doesn't go off at precisely midnight."

"I know," Aline sighs. "But it's looking good, sister. So far everything—the tools, the machines, even the physics—appears to work *exactly* like they would in my real-world workshop."

"A permascape does indeed provide a high-fidelity simulation of the wake," Rew says from her corner, "as long as the Walker masters all involved mechanics, and there are no conflicting wills to disrupt their natural functioning. Woman Speese does seem to display a deep understanding of the concerned technologies."

"I sure as Dem do," Aline gives Edda and Pieter a reassuring smile. "It will work."

"Where is this place?" Pieter asks, looking at the shut door. "In the real world, I mean?"

"Ah," Aline says, extending her arms, "welcome to electric maintenance cabin four, at the south end of Colony Street. It's the perfect place: plenty of discretion and energy, and close to the colonial repeater. Nobody ever comes here unless a big storm breaks something. So a couple of days after the Century Festival I'll just come here on my shift, clean everything up, and nobody will ever know what hit them."

Pieter looks around at the mesh of electric devices merged in a confusion of cables. "And how in Goah's Name are you going to get all this stuff in the real world, love? It looks very expensive."

"Yes," Aline sighs, and nods slowly. "That's a problem. Edda, I need all your savings."

"You got them."

"Good, but that is far from enough. I have some extra savings myself since Gotthard Kraker began his own project for the Trial."

"What is he doing?" Edda asks. Ximena feels the intensity of her curiosity, but she is not worried by the competition. Edda knows that, unless something goes horribly wrong, the trial is theirs for the taking.

"I don't know," Aline replies, "but it involves lots of expensive electrical equipment as well, which I'm helping him procure," she smiles wickedly, "for a hefty fee."

"That's my girl," Pieter says. "Squeeze that asshole dry!"

"So we have enough karma for all our expenses, yeah?" Edda asks.

"Yes, I guess… If I *borrow* some pieces from the Siever's construction site, hmm, and tools, and cables too. But," she frowns lightly, "the problem is *time*."

"Time?" Edda exchanges a puzzled look with Pieter. "We still have a week until the thirty-first."

"Hmm." Aline rubs her neck. "My providers of choice for this sort of thing are the Jansens. Very professional. And discreet. They have a warehouse in Oosterbeek, close to the harbor, in an alley off the Pietersberg Way."

"Sounds good," Edda says. "Especially the *discreet* part."

"Their usual delivery time, door to door, is seven days."

"Seven…?! Pure Sin! That is cutting it *way* too short. Especially with the extra pressure on regional logistics that can be expected this year. Can't you get the stuff from somebody else?"

"Not discreetly."

Edda laughs bitterly. "I hate to risk it all on a courier's time plan."

"I'll take you," Pieter says, eyes on Aline. "On my boat. We'll be back in two days, three max with bad sea. But you'll have to cover my costs for losing those days of catch."

"That is a sweet, sweet offer," Edda says. "Thanks, Piet!"

Aline takes his face between her hands, kisses him and then gently takes a nip on his lower lip. "You'll be *handsomely* compensated."

"**P**lease, my dear professor," Censor Smith says, standing up. "I think I speak for all our students when I say that I am ready to skip the rest of these *preparatory activities* and move on to the Century Festival."

Oh, yes, Ximena thinks, and joins the spontaneous burst of applause that fills the auditorium. Even Mark whistles next to her with loud enthusiasm.

While Censor Smith sits with a pleased expression on his face, Professor Miyagi laughs on stage and raises both hands at his audience. "I hear you, people, I hear you. Fine, fine. Context is clear enough, I think. So, Ank, 31st of December, please?"

TWENTY-SIX

The Lost Colony

A scene comes to life across the amphitheater: a bird's eye view over the colony of Lunteren on a bright winter afternoon. Smoke rises from hundreds of chimneys, the scent of burning firewood intertwines in the fresh air. The sun hangs low over the sea, spreading long shadows over the landscape.

Ximena wets her lips, trying to rein in her anticipation. *It is only hours to the new century.*

Like a bird that has spotted a shiny object, the scene begins to glide down, ever closer to the buildings standing on the south-western edge of the colony. Not far away an extensive array of solar panels follows the sinking sun with obsessive eagerness, next to other structures like wind turbines and what looks like huge silos. Crop fields, barren now in the winter, extend far beyond.

The scene approaches an imposing building right on the edge of the colony: an old Christian church, solid and still proud. The structure—even the tower that rises at the end of the rectangular main body—is aesthetically elegant, walls of red brick under a black slate roof.

The scene *lands* smoothly on the open space south of the church, its bricks bright red in the sun. A large, yellow side door is the only visible entrance.

Ximena turns her head to a sudden, high-pitched *whiz*, in time to see a cycling figure turning a corner at considerable speed. She immediately recognizes Gotthard as he skillfully dismounts the bicycle before it is fully at rest, and parks it among others near the entrance. The sturdy— and yet elegant—bicycle carries a large heavy-looking block attached to the frame, possibly an electric battery; a crude one, judging by the size. The other bicycles in the rack look primitive and worn-down in comparison.

Gotthard takes a wrapped package that he was carrying in the bike's front basket, and strides into the church. The scene's point of view follows behind him.

The inside is lit by direct sunlight streaming in through tall windows, so all electric lamps, placed at intervals on the walls, are off at the moment. The space looks like a factory floor, humming with activity. Grease, sweat and poor ventilation produce an unsavory smell. Workers are busy attending tall, bulky machines placed in two parallel rows.

"Printing presses," Mark whispers in Ximena's ears.

She nods silently, eyes hypnotically fixed on the large cylinders as they rotate with the soft purr of electric power, pressing ink against paper, cutting pages and stacking them on neat piles that younger workers—recent adults not much older than ten—move swiftly away, returning with more ink, paper rolls and other supplies.

Gotthard, wrapped package in his right hand, walks with determined pace across the open space, ignoring the surrounding bustle.

"Man Kraker!" a youthful voice calls to the side, a short, chubby girl, sweating profusely. "Would you mind looking at this blade? The cut is dirty, I think there is a vibration or a—"

Gotthard ignores the girl. At the end of the room, he walks past a vaulted arc into a square area: the base of the tower. As Gotthard approaches a narrow passage of steps, another voice—authoritative this time—stops him. "Gotthard, wait!"

A man already in his mid-twenties approaches Gotthard with quick, short steps. He is carrying a large, elongated object and wears a colorful robe of fine fabric. Despite his skinny, pale face and receding hair, his confident gait produces an almost attractive impression.

"Colder van Althuis," Gotthard says with a stiff smile. "Aws Blessings to you."

The man laughs, glancing back at the main room, where the noise of production shields their voices. "We're alone, young boy. Why so formal? You don't even stop for a *chat* these days." He shoots a wink. "Were you going up to your lair?"

"Sorry, *Simon*. Uh, yes. I want to get some work done before heading off to the Festival."

"You too," he sighs, and shakes his head in frustration. "The whole night shift is refusing work tonight."

Gotthard chuckles. "And you are surprised?"

"I know." Colder van Althuis waves a hand dismissively. "The event of the millennium and all that; but work needs to be done, Goah's Mercy."

Gotthard laughs. "This is not the event of the millennium, Simon. The Century Festival is the biggest thing *ever* to happen in Lunteren's history, and you expect people to miss out? Be realistic. Is that for me?" He points at the bulky object that Colder van Althuis is carrying in his hands.

"That Speese woman left it for you." Colder van Althuis hands it to Gotthard. "What is it?" He stares with curiosity at the long metallic pole and the thick flexible cable, made of the same metal, loosely wrapped around the pole.

"Ah, nothing... just an experiment I'm doing." Gotthard shifts his weight to better carry both the cabled pole and the wrapped package in both hands. "If you will excuse me, I really must..." he staggers towards the stairs.

Colder van Althuis squints up. "You are not using the tower for anything... *inappropriate*, are you?"

"No! Of course not."

"I'm taking a risk here, young man. Leasing it to you. I hope you don't betray my trust."

"Never, Simon. It's just a private science lab, that's all!"

Colder van Althuis smiles. "I know, I know." He gestures at the working space behind him. "Listen, Gotthard. I know you're not on duty today, but we could really use some help."

"What's happened?" Gotthard leaves the bulky equipment on the floor with utmost care.

"We are running behind schedule on the *Wikipedia* batch."

"Let me guess, volume five thousand and sixty-one."

"Yes, the machine assigned to that goahdamn volume is misaligned, I think. But sometimes only. It's bizarre. Could you take a look?"

Gotthard shrugs. "Sorry, but as you can see, I'm very—"

"It's urgent, Gotthard. These ten *Wikipedia* volumes are the most important commission of the year, and the merchants are expected to sail up the Rhine in three days' time. And now the whole goahdamn night shift decides that they would rather go to the Festival. We are in trouble."

Gotthard snorts. "We should have stuck to *Lord of the Rings*."

Colder van Althuis smiles dryly, and sighs. "All right, I'll pay you double tariff. But please don't fail me. This is important for Lunteren."

"Oh, and now you are using the *Lunteren in danger* card. Is this the Colony Elder speaking?" Gotthard asks with a faint smile. "Or the man?"

Colder van Althuis laughs warmly. "For you, my dear boy," he reaches out and places his hand on Gotthard's cheek, "it's always the man."

Gotthard takes a slow step forward until their bodies touch. He leans his head toward Simon's ear to whisper, "I could really use the karma."

Colder van Althuis laughs. "Always the romantic."

"But not now," Gotthard separates from Simon and gives the equipment on the floor an eager glance. "Tomorrow I'll do a double shift, okay?"

"Fine." Colder van Althuis seems pleased. "And you can tell that Siever friend of yours that he's welcome as well, since he's always visiting you up there," he looks up at the tower.

Gotthard laughs. "Perhaps he will. You're not jealous, are you? He's helping me with…" He gives a vague wave of his hand.

Colder van Althuis smiles at him for a few seconds before replying, "My young boy, I don't care what you do, or with whom, as long as I have your full attention when I want your full attention."

Gotthard smiles dryly. "Always the romantic."

The tower room is dark, cold and moist. Ximena folds her arms with a chill while her eyes adjust. A lit electric lamp tries to drive the darkness into the corners, not quite succeeding. The inside of the tower is spacious, especially upwards. A steep, wooden staircase by the bricked wall leads to a higher floor—presumably to where the bells used to call the faithful in pre-Goahn times. The ceiling is but a thin separation made of raw, fragile wooden boards with dim sunlight filtering between them.

Gotthard is leaning over a work bench that extends along the entire wall, soldering a metallic object to an electric circuit. Ximena wrinkles her nose at the sharp solder smell. The room looks like the hobby garage of an electrical engineer with little social life. Machines and components of an electrical nature litter the space.

A knock on the door startles Gotthard. "Gotts!" a muted voice calls from behind the thick door. "It's me!"

"Greetings, Rutger," Gotthard says. "One second."

Many seconds pass while Gotthard keeps working on the circuit.

"Come on!" Rutger knocks again, impatiently. "If Colder van Althuis sees me, he'll try to recruit me."

Gotthard leaves the solder on the bench with a bad-tempered sigh, walks to the door and turns the key.

"Finally!" Rutger says, entering the room. His cream-colored tunic is simple, but made of a fine, silk-like fabric. A gomen—the wide, black, ornate belt of the redeemed—surrounds his narrow waist. "I brought you the battery," he says, pushing his glasses up his nose, as Gotthard locks the door.

Gotthard takes the heavy metallic box from Rutger, and turns it around in his hands, inspecting it carefully. "About time!"

"You're welcome." Rutger rolls his eyes. "We should head off. The streets are already packed, and you should see the Forum, mensa. It's like the whole Geldershire is there. If we don't hurry, we'll not even *fit*."

Gotthard nods, absentmindedly. "Hmm, yes. This should kick enough power." He walks to the bench and carefully places the battery box on the surface.

"I really hope so, because that thing wasn't cheap."

"Nor are the gadgets supplied by Speese," Gotthard says, pointing at the long metallic pole-and-cable that Colder Simon had handed to him, which was lying on the floor. "Good that your Elders were so receptive to our *suggestion* to make a generous contribution to science."

Rutger scoffs. "I still can't believe that worked. They're more easy-going in dreams, I can tell you that." He stares at the mingled electrical equipment, most with their guts wide open, cables poking out and connecting to neighboring devices. "If they knew what we are really doing here…"

"They know," Gotthard says. "A radio telescope."

Rutger chuckles. "To communicate with a colony lost in space centuries ago."

"Hey," Gotthard says with a shrug. "We'll aim our telescope to the heavens and see what we discover. If it happens to be the Lost Colony, and they reveal that a killer asteroid is on its way, then…" He spreads his hands in a gesture of innocence. "That's how science works, mensa. Research. Publish. And change history."

"You know I hear you, Gotts, I really do. But I think you put too much faith in humanity. Whatever we find up there," he points a finger at the ceiling, "I don't think anybody will listen. Certainly not aws Head. And I even have my doubts about the scientists."

"Scientists will listen to the truth, no matter how inconvenient, because we can only survive by dealing with the truth. Oh," Gotthard's face brightens, "and in the process we will win the marai trial. After all, there's nothing more beneficial to humankind than, well, not dying."

"Speaking of the marai, maybe Qoh and the others can help us with the asteroid."

"Maybe. And maybe not."

"Why wouldn't they? The marai always say that they want us to thrive."

"I don't know, mensa," Gotthard says, shaking his head slowly and looking at an empty space on the wall. "We don't really know *their* truth, do we? I'd rather win the trial, learn their secret shadow tricks, and fend for ourselves."

"You really think we can win?"

"Of course, mensa. If we communicate with the Lost Colony before the deadline, the prize is ours."

"I would sure as Dem be more optimistic if we grab that Path in the Shadow by the balls. Then we could *persuade* the Pontifex herself to listen to us."

"It's happening, mensa," Gotthard says with a wink. "Have faith in science. Now, make yourself useful and take that upstairs," he says, pointing at the metallic pole-and-cable on the floor. "Screw it to the rest of the antenna. I'll test the oscillator in the meantime. The sooner we are done here, the earlier we can head to the Forum." He turns his attention to a thick, open book resting on the bench, covered with diagrams.

"Ah, sweet!" Rutger leans down and takes the device in his hands. "For a minute I thought you didn't want to go to the Festival."

Gotthard gapes at his friend. "Are you serious? I

wouldn't miss it for the world!" He chuckles as he lets his eyes fall back on the book. "I bet my ass that whatever Edda and Speese have up their sleeves is happening tonight."

TWENTY-SEVEN

New Year's Eve 2399

The auditorium seems to dissolve in a chaotic mix of loud dance music and the tantalizing mingling of smells—sweet cottons, fried corns, toasted breads, thick syrups, hearty sausages. A bird's eye view of the colony at night sparkles across the amphitheater, gliding gently over the packed streets and squares. Ximena gapes at the sheer overkill of electric light, and at the bright dynamism of colorful hats and tunics; most dancing, many laughing, some singing. Everybody—absolutely *everybody*—is out on the streets tonight.

Lunteren is celebrating like it is the last day on Earth.

The heart of the celebration, where the swarms of light and color seem to converge with the leisurely but sure way of rivers winding into the sea, is the largest public open space in the colony.

"The *Forum* of Lunteren," Miyagi says. "Following the classical Goah's Gift tradition for colony fora: an extensive public area on the colony edge, in direct connection to nature or wilderness. In Lunteren the Forum extends almost five hundred yards across and, as you can see," he gestures with a finger at the long line of trees where a pitch-black forest begins, "more than half of it directly borders the Veluwa woods."

The music, singing and shouting grow louder as the scene glides down over the Forum. It is a flat red-bricked extension able to comfortably host thousands of people, which tonight have claimed the space with bustling enthusiasm. On the far eastern side, next to the Veluwa woods, a large, oval building towers over the Forum like a castle over a medieval town.

"That is the *Eye of Goah*," Miyagi points at the dominant structure, "the heart of the Forum, and aws Head's administrative presence in the colony. See all those annexed rooms and low buildings around the main body? Offices, residences, barracks, archives, storage—you name it. You know how the raw power of the Pontifex flows out of Townsend and spreads throughout the rest of the world? Well, an *itsy-bitsy* piece of it," he brings his index and thumb together, "ends right here."

The scene is already floating close over the heads of celebrating colonists, and Ximena can make out the individuals as they shout and laugh with exuberant joy. Most dance, and jump, and yell like spasmodic maniacs to the thumping, live music.

The Eye of Goah building is surrounded by an elevated terrace, extensive and bordered by elegant columns. A large stage—flooded with blinding, blinking spotlights—dominates the central section of the terrace, beside a diverse assortment of electric equipment: microphones, colossal loudspeakers, radio emitters, knob-covered devices. To the right, a band plays hypnotic music. To the left, shaded from the spotlights, groups of finely dressed colonists with impressive hats walk and mix leisurely in sight of the masses below.

"Those up there," Miyagi points at the elegant figures, "are the *crème de la crème*: aws Head's top bureaucracy, the Colony Elders, industrial families—even Gotthard's family is there. But the real action," Miyagi pauses for effect, "is down here, with the commoners."

With a theatrical wave of his hand, the scene lands right in the middle of the Forum, in the heart of the crowd.

"Here they are, the whole Van Dolah lot." Miyagi points at Edda, dressed in a bright white-and-black-striped tunic framing her dark skin in attractive contrast. Beside her, Willem, wearing a white flat side hat, is talking to Bram, who is carrying little Hans on his chest, comfortably secured in warm cloths.

Edda is keeping to herself, a few steps away from the rest of her family, but her eyes shine with excitement. She throws anxious glances at the people around her and at the still-empty central stage.

"Edda, come over here, girl!" Willem shouts at her.

Without turning, Edda gives him a sidelong glance and says nothing.

"Edda, why are you being such a bitch to Dad?" Bram shouts over the crowd. "This is his last New Year's Eve, Goah's Mercy!"

Edda turns her head, a scowl on her face. "That's precisely why!" she shouts back.

"Ah, here you are!" Quaestor Marjolein Mathus, parting the crowd with a wide smile, walks towards Willem. She is wearing the ceremonial aws Head's purple toga, long and formal, and yet incapable of hiding the exuberance of her petite body. Her long hair falls in elaborate, golden braids to the middle of her back. She usually looks impeccable, Ximena admits, but she has outdone herself tonight.

"Uh, aws Blessings to you, Quaestor Mathus," Willem says, his eyes locked on her. On *all* of her. He blushes.

She laughs, stands on her toes, and kisses him on the cheek. "Oh, come on, Will. I am not exercising office. Not with you."

"How are you, Marjo?" he says. "You must be nervous."

"I am!" She exhales a long breath. "I might not look it, but I'm terrified. *Incredibly* busy, you can*not* imagine how many… tiny details still need my approval, even tonight." She turns. "Aws Blessings to you, Bram, Edda."

"Aws Blessings to you, Quaestor." Bram bows politely, holding the toddler with his right hand. Edda stays silent, her attention elsewhere.

A trace of irritation crosses Marjolein's face. "Aws Blessings to you, Edda!" she shouts louder, walking to her.

Edda turns and stares at her.

In silence.

Willem hurriedly places a hand on Marjolein's shoulder. "Don't mind her. She is giving me the silent treatment."

"Seriously? That is not very pious of you, Edda."

Edda remains silent, facing away.

"Please, let her be," Willem says to Marjolein. "It's nothing."

She purses her lips. "It is most certainly *not* nothing!" Her eyes glare at Edda with rising indignation. "Two mere months to your Joyousday, and this is the family life you must put up with? It's *heartless*! It should be a time of love, remembrance and family."

Edda turns with sudden fury in her eyes. "What do you know of family?!" Edda shouts in Marjolein's face. "You never had parents!"

Marjolein takes a hesitant step back, blinking, eyes wide in disbelief.

"E- Edda!" Willem is horrified.

"You kill our parents!" Edda shouts, tiny drops of spit falling on Marjolein's toga.

"*Edda*!" Willem's furious lashing shout freezes Edda and makes Bram and many colonists in the immediate vicinity startle. "Shut up this instant!" With bloodshot eyes and a brow distorted with rage, his face is almost unrecognizable, as if a demon had taken possession of the always placid Meester.

The toddler in Bram's hold begins to cry like he has just seen a monster leaping out of nowhere, which in a way it has. A large circle of colonists gawk at him.

"I'm *so* sorry, Marjo," Willem says, voice trembling with emotion. "Edda is just upset. She doesn't mean it."

"I do—" Edda begins to speak, but Willem's expression stops her. Tears of frustration begin to well in her eyes.

"Marjo, please forget all this. It's not worth it." Willem takes her hands. "Tonight is the most important moment of your career." He forces a smile. "You alone brought the New-Year's Festival—no, the *Century* Festival—here to Lunteren. All Germania will listen to your words. It is your moment!"

Marjolein's expression softens. "Will, you cannot begin to imagine how many favors I had to call to get us selected. But I didn't do it for me," she says louder, looking around, meeting the glances of the staring crowd with her practiced, professional smile. "I did it for all of us. This honor doesn't belong to me. It belongs to Lunteren!" Some bystanders clap spontaneously, but soon the frenzy of the celebration takes over, and the crowd dissolves into smaller groups, mixing, dispersing.

"Don't worry, Will," Marjolein caresses his cheek, "immature words don't offend Goah."

T he Forum is now considerably more crowded, which would have seemed impossible to Ximena a moment ago. The music thumps louder, the mood more expectant; even the colors feel more vibrant. *Midnight is close*, Ximena thinks, and begins to tap on the bench with impatience.

Edda gives the ticking, mechanical hand-clock an anxious glance. "Shit, it's almost eleven," she mutters, and puts the clock back into a discreet pocket as she turns to her family. "Sorry, I need to do something."

Before Willem and Bram have time to react, she slips through the crowd, and the auditorium scene begins to follow her frantic trot westwards, towards the entry streets into the Forum.

But the progress is slow as she pushes against the current of people still flowing en-masse into the Forum. They are strangers, many of them—in Lunteren just for this one night. And those occasional greetings of the few known faces she crosses, she simply ignores.

With a final gasp, she turns into a narrow, quiet alley off the busy street.

"Goah's Mercy, about time!" Aline says, looking relieved and anxious at the same time. "I thought you'd changed your mind."

"Sorry, it took me forever to... Wow! You look... yummy!" Aline is wearing a long, pale-blue tunic, open on her legs, that shapes her body suggestively. Her long black hair, expertly curled, frames her rosy, beautiful face. "Don't let Piet see you, if you want to keep your tunic on." She laughs.

Aline blushes. "Thanks, you look stunning too, but no time for that." She is holding a clock in her own hands. "Less than a minute to eleven, sister!" She takes a heavy-looking radio receiver out of a cloth bag on her feet and places it on the ground. "Prepare to synchronize."

Edda retrieves her own clock from her pocket and takes it in her hands.

"Wind it up," Aline says, turning the receiver on. Both listen intently to the radio broadcast while Edda turns a knob on the top of her clock.

"… *heavy rain is not stopping the brave* Tczew *colonists from joining in droves their Imperator by the imperial palace, Goah praise their devotion. Imperator Castimer Cisek is waving at the faithful. The coordination ritual will begin any second now. Switching over to his microphone…*"

"*Aws Blessings to you, Hansa.*" A strong, masculine voice soars over the background noise. The roar of an enthusiastic gathering replies. "*It is my duty, it is my privilege, once more, to fulfill the ancestral tradition of the annual coordination!*"

The crowd cheers again.

"*Goah, guide my words as I mark the twenty-third hour of the last Day of Light. Let the same exact time rule inside the borders of the Hanseatic Imperium, from the Atlantic to the Urals. Ready for countdown!*"

The crowd noise dies down, slowly replaced by an expectant murmur.

"*TEN—NINE—EIGHT—*" The crowd joins the count, loud and cheerful, as it progresses down. Edda and Aline listen in silence, fully still, each tightly holding their clock in their hands, their right thumbs ready on top of a protruding knob. "—TWO—ONE—NOW!"

Edda and Aline both press their thumbs at once, as the crowd roars.

Aline turns off the radio device, removes a bundle wrapped in a checked cloth from her bag and hands it to Edda. A delicious warm smell makes Ximena's mouth water. "Nut cookies ala Speese, freshly out of the oven. The note is also in there."

"Goah, the smell is… irresistible!"

Aline laughs. "That's the intention. Piet should be there already, waiting for you."

"Okay." Edda draws a deep breath and smiles silently at Aline.

"This is it, Edda. The point of no return." Aline's voice is calm, her expression serious. "We can still turn around, return to the Festival, and nobody will be the wiser."

Ximena feels Edda's hesitation as the significance of the moment begins to truly sink in. Because it is true, this really is the point of no return. After tonight, lives will be altered forever, beginning with their own. But they can still return to their normal lives and never look back to these crazy rebellious days of youth. They can still live placid, safe lives under the Gift of Goah. Short lives, though. And lonely—Edda thinks of her father with sudden grief. *Powerless* lives.

"We are so doing this, sister," Edda says, a sparkle in her eyes. "This is really happening!"

Aline nods curtly and gives Edda a bright smile.

"Let's be quick about it, yeah?" Edda says. "We need to be back in the Forum long before midnight to avoid suspicion."

They high-five each other and walk away in opposite directions.

TWENTY-EIGHT

Happy New Century!

Professor Miyagi paces the stage of the auditorium, hands clasped behind his back. Ximena awaits with increasing impatience, her eyes staring with anticipation at the frozen scene, where the two teenage girls walk away from each other in a semi-lit alley.

"As historians," Miyagi says, "we all know how the conquest of the Americas by the European powers played out, don't we?"

Some sidetracking, Professor! Ximena thinks, and gives Mark a baffled frown. He shrugs in silence.

"But I'm sure," Miyagi continues, "that few of you are familiar with the story of Pizarro and Atahualpa in Cajamarca."

Ximena chuckles loudly.

"What?" Mark whispers in her ear.

"So funny!" she says, meeting his oh-so-blue eyes. "I watched a sensorial about it just before the seminar! The professor himself—"

Miyagi's words interrupt Ximena's explanation. "You are probably asking yourself what the sixteenth century

Incan Empire has to do with the twenty-fourth century Hanseatic Imperium." He spreads his arms for effect. "You all know the old Twain adage, 'history does not repeat itself, but it rhymes.' Well, Cajamarca and Lunteren are an excellent example. Anybody know what happened in 1532?"

"Here, Professor!" Mark shouts, raising Ximena's arm in the air with frantic enthusiasm.

"Ximena, great!" Miyagi's smile widens. "I'd love to hear your take. Can you summarize Cajamarca?"

Ximena stands, trying—and failing—to rein in her blushing. "Er, Pizarro and his men were outnumbered forty to one. But they managed to capture Atahualpa after massacring his court."

"Yes, in a nutshell," Miyagi says. "They shattered the Incan Empire with a single blow. How did they pull it off?"

"Well, uh, I would say a combination of factors." Ximena shifts her weight from one foot to another. "First, hmm, Pizarro and his men were *desperate*, out of options: they could not engage Atahualpa's army directly, but they could not flee either. Second, Atahualpa's *arrogance*. He was too sure of his power—his divinity—to even conceive a betrayal, let alone a defeat. And third, *technology*. Pizarro had horses, gunpowder, cannons, tactics…"

"Desperation, arrogance and technology." Miyagi smiles at Ximena. "Very well put. Thank you, Ximena."

He paces the stage, hands behind his back, as if lost in thought. Always the showman. "Desperation, arrogance and technology," he repeats, nodding slowly, and then raises his head at the floating Edda and Aline. "Ring a bell, anybody?"

Cody stands up with a raised hand. "You are surely referring to Edda's desperation to save her father, Mathus' corrupted arrogance, and of course, *dreamtech*. You are implying, Professor, that Edda's usage of dreamtech against the Hanseatic Imperium was analogous to the usage of gunpowder-age weaponry by European powers when they civilized the Americas."

"*Civilized*?!" Sky stands not far below Ximena and folds her arms. "For fuck's sake, they killed fifty-five million people—*ninety* fucking percent of the population!—and wiped out a culture extending back thousands of years. And then, to fill the gap, they fucking *imported* millions of slaves from Africa! You call that *civilized*?!"

What in Goah's Name is she talking about?! Ximena gives Mark a frowned glance, but he doesn't seem at odds with Sky's nonsense. Even Miyagi, down there on stage, is watching Sky with professional attentiveness. *Why doesn't he intervene? Is he being polite?*

"I fear you are mistaken, my esteemed fellow Sky," *Yes, Cody. Put her in her place!* "There was no *culture* in the Americas. Not in the civilized sense of the word. There were of course loose tribes of barbarians, fewer than a million in number, but certainly no civilization. I suggest you double-check your facts."

"I can't believe this!" Sky throws her hands up in the air, eyes locked on Cody. "What a fucking—!"

"That's enough, Sky!" Miyagi hastily interrupts. Right on time, because judging by Censor Smith's stern expression, he seemed about to intervene. "Sit, please," Miyagi says. "Everybody, chill!"

It takes him a considerable amount of patience and soothing gestures until the indignant chatter that has gripped the auditorium finally wanes to a murmur.

"Thank you. Fascinating discussion, but outside the boundaries of this seminar. Please, get your focus back on our two ladies, all right?" He gestures at Edda and Aline, frozen in midair. "Look at them, people. So innocent. So hungry to change the world. That hunger that is the eternal curse of youth. And its prerogative. As many youngsters before and after them, Edda and Aline are challenging the status quo. A classic, right? You push, and the establishment snaps you back in place, your young and tender feelings be damned. That's the way of the world. That's how it's always been. Except," he turns around theatrically, looking at the GIA section of the auditorium, "*crucially*," he turns to face the Lundev section, "this time it will work!"

He takes a few more steps in silence. Ximena shifts in place with increasing impatience as she follows the professor's stroll on stage.

"Oh! Their plans will shatter, of course," he says. "The outcome will be far different from what anybody could have reasonably expected. That's the way of history, after all. Capricious. Never playing along. Chaotic. So much so that it's always a challenge for us historians to pinpoint all the factors that lead to world-shattering changes. Take the French Revolution, for example. Why did it happen? Class oppression? The new ideas of the enlightenment? Poor harvests? Which events made it unavoidable? How would history have unfolded if lesser talents than Napoleon had been put in control of a country surrounded by a sea of hate and hostility? With the Lunteren of the Reformation, we historians fight with equal passion about cause and effect. But it is this one night in Lunteren," he raises his finger at the scene, "when *all* of us, without exception, finally agree that the Leap-Day Reformation is truly underway—blatant, vicious, unstoppable. Let's watch."

The scene switches back to the Forum, where Willem and Bram are engaging in casual conversation with neighboring families, while Edda keeps mostly to herself, only giving a polite nod to the occasional greeting.

But she is *burning* inside. Ximena can feel it in her guts. She is constantly mustering her Walker discipline to rein in her emotions, deep breath after deep breath, diluting the tension into raw awareness—focusing on the *now*.

The crowd of colorful colonists surrounds them all the way to the edge of the Forum, and to the streets beyond. The music hammers loud and stimulating. People dance, clap, laugh, and shout words of celebration into each other's ears.

Mark points a finger at the central stage on the Eye's terrace, attracting Ximena's attention. An attractive man is walking forward to one of the standing microphones.

"Aaand… we are back!" the man says, his perfect teeth sparkling under the spotlights. "This is your Master of Ceremonies, Alwin Geissberger, transmitting live from Lunteren, in the beautiful Geldershire of the Dutch Province." His expertly smooth voice—multiplied by loudspeakers scattered around the Forum and neighboring streets—electrifies the crowd to even higher tiers of frenzy. He wears a tunic of flamboyant design with metallic undertones and splashes of screaming colors, and a hat that looks like a fountain of red, yellow and green jelly.

"That was Consul Levinsohn live from Fulda. We thank you, Consul, for your inspiring blessings. In this corner of the country we are surely inspired, aren't we, mensas?!"

The crowd roars across the Forum. Across the colony. Ximena exchanges a nervous glance with Mark. She feels like she is really there, next to the Van Dolahs in the crowd, about to witness history first hand.

"I wish you were here, Germania. Oh, I wish you could see this. The wonderful people of Geldershire are having a *very* good time indeed! Make some noise, Geldershire!"

The crowd goes mad, as Alwin's laughter bursts over the loudspeakers.

A technician approaches and hands him a mechanical clock. He takes it in his hands, and his smile brightens.

"The time has come, mensas. I'm afraid the twenty-fifth century refuses to wait any longer. Three minutes to midnight!"

The crowd cheers. Thousands of beaming eyes stare at the colorful man. Edda's—and Ximena's—breathing quickens. Edda quickly reins hers in, her training kicking in. Ximena can't.

"Colonists of Lunteren," he puts a hand around an ear, as if to hear better, "call your Quaestor, if you please!"

The Forum goes mental, clapping, cheering the name.

Marjolein! Marjolein! Marjolein!

The rhythmic call bounces off the far-off buildings and reverberates across the Forum, hypnotically, entrancing.

The calls turn into screams of delight and awe as Quaestor Marjolein Mathus enters the stage, radiant, sure of herself. She takes her place beside Alwin in front of a second standing microphone.

"Aaand... here she is, Germania! The one and only Quaestor of Lunteren, Marjolein Mathus. I wish you could see her. Whoa, resplendent! Lunteren is flooded with Goah's Blessings, if you know what I mean."

The crowd laughs and cheers. Edda and Bram glance at their father. Willem is blushing.

"Germania," Alwin continues, "it is my honor to receive

the new year—the new century!—by the side of Quaestor Marjolein Mathus of Lunteren. Her impeccable organization has made this magical night possible. Aws Head is blessed to have such talent in aws ranks. Get used to that name, mensas. Goah is smiling upon aws Servant. Marjolein, please." He reaches out to adjust the microphone in front of her down a notch, and then flips a switch.

"Thank you, Alwin." Her voice echoes across the Forum, warm and practiced. "Aws Blessings to you, Germania!"

The crowd goes crazy once more, cheering and chanting her name, drowning the Forum in a tsunami of pride, fanatical reverence, and adoration of their Quaestor.

Alwin leans slightly to show Marjolein the clock that he is holding in his hands.

"Ninety seconds to midnight!" Marjolein says. Her voice, vibrant and clean, echoes across the colony-wide loudspeaker system. "People of Germania, the time has come to bid goodbye to the twenty-fourth century with one last prayer of thanks. Please join me, as we are truly blessed."

The enthusiastic chaos of the Forum turns slowly into a background murmur of devotion as many heads bend down in reverence.

"God Of All Humans!" Marjolein calls. "Your children cherish you. Your children *love* you. We rejoice in your Blessings. We thrive in your care. Oh God Of All Humans, we thank you for our lives, for aws Gift, for aws Compacts, for aws Head, for Pontifex Fahey in Townsend, for Imperator Cisek in Tczew, for Consul Levinsohn in Fulda. Thank you, oh God Of All Humans. And bless our missionaries in the twenty-fifth century, to spread aws Gift and aws Imperia into every last barbaric corner of the world. Praise Goah!"

"Praise Goah!" the crowd shouts as one.

Marjolein is beaming, her smile practiced, her eyes focused. "Germania, join me in the century countdown!"

A mix of screaming and hushing engulfs the crowd as the last seconds of the century tick along. The thousands of heads that fill the Forum to the brim sway like waves on a troubled sea, swept by the invisible hurricanes of exhilaration.

Ximena leans forward, eyes wide in anticipation. *The century countdown!* She knows what is going to happen, and she still feels tense. Even nervous. Mark mutters something beside her, but she is too absorbed to pay attention.

Alwin pulls the clock closer to Marjolein as the thinnest, longest hand races unrelenting to the top. He expertly raises his left hand with his five fingers extended.

"Ten on my mark!" Marjolein shouts. Even her professionally tempered voice seems to quiver now with the weight of the moment, like she could sense deep inside her that her life is about to change forever.

Alwin drops his thumb. Then his index. The middle finger. The ring finger, and as he prepares to close his hand in a fist, a sudden electrical squeak pierces through the loudspeakers, loud and sharp.

The crowd mumbles words of confusion and pain— many colonists cover their ears.

"TEN. Aws Head lies to you!" A distorted female voice thunders out of the loudspeakers, unrecognizable, proud; commanding.

"NINE. Dem is a lie!"

The crowd is silent, mesmerized. Some exchange glances, others simply listen, eyes and mouths lost in the sky.

"EIGHT. Aws Head kills your parents!"

A murmur begins to rise from the crowd, and then voices try to hush them.

"SEVEN. Aws Head kills you!"

Alwin is gesticulating something back at the crew behind the scenes.

"SIX. Goah loves your life!"

Marjolein is staring at Alwin, eyes drenched in panic, shouting inaudible words.

"FIVE. Aws Head is demon-ridden!"

Marjolein runs to the side of the stage and stops, confusion dashing across her face—or is it dread? She runs back.

"FOUR. The Pontifex kills you!"

Ximena and many students across the amphitheater gasp loudly at the words. *The Pontifex? That can't be right!* Ximena sees a blur of movement in the GIA section out the corner of her eye, but she is too enthralled with Marjolein's reaction to look.

"THREE. Cleanse aws Imperia!"

Aws Imperia?! Ximena shakes her head in disbelief as she watches Marjolein fall to her knees, defeated, tears of humiliation in her eyes.

"TWO. Behead aws Head!"

Some sort of tumult appears to be breaking out in the auditorium. A glimpse down on the stage reveals Censor Smith on his feet, talking to Miyagi. Ximena turns her attention back to Marjolein. Her eyes—wet, bloodshot—are eagerly scanning the crowd now. She is searching for something—for *someone*.

"ONE. *Burn* the Joyousday!"

Marjolein finds Edda's eyes. And Edda is staring straight back at her, smug, defiant. Ximena can feel her exultation sending shivers up her spine.

Willem is gaping at his daughter. There is fear in his eyes. No, not fear. *Terror.*

"HAPPY NEW CENTURY!"

"*...* E*xcuse me, they are telling me... Yes. Radio stations from Gallia, Scandinavia and Russia are joining us as well. The whole Hanseatic Imperium is listening—we are broadcasting now Imperium-wide! To our new listeners, welcome. This is Alwin Geissberger, transmitting live the events unfolding right in front of my eyes.*

"*A brief summary for our new listeners: this year Germania selected the colony of Lunteren for the traditional New Year's Festival. Lunteren is a fishing colony in the West coast of Germania. I have the dubious honor of hosting this year's broadcast, transmitting right now live from Lunteren's Forum. The Quaestor of Lunteren, Marjolein Mathus, was the main influence behind the selection of the colony for this year's Festival, and also the chief organizer of the ceremony. A very capable woman, I believe, although after tonight's events, her competence might sadly be called into question. This is what happened: we heard the traditional blessings from Consul Levinsohn and Quaestor Mathus, but when the Quaestor was about to perform the ritual countdown, a rogue radio emission took over. Yes, you heard correctly. An illicit emission of the final century countdown was transmitted in full—country-wide!*

"*I'm still in shock at the words. Johan, have we got a recording already? ... No? ... Aha, I'm told that a recording is being retrieved, but we need a few more minutes to prepare it. Johan, please call in Fulda to see if our free-press license covers us on this one. Might be a problem. I hope we can replay it for our listeners. It was terrifying! The countdown was mocked with blasphemy, calls against the Joyousday and even, Goah forgive me, against our Pontifex and aws Head.*

"*The rogue transmission appears to be the work of professionals, considering the level of sophistication and the precision involved. Our regular transmissions were jammed, while the rogue transmission entered the repeater's network. It was transmitted to all stations in Germania.*

"*Excuse me, a report is coming through… What? … Where, here? … Attention, listeners. A fresh development. Apparently the Joyousday House is on fire. I repeat, the Joyousday House in Lunteren is on fire! More information, one second please… Yes… Okay, apparently the fire started at… midnight? Really? What a coincidence. I guess my listeners are also wondering if this has anything to do with the rogue broadcast. The timing matches. And the symbolism… Wait, more details are coming in… Okay, everything is under control, firefighters are on site. It's an isolated building, no spreading danger. No casualties, the only guard was found sleeping outside, possibly drunk. But the building appears to be irreparably damaged. What a terrible loss for Lunteren. The roof apparently went up in flames and eventually collapsed. The building is still burning. This despicable…*"

TWENTY-NINE

The Lure of Propaganda

Ximena feels her blood warming up with every word Censor Smith throws at Professor Miyagi. *Thank Goah the Grand Censor is here! Somebody has to confront the professor and his one-sided version of truth.*

The historical Edda, a hero of hers since she was first told her story by Abuelo when she was a child, would never have used such words against aws Imperia. The rot Edda fought against was in Hansasia, Goah's Mercy, not in Townsend! What a cheap propagandistic trick—so transparent!—to alter the historical narrative and misuse a revered historical figure to attack a rival regime.

Ximena feels her cheeks warm at the intensity of her indignation. Her *disappointment*. She worshiped this man, this giant among historians, the great Evangelist of History. He represents the peak of what she aspires to be one day. With all his authority and prestige, with the full weight of the oh so illustrious University of Lunteren-Deviss, with all his talk of cold facts and truth, with all his obsessive attention to historical context and detail, how could he stoop so low as to actually falsify such a well-known account as the Century Blasphemy?

"Please, Censor Smith," Miyagi says, raising his hands in a conciliatory gesture. "You are blowing things out of proportion."

Censor Smith is walking across the stage towards Professor Miyagi. "You are using misleading historical records," he shoots an accusing finger at Miyagi, "in an academic seminar no less, and it is me who is blowing things out of proportion? Unheard of!"

Miyagi keeps waving his hands down, and speaks in a calm, soothing tone, "I assure you, Censor Smith, that was the true Century Blasphemy, word by word." He looks up at the white-and-blue section of the amphitheater where half of the GIA students are standing, hands in the air, shouting words of support for their Censor, while the other half exchange words of outrage. "People, there is nothing controversial here, the sources are plentiful, and well preserved."

"Which sources?" Censor Smith asks with a challenging tone.

"The radio broadcast, of course. We have independent, matching copies from the archives of several stations across the world."

"You mean across Hansasia." Censor Smith says the word like it were suspect.

"I'm sure you have your own reproductions stored in Townsend University's archive, but of course I'll send you ours for good measure." Miyagi turns to Ank. "Could you please take care of—?"

"We don't need your tampered recordings," Censor Smith says before the Neanderthal woman has time to confirm.

"Tampered?" Miyagi's eyes widen in disbelief. He seems lost, without words, his eyes locked on the Censor's.

"And very deftly too. Changing just the one word or the other, very tactical; and effective. You made it look like the Century Blasphemy was directed against the entirety of aws Head, and not just the corruption surrounding Marjolein Mathus."

Miyagi is replying something, but Ximena cannot hear his words anymore from up here, since all students, even the Lundev section around Ximena, are now throwing loud opinions over each other. The auditorium has split into a cacophony of dozens of heated discussions.

"Hey, GIA," Sky—the pretty South Asian girl on the front bench below Ximena—has turned and is shouting straight at her. "What's the mensa talking about?"

Ximena still feels too aggravated to speak. Especially to a sassy Lundev brat that dares to argue about the civilizing of the Americas with Cody, an American scholar through and through! How daring ignorance can be.

"Her name is Ximena," Mark says. "And Censor Smith is saying that Professor Miyagi falsified the Century Blasphemy."

"I know what he said," Sky says, frowning at him. "And I want an explanation."

"Perhaps you should ask him yourself," Mark says. "Leave her alone."

"I don't need you to protect me," Ximena says with an icy voice. "Who do you think you are?"

"Ouch!" Sky says, and laughs out loud. "Nice one, GIA!"

Mark blinks at Ximena. "Sorry," he finally says. "Didn't mean to—"

"The Century Blasphemy," Ximena is leaning now

forward, staring down at Sky, "the *true* one, was explicitly—"

"The *true* one?" Sky replies mockingly. "So you're also saying that Professor Miyagi is bullshitting us?"

"Let her speak, Sky," Mark shouts, and gives Ximena an encouraging nod. "I also want to understand."

Ximena glares at him, and then at Sky. "I don't think you really want to hear the truth."

Sky snorts and rolls her eyes.

"I do," Mark says. "I really do. Please."

"Fine," Ximena sighs, and gathers her thoughts. "Everybody knows—or so I thought—that the Century Blasphemies were a call against the Joyousday, not against aws Imperia."

"Well—" Mark begins.

"Let me finish!" Ximena says, a warning in her eyes. "Of course there were also lines in the countdown that condemned aws Head, since it is aws Head that administers the Joyousday. But the *true* Edda van Dolah only denounced the *corrupted* section of aws Head, not all of it!"

"Which corrupted part?" Sky asks from below. All the students in the immediate proximity are silent, following the conversation with great interest.

"The Hanseatic Imperium, of course!"

"The *Hanseatic Imperium*?" Sky says from below. "Edda didn't give a shit about—"

Ximena ignores her. "There was this one line in the Century Blasphemy, in the *true* one, mind you, that said: 'The Imperator kills you!'; and another one was even more explicit: 'Cleanse aws Hansa!'"

"Aws *Hansa*?" Sky spreads her arms in an exaggerated gesture. "What are you talking about? Aws Hansa is not mentioned *anywhere* in the Century Countdown."

"Not in the revisionist version we just heard!" Ximena says, her eyes continually jumping between Mark, Sky and the other listeners. "That's precisely my point. And what does it say instead? It says: 'The Pontifex kills you!' Not the Imperator, no; the *Pontifex*, Goah's Mercy! And instead of calling to cleanse aws Hansa from corruption, Edda here is apparently calling to cleanse aws Imperia!" She chuckles humorlessly, shaking her head in disbelief. "So minimalistic, so *surgical*. A couple of tiny changes in the wording, and suddenly Edda van Dolah is denouncing the entire aws Head hierarchy in the six Imperia of Goah, including Townsend!"

The listening students initially stare at her in silence, like they do not understand, or do not know how to react.

Mark finally clears his throat. "Please correct me if I'm wrong, Ximena. You are saying that Edda van Dolah was not really opposed to aws Head?"

"Not to the true aws Head, no!" Ximena shouts, standing. "Why would she be?! But look at her life," Ximena gestures in the air as if there were a scene still floating there, "plagued by the corruption of Quaestor Mathus and the rest of Hansasia's aws Head."

"*Hansasia?*" Mark exchanges a glance with Sky.

"I mean *Hansa*, sorry. The Hanseatic Imperia."

"I see." Mark nods slowly and looks again down at Sky.

Ximena gives out a sigh of exasperation. She doesn't like how Mark is ganging up with that bitch against her. "How do you think the Dreamwars even began?!" Ximena's voice is more urgent now; louder, shriller. "It was all that corruption, Goah's Mercy, spreading like cancer across the colonies of Germania and then to the rest of the Old World! Van Dolah's *true* fight was obviously against the corruption surrounding her!"

Sky snorts loudly. "Somebody's been fed a large scoop of juicy BS." Again, her eyes meet Mark's.

Raw, burning rage pumps up through Ximena, making her stand at once and lock an accusing finger at the smug girl below. Her legs shake with adrenaline, her heart pumps hatred. "How dare you!"

Mark puts a friendly hand on Ximena's shoulder, encouraging her to sit.

She jumps away. "Don't touch me!" she says, glowering at him, and walks briskly away, making all students in her path stand hastily to let her through.

She doesn't take her eyes off her immediate next step, but the enraged chatter storm that had engulfed the students is waning with every step she takes. She feels the gaze of the whole auditorium falling on her like a judge's hammer.

After a while nobody speaks, as she keeps pushing her way through rows of students, her blush surely visible to all. She doesn't know where to look. First at her feet as she paces along the narrow bench, then at the faces of those standing to let her pass as she mutters words of apology, then at the other end of the amphitheater where she is headed, then at her feet again. *Oh, Goah, it's taking forever!*

She finally arrives at her destination, amid the white-and-blue section of the amphitheater, and without a word, sits next to the wide-eyed Cody O'Higgin. The students next to them hastily adjust their position on the bench to make space for her.

A slow clapping makes its way from the stage. "Well done, Woman Epullan," Censor Smith says.

Ximena raises her eyes to see him and Professor Miyagi side by side, staring at her. There is amusement in Censor Smith's eyes, but in Professor Miyagi's there is something else entirely, something hard to pin down.

"Somewhat melodramatic," Censor Smith continues, "but I celebrate your return to your own people. This is a place of scholarly learning, after all, not of shameless socializing. I trust you agree with me, my dear professor?"

Miyagi keeps his gaze locked on Ximena for a few moments of silence. "This is a place of truth," he finally says.

"Of course it is," Censor Smith says with a chuckle. "But we are seeing here how relative truth really is, aren't we?"

"Truth is not relative," Miyagi says, his usual all-knowing smile gone now. "Truth is the fuel of science. Truth is the blood of our survival in an inhospitable universe."

"Very poetic." Censor Smith gives Miyagi a friendly pat on the shoulder. "I suggest we agree to disagree, like respectful colleagues, and move on. There is still plenty of material to go through, if I am not mistaken?"

Professor Miyagi draws a deep breath. "Yes," he finally says. "Just one last comment to everybody, so that this distasteful moment doesn't go to waste. People, please. You are scientists. Always analyze the evidence thoroughly—and skeptically. You are historians," he points a finger at the crowd, that ends its wide sweep directly on Ximena's face, "and prime prey to the favorite hunting sport of the powerful of all ages: *propaganda*. It is your professional duty to avoid the lure of propaganda. Especially you, Ximena Epullan."

Me?! Ximena blushes at the explicit call out. All heads in the auditorium—every single one—turn to face her.

"Why me, Professor?" she asks, voice quivering from the sudden rush of adrenalin.

"That's a good question," Censor Smith asks. "What's

so special about Woman Epullan? Is it because she was sitting with your people?"

Miyagi purses his lips, still looking at her. But then, after a few moments, waves his hand with a casual, dismissive gesture. "Doesn't matter. My point is, people," he raises his voice, and sweeps his gaze across the entire audience, "that propaganda is like a recreational drug: it feels good, it feels *right*, but it eventually corrupts you, and kills you. So, keep on your toes, all right?"

"Well put, Professor," Censor Smith says. "And for that exact reason, I am sure that you understand that the last section we witnessed—the Century Blasphemy—cannot be published in the Goah's Imperia of the Americas. Oh, why the long face?" He smiles amicably. "I'm not censoring it. Just enforcing a couple of edits for accuracy's sake. Other than that, it is a splendid piece of work!" He laughs, pats Miyagi once more on the shoulder and returns to his seat on the bottom bench.

Ximena, still shaking slightly, is trying to rein in her breathing. She looks down at the stage and finds Professor Miyagi staring right back at her. And now, as she meets his gaze, she sees again that peculiar something in his eyes, but this time she recognizes it: *disappointment.*

An uncomfortable lightness spread inside Ximena's guts, like her soul aches. She turns her look away and keeps her eyes on her lap, too fearful to meet anybody else's glance. But her imagination pictures two beautiful blue eyes staring at her from across the amphitheater. She wants to believe they would look sad—perhaps even hurt. But she doesn't dare raise her head, in fear of meeting only more disappointment.

Professor Miyagi is once more pacing the stage. "We've gone through a lot of material, people," he says, his voice loud and serene. "The Leap-Day Reformation is underway. With the Century Blasphemy we are finally witnessing the first real-world effects of First Contact on the complacent civilization of Goah's Gift. Not unlike Pizarro's fateful arrival to the coasts of Peru, Edda van Dolah and Aline Speese have just left a sour taste in the government's mouth, a taste impossible to ignore. And just like Pizarro, Edda is far from done."

Miyagi stops pacing and looks up at the benches. There are many tense faces in the amphitheater. Way too many. Both the white-and-blue robed students and their more colorful Lundev counterparts look like they have eaten something too unpleasant to admit.

With a sudden, loud clap, Miyagi says, "I think it is a good time for a short recess, what do you say, people? We need to calm our nerves, I think. So I'm going to ask Ank to wake you up, all right? Let's meet back here again in… fifteen wake minutes? Perfect. Use the time wisely, people! Take a nice, relaxing leak, drink a hot glass of milk, whatever you need to chill, all right? See you in a sec!"

Ank stands and walks with that sure step of hers to the center of the stage. Bob, the wudai machine, slides behind her in a frenzy of green tendrils. "You heard the professor," she says, her voice somehow soft and yet clear, as if whispered into every ear at once. "Fifteen minutes. Please set your wu-sarcs for…" she squints at Bob for a second, "01:45 Lunteren wake time, 18:45 Townsend wake time. I repeat: 01:45 Lunteren, 18:45 Townsend. And for those on sleep pills, please, *please*, don't be late!"

With a wide, charming smile and a casual gesture, the students—and Censor Smith, Goah be Merciful—vanish.

Ank and Miyagi are alone in the amphitheater.

Miyagi walks over to Ank and pecks her on her lips. "Wow!" He takes a deep breath. "That was an intense session!"

"And it's bound to get worse before it gets better," Ank says, putting a hand on his cheek. "That's what you get when you mix oil with water, Kenji."

Miyagi laughs. "So true!"

"Do you regret it?"

"What, the Global Program?"

She nods.

"Of course not! If anything, the *worlds* need more global programs, hon. You've seen how they reacted? They went *ballistic* at the first chance! All of them!" He sighs. "It's been over a hundred years since the Dreamwars. It's high time we let the old wounds heal. And history—*true* history—is the only medicine that cures societies long-term."

"I'm not sure about that, Kenji." She raises her head at the benches to her right, which a few moments ago resembled a storm-battered sea of white-and-blue. "Not everybody seems so keen to move on."

Miyagi spreads his arms in a gesture of impotence. "All I can do is what I can do, hon. The universe is a scary dark forest. If we are going to make it, we gotta stick together. And to bring the entire human race into the same boat, truth is the only way. But you know what? I still have faith in good old common sense. Truth is obvious when you use your brain. And propaganda more so. We play them more historical facts, give them enough time to ruminate the cognitive dissonance, and some will come around. You wait and see."

"You are talking about Ximena Epullan."

He shrugs, but says nothing.

Ank gives him a weak smile. "For a minute there I thought you were going to tell her who she really is."

"Yeah," he rubs the back of his neck, "but I got scared."

"Scared?" She winks at him. "Kenji Miyagi got cold feet?"

He smiles. A sad smile. "I'm afraid of what they might do to her if they find out."

"I don't understand. What's the big deal?"

"She could be easily misled, you know?" He wets his lips. "She could be turned into a propaganda tool."

Ank frowns, thoughtful. "Hmm, you think?" She turns her honey-gold eyes on him and takes his hands into hers. "Ximena has the right to know, Kenji. You can't keep this from her!"

"I know, I know. I'm going to tell her, all right? In private. But... I don't think it's the right moment, you know? And anyway, we have a seminar to run."

"How did you find out, anyway? About Ximena, I mean?"

"Ah, yes." He smiles like a veteran recalling a memory of past glories. "It was when I was researching the Inca power struggle. For the Pizarro sensorial, you know? I read this book written by a local scholar: Enrique Epullan, Ximena's biological grandfather. It was dedicated to his dowry mother, Vanessa Kraker."

"Kraker!"

"Exactly, it caught my attention as well. A bit more digging, and I found out that Vanessa Kraker emigrated to the Andes back then, in the thirties, when the GIA was still paying fortunes for Hansasia specialists. And guess where she came from."

"Deviss-Lunteren, of course."

Miyagi nods. "Her biological grandfather was Hans Kraker."

"Gotthard's son," Ank lets her eyes roll to the place in the amphitheater where Ximena was sitting next to Mark, "and Edda's."

"Juicy stuff, huh? Especially for our good friend Grand Censor Jean-Jacques Smith."

END OF DREAMWORMS EPISODE III

Leave a review, Goah's Mercy!

A review, pretty please? Just a line—a word even—suffices. Seriously! Believe it or not, reviews are the oxygen of modern authors. Yeah: No reviews → no sales → there goes my writing career.

Please, PLEASE review now! You can always update your review later if you feel the need.

https://isaacpetrov.com/reviewbook1

OR SCAN THIS WITH YOUR CAMERA!

DREAMWORMS

A POST-APOCALYPTIC FIRST CONTACT EPIC

THE SECOND WAKE

EPISODE IV

ISAAC PETROV

DREAMWORMS Episode IV

ALIEN MASTER

A spectacular blasphemy has been unleashed upon the world.

And the world is now turning her gaze.

AND HER FIST.

All while secretive aliens, hidden behind the barrier of dreams, meddle with whispers of hope.

All while Edda van Dohla plunges in the darkest depths of the Path of the Mind-Walkers in a desperate attempt to save her father from the ritual death known as the Joyousday.

All while Aline Speese makes a discovery that could shake awake human civilization from a centuries-old coma.

Join Ximena Epullan and her fellow students in this new episode of Professor Miyagi's Seminar on *The Rise and Fall of the Juf.*

Join now, and witness humanity's first hesitant steps into **THE SECOND WAKE**.

Join Isaac Petrov's list to obtain a FREE copy of *DREAMWORMS Episode IV: The Second Wake*.

https://isaacpetrov.com/episode4

OR SCAN THIS WITH YOUR CAMERA!

Sign Up — No Bull Sci-Fi

ISAAC PETROV — EPIC SCI-FI AT ITS BEST!

Come over to my site at IsaacPetrov.com and SIGN UP to get fresh SCI-FI updates, discounts and goodies:

https://isaacpetrov.com/book1

OR SCAN THIS WITH YOUR CAMERA!

For Elon Musk and Greta Thunberg.
For the same reason.

Acknowledgments

My wife, Dado—a creature of the Iberian Peninsula—is not widely known for her patience. Yet for what matters, she is. All these weird projects I undertake—be them my latest startup attempt, AI research, or, now, fulfilling the childhood dream of writing stories—she has supported me every step of the way, even as I keep dumping on her my random obsession of the day, day after day, year after year, I hope forever.

That's love.

Dado has sparred ideas with me, from plot to marketing. Thank you. She has witnessed with infinite patience my slow transformation into a very early bird, the product of newly acquired writing habits. Thank you.

I'm lucky my family has been so supportive. Mamá, Nacho, thank you for being proud of me. Vero, Tamara, Eduardo, Ignacio, Gema, thank you for not giving a hard time to your older brother.

To my first alpha, Sam Kassé, thank you for your positive shove. When I sent over to you my first hundred pages, I was so insecure. I didn't know if I could write a good story, or rather, I didn't know if I could get them out of my head and put them on paper for others' consumption. In the entrepreneurial spirit of failing as fast as possible, I was ready to drop it all and get my hand around some new obsession had you found my words lacking. I'm happy you didn't. Also, your sensitive reading skills have been crucial in these—uh, how should I put it? —very sensitive times we live. That's something Isaac Asimov didn't have to cope with, lucky bastard. So thank you, Sam!

The brutal honesty of my developmental editors Chersti Nieveen and Amanda Rutter helped reconceptualize the first draft of Dreamworms into the nine episode long story it turned out to be. Chersti's analysis and personal sessions were crucial to see where Dreamworms fit in the broader world of fantasy/sci-fi literature. Thank you, Chersti, for your deep understanding of story, and your actionable suggestions, which made my work extend perhaps a year over my original deadline. Wow, and I'm not saying that sarcastically. I really mean my gratitude.

Thank you, Maxim Mitenkov, for your wonderful illustrations and cover of the Episodes.

Thank you, Cherie Chapman, for your awesome cover design for the novels. I love what you did there with Edda and Rew—it's quite unique.

Thank you, Claire Rushbrook, for cleaning up my manuscript with such surgical precision. Those are some magnificent editorial powers you have!

And last but not least, I want to thank my beta readers for their feedback. Thank you Dado, Patricio Abando, Eduardo, Tamara, L. A. White, Nicholas Lawrence Carter and Felipe Bertrand. It is thanks to you that the story reaches its final level of maturity, a more nuanced texture somehow. It's hard to explain, but it's real.

About the Author — Isaac Petrov

People, you know how it is when you pick up a book, and it's a *meh*, or even an *ew*? Well, I am one of those poor bastards to whom that happens. **A LOT!**

But, oh, when that rarest of gems, the enthralling, no-bullshit story makes its rare appearance and sucks you whole? Oh, yes! *That* is what I live for, people: a good science fiction book.

Solid, no-bullshit science fiction is all about the playful engagement of the intellect; that mix of escapism and raw realism; that exploration of the human soul under the duress of the most tantalizing of realities. Oh, no other genre comes even close, people. Yeah, I know how arrogant it sounds. Sorry. Doesn't make it any less true.

But hey, this is the page where I get to tell you about my not-so-humble self, and if there is one thing, only one, that I want my readers to know is that **I do love science fiction**. Always have. A true nerd, since way before it was cool (yeah, I'm that old). And my promise to you is that I make the books that I want to read. Nothing less.

If you insist on knowing more, all right. Hmm, let's see. Born in Spain, I'm currently settled in Amsterdam with my wife and young son. Law and economics academic background. Software engineering career. A few start-up failures. Gamer when time allows. And a passion for science since… well, forever—I told you I'm a true nerd!

https://isaacpetrov.com